Poison Lilies

Also by Katie Tallo

Dark August

POISON
LILIES

A NOVEL

Katie Tallo

HARPER

NEW YORK • LONDON • TORONTO • SYDNEY

HARPER

POISON LILIES. Copyright © 2022 by Katie Tallo. All rights reserved. Printed in the United States of America. No part of this book may be used or reproduced in any manner whatsoever without written permission except in the case of brief quotations embodied in critical articles and reviews. For information, address HarperCollins Publishers, 195 Broadway, New York, NY 10007.

HarperCollins books may be purchased for educational, business, or sales promotional use. For information, please email the Special Markets Department at SPsales@harpercollins.com.

FIRST EDITION

Designed by Jamie Lynn Kerner

Library of Congress Cataloging-in-Publication Data has been applied for.

ISBN 978-0-06-321174-2 (pbk.)
ISBN 978-0-06-324788-8 (library edition)

22 23 24 25 26 LSC 10 9 8 7 6 5 4 3 2 1

For Andy, the love of my life

Poison Lilies

Present Day

HER INDEX FINGER TRACES THE MORTAR BETWEEN THE BRICKS. Skirting potholes where sowbugs have built tiny homes. Crushing egg sacs. Her giant-self storms across spider highways. Leaving clouds of sand and lime in her wake. Wreaking havoc. Annihilating anything that dares get in her way.

She is King Kong.

No, she is Queen Kong.

All powerful.

She is a fucking Goddess of Zilla.

And then she's not.

Augusta shrinks to nothing. Her arm hangs limp from the effort of holding it up. And just like that the queen is dead. Crumpled on the clammy cement floor, Gus licks salty tears from the corners of her lips. She sits, her jean jacket draped open. The rough wall of her windowless prison biting her cheek. She presses into the brick harder, but the sting is feeble respite from the profound ache that ebbs and flows inside her.

Gus closes her eyes and listens to the thrumming of her heart.

And another sound. Another thrumming.

She struggles to zero in on the distant chugging, lost deep beneath the rise and fall of her severely compressed lungs. Her mind wanders to the pocket of her jacket, the weight of its contents resting on her hip.

Don't do it.
Don't turn on your phone.
You just checked. It's too soon.
You'll need it later.

But she can't help herself. She can already feel the comfort of its blue glow. Can already see the lovely picture on its home screen of her dog, Levi. He's probably fast asleep this very moment. Snoring. Dreaming doggie dreams. Curled in a furry ball. Cozy and content. He might sense her prolonged absence as he opens one eye then the other. He'll huff but he won't bark. The old dog has no clue that she needs him.

Last time she looked at her phone it was 6:30 A.M. Two hours after she found herself on the wrong side of a locked door in the subbasement of her apartment building.

No cell service. Too deep.

Gus caves. Turns on her cell phone.

11:17 A.M.

Almost seven hours now. Suddenly the screen goes black, and she's pitched into darkness again.

Motherfucker.

She hurls the phone into the black void. Hears it shatter against the far wall. A ghostly window hovers in front of her face, dodging as her eyeballs follow it until she realizes it's the retinal imprint of her phone's glow, taunting her with just how fucked she is. She watches as the ghost phone fades. Along with her hope.

Why didn't you bring a granola bar with you? her stomach moans.

"Fuck if I know," she says out loud.

Stupid girl, can't even feed yourself. You're like a helpless child.
You think I don't know that?

Mouth dry. Throat raw. Hands trembling.

Hey, Stomach, got a question for you. Why are my knuckles sore?

She touches her knuckles gently. Dried blood is crusted over swollen cuts.

Then she remembers.

Pounding, sobbing, screaming, raging for hours at the door. The bloody door that would not budge. The bloody door with no handle on the inside. The solid door. The locked door.

At some point, she gave up. Exhausted. She sat still and listened. For anything. But the silence was almost worse than the screaming. The whole world seemed to have packed up and left. No voices echoed from hallways. No footsteps tapped across hardwood floors. No car horns beeped from Bank Street. No trees rustled in the park. No birds, no dogs, no children laughing.

But wait. There it is again. Did you hear that, Stomach?

Gus hears the faintest sound. She holds her breath. Presses her ear close to the wall.

Yes. There.

A dull plunking in a tempo of threes.

Drip, drip, drip.

Drip, drip, drip.

Water in a rusty pipe, mocking her desert throat.

She exhales. Then unexpectedly something happens.

Water seeps from beneath her. It's not a trickle. More like a confident gush. It startles her. Soaks through her leggings in seconds. Gus sits motionless as warm liquid circles her and reality dawns in the deep darkness. She braces for what she knows is next. Gus takes another shuddering breath and places both hands on her swollen belly.

The baby is coming.

FIRST
TRIMESTER

1

Gish

THE BAD NEWS IS THAT THE ELEVATOR'S BROKEN EVERY OTHER day and Gus's new apartment is on the third floor of an old art deco, four-story building. Levi isn't happy. Part golden retriever, part Spinone Italiano, Levi is a raggedy old man of a dog. Stairs are his least favorite thing. The apartment building was updated and converted to condos decades ago, but it's far from modern. The units are either owned by aging seniors who've lived there forever, or they've been purchased as investment properties and are rented out to people who don't care about outdated kitchens or creaky floors or broken elevators. People like Gus.

The good news is that the rent's dirt cheap, which is perfect because she's currently living off her wafer-thin savings since quitting her job at the pet store. Gus doesn't mind the flickering light fixtures in the stairwell or the weird textured walls of the narrow hallways. Her apartment, number 305, is tucked at the quiet end of the hall near the back stairwell.

The building is in the heart of the Glebe. One of Ottawa's oldest neighborhoods, where the houses have big front porches, old elms shade the sidewalks, and there's a row of shops within walking distance of the building's front door. An entirely new neighborhood where no one knows her face or name. A good place to hide.

Goodbye, Wellington West. Hello, fresh start.

Gus is a master of the fresh start. Although none of hers could really be classified as particularly fresh. For Gus, starting over has been more like a series of hard resets. The first and worst of them began when her mother died and she went to live with her great-grandmother Rose. She was eight. The next came two years later when she was sent to boarding school. Set adrift. Another came at seventeen, when she graduated from high school and moved to Toronto. Alone. Hard resets became a monthly routine when she met Lars. They lived on the road, always moving, always changing locations, IDs, names, personas. Never staying put. Always chasing the next score or thinking up the next con.

At twenty, she thought she was hardened to change, when out of the blue, another reset upended her life. Rose died, and Gus inherited her house. She ditched Lars, moved back to her hometown, and solved her mother's murder. She didn't see that one coming.

After that, Gus was done. At least she thought she was. She got the job at the pet store, a cute apartment nearby, and felt content for the first time in her life.

Cue hard reset number whatever.

This one was her own doing. Well, not entirely her own. It takes two to tango. But she blamed herself nonetheless. She made a mistake she couldn't undo. She had no choice but to cut and run. Gus packed her things in the dead of night, left a rent check on the table, and took off. That was five weeks ago. Late November.

But that was then and this is now. It's hard to believe January is just around the corner. A new year is about to arrive and with it another bone-chilling Ottawa winter. The small city is glazed in a layer of ice and snow that only hints of the deep freeze to come. Gus sits cross-legged in her new living room surrounded by boxes that she still hasn't unpacked. Dusty shafts of sunlight bend through the window, exposing scars in the hardwood floors from decades of furniture scratches and boot scuffs made by strangers who lived here before her. But those people weren't the strangers. Gus and Levi are. These are not her scars. Some date back to 1928 when the building was first built, seventy years before she was born. The place has history in its bones. She can hear it rattling in the water-heated radiators. She can glimpse it in the tarnished bronze around the electric fireplace and in the milky surface of the stained glass framing the mantel.

Soon Levi's untrimmed nails will add new scratches to the hardwood. Soon they won't be the strangers. The Ambassador Court will eventually feel like home. Or at least she hopes so.

Levi made himself at home the first week once he'd figured out where the sun hit the floors in late afternoon. Now he settles there every morning and waits, then basks in the warmth as it slowly drifts across his fur.

Gus is less settled. She's either too cold or too hot. She figures it must be the radiators. One day, she's excited to unpack and organize, the next she's drained of all that get-up-and-go. Most days she defaults to her usual MO.

Box of Honeycomb cereal. Can of cream soda.

Clear shit off the sofa. Feet up.

John Wayne western.

Nap.

Repeat. Only this time with Pop-Tarts and coffee.

But today, something gnaws at her belly more than usual.

A restlessness she can't shake. Gus decides she can't live among boxes forever. She eyes the old blue trunk where she keeps her childhood treasures—old notebooks, crayons, a doll, swimming medals, plastic clip-on earrings in an emerald silk bag. She drags the trunk across the room. Positions it in front of her sofa. On the edge of the trunk is a tiny bloodstain. She spit shines it away, then lifts the lid. She grabs her great-grandmother Rose's nesting dolls and a photo box and arranges them on top of the trunk. The picture frame holds a photo of her late parents taken outside a pub during a weekend leave from Royal Canadian Mounted Police cadet training. They're both in their twenties. Newly dating. Their lives ahead of them. Or so they thought. A year into their marriage, her father was killed just days before Gus was born. He was a rookie on a routine call that went sideways. Her mother died eight years later.

It's no ordinary picture frame. There's a compartment behind the photo where Gus keeps her gun. A purse-size handgun she got for protection. It's remained in the photo box since the day she bought it. She likes knowing it's there, hidden away but handy.

She places a mat at the front door, hangs a curtain in the bedroom, unpacks all the boxes, and puts things away in drawers and cupboards like you're supposed to. But none of this helps. The uneasiness stalks her all weekend. It crawls across her skin when she's lying in bed, and it bubbles in the pit of her stomach when she's getting groceries at McKeen Metro. When she takes Levi for a walk in the park, it sends pins and needles through her fingers. She holds his leash tight as he scratches at the edge of Patterson Creek, trying to free the lily pads from the frozen ice. He does manage to dislodge an old penny from below the bridge. Gus digs it from his mouth and examines it: 1946. She's surprised by how old it is and wonders if it's been in the creek since the forties. She pockets it for good luck.

Sunday, Gus spends an entire day debating what to wear job hunting on Monday.

Monday, she delays the job hunt because decades-old grease has to be scrubbed from under the stove.

Tuesday, she washes all her clothes, carrying the basket down three flights of stairs to the basement laundry room. By the time she's finished washing, drying, folding, and transporting them back up to her apartment, she's not feeling well at all. The smell of detergent and dryer lint is making her want to throw up.

Wednesday, she throws up in the kitchen sink. Gus diagnoses herself with the flu.

That night she goes to bed and sleeps until Thursday night, when something wakes her from her duvet cocoon.

An earworm is going round and round her brain.

A repetitive sound.

A mewing.

At first, she thinks she's dreaming.

Cat dreams.

Gus opens her eyes and listens in the dark. Levi's warm body is pressed against her thigh. She looks at him in the dim light. He's awake. Ears pricked. He's listening too. The mewing stops. The dog turns to her and stares. A *you haven't walked me or fed me in a dog's age* stare. Gus sits up carefully. She's light-headed and shaky. Definitely the flu. Levi jumps off the bed, wagging his tail. Gus rallies. She bare-foots it to the kitchen, wearing the same T-shirt and sweatpants she was wearing thirty hours ago. She prepares the special diet of ground beef and rice that Levi's vet recommended. The mewing starts up again. It's muffled.

Mew, mew. Mew, mew.

It sounds like it's coming from outside. She peers out the living room window to see if there's a stray trapped on a high ledge. Nope. She opens the front door of her apartment to check the dark hallway. A ceiling sconce flickers, but otherwise, nothing furry. Closing the door, she leans an ear to the stucco wall, moving slowly along it. The mewing gets louder as she inches back to the kitchen. Gus stares at a small cupboard door.

Mr. Curry, the building superintendent, said the cupboard was *out of order* so it had been sealed shut. Back in the day, it had been a dumbwaiter, one of four in each corner of the building serving the kitchens of each apartment. One of the peculiar features of the original building that no longer made sense in the modern world. Servants would use it to bring up deliveries from the main floor or send washing down to the laundry, which used to be located in the subbasement, two levels belowground. That subbasement is another of those original features that's no longer practical to keep up. Mr. Curry said it's on account of the annual spring flooding from Patterson Creek Park, a stretch of land beside the building. The park was built over a swampy bog, so there's a lot of groundwater deep underneath it. *Used to flood something awful every year*, he tells her, even though she could care less about some subbasement nobody uses anymore. Mr. Curry likes to hear himself talk. He goes on about how there used to be a secondary level of parking down in the subbasement, along with big storage lockers, and a boiler room. Everything was moved up a level some years back, and the whole thing was blocked off.

Nothing but ghosts live down there now.

❦

Oh and one very pregnant woman.

Gus tries to steady her breath as another contraction comes. She braces one hand against the cold brick while the other cradles her belly. She can feel the baby turning and kicking. It wants out. Gus's thin T-shirt is soaked in sweat. Stabbing pains radiate across her pelvic nerves. She counts the seconds ticking by through clenched teeth. This one was longer than the last contraction, and it came sooner. Then it goes away, giving her a momentary reprieve. In the gap between contractions, Gus tries to focus. She needs desperately to remember what happened. A sliver of memory might save her life. She stares into the darkness, searching, but the fleeting images keep slipping through her consciousness.

All she can hear is that mewing.

Mew, mew. Mew, mew.

That's it. She was standing in front of that sealed cupboard. That dumbwaiter. She remembers now. She ran a kitchen knife along the edges, scraping away the paint and caulking until she was able to loosen the hinges and pry the door open with a metal spatula. The hinges were so old that the wood splintered and the door came off in her hands. Chips of paint littered the linoleum floor of her kitchen. She put the door down and peered inside the narrow shaft. Up then down. The mewing was downward. She groped. Found the rope. Began pulling. The wheels of the dumbwaiter squeaked as it traveled toward her. Finally it arrived, coming level with the cupboard door, clicking into place.

That's when she met Gish. A very large, very angry orange cat. Gish hissed and took a swipe at her forearm, scratching the skin with its claws. Drawing blood. Gus pulled away and the cat bolted into her living room.

At the time, Gus didn't think much of the wooden compartment. The dumbwaiter was no larger than a bar fridge. A useless little elevator hidden inside a shaft in the wall. A shaft running all the way down to the subbasement. That's what Mr. Curry had said.

Jesus Christ.

A daft grin ripples across her sweaty face.

She can't believe it's taken her this long to think of it.

It's a way out.

If she can find it.

Gus is beginning to think she must have hit her head at some point.

Her brain feels like it's idling, revving, then sputtering. Right now it's revved up.

Seizing the moment, Gus stands. She staggers forward, groping along the wall. Palming the bricks, searching for a frame, an indent, a smooth section of plaster, a small handle, a wooden door, anything that might lead her to that stupid idiot of a dumbwaiter. Gus shuts her eyes. Tries to retrace how she got here. She needs to orient herself in the building. The shaft leads from the kitchens in the corner units, near the end of the hall. But where is she?

Think, Gus. Think.

The utility room suddenly comes to mind, and it's quickly followed by a cascade of images. She is standing beside the boiler. Behind it, she finds a trapdoor that leads down to the subbasement. She climbs down a narrow metal stairwell. She sees herself in a dark passageway with crumbling walls. She walks toward the back of the building. The dirt floors are spongy. The air smells like dead fish. Her footsteps echo and multiply, making it sound like someone else is there with her. She's moving south.

And then Queen Kong returns. Suddenly Gus is a giant. She lifts the roof from the apartment building, exposing the walls and stairwells, giving herself a bird's-eye view of the configuration of each floor down to the subbasement. She can see her tiny insect-self way down below in the subbasement. There she is. Walking down a hall, approaching a door at the corner of the building. It's the door to this room, and it's right below the kitchen in her small one-bedroom apartment.

That dumbwaiter is somewhere in this room. She knows it.

In the pitch black, Gus steps away from the wall and takes six steps, imagining the layout of her kitchen. She turns and reaches out. Her fingertips hit wood. Bingo. A cupboard door. She raps her knuckles on it. It's hollow.

Who's the motherfuckin' dumbwaiter now?

She laughs, then doubles over as a torrent of pain spirals across her belly and shoots down her thighs. The shock of it brings Gus to her knees. She cries out. A deep mournful cry that no one can hear. Her head spins as the darkness swallows her. She crumples onto her side in a pitiful heap on the floor. As she loses consciousness, Gus senses her body levitating. She is lifted from the grimy floor of the subbasement. She is weightless as she wafts up through the concrete layer between the floors, into the underground parking garage. Up and up she floats. One floor, then the next, and the next, metamorphosing as she passes effortlessly through the solid hardwood and finally comes to rest on the landing of the top floor of the Ambassador Court. Once there, she sees herself standing outside apartment 405. The one above hers.

Back when her only worry in the world was a stray cat named Gish.

❧

Gus knocks.

She's already tried the apartments directly below hers. A cardboard box held tightly in her arms. Lid closed. A moaning cat inside. 105 wasn't home. The guy in 205 said he didn't own a cat, but likes cats and offered to take it off her hands, but she wasn't ready to give up.

Then Gus climbed to the top of the building to try the

last apartment connected to the dumbwaiter. The one directly above hers.

And now here she is.

Apartment 405.

Knocking on a door that, once opened, changes everything. Brings her face-to-face with the strange and lovely occupant of the sprawling two-bedroom flat. An eighty-five-year-old spinster who has lived in that corner apartment her entire life.

An apartment she hasn't left since the 1950s.

2

Poppy

She's wearing a pastel pink silk kimono tied at the waist with a sash and matching embroidered silk slippers on her tiny feet. A gold chain with a locket loops around her gooseflesh neck. She reminds Gus of an aging Hollywood starlet. She holds the door slightly ajar with one age-spotted hand while softly stroking her long gray hair with the other. She lifts her chin as if smelling the air.

"Can I help you?" she says, her eyes wafting here and there as if she's following the flight path of a butterfly.

Gus realizes the woman is blind.

"I'm in 305. Your downstairs neighbor. Augusta. Do you happen to own a . . . ?"

On cue the cat wails. A smile like a cracked rose blooms on the woman's lips, spreading laugh lines across her cheeks and igniting a sparkle in her unseeing eyes.

"Gish!" yelps the woman, transforming from old woman to delighted child.

"I found it in the dumbwaiter," explains Gus as she opens the flaps of the box. The cat leaps from its cardboard prison.

"Oh, my Gish!" laughs the woman, feeling the cat brush past her ankles.

The tabby corkscrews the woman's legs, then skitters away, back arched, eyes wild as it disappears into the depths of the enormous apartment. Gus can see a flickering light halfway down the wide entrance hall, but much of the apartment fades to darkness. It looks like it goes on forever.

"Augusta, you say?"

"Yes, ma'am. Augusta Monet."

"I do like that name very much. I'm Poppy Honeywell," she says, holding a bony hand in Gus's general direction.

Gus shakes it gently.

"Now that you've saved Lillian Gish from meeting a tragic end, I believe you and I are going to be fast friends. You best come in, love," Poppy says as she turns and strolls away.

The silky tails of her kimono flutter behind her like the tentacles of a pink jellyfish. Her fingers lightly trace the wall as she guides herself confidently down the hallway.

Gus hesitates, then steps across the threshold, closing the door behind her and immediately extinguishing the scrap of light that was spilling inside from the outer hallway. The smell of burnt toast and cat litter mingle in the air. Gus tentatively inches her way toward the flickering light halfway down the hall. She steps on something. It squeaks and she realizes it's a cat toy.

Approaching an archway, Gus turns and finds herself at the entrance to Poppy's spacious living room. A fire crackles in the hearth. Its glow casts over the part of the room nearest the fire, illuminating a cushion-strewn sofa positioned across from two deep armchairs. The furniture is layered with thick blankets and scattered with ornate gold-trimmed cushions. A heavy wood coffee table sits between the sofa and chairs, and an oval-shaped Persian rug spreads beneath them. The edges of the room stay in darkness, accentuating its glowing core. Like a beating heart, the warm light ebbs and swells. The room takes Gus's breath away. She's never seen a place so lovely and warm. The room almost beckons her.

Apart from the fireplace, the only other light source is the yellow moon hanging over the pond in the park just outside the bow window. Heavy red velvet curtains, trussed by decorative tiebacks, partially screen a cushioned window seat. The moon looks like a paper lantern strung in the deep blue winter sky.

Gish is perched on the back of the billowy sofa, glaring at Gus.

"Nice kitty," Gus says.

Gish hisses just as Poppy appears at Gus's shoulder with two bottles of Coke Classic.

"I took that little door off the dumbwaiter years ago. No one was using it, so I turned it into her cubby. She loves it. It must have come off its rails. I imagine it scared the dickens out of her when it fell, poor love. Lucky she wasn't hurt. It's entirely possible she figured out how to operate the dang thing," giggles Poppy. "Gish is a clever little creature. She's forever trying to escape my evil clutches."

Poppy laughs. Gus laughs as well. A bit too loudly. Overplaying the moment for the blind woman's benefit. Gus awkwardly takes one of the colas with a thank-you.

"Miss Gish knows very well that we don't leave the apartment. Never, ever, ever," she coos. "Don't you, my pretty kitty?"

The fat orange cat isn't listening, and instead has begun to lick its anus.

Gus is struck by Poppy's statement, but she doesn't want to pry.

Poppy nods in the direction of the window.

"It's cold out there," she says, as if that explains everything.

"Yes, another long winter ahead of us," says Gus.

"And with winter comes shorter days. I don't mind though," says Poppy rather wistfully. She sips her Coke.

Gus wonders why daylight matters to a blind woman.

"Well now, Miss Augusta, do tell me how a young thing like you came to live one floor below an old spinster like me in a relic like the Ambassador Court," she chirps.

Poppy has a melodic way of speaking that is quite charming. A slight British accent slips in every other word. She reminds Gus of Katharine Hepburn in those black-and-white movies she used to watch with her mother when she was little. Gus warms to Poppy instantly.

"You can call me Gus," she says.

"Oh I like that. Sounds like gusto," Poppy says, raising her Coke for a toast in Gus's general direction. "Gus it is."

They clink bottles.

By week's end, the habit of sharing meals curled up in front of Poppy's fireplace has become an evening ritual. Their mutual love of frozen dinners bonds them instantly. Gus usually arrives around 6 P.M. with hers already microwaved. Levi by her side. She often finds Poppy comfortably seated on one end of the sofa with her TV tray already across her lap and Gish lounging on the back of the sofa. Over beef medallions or baked ziti, the two share more than just dinner. Gus tells Poppy about her parents. She recounts the story of her mother's death and her investigation into it years later. Tells Poppy about Desmond Oaks and his accomplices. How they tried to stop her. How they came after the money Gracie Halladay left her on account of Gus's mother helping Gracie when she was a child. How they even tried to poison Levi. Poppy gasps at this tidbit. She's a good listener and easy to talk to. Partly it's because she's blind. Gus feels like she can be herself, let her guard down, and tell Poppy anything.

Almost anything. She leaves out the humiliating bit about why she really moved to the Ambassador. The unexpected encounter on a snowy night with a man she once knew. And the series of mistakes that night that forced her to abandon the life she'd made for herself. In fact, Gus has pretty much convinced herself that night never happened, so why bring it up?

Poppy shares her story too. At least most of it. There are times when Poppy stops mid-sentence as if she knows she's veered off course and has to pause before slipping into reverse to get back on track. Seems they both have a few delicate threads they don't want unraveled. Gus doesn't mind, but she is curious why the old woman never leaves her apartment. She has everything delivered, from groceries to prescriptions. There are no boots or coats or snowy remnants collecting in the entryway, and she's always wearing slippers. Poppy delicately skirts the subject like a figure skater on the edge of her blade, skillfully altering course mid-sentence with one sweeping turn of phrase. Gus admires her skills.

One subject Poppy doesn't shy away from is her mother, Eva, who Gus learns was the only daughter of a prominent Ottawa philanthropist and entrepreneur. Eva's local lineage goes back to the early 1800s. Her ancestors, the Mutchmores, were one of the Glebe's founding families. Eva married Frank Honeywell and they had a daughter, Poppy, in 1935. Frank was an insurance man. When Poppy was born, Frank and Eva moved into the apartment in the Ambassador Court, at first renting, then purchasing the unit a few years later. Poppy has never lived anywhere else.

As the city evolved and families began migrating to the suburbs, many of the original apartments were divided into smaller units, like Gus's one-bedroom. But not Poppy's. The original corner units were quite grand. Each had a spacious living room with a fireplace, an adjacent sunroom overlooking the park, a kitchen with a pantry, and two large bedrooms at the end of a wide hallway. Poppy's remains just as it was when the building was first built. In more ways than one, Gus is realizing.

The old woman's eyes glisten when she speaks of the sudden death of her father, Frank, who had a heart attack at work. Poppy was only ten. He left one morning and never came home, leaving Eva to raise Poppy alone. It seems Eva was estranged from her family. Poppy's mother never told her why. She just said they were better off without them and their money. Frank's life insurance covered the mortgage on the apartment, and Eva picked up odd jobs as a seamstress to pay the bills and taxes and maintenance fees. They got by. Poppy remembers her childhood fondly. She went to First Avenue Public, rode her bike along the canal, and played in Patterson Creek Park right next to the Ambassador Court. When she speaks of the Glebe neighborhood where she grew up, Poppy's face lights up as if the tragedy that befell her and her mother was soothed by their surroundings. And it's the building she seems to hold most dear.

"This grand old dame has endured more than her share. A Great Depression, a world war, an electrical fire, and a half dozen floods," says Poppy. "Her floors groan a little and her windows rat-a-tat-tat on windy days, but her old bones are as solid as the day she was built."

Poppy loves telling Gus about those early days. Back when the caretaker's young son, Stanley, used to charge a nickel to wash taxis in the underground parking garage. Back when locals hopped on the Ottawa Electric Street Railway right out front and were carried off to downtown office buildings. Back when the more well-to-do residents had live-in maids. Back when there were murphy beds built into the bedroom walls of the maids' quarters and milk doors right outside each apartment. Obsolete in today's world.

As Gus listens, she finds herself gently poking holes in Poppy's stories. Noticing the things she leaves out. The gaps. Like what happened to Poppy's mother. Like why the old woman never goes outside. Like how she lost her sight. Poppy's childhood memories are full of colorful bike rides past pink blossoming trees and green grass and outings with her sticky-faced friends eating red candy apples at the fairgrounds. It's not possible she was always blind. What happened? When did it happen?

The questions linger in the shadows, night after night, as the two sit curled under blankets by the fire, eating packaged dinners from cardboard trays. Despite the epic journey up the stairs, Levi joins them every night, and his calcified bones are rewarded with a warm spot by the hearth. Gish despises Gus but adores Levi. He tolerates her, usually falling asleep while she grooms his velvet ears with her sandpaper tongue.

Poppy seems buoyed by the company. They chat late into the night and Gus sometimes sleeps all day, only rising when the winter sun is setting in late afternoon. They become like two vampires, only moving about in the dark. The lights are never on in Poppy's apartment, and Gus grows to like the dark. Every time she enters the apartment, it's like stepping back in time to the days before electricity, when firelight and moonlight were all anyone needed. In the dark, Gus is free to observe Poppy. The way her hands flit about when she's excited. The flush in her cheeks when she relives the past. The twitch above one eye when she's said too much.

And so it goes for much of January, until something unexpected breaks their nightly rhythm.

It is an evening like any other. Gus microwaves her mac and cheese and heads up to Poppy's apartment. But much to

Levi's annoyance and Gus's surprise, Poppy's door is locked. Gus knocks but Poppy doesn't answer. Listening at the door, she thinks she hears a noise and wonders if it's the cat. But after several tries knocking, Gus gives up and makes her way downstairs, Levi in tow.

Maybe Poppy wants to be alone tonight. Gus listens for signs of life from above as she eats alone. She skims a newspaper she grabbed earlier on her walk with Levi, but she can't focus on the words. She listens for footfalls. For scurrying cat paws. But all she can hear is the winter wind blowing a thick layer of snow across the park outside her window and the steady beating of her worried heart.

The next morning, Gus is up early. She barely slept through the tangle of thoughts in her head.

Poppy is dead.

She's fallen and broken her hip.

Gus did something wrong and now Poppy doesn't want to be friends.

Poppy has gone deaf.

Poppy has choked on a beef medallion.

Gus waits for the sun to rise then heads upstairs. Standing outside Poppy's door, it strikes her that she's never seen the apartment in the light of day. Their friendship has been forged solely by firelight and moonlight. Gus leans one ear against Poppy's door and listens.

"Creep much?" calls out a voice from the end of the hall.

Gus jolts and spins around.

A young girl stands by the doorway of the far stairwell, hands on hips. She's wearing a school uniform under an open snow jacket. Plaid skirt, white shirt and tie, tights, pigtails. Thin legs sticking out from giant snow-caked boots. A backpack slung over one shoulder. A snowball clasped in her mitten. The girl scowls as she cocks her arm, aims, and fires.

3

Marjory Anne Mutchmore-Stanfield

THE KID IS ABOUT TEN OR ELEVEN. BIG BROWN EYES. TIGHT little mouth.

The snowball misses by a mile.

"Can I help you?" asks Gus in her best *I'm the adult in the room* tone of voice.

The girl approaches slowly, giving Gus the once-over. Sizing her up.

"I doubt it. You don't know who I am, do you?" she says, like she owns the joint.

"Not a clue," says Gus.

"Marjory Anne Mutchmore-Stanfield of the Glebe Mutchmores," she says, nose in the air.

It's a look she's clearly perfected in front of the mirror. The girl holds out a soggy mitten in Gus's direction. Gus reaches out to shake her hand, and the girl instantly retracts her arm.

Let the games begin.

"Can't say I've ever heard of the Glebe Mutchmores," Gus lies.

She knows exactly who this is. Poppy's first cousin twice removed. Grandchild of Poppy's uncle Wilfred, Eva's brother. And more importantly, the only Mutchmore who bothers to visit Poppy.

"You must be Mojo?" Gus smiles.

The girl flinches, clearly not fond of anyone but Poppy using the nickname.

"And you are?" asks Mojo.

"Augusta. I live downstairs. I'm Poppy's friend," she says, folding her arms in triumph. "We have dinner together every night."

"That's weird. Poppy's never mentioned you," Mojo says with a smirk, "and I stop by to see her almost every morning on my way to school."

Gus realizes this game is going nowhere fast, and there are more urgent matters at hand than one-upping a grade schooler. Like Poppy's well-being.

"Here's the thing, Mojo, I'm worried about Poppy," she says. "She didn't answer her door last night. Have you heard from her?"

The girl folds her arms, ignoring the question.

"You must be the one Poppy calls Gus," says the girl as she pushes past Gus and knocks loudly on Poppy's door.

They both wait. Seconds go by. They hear a scratching sound on the other side of the door. Then a mewing. Gish. But no footsteps. No Poppy. The girl knocks again, shaking the snow off her boots and coat, as if she's expecting the door to fly open at any moment.

"Poppers, it's me," Mojo shouts into the crack of the doorframe.

Nothing. Mojo's face dissolves from smug to scared. From brat to child. She pulls a key from her pocket but hesitates.

"Do you want me to go in first?" asks Gus softly.

"Poppers never goes out," she says to herself, staring at the key.

"I'm sure she's okay," says Gus, trying to comfort the girl, who looks like she might cry.

Gus reaches for the key. Mojo pulls it away from her, pushes the key into the lock, and slowly slides the bolt sideways. She eases the door open. Gish meows as she circles Mojo's boots, then scurries back into the dim apartment, disappearing into the living room. A man's voice can be heard faintly in the distance.

Mojo looks at Gus. Gus at Mojo.

Gus goes in first, Mojo staying close, one hand on Gus's elbow. They make their way down the wide hallway into the apartment, shuffling along as one.

The voice grows louder as they approach the living room. It crackles with static and Gus realizes it's a voice on a radio or TV. She braces herself, unsure of what they're about to find. Hoping it's not a body. They reach the arched entryway and peer into the living room. At first glance, Gus is confused by what she sees. She doesn't recognize the room. Sunlight streams through the open curtains of the large bow window, bringing to life details of a room that, until this very moment, had been hidden in the shadows of wintery nights.

Intricately designed gold-and-blue floral wallpaper adorns the walls. Books line the shelves of two bookcases on either side of the hearth. Heavy framed artworks cover the walls, mostly still life paintings of bowls of fruit or landscapes with green pastures and weeping willows. One is a portrait of an aristocratic couple, the man standing in top hat and tails, the woman sitting in front of him wearing a long blue dress. A massive radio the size of an oven sits in a corner of the room next to a vintage wind-up gramophone and a box of records in brown paper sleeves. Gus always felt she was stepping back in time when she visited Poppy, but only now does she realize how true that was. The room is frozen in time.

Even the voice warbling from the antique radio sounds like it's from a bygone era.

Then Gus spots her. Or rather spots her silk slippers poking out from under one of the curtains in the bow window. Mojo sees them too. The kid gasps. Gus moves closer so she can see around the curtain. Mojo stays put. Poppy is sitting in the window seat, hands in her lap, face hidden by the velvet curtain. She's stone still.

"Poppers?" Mojo says in a thin voice from across the room. Nothing.

❧

There was a lot more that Gus hadn't seen on her nightly visits to Poppy's apartment. Not just the details of Poppy's timeless living room. Some other things. They had been there all along. Hidden in the dark hall. She hadn't noticed them that morning. Her focus had been on finding her friend, not on the walls of the old woman's hallway. And definitely not on what hung on those walls.

Gus now waits in that hallway as Mojo says goodbye to Poppy. She stares at the walls with fascination. How did she miss them? Displayed down the entire length of one wall, top to bottom, is a collection of papers of varying sizes and colors and shapes. All of them are lost pet signs. Some with frayed corners or water stains. It's like a bizarre art installation. There must be dozens of postings. Most bear pictures of cats or dogs. One shows a parrot, another a ferret, and two others, hamsters. Some are handwritten. Others are neatly typed printouts. All have one thing in common. A loved one is missing. Gus lets her eyes wander across the sad, macabre exhibit.

Meadow is diabetic and needs her daily shots.

Fluffy is a touch skittish. Approach slowly.

Rambo might take shelter in a garage or shed.

Sadie is afraid of men and loud voices.

Please help us find our darling Sam.

Shadow comes when called.

Finnigan loves bacon.

Lark.

Chai.

Riley.

Chester.

Beloved.

Family.

Missing.

Heartbroken.

Devastated.

Lost.

Mojo stands in the hall watching Gus. She points proudly at the display.

"I collect them for her, you know. It was my idea to put them on the wall. So Poppers can visit them whenever she feels like it. This was the first one," she says, pointing to a small poster about a missing teacup Chihuahua named Chamomile.

"I found it right outside, just lying on the sidewalk. I picked it up and brought it to her and read it out loud. It was like a story, she said. So I kept bringing them. I read them to her and then I find a spot for them on the wall. I think she likes knowing they're here even if she can't see them. She likes the company," Mojo explains.

Gus wonders if Poppy is just indulging the kid. What

possible enjoyment could a blind woman get from bits of old paper she can't read for herself? Then Gus reaches out and traces her hand along the wall, feeling the curled edges of one sign, the torn corner of another. There's even one with little phone numbers written along the bottom edge all in a row. Some are missing. The leftover numbers dangle like tassels.

Gus recalls how Poppy always seems to run her hand along this very wall when she navigates her way to and from her front door. She realizes the old woman doesn't do it because she doesn't know the way. She's touching the lost pet signs. Perhaps it's her way of connecting with the stories that cling to the wall. Maybe Mojo is right. They do keep her company.

"I get most of them from the assistant manager at the Metro. He saves them for me when he clears the community board once a month. This one I found tossed in the garbage. If I see one posted on a telephone pole or something, I don't touch it. These are only the pets that were found," she explains, like it makes perfect sense.

"How do you know that?" asks Gus.

"Well, I don't, but I'm sure most are found. And if they're lost-lost, then this wall makes sure they're never forgotten. That's what Poppers says."

Mojo heads for the front door.

As they leave, Gus's mind flits back in time to another wall. Her great-grandmother's living room wall, where Gus once hung bits of paper in the hope of making sense of the world. Maybe that's what Poppy and Mojo are trying to do with all these lost pet signs. Bring some sense of order to the chaos. Give some meaning to random, heartbreaking loss.

"We should go. Let her rest. She's asleep now," says Mojo.

Gus follows.

The ambulance has come and gone.

After they found Poppy sitting in the window seat, pale

and hollow-eyed, her blind eyes staring down at the park almost as if she could see, unable to move or speak, they'd dialed 911. The paramedics said Poppy was suffering from dehydration. Said it like it was nothing. They'd seen it a million times, especially with the elderly. They administered an IV, took her blood pressure, checked her heart. Said all she needed was some rest and she'd be good as new.

But Poppy clearly wasn't good or new. In fact, she looked like she'd aged ten years as she leaned back against the propped pillows, clearly uncomfortable with all the attention. She barely spoke a word except to answer the paramedic's questions with a simple yes or no. After they topped up her fluids, they rolled the empty stretcher out the door. They weren't equipped to measure her state of mind, nor did they try.

As Mojo locks the door, Gus knows there's more going on with her friend than simple dehydration.

Why hadn't she answered her door last night? Why was she sitting in the window as if she was staring outside? Had she been there all night?

Gus hadn't heard footsteps. Nothing. Not even the radio. But it was on.

Gus's head is reeling with more questions than answers when a text chimes from inside Mojo's backpack. The girl checks her phone. Her face darkens. She shoves the key to Poppy's apartment into Gus's hand.

"Check on her later, okay? Mummy's waiting out front and she's gonna be super mad because Headmistress Cochrane says you can't be late to school without a note or a parent so Mummy's had to come get me. Like it's my fault Poppers got herself all dehydra . . . dehydrogenated or whatever."

Clearly flustered, Mojo turns on her heel and takes off. Gus watches the girl run down the hall. As she enters the stairwell, she calls out.

"I'll be back tomorrow." And with that, she's gone.

Her mother's curbside pickup bugs Gus. The woman couldn't even get out of her car? No check on Poppy. No offer of help. No hello or thank-you to the neighbor who called 911. Just *super mad*. Gus hasn't met Mojo's mother, but already she doesn't like her.

That afternoon, Gus does check on Poppy, who pretends to feel much better. Propped up in bed, she smiles and sips her water and takes a few bites of the chicken parmesan penne that Gus prepared for her. But Poppy is distant. It's as if the daylight has made them strangers.

As she lets herself out the front door, Gus glances back into Poppy's apartment down the long hall, toward the end that is usually pitch-black. There are three doors. One leads to Poppy's bedroom, the open door is to her bathroom, but a third door is closed. Gus wonders if it was Eva's room. Poppy's mother. Maybe Poppy uses it for something else now. A storage room perhaps. A sunbeam cascades from a window in the bathroom and bends toward the door, illuminating a cobweb stretched across its frame. Clearly no one has been in that room in a long time.

Gus had suggested they have dinner together, but Poppy said she was tired. Not tonight. A lump had formed in Gus's throat as she cheerfully said goodbye.

Back in her apartment, an emptiness fills her chest. Gus feels silly for being hurt. Silly that she was banking on their routine lasting forever. Silly that her eighty-five-year-old neighbor has become so important to her. Gus stumbles around her apartment like a wet dishrag as intrusive shadows from her past lurk in the corners. She dusts the top of her old trunk and sweeps fur balls out from under the sofa, hoping to ward off faces she'd rather forget. One in particular. She checks the want ads and draws frowns in the frost on the windows. He lingers.

After an hour of feeling sorry for herself, Gus pulls on her winter coat and takes the dog for a walk. Levi wags his tail as the crisp air hits his nostrils. He trots along like a pup. By the time they've gone along the canal, circled back down Linden Terrace, and entered the eastern edge of Patterson Creek Park, Gus is feeling less sulky. Levi pushes his nose deep into the fresh powder. When he finds a particularly smelly patch of snow, he rolls on his back, his hind legs kicking like a jackrabbit. As they approach the stretch of park beside the Ambassador Court, they find the path blocked. It's been cordoned off, and the snow has been trampled where caution tape circles the pond's edge near a stone footbridge. The ice in the pond is broken. Kids must have been playing on it and fallen through. She hopes no one was hurt. It doesn't surprise her that she hadn't noticed any commotion in the park below her window. The drafty diamond-paned casements have been frosted over for weeks now.

Later that evening, Gus eats dinner alone again. It feels strange. The pattern of sharing dinners with Poppy has formed a deep groove in her life. And now with that indentation empty, the familiar restlessness she felt after moving in has returned to fill it up. Gus goes to bed early. At 3 A.M. she gives up trying to sleep. Her body is all pins and needles.

But it's her twitchy mind that finally gets her out of bed.

She paces her apartment wondering if it's too early for coffee.

Gus takes a shower. As she stands in the stream of hot water, eyes closed, a series of images cascade around her.

A wall of lost pets.

A cobwebbed door at the end of a hall.

A living room frozen in time.

An elderly woman sitting alone in a window seat.

A snowy park below the window.

Caution tape around an icy pond.

The images string together, flowing across her mind, then brushing down a wide hallway, through a large living room and coming to rest behind that velvet curtain alongside Poppy's ashen cheeks.

Gus opens her eyes and the images are gone.

She wraps a towel around herself and wanders through her dark apartment toward the large living room window. It's framed by two smaller windows, creating a bow effect that offers views of the length of the park, at least when it's not frosted over. Hers is almost the same view as Poppy's. Then it hits her. What's been tweaking her brain.

When they found Poppy sitting in the window seat, the window next to her had been cleared of its icy layer. It was usually frosted over like Gus's. But the ice had been scraped away as if Poppy had been trying to see out. Only she can't see.

Gus grabs a metal spatula and scrapes the frost from the inside of her window. Down below she can make out the large oval pond fed by a long creek that winds its way eastward to the Rideau Canal.

What was she hoping to see with her sightless eyes?

The creek's entire length is snow-covered, but the pond has been cleared as a skating rink for local kids. Gus can make out the stone footbridge arcing over the pond where the ice has given way. She wipes away the flakes dusting her window and looks more closely at the park. She's surprised to see a lone figure walking toward the bridge at such a late hour. Then she spots a flash of pink as the figure crosses through a pool of light cast by a lamppost at one end of the bridge.

Poppy's pink kimono.

❧

The sky moves from black to deep blue as morning inches toward the wintery horizon. Poppy is wrapped in a warm blanket by her fireplace. The old woman's lips and fingers have gone from blue to pink. Gus is thawing too.

She'd run outside wearing nothing but boots and a long winter coat, her wet hair becoming a frozen helmet.

Now that their chattering teeth and body chills have calmed, they sit quietly, sipping hot cocoa in the waning darkness. But Gus can't be silent for much longer. She needs answers. Gus is about to speak when Poppy's face lifts from gazing down at her mug.

Gus holds her tongue. Poppy is ready to talk.

And she doesn't stop until sunlight floods the living room.

Her story begins thirty hours earlier. She was listening to CBC on the radio. She listens every afternoon to her favorite show, *Now or Never*. She likes the hosts, Ify and Trevor. At the top of the hour, there was a news break. She was only half listening when the words *Patterson Creek Park* caught her attention. It was a news story about a city worker who'd found a suitcase and a shoe protruding from the splintering ice at the edge of the pond. A water main had burst in the freezing weather. A municipal crew had been deployed to deal with the flooding storm drain. It was connected to the pond, and water had poured into the pond, stirring up its murky depths, which had begun to gush upward, breaking through the ice.

When Poppy was a young girl, she was warned not to play near the pond's edge. Her father said it was bottomless. She imagined its depths leading all the way to the earth's core. When the chorus frogs came back to life every spring, she believed they took refuge there, warming their hearts next to hot lava. As a teenager, she learned the simple truth: the park had been built over a deep, mud-bottomed bog.

The suitcase, circa 1950, was found under the bridge.

Gus's mind flashes back to the penny Levi scraped from the pond's surface. A 1946 penny. Then she remembers the tape surrounding the ice. It now strikes her that the caution tape around the pond might have been police tape.

Gus watches Poppy's expression darken. Her voice slows as if her mind is creeping toward the edge of a cliff. She continues her story.

Over the radio, a police spokesperson gave a detailed and chilling account of what the city worker found inside that shoe. The skeletal remains of a human foot. The bones were still bound in the threads of a wool sock. The suitcase contained the soggy remains of a shaving kit along with some men's clothing. Divers were called in. The pond was searched. And a few hours later, an entire skeleton was pulled from the thick muck.

Poppy shudders as her eyes glaze over. She looks much like she did when Gus and Mojo found her behind the curtain. Shaken and mortified. As if saying the story out loud has once again ripped open the fabric of the universe and revealed some horrible truth. A chill grips Gus. She touches her hair to see if it's still frozen.

Then a loud knocking shatters the silence.

Both women jump.

It's coming from the front door.

Poppy turns her head in the direction of the knocking.

Her expression is almost one of relief.

"They found him," Poppy whispers.

Gus shivers.

4

Constable Laframboise

SHE HAS A FLAT FACE. SORT OF PRESSED LIKE A PANINI. HER uniform is starched stiff. She looks fit. All angles and sharp edges. She introduces herself as Constable Laframboise of the Ottawa Police Service. A junior investigator with the Missing Persons Cold Case Unit. Her assignment is to canvass the neighborhood and to interview any residents near the park who might have lived in the area in the 1950s. Poppy tells her she's lived in the building her whole life.

Laframboise shows them her badge and takes a seat in one of Poppy's living room chairs. She pulls out a pocket-size notepad and retractable four-color pen. She clicks the pen every time she asks a question as if she's changing colors depending on the answer. An impressive number of bobby pins secure a brunette bun to the back of her skull. And her speech pattern matches her appearance. By the book. It reminds Gus of the way Siri speaks. Assembling words into sentences without emotion or thought to their meaning.

"Human remains were extracted from a small body of

water in the adjacent park on the morning of January 30.
Identification papers were found intact in the interior coat
pocket of said remains. Does the name Leo Ewart mean anything to you?" she asks.

Poppy sucks in a breath as she hears the name.

"Yes, I knew him."

The constable looks surprised. Her first lead of the day.

"Good, good. Did Mr. Ewart live in the building?"

"No. He lived on Fourth near Bronson," Poppy says, eyes
blinking.

"And what was the nature of your relationship?" asks Laframboise.

"As I said, we were friends," answers Poppy.

"Actually, you did not say," says the constable, looking
down at her notes to check.

"Didn't I?" asks Poppy, drifting a little.

"Do you remember when you last saw Mr. Ewart?" asks
the constable, trying to catch Poppy's eye.

Gus realizes the constable has no idea Poppy is blind.

"October 31, 1953," answers Poppy instantly.

Laframboise writes something on her notepad. Most likely
the date. The cop speaks without looking up. Gus figures she's
doing this so Poppy won't feel watched and will let her guard
down. Interviewing 101. Only it doesn't quite work when the
subject is blind.

"That's very specific. You're sure of the date?"

"I'm sure" is all Poppy says.

The constable looks up. Waits.

"It was Halloween," adds Poppy. "It was his favorite day
of the year. Leo loved the costumes and the theater of it all."

"What was he doing when you last saw him?" asks the
constable.

"He was walking across the park. I saw him from my window, midday," says Poppy.

"He was wearing a costume?" asks the constable.

"No. Just his wool coat," answers Poppy.

Something twigs in Gus's brain. Poppy just said she saw Leo from her window. Which means that Poppy wasn't blind in 1953. She can see a young Poppy sitting in the window, but the image is instantly replaced by the old Poppy from the other night, staring out as if seeing. Gus watches her friend's face closely. Watches her pupils. Wonders if she's just pretending to be blind. Gus suddenly feels ridiculous for even thinking it. She laughs out loud, quickly covering it up with a cough.

Laframboise shoots her a look then continues.

"And you never saw him again?"

"No, never again," says Poppy, obviously tiring.

"We couldn't find any archival records of a missing person by his name," she says. "You didn't report him missing?"

"I didn't know he was missing," says Poppy.

"How's that?"

"What?" Poppy seems confused.

"Didn't you wonder why you never saw your friend again?" says Laframboise.

"Wonder?" Poppy says. "Yes of course" is all she offers by way of explanation.

"Did he have any next of kin?" she asks.

"No," says Poppy.

"Is there anything you can tell me about him that might explain how he ended up at the bottom of a pond outside your building?" the constable asks.

Poppy visibly shrinks. Gus picks up Poppy's cocoa from the coffee table and guides it to her hand. The old woman takes a sip. Only then does it dawn on Laframboise that she's blind.

"She's been up all night. Will this take much longer?" Gus asks.

The constable looks at Gus, then tilts her head as if seeing her for the first time. Gus suddenly feels the need to explain herself.

"Augusta Monet. I'm her neighbor. Well, her friend. I live downstairs," she babbles.

Laframboise's eyes flick to the floor as if she has X-ray vision and can see into the messy apartment below to verify the statement. Then she goes back to ignoring Gus.

"Where did you think Mr. Ewart had been all these years?" she asks Poppy.

"Not in the pond," answers Poppy.

"We did find an employment record for a Leo Ewart in a company directory from back then. A business known as The Trichborne Group." She adds, "Does that sound familiar?"

"Leo worked there," confirms Poppy.

"Odd that his employers didn't report him missing?" muses the constable.

"He'd just quit his job," says Poppy.

"Why did he do that?" asks Laframboise.

"People quit," says Poppy.

"Was he planning to move? Did he have another job lined up? Was he in some sort of trouble? Gambling debts? Any disagreements with someone, anything?" asks the constable.

Poppy shrugs.

"Nothing? You were friends and he told you nothing?" says the constable.

Poppy's eyelids flutter.

"Not a word," says Poppy, more to herself than the constable.

Poppy seems like she's checked out. Gus sighs and slaps her hands on her knees, trying to signal that it's time to wrap this up. Laframboise closes her notepad, tucks it in her belt, and places her pen neatly inside her breast pocket.

"That will be all for now, Miss Honeywell," she says, rising from the chair, making it clear that it's her decision.

"How did he die?" asks Poppy in almost a whisper.

Laframboise raises one eyebrow, but otherwise stays perfectly still.

"The remains and personal effects have been sent to our forensics lab for examination. They were well preserved by the mud, but it's hard to say if a cause of death will be easily determinable with so much time passing," says the constable. "If forensics can confirm it, they will. All indications point to a simple case of accidental drowning," she adds.

She says it like the case has already been solved in her mind. Like she was only talking to Poppy so she could practice her interview skills. Like she doesn't give a shit what really happened. Like it is just another cold case that she got stuck with until something juicier and more career advancing comes along. At least that's how it feels to Gus as she watches the constable reach out to shake Poppy's hand, then retract it awkwardly when she remembers the old woman can't see it.

"Sorry for your loss, ma'am. We'll let you know the findings."

Gus shows Laframboise out. Back in the living room, she finds Poppy standing at the window, her back to Gus.

"He was handsome. The bluest eyes you ever saw. He was just twenty-three," says Poppy.

"You loved him?" Gus asks, knowing the answer.

Poppy turns. Tears stream down her face.

"With my whole heart," she says.

Beyond the window, the sun is a misty peach ball, ticking

higher and higher in the sky. But inside the apartment, time seems to stand still.

And then it moves in the other direction as a story unspools.

Rolling back some seventy years.

5

Leo

IT WAS 1950. POPPY RAN INTO ONE OF HER MOTHER'S CHILD-hood friends one day on the street. A wealthy entrepreneur named Teddy Trichborne. He was the one who introduced them. Leo had just moved to Ottawa and Teddy had taken the young man under his wing, offering him an internship at The Trichborne Group. Leo didn't know anyone in town. He lived nearby, so he and Poppy often met for late-afternoon walks along the canal.

In the beginning, Poppy hid the blossoming friendship from her mother. She was only fifteen and Leo was twenty, and she knew Eva would disapprove of her keeping company with a man without a chaperone. Leo was sweet and soft-spoken and funny and loved to make her laugh by imperson-ating their favorite screen actors. Humphrey Bogart, Jimmy Stewart, Marlon Brando. And he was good at it. Always the gentleman, he offered his arm when they descended the steep steps into the park and insisted on paying when they rode the electric tram or stole away for a Sunday matinee at the Glebe Theatre. They'd sit in the dark and whisper about traveling the world. They would climb the pyramids in Giza. They would explore the Mayan ruins of Chichén Itzá. One day.

Poppy pauses. Then she asks Gus to get her handbag from the front hall. When she has it, Poppy roots inside and pulls out a small bundle of notes neatly tied with string. She unties the bundle. Something is hidden among the papers. She hands it to Gus. It's a strip of faded photo booth images. A young couple sits close together in the photos. In one they're laughing, in another they're sticking their tongues out toward the lens, and in the last, they're covering their faces with their hands. Leo is peeking through his fingers, looking at Poppy. He is handsome, despite his crooked smile or perhaps because of it. His eyes dance. He's clearly in love. Poppy is a beautiful young woman with long dark hair that cascades across her shoulders. Her smiling eyes are so bright and alive. The pair looks blissful.

Gus's gaze wanders across their faces as Poppy continues her story.

For three years the couple hid their courtship from her mother. But when Poppy turned eighteen, they decided it was time. She told Eva about Leo. At first, her mother was amenable, even pleased for Poppy. She met Leo and liked him. Or at least she seemed to. But in early October, everything changed. Almost overnight, Eva turned against their relationship without explanation. She forbade Poppy from seeing Leo, going so far as to keep her under lock and key.

The building caretaker's son, Stanley, became their go-between, passing notes back and forth. As she recounts this part of her story, Poppy gently pats the bundle in her lap, and Gus knows they must be those same love notes.

The couple soon realized their only option was to run away together. Leo quit his job and immediately began arranging their travel papers and tickets out of the country.

He promised to let her know when everything was ready so she could get her belongings packed at the last minute. They agreed upon a signal. He would walk through the park wearing a red cap at noon, and that would be the night they would elope. Stanley was to bring her a note telling her when and where to meet Leo. That October, she watched from her window every day at noon. Then the day came. Poppy saw Leo walking across the park in a red cap.

It was October 31, 1953.

But the note never came.

Poppy's eyes look far away as if she's seeing the events of the past unfold.

It was unusually cold for October. A blustery arctic front had swept thick dark clouds across the sky. She ate minestrone soup with her mother, thinking this would be their last supper together. She wondered when Stanley would bring her the note with the final details of the plan. She was sad, but excited and hopeful. If only she could tell her mother. If only Eva could be happy for her. Perhaps, in time, her mother would come around. She hoped one day that would be true. Eva was quiet. Almost as if she knew. Her mother didn't eat, just fiddled with her spoon.

Before bed, Poppy checked the usual hiding spot in the milk cupboard for the note. Still nothing. She went to her room and busied herself packing a small bag. Drowsy, she lay down, planning to check again for the note in an hour. The next morning when Poppy rose from a deep slumber, she was alarmed that she'd slept through the night. She didn't even remember falling asleep. The previous night was blank. She panicked. Before her mother woke, she ran out of the apartment. She tried Stanley but he wasn't home. She ran for blocks to Leo's apartment. She asked his neighbors and his landlord. No one had seen him. She tried his former workplace. His employer, Teddy Trichborne, seemed the most troubled. His protégé had quit out of the blue and left no word as to why or where he was headed. A newspaper boy on the corner who knew Leo said he'd seen him jump on the tram with a suitcase sometime yesterday.

Leo was gone.

Poppy's heart ached without answers. Had something happened to him? Why had he signaled her and then left no note? Had he changed his mind? Had she gotten the plan wrong? She began to wonder if she'd imagined their feelings for each other. Then she remembered the milk cupboard. She'd forgotten to check it this morning. She returned home and found a note in their hiding spot. And that's when she knew the inexplicable yet horrible truth. The note simply said, *I'm sorry, please forget about me. Leo.*

He'd left without her. Poppy was devastated.

Days turned to weeks and winter settled in deep. A chilling reminder of her loss. Her mother tried to get Poppy to focus on the future. On a career or higher education. On something to look forward to. But Poppy couldn't see her way out of the darkness. Her eyesight began to deteriorate. She wouldn't leave her room. Eva tried coddling her, then she switched to ignoring her, then scolding her. Nothing worked. And then Poppy went completely blind. The doctor said it was hysterical blindness and in time her sight would return. Poppy was young. She'd bounce back. What concerned the doctor more than the young woman's hysteria, though, was Eva's bizarre state of mind.

She was clearly more ill than she let on. Eva's hands shook uncontrollably, and her pupils were cloudy. She couldn't keep food down. Her blood pressure was gravely high. By Christmas, Eva's mind seemed to be tumbling away from her at breakneck speed. She could barely formulate sentences or perform simple tasks like brushing her own hair. When touched, she had violent outbursts. She heard voices and claimed to see ghosts. Poppy was frightened. By late December 1953, Eva's brother, Wilfred, intervened and had Eva committed to a hospital for the insane in Brockville, Ontario.

Poppy was eighteen when her mother was taken away. She was left to fend for herself on a meager monthly allowance provided by her uncle Wilfred. Having relied on her mother's eyes for weeks, Poppy was afraid to go outside. Soon, Poppy had arranged her life so that she wouldn't have to venture out, relying on delivery services and the help of a few residents of the building to get by. Until last night, Poppy had not stepped foot outside her fourth-floor apartment in decades. The world had nothing left for her.

Hearing her story, Gus is heartbroken for Poppy. For the terrible losses she has endured. She was so young. So alone. She could have found love again. Had a family, traveled, had children, a life. But instead she lost sight of everything. Literally. Of all that could have been. Loss has shaped her very existence. It has shaped Gus's as well. In their own way, they have each held on to the past because it's inhabited by the people they love.

This is why Poppy's apartment remains exactly as it was in the 1950s and why Poppy, wrapped in her pink kimono with her silver hair cascading around her shoulders, also remains the same. She is a young girl trapped in an old woman's fading shell.

"We took those photos our last summer together. On his birthday," Poppy says, like she knows Gus is looking at the images.

"I'm so sorry, Poppy" is all Gus can think to say.

"Oh, sweet girl, there's nothing to be sorry about," says Poppy, her voice wistful. "You see, it wasn't true after all. Leo never left me. He was in the park this whole time."

Poppy nods toward the bow window and the strange events of the past twenty-four hours become clearer. Gus understands why Poppy wasn't herself at first. Why she sat unable to speak in the window. Why she ventured outside into the park. She was shocked by what she'd heard on the radio, and in her heart, she knew they'd found her Leo even before the constable confirmed it. She wanted to be close to him. Close to his resting place. And now, as the initial shock begins to lift, Poppy is experiencing a revelation. Gus can see it in her expression. The worry lines have eased. The flush has returned to her cheeks. Knowing her lover did not abandon her all those years ago has lifted a heavy burden she's carried for decades.

Gus glances at the small bundle of handwritten notes in Poppy's lap. The old woman kept them all these years. Love notes on faded blue writing paper. It's all she has left of Leo. Tender messages about a future that never happened. Hopes and dreams laid out in ink on paper but never lifted from the page to become real. And that last note. The apology. Gus wonders what he was sorry about. It sounded like he'd gone without her. But he hadn't. So what did it mean?

Gus can't keep her mind from meandering through possible answers as she looks at the fragile folds in the notepaper. Time has made them brittle. Time is like that. It creases and bends until it finally breaks apart. Gus can almost see the tenuous folds between the past and the present thinning before her eyes. She holds her breath, but she can't hold it together. Everything in front of her begins to disintegrate.

No, no, no, don't go there.

It's too late.

The past collapses and slides away.

～⌒～

Gus is pulled violently into the present.

Back to her subbasement prison cell.

Back to a new surge of pain that rips across her belly and down her legs.

The stone floor is cold against her spine. She must have fainted again. How long has she been out this time? Gus tries to see through the pain to what she was doing before she blacked out. She was searching for something. She tries to slow her breathing, but it's coming in sharp gasps. The pain is unbearable. All she can do is scream. Long and loud. The release of energy triggers a shift in her belly, and the contraction slows. Almost as suddenly as it came on, the agony mercifully wafts away.

Gus closes her eyes and basks in the momentary calm. Slowly, a memory comes to her. There's a sound in the memory. She's in this room. She is rushing toward the door after it shuts behind her. As she reaches it, she hears the sound. A key clicking in the lock.

Gus opens her eyes. This new memory brings with it a chilling realization. Someone locked her in this room intentionally. She didn't get trapped down here by accident. But the realization also gives her hope. It means someone knows she's down here. They know she's alone, without food or water. They have to know she's pregnant. They have to feel something. Remorse. Regret. Pity. They'll come back to free her.

The fuck they will.

Hope limps away across the dank floor like an injured rat. Gus knows they're not coming back.

The queen is royally fucked.

And she also knows it's her own fault.

She dug too deep. Asked too many questions. Pushed too hard.

Like before.

She didn't stop when she knew it was getting dangerous.

It's not the first time she's gone after the truth, no matter the cost.

Now she knows too much.

Someone wants her dead.

The baby kicks her ribs. She looks at her belly. At her baby. Knows she can't give up. Gus takes a deep breath and refocuses. A word dances into her mind.

Dumbwaiter.

That's what she was searching for. That stupid little elevator where she found the furry stowaway. It's her way out. Gus draws her knees as close as she can to her large belly, making herself as small as possible. She's not small at all. Not in a million years will Queen Kong fit inside that dumbwaiter.

She needs a Plan B.

As an idea takes shape, Gus hears a soft murmuring from across the room.

She stays perfectly still and listens.

Someone is there in the dark corner.

Do you see, Honey Pie? the voice whispers.

It's a voice she knows by heart.

Not yet, Mama.

Gus closes her eyes and drifts back.

Back to when she first met the Mutchmores.

Back to when she had no idea what they were capable of.

6

The Mutchmores

It's been two weeks since Leo's foot poked from the icy pond. The police tape is gone and February is full of bluster. The cracked pond has frozen over again like nothing happened. Even the freeze-dried lilies are covered in a new layer of ice and snow.

Levi hates the bitter weather. The salt on the sidewalks stings his paws. Gus tried putting plastic booties on his feet but he hated them. He'd do a weird high step then lose his balance, fall over, and tug them off with his teeth. But without them he's impossible to walk. Every couple of feet he does a three-legged hop or stops to lick the salt away, which only hardens it to his paws. The pair usually only make it halfway across the park before he sinks to his belly, refusing to go farther. Now that they're back to having nightly dinners with Poppy, Levi is stubbornly attached to this ritual, and late-afternoon walks only cut into the time he gets to spend stretched in front of the fire while Gish licks the pads of his tender paws.

Heading back to the Ambassador, Gus contemplates her shrinking funds, her lack of motivation in the job hunt department, and her persistent belly issues. Gus feels herself slipping into hibernation mode as winter deepens. She knows it's not healthy for her to retreat, to ignore the seesaw of life's ups and downs, to fight the inevitability of what may be coming, to act like the indefensible missteps she took that November night never happened. She can still see the blood splatter on the snowy sidewalk as if it was yesterday. For now, she puts her head down. One foot in front of the other. Mostly she can't wait to get bundled up in bed each night.

Meanwhile Poppy seems headed in the opposite direction. She's slowly coming out of her shell. She gets dressed every morning, reserving her pink kimono for evenings only. She's taken to pinning her long silver hair into a loose bun on top of her head and powdering her nose. She sometimes puts lipstick on, with mixed results.

She ventures into the halls and, when it works, she uses the elevator to go down to the laundry room or the lobby to collect her mail. She's even begun to navigate the stairwells, after a few practice runs with Mojo.

Poppy and Mojo have started a new routine. They bake cookies or chewy squares every Sunday and hand them out in pretty tins to neighbors in the building. It's as if Poppy wants to do something for the people who've helped her out all these years. One of those people is the former caretaker, who still lives in the building with his sister, Alice. His name is Stanley Croft. He and Alice always get a batch.

Poppy tells Gus that Stanley joined the army in the early fifties. At the time, his father, William, was the building's caretaker. But not long after Stanley went away, William died, and Stanley was honorably discharged so that he could return to care for his younger sister, Alice. He took his father's place as caretaker, and even though he's long retired and there's a new building superintendent, Mr. Curry, the siblings have lived in their two-bedroom apartment on the first floor ever since. Neither ever marrying. They've been helping Poppy for years.

As Gus and Levi return from their walk and approach the entrance of the Ambassador Court, she spots a figure in the archway.

She can't believe who it is.

"Is that Mr. Levi, my furry friend?" Poppy smiles as Levi rubs against her leg.

"Would you like to go for a walk?" asks Gus.

"I've got a better idea," says Poppy, handing Gus an envelope embossed with a crest and gold lettering. "I'd know the feel of that crest anywhere. Open it."

Gus opens the envelope. Inside is an invitation to the Annual Mutchmore Winter Gala.

"Tell me I'm wrong, but I bet that's an invitation to a gala, isn't it? Comes every year," says Poppy.

"You're right," says Gus.

"How would you feel about going to a party, love?" Poppy asks with a hesitant shrug. "I don't know if I dare, but if you'll agree to come with me, I think I just might. Dare, that is."

Her words echo off the stone archway and seem to drift away on the bitter wind.

Gus looks down at her hand. The envelope disappears.

Levi and Poppy dissolve before her eyes.

And the fragile moment is lost just like that.

❧

A violent body shudder pulls her back to the present. She's covered in a cold sweat. She shivers. Her throat is raw. Gus knows she has to move. To keep the blood flowing. She lifts herself off the floor to a seated position. She presses her palms against the rough brick wall and pushes herself to a standing position. Her back aches. Her knees nearly buckle but she grips the wall. Steadies herself. Feels around for the wood door to the dumbwaiter. Finds it. Gus pulls on the door handle. It won't budge. She slams her fists along the edges of the door to loosen the grit. Tries again. The wood cracks, groans, then the door opens, letting loose a cloud of stale dust. Gus coughs, waving the dust away. She sticks her head inside the shaft and looks up. It's dark. She opens her mouth and tries to yell up the shaft, but she can only manage a croak. Her voice is shot. Raw from all the screaming.

She needs all her energy to execute Plan B, so she gives up on trying to get her vocal cords to cooperate. She needs to move fast before another contraction takes her legs out from under her. Gus reaches inside the small elevator shaft, feels for the rope, and begins to slowly lower the dumbwaiter. She can hear the squeaky wheels of the pulley turning. She pulls and pulls until finally the compartment is locked in place, right in front of her. She drops to her knees then begins to crawl across the floor in the dark. Finds what she's looking for. The shattered pieces of her cell phone. Amazingly, the phone is still intact—the protective case is the only thing that shattered. She grabs a piece with a sharp edge. Takes a handful of her long red hair and runs the shard across it until she's cut off a chunk. Then she rips a strip of cloth from the hem of her T-shirt and ties it around the lock of hair. She crawls back to the compartment and suspends the hair from the slates in the top of the dumbwaiter so it dangles near the opening. Impossible to miss. As an added touch, she carefully scratches some words into the floor of the dumbwaiter using the shard.

A message.

She's hoping that he's already wondering where she is.

That he's searching for her. He'll come for her. He'll see her SOS. He'll save her.

Just thinking about him causes her breath to catch in her throat and her heart to ache.

She wants to see him again.

The memory of the first time they met comes flooding back.

It lifts her from her dungeon and places her gently in a beautiful palace strung with white lights. She can hear the quartet playing. She can smell the forget-me-nots.

&

Framed by ushers in military dress, Poppy clasps Gus's elbow as they pass through the grand entrance leading into the gala. The venue is spectacular. Floor-to-ceiling windows reflect the strings of bulbs looped across the beams of the massive, vaulted ceilings. A round stage seems to float in the middle of the room, where a quartet of musicians plays, surrounded by dozens of round tables set with white linens, place settings for ten, and exquisite centerpieces of blue forget-me-nots. Several men in uniform ring the outer edges of the room. Guests dressed in fancy gowns and tuxedos mingle and clink champagne flutes.

Gus can't believe she agreed to this. She feels like an impostor, especially because she's not even wearing her own clothes. Poppy had some dresses from when she used to go out stored in a garment bag in the back of her closet. Gus is wearing an emerald-green dress with a flowing princess waist. She's put on some weight the last few months, and it was the only one that fit her. Poppy wears a silver gown with tiny pearls embroidered into the bodice. It fits Poppy perfectly, like she's been the same size her whole life.

Visions of the tiny clasp at her neck coming undone and the dress cascading to her ankles sets Gus's heart racing.

But she quickly forgets her own anxieties when she realizes Poppy is gripping her arm like a vise. Her friend is shaking.

"We can go," Gus offers. "You don't have to do this."

Poppy takes a deep breath. Shakes her head and steps forward.

"Tell me what it looks like," she says, her voice catching in her dry throat.

Gus describes the room for Poppy as they make their way toward the seating chart. She keeps her voice calm and low and the pace slow so that Poppy can get used to the sounds and the feel of so many people around her. She knows her friend must be overwhelmed, but Gus can see the worry lines on Poppy's brow slowly beginning to fade with each step.

Mojo intercepts them.

"Poppers! You came, you came," she squeals, hugging Poppy and raising an eyebrow at Gus and her borrowed gown.

Gus returns the look by giving Mojo's blue velvet pantsuit the once-over.

Ever since the two of them discovered Poppy sitting shell-shocked in her window seat, Gus and Mojo have tolerated, but mostly avoided, each other. Mojo comes by weekdays before school and on Sunday afternoons. Gus visits in the evenings. Their paths rarely cross. Gus knows the kid is out of joint because of Gus's growing friendship with Poppy, but she also knows they both care deeply about the woman so she can't entirely hate the kid.

"I told Mummy you were coming and she didn't believe me. She said hell would freeze over before you'd show your face. But here you are, so I was right."

Mojo jumps up and down, then spots someone else she knows and prances away like a puppy distracted by a tossed ball.

"Footsie! Yo, Foots!" she hollers to a girl her age wearing a sequin romper.

Poppy squeezes Gus's arm.

"Welcome to hell," Poppy whispers.

She looks like she's only half kidding.

Gus checks out the seating chart, and to her relief, they're not seated at the head table with the Mutchmore clan. And yet a tiny part of Gus is insulted on Poppy's behalf. *How dare they?* Considering they're the hosts of this bloody gala, not one of her family members, aside from bratty little Mojo, has come over to properly greet her. Gus isn't even sure who Mojo's parents are until they make their grand entrance, and even then, they're so far across the room that she can't get a proper look at Ricker Stanfield and May Mutchmore-Stanfield.

Poppy and Gus make their way to table 47, tucked in a back corner behind a pillar that partially obscures the stage. Gus is overjoyed to be out of the way. At the kids' table. And it seems their tablemates have also been banished for reasons that quickly become apparent, turning Gus's initial joy into bubbling rage within the hour.

First up in the gallery of misfit tablemates are the McClintocks, who begin their introductions even before the others are settled into their seats. They casually let it slip that they live in a mansion in Rockcliffe Park. She's an art collector. He's in banking. But despite having all the right credentials to earn seats at a better table, here they are at table 47. Gus soon figures out why. They've brought along their four astonishingly ill-mannered children. The youngest has already urinated on the floor, causing a near-disaster when a waiter carrying a full tray of wine glasses slips in the puddle. He recovers at the last second. The middle two devil-spawn are twins whose faces look like they got squished together at birth and never got unsquished. Together, they've dismembered the floral centerpiece and are now eating the forget-me-nots. The oldest is playing a video game at full volume on his phone. The game involves a lot of semiautomatic gunfire and screaming. The McClintocks appear helpless to stop the mayhem. So they ignore it. Pouring more wine and waving at friends while their monstrous brood goes wild.

Incredibly, there's another misfit who beats out the McClintocks for most annoying tablemate. A distinguished-looking man in his fifties who introduces himself as Dr. Braddish Billings III. Strike one is when Gus catches him swapping his name card for hers so he can have the better view of the stage. Because of him, Gus is no longer sitting next to Poppy. When she protests, he pretends not to hear her. Strike two comes later when he loudly berates a member of the serving staff when he moves his arm, bumps hers, and she accidentally splashes a drop of wine on his sleeve. His fault. He tells her she's ruined his suit and she'll have to pay for the dry cleaning. She rushes off, tears in her eyes. Strike three: he sneezes into his napkin, then switches it with Mr. McClintock's.

But as the evening progresses, Gus lands on the real reason he's been seated at the kids' table. All night, guests have been passing by on their way to use the toilets located next to table 47. Many of them pat him on the back or say a quick hello or offer him a wave, but each one dashes off quickly as if they have to get to the bathroom fast. These people know him, and she's absolutely convinced that every one of them put in a special request that he not be seated at their table. In part because he's a total dickhead, but mostly because he's a complete and utter bore. He literally never stops talking, even when his mouth is full of food. He was only invited because the Mutchmores need him. Gus knows this because he hasn't stopped yammering on, loudly, about his life's work. Braddish is the undisputed authority on all things Mutchmorian. He drones on about his prominence as a tenured professor of history, a biographer, and an author of innumerable, no doubt dull as dishwater, books about the family, their ancestors, their foundation, their legacy.

Poppy has the misfortune of being seated right next to Boring Braddish. Her polite expression has transformed over the course of the meal to one of stunned silence as she wilts under the onslaught of Braddish's navel-gazing monologue. And worse, bits of food keep flying across the table as he picks his teeth with one of the wood skewers from his shrimp kebab appetizer.

Meanwhile, Gus has her own issues. She's squeezed between the gamer kid and a gangly young man who looks like his suit is two sizes too big and he forgot to brush his hair. His curly black mop, scruffy facial hair, thick glasses, and slouching posture remind Gus of an old man, not a guy in his twenties. His food even looks like old man food. He must have pre-ordered some special dietary option. It looks like bean-and-rice slop. It's making her nauseous watching him eat, painfully slowly. The guy hasn't uttered a word since sitting next to her. At first he was too busy wiping his utensils with wet wipes. Now, he's the last to finish eating. The waiters hover. Gus wills him to finish so they can get on with dessert and get out of there.

The band strikes up as the dinner dishes are whisked away by serving staff who glide through the tables, trays high above their heads, maneuvering with the agility of ice dancers. Gus tries to enjoy the music, but she can't seem to tune out the war zone exploding from the McClintock kid's phone.

Poppy looks just as miserable. Gus has to rescue her. They need an escape plan. She scans the room for exits. Looks one way, then turns the other way just as the young man next to her is leaning toward her. Their noses touch. His breath smells like coffee and cookies, even though dessert hasn't been served. They both jerk their heads back.

He says something, but she doesn't catch it.

"What?" Gus shouts.

"I was trying to introduce myself," he says, louder.

Gus shrugs.

"I was leaning into your ear," he says, pointing to her ears.

"That's right, I can't hear you," she says, nodding.

"My name is Howard," he shouts just as the music ends. His name rockets across the hall. Several people twist in their chairs to register their disapproval. Howard gives Gus a toothy grin that turns him from old man to young boy in a flash. Gus can't help but smile back. It's taken him the entire meal to work up the courage to speak, so she feigns interest.

"Augusta Monet," she says, holding out her hand. "What do you do?"

He shakes her hand and says something. Again, Gus can't hear him. The bursts of gunfire on the kid's phone have intensified. Howard pauses, looks like he's given up, but then he does something that surprises Gus. In one swift motion, he reaches in front of her, yanks the phone from the kid's hand, and drops it in a full glass of water in front of the boy. It happens so fast the boy doesn't seem to register who did what or how. He stares wide-eyed at his drowned phone.

With a ceasefire in hand, Howard turns to Gus and reintroduces himself. It turns out that Howard Baylis is a blogger who also freelances for a community paper called the *Kitchissippi Times*. It's why he's at the gala. He's doing a society page piece on the annual event.

He offers her a wet wipe. She takes it. Smells like lemons.

Gus doesn't know what to make of Howard. He's weird and awkward and sort of geeky, yet oddly likeable and buoyant and sure of himself. It's like he knows he's a square peg but he's okay with it. He looks out of place in this stuffy crowd. But he doesn't seem to care.

Howard points at the forget-me-not petals strewn in front of the McClintock twins.

"Myosotis," he says.

Gus raises an eyebrow. He goes on.

"It's the Greek word for a forget-me-not. Loosely translates to mouse's ear. You know the juice from the leaves of a forget-me-not can be used to stop a nose bleed. I doubt that's why the Mutchmores chose them, though," he laughs. "That'd be weird. I'm betting it's more a symbol of remembrance for the fallen soldiers and all that. Veterans' hospice. Makes sense. Yeah, it's probably not the nose thing, or the ear thing."

Howard's eyes dart upward as if he's accessing a database of factoids stored in his brain. He types a short note into his phone as if some gem just came to him that he has to write down before he forgets it. Definitely an odd duck.

The lights dim, the hall darkens, and the stage becomes illuminated. All eyes are pulled to the center of the room. Everyone stops talking, including Braddish. A silhouetted figure carefully ascends the steps, approaching center stage, mic in hand.

Wilfred Mutchmore introduces himself in a wilting voice. This must be the Uncle Wilfred that Poppy spoke of. The one who put her mother in a hospital for the insane. Gus glances at Poppy but can't read her face in the dark. A live video feed of the old man's face is projected behind him on an enormous, invisible screen. The image floats like a see-through hologram. Observable from every angle of the room. Too observable. The camera is insanely close. Every wrinkle on his haggard face is on display. Wilfred's shiny eyes peek out from under purple, sagging lids. He looks fossilized.

As if reading her mind, Howard whispers into Gus's ear. He tells her that he did a piece on Wilfred's one hundredth birthday party a couple of years ago at the Ottawa Hunt and Golf Club.

The elderly man stumbles through a raspy introduction of the foundation. It is a history tangled in the roots of a prominent family tree, reaching back to the early twentieth century when Wilfred's parents, Robert and Cora, lost their firstborn son, Felix, in the Great War. When the war ended, and they saw so many returning veterans in need of housing, they created the foundation to honor their fallen son and to help hundreds of war heroes get back on their feet. After the death of his parents, Wilfred vowed to carry on his family's good works, honoring his parents' rich legacy of service. Wilfred expanded the foundation's land holdings and programs, which continue to serve the needs of veterans to this day.

Gus glances around the dark hall. She doesn't see any uniforms other than the military guard serving as decoration at the fringes—none on the guests. She's guessing the veterans' needs don't include black-tie dinners. This gala is for wealthy donors only.

Wilfred thanks his wife, Charlotte, for her years of dedication to the foundation. He nods to a white-haired woman at the head table. A roving spotlight finds her. Charlotte looks quite a bit younger than her withered husband.

Howard whispers that the pair married in 1953 when Wilfred was thirty-four and Charlotte was just eighteen. A young secretary at the foundation. Quite the eyebrow raiser at the time.

Gus looks at Howard. She's impressed.

"It's my job to know the who's who of O Town," he smiles.

Charlotte acknowledges her husband with a drunken salute of her champagne flute, then downs the contents. A dull chatter dances across the hall as the guests tire of the old man. He clears his throat.

"It was a different time, a different century, when I took the reins of my father's foundation on his passing. I admit, they had to pry those reins from my grip when the time came for me to retire"—he pauses for the obligatory laughter from the audience—"but as we ushered in a new century, a new generation came along with it. And take those reins they did. The foundation has flourished under their leadership, and before I introduce the couple of the hour, I want to thank you for allowing an old man a final moment in the spotlight."

Again he pauses. The requisite claps sputter and die quickly.

"Without further ado, allow me to present your hosts, May Mutchmore-Stanfield and her husband, Ricker Stanfield, the son I never had," declares Wilfred with a sweep of his hand toward the head table.

The spotlight catches Ricker in the middle of dabbing napkins into the tablecloth where his mother-in-law, Charlotte, has spilled something. Charlotte is batting him away, as utensils clatter to the floor. The thunderous applause catches him off guard, but Ricker composes himself instantly, takes the arm of the beautiful woman sitting on the other side of him, and together they float toward the center of the hall like they own the place. The spotlight follows them. Gus can see Mojo waving to her parents as they pass. The video zeroes in on the couple as they smile their perfect smiles, step onto the stage, and wave like a newly crowned royal couple. May glitters from head to toe. Ricker is dapper in tux and tails.

"Exclamation mark," says Howard, looking gobsmacked.

Gus nods. The Mutchmores make a charade of attempting to quiet the crowd, and after waving to a few chosen guests, Ricker introduces the real star of the evening. The video screen flickers, and a large image of a soldier appears behind them. It's a black-and-white archival shot of a young man in uniform. Below the image, a caption reads: PRIVATE FELIX MUTCHMORE, 1900–1916.

May tells his story in a practiced voice oozing with passion.

Young Felix lied about his age so that he could voluntarily enlist to serve his country and fight in the Great War. Tragically, he was one of over a thousand Canadian Corps soldiers killed in action at the Battle of Mount Sorrel in Belgium.

"A Canadian hero and a Mutchmore son, Felix lost his life that day in June," May says, her voice wavering with emotion. "Young Felix believed in self-sacrifice, bravery, honor."

Ricker continues the story in a rehearsed transition. "Ideals that May and I strive to live up to each and every day." He places his arm around his wife. "These are the principles upon which this foundation was built"—he nods to his father-in-law—"and the reason it was named for a Mutchmore hero."

May chimes in: "In the name of my uncle, who gave his life so that we could all be free, a soldier who I am proud to call family, let us raise our glasses." And just like that, a waiter materializes from the shadows of the stage with a tray carrying two champagne flutes. The couple each take a flute, raise it, and speak in unison.

"To Felix Mutchmore."

Cameras flash as everyone in the room stands, raising their glasses toward the pair as a chorus of *hear hear*s and *bravo*s echoes across the hall.

As if pulled by a force field, Gus and Howard, and every misfit at table 47, rise to their feet, smiling like Cheshire cats, unable to help themselves from being caught up in the moment. The image of the war hero on the screen behind May and Ricker is replaced by a live feed of the golden couple.

The quartet returns to the stage. May and Ricker descend

to circulate among their people. Dessert is served as guests mingle. The world is aglitter.

And then things go south.

The Mutchmore matriarch, Charlotte, stumbles past table 47. She spots Poppy, evidently for the first time.

"Oh my goodness, look who it is," she calls out, detouring around their table.

Heads turn. Eyes widen.

Charlotte grabs the back of Braddish's chair to steady herself. He rises to offer his hand. Clearly he thinks she's talking about him. She shimmies past him and takes his seat next to Poppy. Embarrassed, Braddish drifts away into the crowd.

Charlotte's face is inches from Poppy's. Poppy looks gray. Not sure what's happening, Gus rises and tries to get around the table, but the mingling guests block her way. She glances across the room. She spots May Mutchmore-Stanfield whispering in her husband's ear then heading in their direction. The guests part for May as she makes her way to Charlotte. She gets there before Gus can. May lifts her mother by the elbow, trying to ease her from the chair. May thinks she's got things under control, but Charlotte squirms from her grip. Gus is closer. She can hear Charlotte's slurring words.

"It's Poppy. Don't you recognize her? I was speaking with her," snaps Charlotte, trying to sit back down.

"Darling, don't make a scene," says May, her eyes darting around the room.

"Did you know her mum and I were close? She said it was like she had another daughter when I married into the family," Charlotte says, swaying a little.

"That's nice," says May. "Now let's go freshen up, Mother."

"Stop it. Stop trying to manage me, May," shouts Charlotte.

A hush descends around them.

Charlotte looks around. Realizes what she's done. She pastes a smile on her face and relents a little by taking May's arm. Gus is beside them. She maneuvers behind Poppy and rests a hand on her shoulder to let her know she's there. Poppy turns her head in the direction of May and Charlotte, who seem engaged in a barely visible tug-of-war.

"It was so kind of the family to invite me every year, I thought I might as well come see what all the fuss was about," says Poppy, smiling.

This sets Charlotte off again. She lets go of May's arm and tries to shoo her daughter away. She sits next to Poppy.

With an almost imperceptible lift of her finger, May signals for reinforcements.

"You have your mother's cheekbones," Charlotte says to Poppy. "The Mutchmore cheekbones. High and mighty."

Poppy bristles a little.

"She wasn't so high and mighty in the end though, was she?" says Charlotte.

Most of the guests within earshot pretend not to be listening. Others have their phones out, pointed nonchalantly in the direction of the unfolding drama. Gus whispers in Poppy's ear and helps her to her feet. Charlotte notices Gus for the first time.

"Leaving so soon?" says Charlotte, staring at Gus.

The pong of alcohol oozes from the older woman's pores. Her face falls when she sees the troubled look on Poppy's face.

"I'm sorry," whimpers Charlotte, "I should have done more for Eva. And I should have come to visit you years ago."

May has extricated herself from the situation. She's nowhere to be seen.

Before Poppy can say anything, Charlotte grips her arm and pulls her close.

"Do you think Eva knew this family is cursed? Did she

tell you why there haven't been any more sons? Did she?" Charlotte stammers, as if she can't stop the thoughts in her wine-soaked brain from spilling out.

Poppy looks confused. Gus unravels Charlotte's fingers from Poppy's arm. Charlotte loses her balance, and as she does, her elbow flies up and catches Gus on the chin, toppling her into the table. A glass shatters to the floor. People gasp.

Howard is suddenly there. He nods for Gus to go and steps in front of Charlotte.

"Mrs. Mutchmore, how are you? It's me, Howard Baylis. We met last year," says Howard.

Charlotte tries to look past Howard, but he shifts to block her view. Gus links Poppy's arm and leads her through the crowd. Glancing back, she can see Ricker smoothly winding through guests and tables and serving staff, face relaxed. Mr. Cool. When he reaches Charlotte, Ricker whisks his mother-in-law away. Howard gives Gus a thumbs-up to see if she's okay. She nods then weaves Poppy toward the exit. May appears out of nowhere and stands in their path. A smile spreads across her elegantly painted face.

"You're Augusta Monet?" she says. "Marjory has told me all about you."

Gus nods. Figures she might as well be polite. She offers May her hand. May looks at it but doesn't take it. Instead, May moves past them as if she's seen someone else more interesting. As she does, she bumps Gus in the shoulder.

"Be careful now, Ms. Monet," she whispers in her ear.

The words send a shiver down Gus's neck. Poppy squeezes her arm tight.

Fifteen minutes later, Poppy and Gus are in the back of a cab heading for the Ambassador.

"Are you okay?" asks Gus.

"I'm all right, love. I know my mother wasn't exactly a

shiny penny in the Mutchmore change purse, not like her eldest brother, Felix," says Poppy. "Charlotte meant no harm. She just had one too many chardonnays."

Gus isn't so sure.

"But let's forget her. Weren't those shrimp thingie-kebabs simply the bee's knees?" says Poppy.

Gus laughs. Poppy is amazing. She just attended her first social event in decades. A huge party, no less, where her relatives didn't exactly make her feel welcome, and yet she seems lighter than she has in weeks.

"How are you feeling?" Poppy asks, out of the blue. "Still a bit . . . off?"

Even blind, Poppy is observant. Gus tries to brush it off.

"Just a bug. It's nothing," she says.

"Your monthly visitor hasn't come calling in a while," Poppy muses.

"My what? Oh. No. How?" Gus stammers.

"You'll be light in August. That's my guess," Poppy says with confidence.

"Light?" Gus mumbles.

"When the baby comes," says Poppy, "you'll be light."

Gus looks down at her lap. Her coat hangs open and the emerald dress rests across her belly. Her belly that's been growing each passing week.

The baby.

How did she not know this? Or did she? Clearly Poppy knew.

"And the progenitor?" asks Poppy. "Is he still in the picture?"

Gus doesn't know what the word *progenitor* means, but she can guess.

"He's dead," she lies.

Poppy gasps and reaches for Gus's hand.

"I'm so sorry, my dear," she whispers. "I shouldn't have pried. Everything's going to be okay, love."

Gus doesn't believe her.

Then suddenly time flips upside down and everything comes at her like a freight train from a tunnel. That snowy November night three months ago barrels toward Gus. The mistake she made. The reason she moved.

She can't look away.

She's there.

And he's there too.

7

Tommy

HE'S STANDING ON THE SIDEWALK OUTSIDE THE PET STORE,
tapping on the glass to get the dog's attention. Levi is sunning
in his usual spot in the front display window surrounded by
chew toys. One ear twitches. His good eye opens then he
rolls onto his back, front legs dangling over his chest like two
broken sticks, hind legs spread eagle, exposing himself to the
world. A sigh ripples his blackish pink lips as he surrenders
to the sweet tug of sleep, indifferent to the stranger in the
window.

Levi doesn't recognize him, but Gus does.

It's a man she'll never forget, because he tried to kill her.

It's Tommy Oaks.

Gus met Tommy when she was looking into her mother's death. He was a sweet cop who told her his name was
Stu. He helped her with the investigation and they became
friends. But it was a lie. He wasn't a cop at all. He was doing
the bidding of his brother. A bad dude named Dez. When
everything unraveled, Tommy went to prison for killing a

real police officer. Gus witnessed the murder. She escaped with her life, gave evidence at his trial, and watched as he was sentenced. No possibility of parole for twenty-five years.

All of it feels a lifetime ago. And yet it was only two summers back, on that dark August day, when Tommy aimed a gun at Gus and fired.

She remembers the last time she saw him. He was being led from the courtroom in handcuffs. And yet here he is. Peering through the window of Global Pet Foods.

Did he somehow get early parole? Or escape?

How did he find her?

She does still live in the same neighborhood.

Has the same name.

Walks her dog the same route every day.

She made it easy.

But why is he here?

To make amends? Not fucking likely.

To avenge his brother's death.

To finish what he started.

They make eye contact through the window.

Shit.

Gus ducks behind the counter and looks for a weapon. All she can find is a dog bone. Like that will protect her. She hears the door chime announcing that he's coming in.

"You got any Taste of the Wild?" says a loud voice behind her.

Gus jumps out of her skin. She turns to see that it's a regular customer, Mr. Higgins, standing over her. He's giving her away, and unfortunately, he's way too frail to defend her.

"I'm looking for the Ancient Wetlands recipe," he chirps, oblivious to the fact that she's hiding from someone.

Gus stays low and points the dog bone toward the back aisle.

"Bottom shelf on the left marked Canine Formulas," she blurts out.

Mr. Higgins shuffles down the aisle and calls back over his shoulder.

"That's grain-free, right?"

Shut up, man.

There's no point in hiding any longer. Clutching the bone, she rises slowly and locks eyes with Tommy, who is now standing on the other side of the counter.

"Hey, Red."

He smiles.

Killer dimples.

⁓

It's just before sunrise and her bedroom has a muddy glow. Late November frost creeps along the edges of her window. Gus lies on her side facing the bedroom door. Levi stands in the doorway, head dipped and eyes sullen. He's pouting. Gus rolls over. Tommy is sleeping in Levi's spot. She gags.

Gus, naked, slips out of bed. She grabs her robe, steps over Levi, and tiptoes down the hall to the bathroom, closing the door gently. Gus splashes cold water on her face. Gargles with Listerine. Her skin is ashen with dark circles rimming her eyes. She shakes her head.

What the ever-loving fuck have you done?

Gus fast-forwards through her short love life. The scenes flicker past like a disaster movie costarring loser number one, Lars, her first boyfriend. A petty criminal who she finally dumped after he broke into her house and attacked her and her dog. Costarring Tommy. The second man she's slept with in her twenty-two pathetic years. And this particular Romeo tried to shoot her in the back.

But the star of this epically rotten tomato is the ridiculous redhead staring back at her from the other side of the mirror. A moth to the flame. Fly close, burn a little, circle away, miss the pain, fly close, burn a little again. Cauterizing the wound each time, but never healing it. This was her pattern. She thought she was done with it, but as she scans the mirror for the version of herself that solved the mystery of her mother's death—that strong, resilient, smart woman she thought she'd become—she can't see her. All she sees staring back is the other Gus. The reckless one. The thoughtless one. The one with a thing for danger. The one who can't resist a bad boy.

And there it is.

The End.

Roll credits.

Gus moans and tries to block out the ugly truth of last night, but it floats around her reflection, scowling at her.

❧

Tommy is leaning on the counter in the pet store. Smiling. Gus is waving the dog bone in his face. Shouting. Mr. Higgins finally realizes what is happening and scurries for the door, abandoning her. Levi rises to his feet, lips quivering, and Tommy backs off, raising his hands in surrender before leaving. Gus locks the door, turns out the lights, and watches the street for a while.

When the coast seems clear, she closes up shop. It is already dark out. The street is deserted. Heavy snow falls as Gus and Levi walk home. Then Levi growls.

Tommy comes out of nowhere, approaching them too fast. Gus freaks and reaches inside her satchel. Once she finds what she's looking for, she pulls it out and fires in his direction.

ംട്ടെ

Gus closes her eyes hoping to freeze the events so she doesn't have to continue reliving them. But they stutter and skip a moment, then keep playing.

No pause button. No way to undo what happened.

ംട്ടെ

Tommy's hands shoot up to his eyes. He lets out a wail that sounds more animal than human. He didn't see the stream of pepper spray until it was too late. Got it full in the face. He twists sideways and topples, cracking his skull against the corner of John's Family Diner, where Gus eats breakfast every morning before walking the eight blocks to work. She lives above John's in a tiny one-bedroom that smells like bacon. The rent's cheap and it's in the same neighborhood where her great-grandmother Rose's house once stood, so it feels like the closest thing to home she could hope for. She's settled. Safe. Content.

At least she was.

Tommy sinks to his knees. Blood pours from a gash in his temple and drips from his chin. He puts his hands in the snow to keep from falling on his face. His eyes are shut tight and tears squeeze from their corners, mixing with blood. He looks like he might pass out.

Gus is frozen. Levi looks just as stunned.

It's after 7 P.M. and the moonless winter sky is dark and thick with snow. A streetlight illuminates the red splatter on the fresh powder. Levi inspects the bloody snow. It looks like a crime scene. Thank God the diner is closed and the streets are empty. Or they were. A block away, a couple rounds a corner and strolls toward them. Gus wants to duck into her apartment.

Do it.

Before they see you.

He can be their problem.

The couple are getting closer. The woman is pointing in their direction.

Fuck, fuck, fuck.

They've seen her. They'll call the cops if she runs.

Even though both her parents were police officers, Gus doesn't fully trust the men and women in blue. They've messed with her before.

Without thinking, Gus grabs Tommy's elbow, lifts him to his feet, and hauls him into the stairwell of her apartment. It's like dragging a blind drunk. Levi follows as fast as his geriatric hips will allow.

The ungainly threesome makes it to the top of the stairs, leaving a trail of blood. Gus gets her apartment door open and guides Tommy over to the lumpy sofa that takes up most of her tiny living room. He dissolves in a heap. She drops her satchel at his feet, kicks off her boots, stumbles to the bathroom, and roots through her vanity for first-aid supplies.

She grabs a bottle of rubbing alcohol, a box of children's Band-Aids, a miniature sewing kit, and a towel. She hurries back and sits perched across from Tommy on the old trunk that doubles as her coffee table. He mumbles half-coherent explanations that include words like *bail* and *appeal.* He says his brother made him do it. He was out of his mind with grief when he tried to hurt her. And on and on and on.

Gus doesn't say a word. She slows the bloodletting by pressing the towel to his forehead, then begins haphazardly trying to stitch the laceration closed with a needle and thread. The wound discharges beads of blood onto her fingers with each poke of the needle, but she keeps sewing.

Tommy cringes and sniffles. He babbles on about never

wanting to hurt Levi or Gus. Dez lied about everything. Her and the money. All of it. He sees that now. But Dez was a violent man. A tyrant. He'd bullied him ever since they were kids. Tommy lost all his friends and eventually his job. He was at the beck and call of his invalid brother 24/7. He had to do his bidding. He lived in fear. Dez would wake him in the middle of the night and put a gun to Tommy's head. Once he shot the gun off right by his ear to teach him a lesson.

Gus gives up on sewing the wound shut and tapes a bunch of Hello Kitty Band-Aids across the gaps. Surprisingly, they hold. Tommy's voice is getting raspy. He's moved from confessing to self-flagellation. He calls himself a coward. Pathetic. A fucking loser.

"Red," he says.

Gus says nothing.

"I'm so sorry," he says, "for everything."

She busies herself picking up the Band-Aid wrappers.

"How can you be out?" she finally says, unable to resist asking.

"Judge made a mistake at the trial," he says.

Gus thinks back. She remembers the cramped courtroom. It smelled like feet. The judge was short. She looked tiny behind the large raised bench. There was a detached expression on her face, as if half the time she wasn't even listening.

"When she instructed the jury, she made it sound like their only option was first-degree murder, not manslaughter," he tells Gus.

"That was wrong?" she asks.

"It was. I never intended to do it. That's manslaughter. Anyway, my lawyers won the appeal. They put my psych assessment forward as new evidence. I've got PTSD. At least that's what they tell me," he says, hands trembling.

Then he starts to weep.

Between sobs, he tells her that he wasn't always that way. He was good once. A good son. A good brother. A good man. Then it all went to shit.

"I don't know who I am anymore," he cries. "I don't know what I'm doing here."

Gus doesn't know what to say or do, so she turns her attention to the red blisters forming around his wet eyes.

"Hey, Siri?" she says, greeting her phone as she lifts it from her satchel. It beeps. "What do you do if you've been pepper sprayed?" she asks it.

Siri answers in her usual humorless voice. "Okay, I found this on the web for what to do if your penis tastes like pepper."

The link displays an article entitled "10 Smelly Penis Cures."

Gus jabs her finger at the home button to reset. She tries again. This time she types her question into a Google search and finds exactly what she's looking for.

How to Relieve Pepper Spray Burns.

It still strikes her as oddly sinister that her phone knows all. A luddite most of her life, Gus finally got a smartphone a few months back and ever since, she's been equal parts infatuated with and wary of her all-knowing, all-seeing device. She reviews the options in the article.

Dish soap and water.

Cold milk spray.

Vegetable oil lotion.

She has no milk and has never bought vegetable oil in her life, so it will have to be soap and water. She intends to make sure he can see before showing him the door.

After filling a bowl with one part dish soap and two parts cold water, Gus gently dabs Tommy's closed eyelids with a soapy dish cloth. His face is a mess of red blisters. It reminds her of the first time she met his brother, Desmond, whose face had been charbroiled in a terrible fire. His deformed features turned out to be the perfect reflection of the monstrous soul inside the man. The man who strangled her mother.

Gus's hand trembles violently at the thought of her mother's death. She stops what she's doing, stands up, and heads back to the kitchen. She dumps the dirty water into the sink and shakes off the grainy video image of her mother's final moments. It's more shakable now than it was in the weeks and months after she found the terrible recording. The deep grooves that scarred her mind back then have smoothed over, filling in with time. Knowing the truth of what happened helps. The mystery of her mother's demise no longer haunts Gus. The past stays in the past where it belongs, and she lives in the present now, in her cozy apartment with her trusty dog, Levi, by her side. She can walk to her job through the neighborhood where she grew up. She knows every crack in the sidewalk, every newspaper box and street sign. She knows when the OC Transpo bus is due to come down Wellington. She can recognize the postman from four blocks away and she knows the produce guy by name at the local Farm Boy.

The past has no right to come knocking.

The kitchen sink is just about to overflow. She turns off the tap, dips the bowl in the clean water, adds more dish soap, and goes back to the task at hand. Getting rid of Tommy.

Tommy has stopped talking. It's as if he's run out of words or the ability to form them. He barely moves. Winces at her touch every so often, but mostly he sits still in the middle of her secondhand sofa, his hands in his lap. His breathing steadies. His swollen eyes stay shut.

As she gently wipes his skin, Gus finds her eyes wandering across his face. He's still got that Boy Scout thing going on. Blond, blue-eyed, handsome. A little older than when they first met. He's holding tension around his jaw, likely from the pain, and there's a hollowness to his cheeks, but he's still got those dimples at the corners of his mouth. She scans his torso while dabbing his face. Fooling herself that she's just being analytical. He's still lean. A little more muscular in the biceps and chest. It must be prison life. Weight lifting, no doubt.

Gus feels a pang of longing for something she can't have. For Stu. For that sweet cop. For the time she lay next to him in a motel room. She slept under the covers and he stayed on top, fully clothed the whole night. He was being a gentleman. He was comforting her. She remembers kissing his mouth. She remembers giggling when he said something funny. Stu was good once upon a time. And he was kind to her. But not really.

That sweet guy was a lie. Some persona he invented to fool her. He was an illusion. She could touch him, talk to him, kiss him, and then she couldn't. He disappeared in a puff of gun smoke. Gus lets herself bear the full weight of her feelings for Stu. For the first time in over two years, she gives in to the sickening and sad realization. She misses him. He was the one person she trusted when everyone and every-thing else seemed to be against her. He felt real.

Gus tries to clear the lump in her throat as she goes back to wiping the oily pepper spray from under his hairline. Tommy opens his puffy eyes. Her face is close to his. He sees how she's looking at him. Their eyes meet. Before she can stop him, he leans in and kisses her on the mouth. Instead of pulling away or stabbing him in the throat or clawing open the cut in his temple, Gus kisses him back. He puts his hands on her waist and pulls her off the trunk and onto his lap. Her knees straddle his hips. She presses her body against him as their kiss deepens. Gus can't breathe, but she doesn't want to. She doesn't want to breathe or think. Right now he is all the air she needs. All the thoughts and feelings she desires. Her loneliness mingles with his. Gus senses the walls around her heart blowing apart. Splintering into nothingness. Her heart aches as she bares it to him fully.

Like electricity, she can feel the unfinished business surging between them. She never let herself get too close. Never crossed the line. Never felt how this feels right now. He vanished before she got the chance. She never got to say goodbye to Stu. And even though, deep down, she knows none of this is real, Gus vanishes too. She turns her back on the woman who built those walls and steps into the body of another.

A woman wild and reckless and lovesick.

A woman stumbling to her bedroom, lips locked on a cute guy named Stu.

A woman nothing like Augusta Maggie Monet.

❧

Levi is thoroughly unimpressed by the events of last night. As Gus emerges from the bathroom, he is facing the kitchen, his back to her. He doesn't turn to look at her. Gus heads for the bedroom and sits next to Tommy. She glances back down the hall as the old dog slowly lifts himself to a standing position. A painful display of osteoarthritis and disapproval. The floorboards groan in harmony with his creaky bones. He shoots her a look, then heads for the kitchen, his fluffy hindquarters wiggling as he walks away. The dog's pissed.

Shame washes anew through Gus's chest as she stares at her sleeping felon. Tommy rolls onto his back, sputters, then continues to snore, eyes swollen shut. His face is a disaster. His blisters are raging, and his cheeks have ballooned like a boxer's after a fight. An angry purple bruise bulges from his temple where he hit John's brick wall. Blood crusts his hairline. A single Hello Kitty Band-Aid dangles from his brow. The rest of the blood-soaked sweethearts are scattered in the bedsheets. The pillow under his head is bloodstained. A secondary crime scene, but this time she is his accomplice, not his assailant. Despite the damage, Tommy looks oddly peaceful.

Gus is far from it. She knows what she has to do. Hard reset.

A checklist is already formulating in her head as she watches his chest rise and fall.

Tell no one what you've done or who you've done it with.

Give Tommy the slip.

Quit your job ASAP.

Find a cheap apartment in some other part of town.

Disappear in the dead of night.

Pretend this never happened.

Hide this list.

Do not pass Go. Do not collect $200.

Go back to square one.

Again.

❧

Lying in bed the night of the gala, Gus stares into space as she contemplates her new reality. The one she was refusing to acknowledge. The one living inside her that she can no longer pretend isn't there. The one lasting result of a mistake she made last November that she can't undo. She glances at her phone on the side table and calls out to Siri.

"How big is an unborn baby at three months?"

The answer? As big as a plum.

Gus hates plums.

SECOND
TRIMESTER

8

Unidentified Male

TWO WEEKS LATER, POPPY COMES DOWNSTAIRS TO SEE GUS. Another first. Poppy is fidgety, like a schoolgirl waiting for the bell to ring so she can run outside and play. Poppy has just had a visit from Constable Laframboise. She's holding a piece of paper in her hand. Gus gets her a glass of water, but Poppy can't sit. Instead, she paces back and forth. The water splashes on the hardwood close to where Levi was trying to nap in his favorite sunny spot. The dog is watching Poppy's back-and-forth dance with one eye open. He doesn't get up. Instead he stretches his neck as far as it will reach toward the water and licks sideways at the puddle, barely lifting his head.

Poppy seems overly excited by the constable's visit. Almost giddy. Laframboise had stopped by to give Poppy a copy of the forensics results. As a courtesy, she said. The constable had read the findings out loud to Poppy.

A deep crack was found in the skull. Based on where the remains surfaced, this was *deemed consistent with an accidental fall whereby the deceased's head struck the low stone barrier of the bridge as he fell into the water.* The skeleton was completely intact, other than the right foot, which likely detached over time. DNA samples proved fruitless in identifying the man since databases only go back to the late eighties. So no match there. The police anthropologist did conclude that *the unidentified male was Caucasian, six foot two inches tall.* The bones were estimated to be about seventy years old, and the man was likely in his twenties when he went in the water. The ID in the coat pocket and the timeframe that Poppy said her friend went missing both point to the same conclusion. *The remains are those of Mr. Leo Ewart.*

The case has been closed.

Poppy holds up the copy of the report. Her eyes are bright. Gus wonders if she's in shock. She looks almost happy.

"That must have been hard to hear," says Gus.

Poppy shrugs. "It's not him," she says matter-of-factly.

Gus isn't sure she's heard her right. "Not who?" she asks.

"Leo," says Poppy. "Oh believe me, love, there is a part of me that wishes it was him. Prayed it was him. Because, you see, then I would know for certain what happened to him. But now, I'm happy it's not him. I wouldn't have wanted such a horrid end for my Leo. No, whoever died in that pond all those years ago was someone else. And he was wearing Leo's coat."

Gus stares at Poppy. Wonders if she's in denial.

"But you were so sure it was Leo," says Gus. "The report says it's Leo."

Gus points to the paper in Poppy's hand, then stops herself. Poppy can't see her.

"This dang forensics report is how I know it's not him." Poppy smiles, handing it to Gus.

"Leo was five nine. It's highly probable that a skeleton can shrink over time, but can it grow five inches? And that's not the half of it. The constable said, other than the right foot, the man's skeleton was intact. Completely intact. So it can't be Leo then, can it?"

Gus is dumbstruck. She stares at the report. Not seeing what Poppy clearly does. Poppy lifts her left foot and wiggles her toes.

"Leo was missing a toe on his left foot. Cut off at the bone in a mishap when he was a child. I'm betting a toe can't magically rematerialize, now can it?"

Gus can't argue with that.

Poppy joins Gus and Levi for their afternoon walk in the park. She can't be alone right now. The woman is bubbling with questions and theories. Gus gets it. Poppy just wants the truth. She's no longer afraid of it or content with a bittersweet ending. And yet she didn't say a word to Laframboise about the discrepancies. Why not? Why not help the police with their investigation? Doesn't she trust them? Does she have something to hide?

Gus lets it go. She doesn't press her friend.

Gus holds Poppy's arm as they descend the stone steps that lead to the snowy path running alongside the apartment building. Poppy wears a long tweed coat and a pair of old-fashioned lace-up boots with fur trim that don't look very warm. They head down the hill toward the creek. The wintery light makes everything sparkle, including Poppy's eyes.

"Do you think Leo had something to do with U.M.'s death?" says Poppy out of the blue.

Gus is in the middle of bagging Levi's poop. She pauses and looks over at Poppy.

"U.M.?" she asks as Poppy continues walking, unaware that Gus has stopped.

"Unidentified Male," says Poppy as if it should have been obvious.

"He was wearing Leo's coat. Maybe they knew each other," says Gus, catching up.

Poppy seems at ease walking without her help. She links her arm through the old woman's bent elbow just in case.

"Maybe he's the reason Leo disappeared," says Poppy, her breath puffing white.

"You think Leo saw what happened to U.M.?" Gus tries.

"Leo was compassionate. And it was cold. Maybe he gave his coat to a stranger. A homeless man who then fell into the water. Perhaps he tried to save him," Poppy says.

"But why leave without a word if it was an accident?" says Gus carefully.

Poppy slows her pace, deep in thought. Gus can almost see the possibilities interlacing with the lines on her face. Her expression darkens. "Unless Leo and the man, somehow, had a fight and . . ." Poppy's voice falters. She stops walking.

"You think Leo kil—" Gus starts to say what they're both thinking, but Poppy cuts her off, squeezing Gus's arm tighter.

"That's why I didn't tell the policewoman that it wasn't Leo. I need to know the truth, but perhaps the whole world doesn't," says Poppy, shivering.

Gus doesn't know what to say. She knows the feeling. That desperate, almost primal need to know what happened to someone you loved and lost, even if that truth scares you and could hurt you or possibly change how you see that person forever. Gus has been down that hard and lonely road.

"I need your eyes," says Poppy, turning to Gus.

Gus lets go of Poppy's arm and moves away from her.

Levi turns, ears perked, sensing something's up.

"You've looked into the past. You've investigated a miss-

ing person. You solved the mystery of your mother's death—
you told me so yourself. You dug and dug until you got at the
bare-bones truth," Poppy says with a voice stronger than Gus
has ever heard her use before.

Gus wishes she hadn't told her anything about her mother.

"Augusta, I can't do this without you. You're the only one
I trust. The truth is the only way I can move forward. You
can help me," she says, her feet firmly planted.

"But I don't know what I'm doing," Gus says weakly.

"That's where you're wrong, sweet girl. You know more
than most. Because you've been there before. You know your
way around. Not many people can say that," says Poppy, then
she adds, "I want to hire you."

"I'm not who you think I am. I'm no detective. I'm a
pregnant, unemployed pet-store clerk," she blurts.

Poppy smiles and reaches out for Gus's arm. Gus moves toward her. Poppy sighs, doesn't say anything else. Together, they
circle the pond, cross the bridge, and head down the snowy
path and up the steps to the street above. Levi brings up the
rear, struggling a little on the steps, finally scrambling up to
the sidewalk a few feet from the Ambassador Court's front
entrance.

I will let Poppy down easy.

This is what Gus is thinking as they step onto the fourth-
floor landing outside Poppy's apartment. But when she spots
the door ajar and catches a whiff of a terrible smell coming
from inside, Gus realizes that the past isn't going away quietly.
It has been tugging at the hem of her winter coat ever since
she came to the Glebe. Double-daring her to move into an
old building and befriend an old woman. Laying all its cards
on the sure bet that Gus is more at home in the past than the
present. It's been strutting and sweet-talking her for months

now. Making her feel like she belongs somewhere. Like she's not alone in the world. And now that it has her right where it wants her, it's about to reveal its true intentions.

It has brought her another cold case.

One that someone definitely does not want warmed up.

9

Shannon

LEVI SNIFFS THE AIR AND LOWERS SLOWLY TO HIS BELLY. HE'S not going in. He knows something bad has gone on inside Poppy's apartment. They can all smell it. Burnt flesh. Gus and Poppy creep arm-in-arm down the long, wide hallway toward the living room. A thin cloud of smoke snakes across the ceiling. Gus stops. The first thing she thinks of is the fireplace. She lets go of Poppy's arm. She'll go first. She walks ahead of the old woman into the living room. Nothing looks out of place. There's no fire in the hearth. A sound draws Poppy across the hall toward the kitchen. Gus hears it too, a second too late. She turns. It's the sound of water running. Gus is within an arm's reach of Poppy when she spots the overflowing kitchen sink. A small waterfall pours down the front of the cupboard into a lake of water on the floor. Poppy's toaster hangs by an extension cord over the edge of the counter, resting on its side in the puddle.

The cord is plugged into the socket.

Gus inhales sharply as she fully grasps what's about to happen. She reaches for Poppy, grabbing the collar of her coat just as the toe of her boot dips into the edge of the puddle. Poppy's body jerks violently as electricity surges through the fabric sole of her boot. A jolt of fire burns through Gus's fingertips, shoots up her arm, and pierces deep into her shoulder blade like a knife. The two of them spill onto the hall floor, both flat on their backs. Poppy twitches then goes still, eyes closed. Levi races toward them from the front door. He hovers over Gus and licks her face, whimpering. She manages to grab hold of his collar, fearing he might step into the pool of electrified water inching toward them.

Gus turns her head, and that's when she sees the body in the kitchen. The charred remains of Gish. Black where she used to be orange. Brittle where she used to be soft.

That was the smell. Toasted cat.

Three hours later, the ambulance, police, and hydro electric crew have come and gone.

The paramedics took Poppy to the hospital. She was unconscious but alive. Gus had tucked Poppy's purse by her side on the stretcher, made sure she had her health card, and told her not to worry. She'd be back home soon. Poppy couldn't hear her words, but it felt good saying them anyway. One of the hydro workers who disconnected the main power to the kitchen kindly offered to dispose of what was left of Gish.

Gus and Levi stumble down to the third floor after she gets the super to lock up Poppy's apartment. She kicks off her winter boots, drops her coat on the floor. She doesn't bother to turn on lights or undress or brush her teeth. Gus and Levi curl up on her bed, and despite the disturbing incidents of the last few hours, they're both asleep in seconds.

For the first time in years, her mother makes an appearance. Shannon just walks right into Gus's dream like she owns the place. Makes herself comfortable. No apologies for leaving. For dying. She just waltzes in and stands next to Gus on the bridge above the pond. It's summer. Gus has never even seen the bridge in summer, but this insight isn't enough to untangle her from the dream. Gus looks down into the pond below. Their wobbly faces are reflected side by side, crowned by floating lily pads.

"This where he went in?" Shannon asks, like she's interviewing a witness.

"I guess so," answers Gus.

"Well, is it or isn't it?" asks Shannon.

"I wasn't there," says Gus.

"No, but you could go there," says Shannon.

"Where?" asks Gus.

Shannon gives her a look like Gus knows exactly what she means.

"I understand that U.M. was wearing Leo's coat?" Shannon says, moving on.

"Yeah," says Gus.

"Strange, don't you think?" prods Shannon.

Gus sighs, says nothing.

"Maybe if you can figure out who U.M. was, you'll find Leo."

"Please stop," says Gus.

"Or if you find Leo, maybe he can tell you who U.M. was," Shannon says, her face distorting as tiny waves disturb the pond's surface.

"This has nothing to do with me," says Gus. "I don't know these people."

"You know her. She's like you. An orphan," says Shannon.

Gus stares at her mother. She feels the stone bridge shift. "No, I can't help her" is all she can think to say.

Shannon looks at her daughter with a sharp turn of her head, a scold on her brow. Then just as suddenly, her expression of admonishment changes. She smiles.

"Ha, you're right. The old doll can hire someone else to do her silly detective work. I mean we're all replaceable, right?" says Shannon. And then in a singsongy voice, she adds, "Tommy with Stu. Me with you."

Gus covers her ears.

"Stop it," she says. "I can't do it."

Shannon's smile fades. Gus looks away from her mother.

"I can't go back," Gus says.

"You can if you want to, Sugar Bunch. Just jump," says Shannon.

Then, without warning, Shannon hikes herself up onto the stone parapet of the bridge, and before Gus can stop her, she launches herself over the edge. Gus reaches out. She's too late. Shannon splashes into the pond below. Gus leans over, watching helplessly as her mother's face disappears under the dark water.

"Mama!" screams Gus. "Don't go!"

Gus is jarred awake. She sits up in a cold sweat. The residue of the dream lingers. At first it's right under her eyelids, but by morning the dream hovers a thousand miles away in a tiny corner of her brain. A wobbly vision she can barely make out.

Gus didn't shut her bedroom curtains last night. Sun floods the room. She is blinded by the light. As she lies in the warm rays, eyes shut, she tugs at the best parts of the dream, drawing them close again. The lovely feeling of spending a few moments next to her mother, the dogged police officer, Shannon Monet. The woman who raised her until she was eight. The feisty detective who never ignored her gut, never stopped asking questions, and never thought twice about putting herself in danger to get at the truth.

She opens her eyes.

She is her mother's daughter.

Gus sits up in bed.

Poppy could have left the tap running. Maybe a rag fell into the sink and stopped up the drain. Maybe the cat knocked the toaster off the counter. Maybe Poppy left her door open. A lot of maybes. The bone-chilling alternative is that someone intentionally laid a trap for Poppy.

❧

The next morning, Gus looks up the nearest ob/gyn. She calls and the receptionist tells her that someone just canceled so they can fit her in that morning. Poppy had been gently encouraging her to see a doctor, but Gus was reluctant. She didn't do doctors. But she also realized that ignoring her pregnancy wasn't going to make it go away. And deep down she wanted to make sure the plum was doing okay after the near-electrocution.

Doctor Chandra was bubbly and smiled way too much. But she was kind and gentle and didn't ask personal questions, which Gus appreciated. The doctor told her everything was progressing well. She measured her belly, took her blood pressure, and listened to her heart. She told her to reduce her sugar intake and to take maternity vitamins. Beyond that, she said Gus was young, healthy, and should have a normal pregnancy. Gus wanted to believe the good doctor but nothing about her life right now was normal, including the plum.

Doctor Chandra scheduled her for monthly visits, and Gus was feeling pretty proud of herself by the time she left the clinic. Almost like a responsible grown-up. On the way home she even considered popping into Winners for some maternity clothes. At the entrance, she changed her mind. She couldn't bring herself to enter the world of helpful salesclerks with their inevitable small talk about the baby's sex and her due date and the names she'd chosen and the loving father who must be so excited. The thought of it made her heart race and her palms sweat. She had stretchy T-shirts and leggings at home. They would do just fine.

How big could a baby get?

Gus wishes she hadn't asked Siri.

As big as a watermelon was the answer.

❧

A few days later, Poppy regains consciousness and is out of the ICU. Gus heads to the Civic Hospital to visit her friend, arriving at the exact same time as the Mutchmores. May, Ricker, and Mojo. Bad timing. She was hoping to talk to Poppy alone. Poppy is weak, but strong enough to insist that Gus be allowed to stay in the room when the doctor comes in to update the family. Poppy says Gus is practically family. May visibly cringes at this, but bites her tongue.

The doctor states the obvious: Poppy's heart took a bad jolt. Then he says something that strikes Gus as odd. The electric shock has "disorganized" Poppy's heart. *Wasn't it already disorganized?* He calls it *arrhythmia.* Says they'll be keeping her a while for observation. Possibly a few weeks. Poppy has some nerve damage. Numbness in her toes. In time they'll know if there is any lasting brain damage. She has some amnesia, which the doctor says is to be expected. She doesn't recall much about the incident. Just the sound of water running and then blackness.

Mojo sits on the end of the bed, gently rubbing Poppy's toes. Poppy looks confused. May and Ricker don't help. When the doctor leaves, they stand on either side of her bed, having an awkward conversation about the unusually cold weather this winter, as if she's not there. Gus has planted herself in a chair in the corner, trying to give the family space. She leans over to smell the cheap blue carnations the Mutchmores brought wrapped in cellophane. The flowers look dyed and have no smell. *Why would you bring a blind woman unscented flowers?*

Poppy's eyes flit back and forth from May to Ricker as if she's trying to catch up with the sound of their voices. Mojo chatters on about how lucky Poppy is to get her meals brought to her on a little tray.

No one mentions Gish.

Ricker checks his watch for the millionth time. May nods. The Mutchmores' visit is over. May pats Poppy's hand like she's petting a dog, then nods to her daughter. Mojo wants to stay. The girl doesn't budge. She folds her arms and pouts.

"Cousin Poppy needs her rest," May says.

It just now hits Gus that May and Poppy are cousins despite their age difference. May's father and Poppy's mother were siblings—Wilfred and Eva. But May was born forty years after Poppy. Then Gus remembers Howard saying that Wilfred married a much younger woman in Charlotte, May's mother. In fact, Charlotte is Poppy's age.

May smiles and explains to her daughter that it's not polite to overstay one's welcome. She glances across the room at Gus, who smiles back.

Message received. And deleted.

May follows her husband out the door. Mojo kisses Poppy's forehead, then skips out of the room with a little wave.

Finally, they're alone. Gus fluffs the pillows behind Poppy's head, tops up her water glass, then sits on the edge of the bed. She takes one of Poppy's frail hands in hers, noticing that she's clutching something in the other.

"What's that?" Gus asks.

Poppy uncurls her fingers. A gold locket on a thin chain rests in her palm.

"I was with Leo when he bought this for me. He didn't

have a picture of himself to put inside, and in true Leo style, he pulled some strands of hair from his head and placed them inside the locket." She smiles. "I laughed. It was so silly and romantic. He said it was so I could carry a little piece of him wherever I went, right next to my heart," she says softly, her smile fading.

It's the most Poppy has spoken since Gus arrived. She's relieved to hear her sounding like herself. *Brain damage, my ass*. Poppy hands the locket to Gus.

"I was hoping you might hang on to this for me and keep it safe while I'm in here?" she says. "I'd hate to lose it."

Gus swallows hard. Touched that Poppy would trust her with such an intimate possession. She takes it and holds it. The feel of the delicate keepsake solidifies her resolve.

"I'll do it," Gus says.

Poppy doesn't immediately understand her meaning, but then the old woman's eyes brighten, her shoulders ease, and her breath steadies. She smiles.

"How does two hundred dollars a week sound?" Poppy asks. They shake on it.

"I'll call my bank manager and set up a weekly transfer," she adds.

Gus tells her friend she'll begin right away. She'll come by with updates every chance she gets.

Poppy tells Gus where she can find the strip of photos of her and Leo, along with the bundle of notes he sent Poppy. They're tucked under the pillow on her bed back home.

"You take them. Look through them. They can be your first pieces of evidence," says Poppy with a smile.

"But they're private," says Gus. "I can't."

"Oh of course you can, love. They're of more use to you than me right now," she says.

Gus recalls the photos of the young couple on the verge of falling in love.

"I'll find out what happened to your Leo, I promise," Gus says without thinking.

The second the words leave her lips, a lump forms in her throat. A promise is a bond. A contract. An unbreakable, irrevocable vow. With all her heart, Gus wants to do this for Poppy. She wants to solve the mystery that's haunted her for so long. Wants to bring her the peace she deserves. Wants her to feel the contentment that washes through your soul when you finally and fully know the truth about someone you love.

Why the fuck did I promise?

Regret sinks into her bones. She's in over her head and she hasn't even begun.

Gus has absolutely no idea where to start.

But as it turns out, Poppy does.

The old woman reaches for her handbag on the side table next to her. She digs in the bottom. Finds what she's looking for. Her key ring. She holds it up. Three keys dangle from it. Gus recognizes two of them. They're similar to her own. One is a key to the main entrance of the Ambassador Court. The other is the key to Poppy's apartment door.

The third one is unfamiliar.

Poppy feels along the ring, then holds the key between two bony fingers.

It is long and made of brass.

A skeleton key.

Gus takes the keys. She places them in her palm. As she stares at the skeleton key, it disappears as if she's conjured a magic trick. But it's not magic that disappears the key, her palm, the hospital room, and Poppy with it. It's a trick of the mind that she can only sustain for so long, it seems. She lets go

of the moment and slips back into the present, where the plum
has become a watermelon and the world is dark and damp.

∽✦∾

Gus is startled to find herself hauling on the rope. She must
have slipped away while concentrating on the task at hand.
Instantly she refocuses on what she's doing. She pulls and pulls
and the dumbwaiter rises. She feels a light clunk as it passes
each level. Basement, first floor, second, and third. Her floor.
Her apartment. She lets it rest there. Not all the way to the
top. The fourth floor. There's no point. Poppy is not in her
apartment anymore. Gus releases her grip on the rope. The
compartment should be facing her own kitchen now. The
cupboard door has been pulled off, so it's visible. Maybe Levi
heard the dumbwaiter. He might have wandered over and
spotted the bait. Sniffing as he picked up the scent of her lock
of hair.

She listens up the shaft. Hears nothing. No barking.

Then another nugget comes loose in her concussed brain,
and she remembers.

Levi is not there either.

Gus sinks to her knees, despair weighing her down.

The watermelon is heavy. It shifts like an earthquake,
heaving under her skin.

A new wave of pain rolls in. Gus lets herself be carried
away on its wake. Resistance is futile. She's done all she can.
She has sent her dispatch through a tin can telephone. She
has floated a message in a bottle across an ocean. Efforts her
eight-year-old self would think clever, which now seem ut-
terly stupid and hopeless to her grown-up self.

If only the past hadn't come after her again.

If only she weren't just like her mother.

Relentless and reckless.

10

The Irishman

A HINT OF SCORCHED LINOLEUM HANGS IN THE AIR AS GUS enters Poppy's dark apartment. Levi's asleep downstairs. It's late. 3 A.M. She tried to get some sleep herself, but couldn't. March is half over. The clocks have sprung forward. Gus has a new case. A job. A purpose. She's vibrating. Or maybe it's her body and mind accepting the inevitable that's brought this surge of excited energy to replace the nausea of the past few months. Whatever the reason, Gus is itching to try that skeleton key and waiting until daylight now seems ridiculous. Poppy told her it was the key to her mother's room. She has to see that room.

Gus flips on the hall light and scoots past Poppy's kitchen with a shudder, pulling her robe tighter. She can't bring herself to look, even though she knows there's nothing left but the burn mark in the linoleum where they found Gish.

Poppy's longtime friends Stanley and Alice, from the first floor, insisted on helping Gus clean the mess. The trio mopped and toweled the floor, cleaned out the fridge, removed any food that might go bad, disposed of the cat litter, and boxed up Gish's cat toys and dishes. Together, they did a quick tidy of the apartment, readying it for Poppy's return. The pair were sweet to help, but with Stanley pushing ninety and his elderly sister spending most of the time fretting that he might break a hip, Gus did most of the heavy lifting.

But despite their efforts, the smell of death lingers.

Gus wanders to the far end of the hall, past Poppy's bedroom door. Past the bathroom. To the end, where a cobwebbed door sits closed. She stares at the web. Inside its beautiful and delicate design, she sees myriad questions strung from right now to back then. She touches the web. It sticks to her fingertips. That's what the past does.

Gus knows she must take her time. Tread lightly.

She holds out the skeleton key, pushes it into the lock, and turns it gently. The lock clicks, the hinges groan, and she slowly pushes open the door to Eva's bedroom. A dust bunny circles the iron leg of the bed, brought to life by the sucking of stagnant air from the room as the door opens.

The hall light illuminates a narrow section of the room. It's hard to believe, but this door hasn't been opened since December 1953. The day Poppy stood helplessly by while her mother was dragged screaming from her home. Poppy was just eighteen. She locked the door to her mother's bedroom because she didn't want her relatives snooping in her mother's things. She wanted everything left just as it was for when Eva got better and came home. But her mother didn't get better. She didn't come home. She died three years later in the asylum. She was forty-three.

Poppy couldn't bring herself to open the door again once her mother was gone. It was too painful. It felt like an intrusion. Her mother's bedroom had been Eva's private sanctuary, where she spent her evenings writing, answering correspondences, or reading her books. It was also where she did her work as a seamstress. Poppy kept the room locked.

Until now.

When she handed Gus the key, Poppy called the room a time capsule. The words gave Gus shivers. Poppy suggested Gus begin her investigation there. Perhaps something in that room held a clue as to why Eva turned against Poppy's relationship with Leo. Why she went mad. A clue that's been frozen in time since 1953.

Hell yeah.

Gus's excitement intensifies as she steps into the room, dust on her tongue, mold in her nostrils. She can taste the past. There's a small double bed in one corner of the room. It's covered by a floral quilt, topped with two pillows in lace-trimmed cases. The room is dark. Gus spots a lamp on a small side table by the bed. She walks over and pulls the cord. The bulb is dead. She walks back to the door and pushes it wider. The hall light illuminates the side table. She walks back over. On the table sits a heart-shaped, porcelain pill box. Gus lifts the lid. The box contains several large yellow pills. There's a *Life* magazine sitting next to it. She brushes dust from it. There's a fold inside the magazine as if Eva was in the middle of reading it. A young brunette woman is on the cover and the date reads November 23, 1953. A few weeks after Leo disappeared.

Gus takes in the rest of the room. Scarves of dust cling to the ceiling corners like decorative bunting. An armchair is positioned on a wool rug under the window. Next to it, a bookcase is stacked with paperbacks. Blue curtains drape the window. There's a wardrobe at the foot of the bed. In the far corner, a sewing machine rests on top of a table next to a cabinet with a fold-down ironing board. On the cabinet's shelves are the tools of Eva's trade. Spools of thread, scissors, a tape measure, sewing patterns, and bolts of fabric. Set against the opposite wall is a cherrywood vanity with a tilting mirror and matching chair. The antique set is carved with ornate flowers and vines that trim the large mirror and the chair legs. The desktop of the vanity is cluttered with glass bottles, perfumes and lotions by the looks of them, an ivory hairbrush and comb set, a jar of cotton balls, a pewter jewelry box, a collection of envelopes, writing paper, a letter opener, and a few utility bills. This is where Eva beautified herself for evenings out. It's where she wrote, paid her bills, and likely looked at her reflection in the mirror and pondered her sanity.

The mirror is cloudy. All Gus can see are shadows. The ghosts of the past. Gus wipes the mirror with the sleeve of her robe. As she does, it swings on its hinge and something topples off the top edge. Gus picks it up. It's a tiny key. She scans the desk. No locks on the drawers. She starts opening the drawers, and after some sifting, she finds a small book with a lock. The key fits.

Gus opens the book. On the front page are words written in beautiful flowing cursive. *Diary of Eva Honeywell, 1953.*

Gus gasps.

Hands shaking, she flips through the first few pages. They are filled top to bottom with lines of prose, carefully written in precise penmanship. Gus closes the diary and holds it to her chest, her heart beating fast. *Jackpot.* A window into Eva's mind. Amazing. Gus can't stop smiling.

But her joy is gut-punched by an unexpected sound. Until that second everything had been dead quiet. The residents inside the building were asleep. The night air was calm and windless. No whispering trees, no rattling windows. No traffic. The city had gone to bed. The only sound had been her own steady breathing.

Until it wasn't.

She hears it again.

This time there's no mistaking it. It's the sound of a floorboard creaking under the weight of someone moving, slowly.

She is not alone in the apartment.

An icy chill tingles the back of her neck.

Gus looks at the bedroom door. It stands open. Her eyes dart under the bed, then to the wardrobe, searching for a hiding spot.

Another creak.

Fuck.

There's no time to hide. She needs a weapon. Gus scans the room, and her gaze lands on a long wood handle poking out from beneath the bed. She grabs it. At the other end of the handle is a heavy, brass warming pan. *This'll do nicely.* She holds the pan like a bat, tiptoes through the doorway into the long hall. It's empty. She slides along the wall toward the living room. She hears a noise. The sofa leg squeaks against the hardwood like the furniture's being moved. She peers around the entryway into the living room. A man is leaning over the sofa, lifting cushions. His back is to Gus. She enters the room, holding the pan high.

"Who the fuck are you?" she shouts.

"Jesus, Mary, and Joseph!" he yelps as he spins around.

He's got a thick Irish accent. He loses his balance and nearly falls back into the sofa. Gus does a quick body scan. Dark curly hair. Wide mouth. One eyebrow broken in two. She's guessing a scar runs through it. About six one. Athletic. Dark suit. Shiny black shoes.

"You scared the livin' daylights outta me, lass," he says, his black eyes shining.

"You gonna answer me?" demands Gus, a quiver in her voice betraying her nerves.

"I could ask you the same thing," he says with a sly grin.

"I'm a friend of the woman who lives in this apartment," she adds.

"Yes, Miss Poppy Honeywell." He nods, like they're in agreement.

Gus is unnerved by the Mister Nice Guy routine.

"I called 911," she lies, wishing it were true.

"Oh you have, have you?" he says. "That's a crying shame, sweetheart."

He turns and straightens the sofa cushions, then heads straight for her. Gus raises the warming pan. Ready to smash it into his pearly whites. He stops, lifts his crooked eyebrow. Then, giving her a wide berth, he passes by, hands up in surrender, and heads for the front door. She follows at a distance. As the Irishman opens the door, he turns back. Stares a little too long.

"You were at the gala," he smiles.

He looks friendly, but something else emanates from this guy. Menace. She's felt that kind of dark energy before.

Gus can't speak.

"You're the one they call Augusta Monet. Don't tell me, let me guess"—he holds up a finger as if to quiet her—"apartment 305. Am I right?"

Gus feels the heavy brass pan shaking in her hands.

The Irishman's smile melts. He crooks his neck, one way then the other, like a fighter preparing to enter the ring, never taking his eyes off hers. The warming pan rattles.

"Good thing you were there when the old bird nearly shocked herself to death," he says.

Then he disappears down the hall, leaving the front door wide open.

Gus drops the warming pan, runs for the door, and slams it shut. She puts one ear to the door. Hears the fire exit door close. Hears echoing footsteps getting farther away as he descends the stairwell. Stays there for a long time, waiting for the silence to return.

Then she moves fast. She does a speedy search of Eva's bedroom, retracing her steps from the bed to the vanity. She finds an old newspaper clipping tucked inside the *Life* magazine where it was folded. Pockets the clipping without reading it, grabs the diary, and locks the room. Next, Gus grabs the strip of photos and the love notes from under the pillow in Poppy's bedroom. Then she gives the living room a half-assed search as questions spin around her brain.

What was the Irishman looking for?

And why was he here in the middle of the night?

How does he know her name and where she lives?

Gus spots Poppy's tweed coat on a coatrack. Gus had hung it there after Poppy was taken to the hospital. She searches the pockets and finds the forensics report.

Gus hurries down to her apartment, already planning her next steps.

She knows what will help her make connections and see patterns.

An evidence wall.

Sleep seems like a waste of time, so Gus brews a pot of coffee and begins. By 7 A.M. she's moved everything away from one wall in her living room and situated her sofa and trunk directly across from it. She's gone to a twenty-four-hour Shoppers Drug Mart and returned with supplies. She's arranged them on top of her blue trunk.

Red marker. Check.

Pushpins. Check.

Notebook and pen. Check, check.

Box of Honeycomb cereal. *Hell yeah!*

Gus eats handfuls of sugary combs as she stares at the bare wall.

The sun is rising when Levi makes an appearance. He ambles from the bedroom, fuzzy-headed and drooling. As the sun's rays bend through the thick windowpane, they splinter into rainbow-colored orbs that hover across the wall. Levi watches them. He stares at the bare wall. Then at the new position of the sofa and coffee table. Then at Gus. He yawns.

"It's a work in progress, dog," she says, shrugging him off.

Levi ambles away to find his water dish. She hears his tongue lapping.

Gus picks up the red marker and writes a date at the center of the bare wall.

October 31, 1953.

The epicenter of her investigation.

The last time Poppy saw Leo.

Gus gathers her evidence, or as her mother used to call it: exhibits.

Exhibit A: The newspaper article she found tucked in Eva's magazine by her bedside. It's a half-page feature from the business section of the *Ottawa Citizen*. It's about the Trichborne Group, their recent stock market launch, and the grand opening of their new suite of offices on Metcalfe Street. Prominent on the page is a photo of Trichborne's executives and staff gathered in the opulent marble-floored lobby of their new office building. Teddy Trichborne, founder and CEO, is front and center. A young man stands next to Teddy. Gus doesn't have to cross-reference his face. It's Leo.

Exhibit B: The strip of photos of Leo and Poppy. A faded date runs along the bottom.

Exhibit C: The bundle of love notes from Leo written before he disappeared.

Exhibit D: The forensics report that Poppy pointed out describes human remains that are too tall and too skeletally intact to be Leo's.

Exhibit E: Eva's diary, and tonight's bedtime reading.

It's a start. A newspaper article, a strip of photos, love notes, a forensics report, and a diary. Gus sets the diary aside then pins the other items carefully to the wall, arranging them in a circle around the date. Using the red marker, she draws a line from each item, creating a red web. Across each line, she adds some basic information.

Exhibit A: Trichborne Article.

Exhibit B: Lovebird Photos.

Exhibit C: Dear Poppy Notes.

Exhibit D: Forensics Report.

Gus steps back, tilts her head, examining the wall of evidence. She tries to see what's missing. What questions need answering. Across the top of the living room wall, above her web of evidence, she adds three questions in bold red marker.

What happened to Leo?

Whose bones were in the pond?

Who is the Irishman?

There are plenty of other questions, but for now these ones press hardest on her tired brain. Lack of sleep closes in like fog. After wolfing down a tuna sandwich, feeding Levi, and gulping a full can of cream soda, Gus flops on the sofa. She looks at the evidence wall. It doesn't feel like anything yet. Her mother's evidence wall felt alive. Shannon's fingerprints and sweat and tears were all over it.

Gus is struck by the difference. Is hers just a pretend version of the real thing? Is she playing at being a detective? She's taken Poppy's money, and now looking at the wall, she feels ridiculous. Like a fraud.

What was she thinking?

She needs to take it all down before anyone sees it.

Did she even buy washable markers?

The wall stares back at her. A bright red, indelible grin.

Gus closes her eyes and crumples to her side in a fetal position. She's beyond exhausted. She falls into a dreamless, deep, dark sleep.

A rapping at her door wakes her like a slap in the face. She wipes drool from the corner of her mouth. The sun is low. It's late afternoon. She's been asleep for hours. Gus pulls herself up and tiptoes to the door. Groggy and unsteady. She looks through the peephole.

It's not the Irishman.

It's the Mutchmore brat.

Gus glances behind her, hoping she only dreamed that she created an evidence wall.

Nope. Gus opens the door a crack.

"Hey, what's up?" she whispers, pretending like she's trying to be quiet.

Mojo narrows her eyes, already suspicious of the half-cracked door.

"The dog's sleeping," explains Gus.

Right on cue, Levi appears below her and pokes his nose through the crack.

Mojo rolls her eyes.

"I'm kind of busy right now," says Gus.

"Too busy for this?" says Mojo, holding up a Polaroid of a very dead Gish splayed on the scorched linoleum of Poppy's kitchen floor.

"What the fuck?" says Gus, opening the door.

Mojo explains in a shaky voice that she discovered the grisly photo taped to the lost pet wall in Poppy's apartment. She'd gone over to post some new signs as a surprise for Poppy's return. Despite acting all tough, Mojo's hand is trembling. Gus takes the photo so the girl can stop holding it out in front of her. The kid looks relieved.

"Whoever took that photo killed Gish," Mojo declares,

then she walks past Gus and into her apartment. She sits on her sofa, her wet boots dripping a puddle on Gus's floor. Levi follows Mojo, licking the puddle then her hand. She pets his head robotically. Her lower lip trembles.

Gus stares at the Polaroid. It's like some sort of bizarre crime scene photo. Exhibit F. She can guess who put it there.

"The Irishman," Gus mutters to herself.

"Who?" asks Mojo.

"Just this guy I caught snooping in Poppy's apartment last night. Irish accent," she says.

Mojo bursts into tears. Gus isn't sure what to do. She grabs a couple of cream sodas from the fridge. When she returns, Levi's nestled against Mojo's hip on the sofa. The girl has stopped crying. She's staring at the evidence wall.

"Ignore that," says Gus, standing between Mojo and the wall, blocking her view.

Mojo leans to one side for a better look.

"What is it?" she asks, scrunching her nose.

"It's a sort of evidence wall. I mean it's the beginning of one, of course." Gus hands her the soda.

Mojo squints like she doesn't understand. Gus suddenly feels defensive of her wall.

"I'm investigating a disappearance for Poppy. She hired me, and this is how I work things out," says Gus.

Mojo slurps foam from the rim of the soda can. She doesn't say anything, so Gus fills the space, feeling the need to justify her methods to an eleven-year-old.

"I'm like a detective. Well not officially one. I have done it before, on, like, an amateur basis," Gus says, digging her fingers into her palms.

Stop talking. Stop talking.

Gus feels naked as she watches Mojo examine her wall. She braces for a snarky remark.

"Cool," says Mojo.

Gus looks from Mojo to the wall. Then she sees what Mojo sees. What her younger self would see. A living room where grown-up rules have been chucked out the window. Where you can draw on the walls with red marker. Where you can pin up whatever you like, however you like. Mojo and Gus sip their cream sodas, and in that moment, they are just two kids smiling at a messy wall.

"How come you're not in school?" asks Gus.

"March break," says Mojo.

"Cool." Gus nods.

"I could help with the detective stuff," says Mojo.

"It's okay, I got this," Gus says, trying to let her down easy.

"I've done it before too. I have a talent for it. Miss Travis says so. In her class, we did this family tree project and mine was the best. It was so easy doing all the research. There's all this stuff online. I got extra marks for mapping out what countries my ancestors come from. And a gold star."

Gus nods, although she's not sure how any of this qualifies the kid to be a detective. Not that she's one to talk.

"There's tons of stuff missing," says Mojo.

And now she's a critic.

"Like I said, I'm just getting started," Gus says, trying to wrap things up. "You know what? I was just about to walk Levi so I should really . . ." Gus nods toward the door. "Do that."

Levi snorts and curls deeper into the sofa. He's not backing her up. Mojo rises and walks over to the wall. That's when Gus spots the diary sitting in plain view on her blue trunk.

"Tons of stuff missing," Mojo says, pointing her soda to the questions written at the top of the wall. "The Irishman's name, for one."

Gus shoves the diary off the trunk and kicks it under the sofa.

"And another thing, when Gramma Char-Char heard those bones were found in the pond outside Poppy's, she flipped. She called it an omen. Grown-ups say anything in front of me because they don't think I'm listening. Only I am," Mojo says. "I hear tons of stuff."

If she says *tons of stuff* one more time, Gus is going to scream.

"So who's the Irishman?" Gus asks, taking the bait.

"I bet it's Malachy," says Mojo. "Grandpa Wilfred's driver."

"Tall. Dark curly hair. Weird eyebrow?" asks Gus.

"That's Malachy," says Mojo like they've cracked the case.

Interesting. Old man Mutchmore sent one of his lackeys to Poppy's to find something. Did this Malachy guy try to electrocute Poppy? Clearly they have access to her apartment. There's no way Gus left the door unlocked when she was searching Eva's room. Or did she? The plum has been messing with her mind lately. Or is it an apple now? She's been more forgetful. One thing she can't forget is that look the Irishman gave her before he left. Gus shudders.

Mojo steps closer to the wall and peers at the photo strip.

"Hey! That's Poppers and her boyfriend Leo. She showed me those once. OMG! Is that who disappeared? She never told me he . . . is it him? Is that who Popper's hired you to find? Is he the one in the pond? Is he?" Her mouth forms a perfect oval as she points to the question, *What happened to Leo?*

"Yes. No," Gus falters. "I don't know yet. He disappeared years ago, but Poppy doesn't think the bones in the pond are him. Even though he was wearing Leo's coat."

"A mystery. I love mysteries," declares Mojo, kicking off her boots. "I'm in."

"No, no, no. This isn't a game. You're just a kid," Gus says in a tone that reminds her of her mother.

Mojo jumps on the sofa, her soda dappling the cushions and the dog with pink droplets. Levi slides nonchalantly to the floor and shuffles into the hall to find a less chaotic spot to lie down. Mojo stops bouncing. She sticks out her tiny chest and states her case.

"I'm practically in middle school, and you need me," she says. "I know how to do all kinds of online research. I'm already signed up with the best genealogy databases and their sister sites—the ones that are all about DNA. And I'm super good at finding records. Even stuff going way back. Birth, death, adoption, marriage, dental. Need I say more?" Mojo folds her arms, case closed.

Gus knows that posing a simple question to Siri sums up her own tech skills, but she can't stoop to using the kid for her online prowess.

"Tell me you've got DNA kits?" says Mojo, jumping off the sofa.

"What?" asks Gus. "No. Why would I?"

"To identify genetic markers," she says.

Gus shrugs. Mojo sighs.

"Okay, so there are these little things in your DNA that go, *hey this is where you come from* or *this is who shares your DNA*, stuff like that," says Mojo. "So like me—I come from the Isle of Skye off the coast of Scotland. That's what my genetic markers tell me. And I share some of my DNA with my mom, my dad, and my grandpa . . ."

"I get it," Gus says, cutting her off.

"Every real detective has DNA kits in their toolbox," says Mojo. "It's kind of basic."

"I know," Gus snaps, wondering why she's letting this kid get under her skin.

"Let me do it for Poppers," she whines. "Mummy says

you're up to no good, but I don't think that's true, I wanna help."

Gus bristles at being unfairly judged by the perfect May.

"I think Poppers needs us both," says Mojo. "I am her family."

Then Gus sees the girl's true usefulness. She's an insider. She can give Gus access to the Mutchmores. They're a big part of Poppy's story. They're her family. Some of them were alive when Leo disappeared. And they're up to something. Mojo could be Gus's eyes and ears at the Mutchmore dinner table.

March break is short, right? What could it hurt?

Gus has never been a team player, but short-term, Marjory Anne Mutchmore-Stanfield has value as an informant and as tech support. Against her better judgment, she opens the door a crack.

"I can't pay you," Gus says.

Mojo squeals. Levi scrambles to his feet and races from the hall. He slides on the floor and bumps into the wall, then shakes himself off and stares at Mojo.

"I'll start in two days. No, three. On Thursday," says Mojo, pulling on her boots. "I'm going skiing with Mummy at Mont Tremblant tomorrow for a couple days. I'll bring Alma with me when I come back. See you then."

She waves and dashes out the door.

"Who's Alma?" Gus calls out, instantly regretting her decision.

But the girl is gone.

Gus hopes Alma isn't a school friend. There's no way she's babysitting a couple of sixth graders.

In red marker, Gus writes *Malachy* beside the question *Who is the Irishman?*

She pins the Polaroid of Gish to the wall.

Then Gus remembers something Mojo said earlier.

When Gramma Char-Char heard those bones were found in the pond outside Poppy's, she flipped. She called it an omen.

She writes *omen* beside the question *Whose bones were in the pond?*

Gus steps back, absorbing the images and words.

❧

She can see herself standing in her living room, gazing at her newly created evidence wall. Then she watches herself step forward and move right through the wall as if permeating a membrane into another dimension. Her body disappears from that place in time when she had more questions than answers, and it tumbles forward five full months into the dark, damp present where the answers lie in tatters at her cold feet.

She doesn't want to open her eyes. Doesn't want to leave those dreamy rememberings. Her hallucinatory visits back to those early days of her investigation are not only comforting, they are the key to her finding her way out of her present hell. It's an old coping mechanism of hers. Even as a child, she'd travel back to when her mother was alive, escaping the painful present. She would visit with her, and sometimes their time together felt more real than when she actually lived with Shannon in that little house in Hintonburg.

A rustling noise in the corner of the room brings her fully back into the pitch-black basement. Gus can't see, but she can hear something. She crawls toward the sound on hands and knees. It feels good to move her swollen body. To hang the weight of her belly under her, away from her aching spine.

"Mama?" she whispers as she crawls, her voice still sandpaper.

She reaches out. Hears a fluttering coming from above. Gus pulls herself to her feet, bracing one hand against the wall and stretching the other hand up. Something lightly brushes past her fingers. A feather. A bird. She can hear it whooshing overhead, then scrabbling in the corner.

Then it's gone.

"Come back?" she croaks.

But it's the lucky one. It's found a way out. It's escaped through a tiny crack in the ceiling she cannot see. That she cannot fit through. Then she hears something hit the floor. Kneeling, she feels around. Her fingers touch a small object. Sticks. Straw? No. It's circular. It's a nest. A small basket no larger than the palm of her hand. She dips her fingers inside and touches something fleshy and cold. She pulls away, knowing what it is. A newborn bird. It's dead.

Her heart skips a beat.

There are no such things as omens.

Gus places the nest gently in the corner. She sits very still. Holding her belly. Her baby.

There are no such things as omens.

The watermelon moves, pressing against her hand. Gus winces as a flood of emotion overwhelms her. She loves this watermelon with her whole heart. How is that possible when months ago she was pretending it didn't exist? But in this moment, her love is undeniable and fierce. She knows she will do anything to protect her. And she knows it's a girl. A girl who is almost ready to enter the world.

But is this feeling enough? Will she be a good mother?

A diary flutters into her mind like a winged vulture—a confession about an unwanted child clasped in its teeth. A mother tormented. A chill runs through Gus as memories swoop in and carry her away to the night she first read Eva's diary.

Back then, she was fumbling blindly through the beginnings of a so-called investigation. Lying in her bed that night, Gus could never have envisioned the truly devastating circumstances that unfolded decades before that moonless Halloween night when Leo disappeared.

Back then, she did not know that a perilous secret had long ago slithered around the roots of a family tree. A poison had taken hold, turning those roots black.

11

Eva

LEVI IS SNORING NEXT TO HER. GUS EATS COLD POP-TARTS from the box as she gently turns the brittle pages of Eva's diary. She notices that the writing transforms the deeper she gets. The dates change from winter to spring to summer to autumn of 1953. And the pristine penmanship changes as well. Words are scribbled over, pages are torn out, leaving tattered edges. The writing deteriorates to a spidery scrawl by year's end. But it's the last page that stuns her. The penmanship is violent and the words are harrowing. Scratched so deeply into the paper that Eva's pen sliced it in places, leaving gaping wounds. The paper is barely holding together. Gus can't help herself. She reads this last page first, and when she's finished, she is more certain than ever that clues to Leo's disappearance lie hidden in the inky pages of Eva's diary.

Hell is close. The fine gauze of existence barely separates me from its scorching fire. How my skin burns. How my perfidious heart shrivels inside my blackened chest. I am damned and the devil knows it. He taps at my door each night. His flames lick at my heels by day. And now he has taken my Poppy's eyes. A cruel warning.

He wants me to see what I have done. To see my daughter without vision, without dreams. To see the baby boy I abandoned. What mother forsakes her own flesh and blood? I am no mother. I am the devil's mistress. I lay in his bed and my daughter and son have paid the price. The dark hood knows what I have done. Who I discarded, who I deceived, who I killed. All the ways in which I have sinned. He beckons me. He sends the ghost of my son in his stead. I cannot defend myself. I am weakened, fearful, horrified. I am at hell's door and I cannot turn away. I must enter. I must burn for what I've done.

The entry is dated December 22, 1953. According to Poppy, this was around the time Eva was committed. She was clearly tormented by what was happening to Poppy and by things she'd done in the past. Did she really give up a child? A boy? Did she commit murder? She writes of a ghost and the devil. She was obviously delusional at the end. But what about the months before?

Gus flips back to page one.

January 1, 1953.

Gus bends the spine of the small diary, and as she does the cover bows and out slips a piece of blue paper that was tucked inside it. Gus flashes to a memory. Last year, when she was investigating her mother's murder, she made a chance discovery. She found documents hidden inside the sleeves of her elementary class photos. It looks like Poppy's mother hid things too.

Gus recognizes the blue paper. It is the same paper Leo used to write his love notes to Poppy. Gus reads it and realizes that Eva didn't mean for this to be found. Ever. It is the note that never came. The one that Poppy waited for that fateful night. Eva must have somehow intercepted it. She knew what they were planning.

My darling Poppy, I cannot wait until the moment when I can hold you in my arms. Everything is arranged. When your mother retires for the evening, meet me on the footbridge in Patterson Creek Park at 11 pm. There is to be good cloud cover on All Hallows' Eve, so darkness will be our friend. I have bought us train tickets to Montreal and then on to Boston just as we planned. Soon we will be together. Yours now and forever, Leo.

A bitter March wind blows across the park outside Gus's window as winter digs its heels in, determined to stick around a while longer. She scrapes frost from the pane and can just make out the footbridge below. Snowdrifts shift and reshape in the wind, forming frozen waves. She closes the curtains and snuggles next to Levi. He's toasty warm.

Gus reads the entire diary and finishes off the Pop-Tarts, vowing it will be her last box. As the sugar begins to tug her toward sleep, she turns the pages over in her mind. Ponders everything she's read. How much of it to share with Poppy. How much to spare her from ever knowing.

Eyelids heavy, Gus watches a spider drop into the ceiling lamp. Its shadow moves across the glass dish. An alien circumventing a crater on a faraway planet.

She feels a fluttering in her belly.

Another alien.

But this one is not in some far-off galaxy.

It's right here, inside her.

Floating in a universe made for one.

One apple that is now an avocado.

12

The Babies

VISITING HOURS AT THE CIVIC HOSPITAL ARE 2 P.M. TO 5 P.M. Gus arrives at 2 P.M. on the dot in hopes of getting Poppy alone. Gus peers behind the curtain surrounding her bed. No Mutchmores. Just Poppy. Under the blue fluorescent glow, she looks bloodless and hollow-eyed. A vampire. Her voice is a soft quiver. She looks worse than the last visit. Electrocution has severely rocked her eighty-five-year-old system.

Gus is nervous, this being her first official update. She tells Poppy about unlocking Eva's room and finding her mother's diary. She mentions the newspaper clipping in the *Life* magazine and running into Malachy, but skips the part about Gish's grisly Polaroid and Leo's missing note. Both might be too disturbing for her frail state. Poppy listens with interest. Gus shares that she created an evidence wall. She's secretly thankful Poppy won't actually be able to see it. Gus shifts the conversation to Poppy. They talk about the nurses and the tests and the food and the charming orderly Poppy has taken a shine to.

Gus listens, but her mind wanders to an entry Eva made in her diary on October 31. She wrote of finding Leo's note and then went on to describe how she drugged the soup, which explains why Poppy fell into such a deep sleep, and why Eva didn't eat that evening. The entries in the days that follow don't reveal what happened later that night. It's as if she doesn't dare write about it. Instead she writes of being haunted by nightmares and ghosts. The entries in the months before are even less helpful. Eva doesn't write about why she wanted to keep Poppy and Leo apart. Something happened in early October that sets her reeling, but again, she seems too hesitant or fearful to put it in writing. She weaves around the truth with strange musings about protecting Poppy's soul.

As if reading Gus's mind, Poppy asks about the diary. Gus treads lightly. She focuses on the spring and summer months, which are much less harrowing. In fact, they're dull. Dull is good. The pages are steeped in the minutiae of Eva's life. She was a meticulous chronicler of her daily errands and social engagements, doctor appointments and client fittings. 1953 was a busy year.

Until it wasn't.

On October 2 she had a meeting with someone she called *Pug*. After that, her diary takes a dark turn, and on the last day of October she wrote:

Today I finished the lace hem on Alisha Holbrough's wedding dress. I went along to the shops because we needed flour, but I forgot the flour. After running into the Croft boy in the hall, I made mine-strone soup seasoned with sleeping salts. Poppy and I read by the fire after supper. She soon became heavy-eyed and retired for the night. I am wide awake as I write this. My heart races. I watch the clock. It is almost time. It is the only way. I must do this for her.

Gus doesn't want to share this with Poppy. She's concerned that finding out that her own mother sabotaged her elopement might do her in. She tells herself that she'll share the discovery when Poppy's stronger. She's glad Poppy can't see the diary and how Eva's entries became jagged and incoherent through November '53. It's a terrifying glimpse into Eva's tortured existence. The woman seemed incapable of stopping herself from hurtling into the blackest parts of her mind, culminating in that hellish final entry.

"Did your mother ever mention anyone named Pug?" asks Gus.

Poppy looks surprised. "Oh my, I haven't heard that name in years." She smiles, but it looks forced.

Gus waits, examining Poppy's face.

"He was Leo's boss. Teddy Trichborne was his name. My mother knew him when they were children. She was the one who nicknamed him Pug," Poppy says. "Why?"

"Eva wrote about a meeting with him in early October," says Gus. "Do you know what they were meeting about?"

"They were friends." Poppy shrugs. "I don't know, love."

Gus pulls out her notebook and pen.

Pug = Teddy Trichborne.

"Didn't you tell me that Leo's boss introduced you two?" confirms Gus, looking up from her notes to see Poppy nodding.

The old woman seems distracted. She sips her water. She's fading.

One more question.

"Did Eva ever mention a baby?" asks Gus.

Poppy doesn't seem to understand the question.

Before Gus can elaborate, Charlotte Mutchmore clears her throat and emerges from behind the curtain. Mink coat, pashmina scarf, leather boots, matching purse. Gus rises.

"Poppy, darling, you're looking well. And you have a visitor," she says with a glossy smirk.

Poppy smiles weakly in her direction.

"Poppy and I made up after our little misunderstanding

at the gala," she says, leaning across Gus and squeezing Poppy's arm.

"Give us a wee sec, will you, darling?" she says to Poppy. The elderly woman links arms with Gus like they're old school chums, then she steers her from the room. She's surprisingly strong. Gus doesn't even have a chance to say goodbye to Poppy. The second they're in the hall, Charlotte drops her arm and brushes off her sleeve like she's ridding her expensive coat of Gus's unworthy pedigree. Charlotte sways close to Gus. Her peppermint-coated boozy breath pollutes Gus's airspace.

"You are everywhere these days, aren't you?" she says, stabbing a bony finger at Gus. "And we, the Mutchmores that is, all so appreciate your whatever-this-is, your little friendship with our Poppy. But I must insist that you give our family a wee bit of space during this oh-so-trying time. Poppy has been through a frightening ordeal, and these spontaneous visits of yours, these questions you're asking, they simply must stop. I'm sure you understand, and I will be letting the good nurses in this ward know that we are her family and we can take care of her. You do understand, sweet little Augusta Monet."

She smiles, ending her oh-so-sickly-sweet *Get the fuck out and stay the fuck out*. But Gus is not going quietly. She remembers something Charlotte said at the gala.

Did you know her mum and I were close?

"You knew Eva well?" Gus asks, smiling.

"She was family," she says, uncertain as to why the girl is not running away in tears.

Gus stands her ground. Poppy is her friend and employer. And there was something else Charlotte said.

"Your family is cursed?" Gus pushes. "Isn't that what you said?"

Charlotte winces and lets her gaze fall to her age-spotted hands. "Not so much a curse as a cull," she says, more to herself than Gus.

Then Charlotte looks as if she's realized something has been said that can't be unsaid. But just as quickly she gathers herself and smiles.

"I like you. You're fearless. I used to be. Now everything frightens me. You'd think with age things would get easier, but the older you get the more death just sits there in the shadows waiting," she muses.

They look at each other. The silence seems to hold them both frozen in place, connecting them, if only for a moment. Charlotte is the first to break the ice, her words sounding more like a genuine offer of advice than a threat.

"You best stop asking about the babies," she says softly, then turns and walks into Poppy's room, closing the door behind her.

Far off, an alarm bleats from an intercom.

A voice calls out a code.

Gus stands alone in the empty hall.

The sound of running feet and squeaky portable machines being wheeled toward the bleating emergency reverberate down a corridor of the hospital.

But Gus hears nothing.

Her ears are ringing with Charlotte's words.

Two of them.

The babies.

13

Squirrel

Mojo holds her phone up to Gus's face. On the screen is a photo of a man in a dark suit leaning against a limousine, smoking.

"That's the Irishman," nods Gus.

"Malachy," says Mojo. "Told you. I printed it. For your wall." And without asking, Mojo pins the printout under the word *Malachy*.

Then the girl pulls a slender MacBook from her backpack and sets it on Gus's blue trunk. She kneels in front of it and looks up at Gus, who sits across from her on the sofa. She bounces on her heels, full of bubbling energy.

"This is Alma!" announces Mojo with a little squeal, pointing to the laptop.

Levi lifts one ear. He's been desperately trying to get some shut-eye in his favorite sunny corner, but Mojo's voice keeps piercing the membrane of his drowsy dog-brain. He snorts and buries his muzzle between his paws.

"Oh, your laptop," says Gus. "Why Alma?"

"Hungarian for *apple*," says Mojo, delighted with herself.

"Haha," says Gus flatly, nursing her third cup of coffee.

It's way too early in the morning for any of this. Gus forgot Mojo was coming over. She forgot it was Thursday.

"Tell me about your family tree," Gus says, hoping to lasso some of Mojo's energy.

Mojo claps her hands and springs to her feet.

That didn't work.

She dances over to the wall and grabs the red marker. Mojo looks back at Gus expectantly, the marker inches from a blank space on the evidence wall, ready for the starter's gun. Gus nods and off she goes. Mojo draws a tree trunk. As she adds branches, she describes the Mutchmore family history just like she's giving a school presentation she knows by heart.

"The first Mutchmores came from Scotland, all the way to Upper Canada, in the 1700s," begins Mojo.

Gus watches as generations of settlers sprout from the upper branches of Mojo's tree. Her great-great-grandfather Alasdair is the third generation.

"In the late 1800s, when some important men wanted to build this train track through his land, Alasdair got shares in the Canadian Pacific Railway Company. The company blew up, and I mean in a good way. Hotels, shops, shipping. That's how we got rich," she says, smiling.

Mojo's great-grandfather, Robert, is added to the tree. Alasdair's son.

"Great-Grandpa Robert inherited everything when he was only nineteen years old. And he married Cora and she was even younger than him. She was really pretty. This one article said they were the toast of town. They threw parties at their big mansion on Queen Elizabeth Driveway. Cora did charity balls at the Château Laurier, which they owned, and Robert was friends with all the really important and fat people in the national capital," she says.

"Fat?" asks Gus.

"Fat cats," she says without missing a beat. "That's what Mummy calls rich people, but not us."

Gus sits back on the sofa and smiles. The kid is entertaining, that's for sure.

Mojo adds a branch for Felix, the war hero.

"And then they had a son. The heir to the Mutchmore fortune. Felix. He was born right when a new century started. Nineteen hundred. Thirteen years later, they had a daughter, Eva." Mojo adds a branch.

"One boy, one girl. The perfect family. Robert and Cora had it all, but then, dum-dee-dum"—she pauses for dramatic effect—"tragedy struck when Felix ran away to join the war at sixteen and was killed dead by the Germans."

Mojo scribbles out the branch bearing Felix's name.

"They were heartbroken. No one could replace their Felix. Until," she says, adding a new branch, "someone did. In 1919, Cora had another son. Wilfred. My grandpa."

Mojo proceeds to add spouses, using little heart-shaped leaves to connect the names.

"When the kids grew up, Eva married a guy named Frank, and they had a daughter, Poppy. Then, after being a bachelor for a really long time, Wilfred finally married Charlotte. And after trying to have a baby for a really long time, they finally had May. So now both of them had kids of their own. Poppy and May," she says, adding their names below their parents.

"Poppers never got married or had any kids, but May did. She married Ricker Stanfield and they had a charming little daughter." Mojo adds a branch to the bottom of the tree.

She turns to look at Gus with a toothy grin.

"Me. Marjory Anne!" she squeaks, adding her own name to this last branch.

"Ta-dum," she says proudly, extending her arms toward her masterpiece like a game show presenter revealing a prize.

Gus smiles and claps politely, feeling a little sorry for the girl. Mojo's story and the one Gus heard at the gala say a lot about the family. Sons matter to the Mutchmores, especially when it comes to their precious legacy. Maybe Wilfred is content to leave his fortune in the hands of his son-in-law, Ricker, but Gus is beginning to get the feeling that the male bloodline matters a great deal to the Mutchmores. And there has been no Mutchmore son since Wilfred.

Charlotte said it.

This family is cursed . . . there haven't been any more sons.

It seems the weight of that legacy now rests on the tiny shoulders of Marjory Anne Mutchmore-Stanfield.

The caffeine has kicked in. Gus throws the girl a bone. She points out the new additions she made to the wall since Mojo was last here. The hidden note from Leo that Eva intercepted. And another tidbit from the diary that Gus added to the wall.

Eva's meeting with Pug (Teddy), October 2, 1953.

"Pug, that's funny," says Mojo.

The last time Mojo showed up uninvited, Gus had hidden Eva's diary. She wasn't sure why, but now that Gus has read it, she's glad she did. An eleven-year-old doesn't need to read about murder and ghosts and hellfire. Although she almost thinks Mojo would eat it up.

"Why is a meeting important?" asks Mojo.

"Not sure if it is," Gus says, trying to keep things vague.

"How'd you know about it?" presses Mojo.

"Poppy remembered it," she lies.

If the diary is accurate, something changed in Eva after that meeting. But Gus can't tell Mojo that or she'll have to reveal the diary. She'd wanted to ask Poppy more about Pug, but Charlotte had interrupted them.

"Babies?" asks Mojo, pointing to another new addition to the wall. Gus added a new question after her encounter with Charlotte at the hospital. She wrote it next to the others.

Who are the babies?

Gus figures she might as well tell Mojo what Charlotte said. See if it twigs anything.

You best stop asking about the babies.

"What babies?" asks Mojo.

"Exactly," shrugs Gus.

Now that the can of babies has been opened, Gus presses on.

"Did you ever hear talk of Eva having a son?"

"No, and I would know," she says, pointing to the family tree she drew on the wall.

"Maybe before she was married," suggests Gus.

"Who told you that?" says Mojo, her lower lip stuck out in a pout.

"It's just something I remember Poppy hinted at," Gus lies.

"Is that who the babies are?" guesses Mojo.

"Maybe. Or Charlotte meant something else," says Gus.

They plunk side by side on the sofa, staring at the wall.

"Your grandma said the bones in the pond were an omen," Gus says.

They both look at the word written on the wall. *Omen*.

"She kind of thinks everything's a sign," says Mojo.

"What did she say, exactly?" asks Gus.

Mojo takes a deep breath and then gives a motor-mouthed rundown of what happened.

"So I was sleeping over like I always do on weekends so Mummy and Daddy can do their charity stuff, and we were sitting at the breakfast table on Sunday morning and she was reading the paper and she kind of made this sound like she couldn't breathe and that's when she said it. She pointed at the paper and said, *It's an omen*. She was pointing at a thing about the bones they found in the ice. Grandpa almost choked on his English muffin. She got up and shoved the paper at him and then she ran upstairs. She didn't even finish her eggs."

Gus considers Charlotte's words. She can't see the link between decades-old bones and the Mutchmores. Gus thinks on her recent encounters with Malachy and Charlotte, even May. Each, in their own way, was trying to veer her off course. The Mutchmores are afraid of something.

That's always good. Fear means there are secrets to be uncovered.

Time to tap Mojo's tech skills.

"You said you could find records?" she says, pointing to Alma.

"You bet I can," says Mojo, flopping in front of her laptop. "What d'ya need?"

She beams, both hands hovering over the keyboard.

"How about birth records? Or even adoption records? Poppy said something about Eva giving up a baby," says Gus. "Anything with the name Eva Mutchmore."

After a few clicks and sighs and furrowed brows, Mojo comes up empty.

Maybe Eva had the baby after she was married.

"Try Honeywell," suggests Gus.

Mojo finds only one record. Poppy's birth registration.

"I'll try putting some keywords in a few database search engines," she says. "Maybe Eva didn't use her real name."

Gus paces the room and eventually goes in the kitchen and puts on more coffee and makes herself a bowl of Honeycomb. The morning disappears. She goes over her notes and tidies up a bit. The whole time, Mojo clicks and types, clicks and types.

Finally, Mojo shrieks, "I found it!"

Gus jumps. Levi is jolted from his sleep. He barks.

"I can't believe I missed this when I was doing my family tree," she says.

The dog drags himself to his feet and stands by the front door, head bowed. He's done napping and he's ready for his daily walk. Gus ignores the dog. She circles behind Mojo and stares at the laptop's screen, no idea what she's looking at.

"It's a birth registration for a Baby M. And there's adoption orders attached to the file. Both records are sealed, so no birth parents are named, only dates. But look there"—she points—"that's the name of the adoption agency. See?" She squeals.

Gus shakes her head, not seeing what Mojo sees. The girl keeps clicking back and forth between the two documents. It's dizzying.

"Okay, so first off, look at the date the baby was born. August 2, 1930. Eva would have been seventeen. She wasn't married yet, so she would've had to give up the baby for adoption, right? And second, they called it Baby M. As in Mutchmore," says Mojo, as if it's obvious.

"That's all? Baby M and a random date?" Gus sighs. "M could stand for anything."

Mojo smiles, undeterred.

"You're right, it could. But it doesn't. You know how I know it doesn't? You know how I know this is a Mutchmore baby?" sings Mojo, toying with Gus.

Gus strains to keep her *excited to hear what you're thinking* face from dissolving into a *just spit it the fuck out* face.

"The Ladies' *something* Association of Ottawa. Benevolent, that's it. They, like, did adoptions and stuff. My great-grandma, Cora, was the head of the whole thing," she says, clicking open a folder on her desktop.

In the folder are several jpeg images of black-and-white photographs glued to the pages of a family album. She clicks on one image, and it becomes full screen. There are names printed neatly below the photo. Cora Mutchmore is dead center.

"That's the LBA, and that's my great-grandma. Cora Mutchmore. She did all this fundraising to build a new orphanage. This was taken in front of the building. I think it was on Carling Avenue."

"It's definitely a connection, but it's still a stretch," says Gus, looking at the grainy image of a group of women in fancy hats, their white-gloved hands clutching purses as they pose, grouped around a man who is cutting a ribbon.

"You're the one who said Eva had a baby," Mojo whines.

"We need proof. We need names, not initials," says Gus.

"The couple who adopted the baby have names, see?" offers Mojo.

Mojo jumps from the photos back to the browser, opening one tab, then another.

"Wait, slow down. I better get a record of all this," she says.

Gus uses her phone to take photos of the documents. She briefly glances at the adoption record.

"This could be anyone's baby," says Gus. "We have to find something more concrete. Something with names. Can you get records unsealed?"

"I don't think so," says Mojo, deflated. "Investigating is hard."

Mojo slumps and sticks out her lower lip. Then something dawns on her.

"What time is it?" asks Mojo, looking like she might be in trouble.

"Your parents don't know where you are, do they?" says Gus, knowing the answer.

"They . . . um," she stammers.

Mojo flushes. Gus gets why she didn't tell them. It's clear the family doesn't like her.

"There is one thing I guess I could try before I go," she says quietly, as if she's not sure she wants to say it.

"What?" asks Gus.

"I don't know if it'll work but I could run a deep search."

"And that is?" Gus asks.

"It's this plug-in that scans the web and finds all these sites and random links that don't come up in regular searches," she says, her hand hovering over the mouse, hesitating.

"Do it," says Gus.

Mojo clicks on a circular icon on her desktop.

"Nothing's happening," says Gus.

"It's scanning in the background. It can take hours. Days. You have to leave the laptop open or all the data will be lost, so don't touch it," says Mojo.

Gus has no idea what a plug-in is or what Alma is doing, but she goes with it. While they wait for the scan, Gus suggests they take Levi for a walk around the park. He's long overdue.

The smell of March's moldy retreat hangs in the air. Patches of dirty snow are beginning to melt, revealing brown squishy mats of glistening autumn leaves from last year. Levi pushes his snout through the wet piles, licking their slimy underbellies. Gus has to drag Levi away from his favorite corner of the park under the honey locusts. They circle back along the path toward the steep stone stairs leading up to the street. The damp chills them to the bone, but when they get back to Gus's apartment, an even more chilling gift awaits them outside her door.

A dead squirrel.

The twisted corpse looks like it's been hit by a car. One of its hind legs juts in the wrong direction. But stranger still, it doesn't look like it was just picked up off the road and deposited on her threshold. It's been patched up and sewn together, albeit in a bit of a hurry.

Mojo spots it first. She's plastered against the wall. Eyes bugged out, mouth gaping. Levi catches the scent and darts ahead with surprising speed. That's when Gus sees it. Before she can stop him, Levi gets hold of his new chew toy. He dances about, evading Gus's frantic hands. She grabs hold of his jaw, which is clamped down on his catch like a vise. Gus manages to pry it open wide enough to yank the roadkill from his frothing mouth. She holds his collar and flings the carcass down the hall just as May Mutchmore-Stanfield steps off the elevator. It lands at her feet. The elegant woman barely flinches. She looks down at the dead squirrel. Then she slowly lifts her chin and turns her gaze down the hall toward Gus and Levi and her daughter, who's white as a ghost.

The only thought that flits across Gus's mind is that the fickle elevator must be working again. It's old and cranky and only seems to run when it feels like it or when Mr. Curry feels like fixing it.

No one says a word. Levi pulls and whines, nose twitching, a bit of fur stuck to his lip. Gus holds him tight. May motions her daughter. Mojo obeys like a trained dog. She runs to her mother's side. May presses the elevator button rapid-fire in a futile attempt to bring it back faster. Gus hauls Levi toward their door. He yowls and squirms. Then a sudden loud rattle emanates from the elevator shaft. Levi freezes. A gear can be heard grinding to an echoing thud. May rolls her eyes, grabs Mojo's elbow, and the two of them head in the opposite direction, toward the far stairwell.

"It's not my squirrel" is all Gus can think to call out.

May turns and shoots daggers in Gus's direction.

"You and that ugly mutt, keep away from my daughter from now on," shouts May, before disappearing into the stairwell, Mojo at her heels.

Gus looks at Levi. He looks up at her.

"That was uncalled for," Gus says. "You're a beautiful boy."

Levi licks the fur dangling from his lower lip and eats it.

Gus deposits the cadaver down the garbage chute, much to the dog's dismay. As she watches it disappear down the metal shaft, Gus is reminded of a dead possum that was once left for her to find. A gift from Gracie Halladay, a reclusive woman who had a penchant for transforming roadkill into her little taxidermy friends. But this can't be Gracie's handiwork. Their paths were disentangled over two years ago and Gracie is long gone. Probably in the States with her surrogate family, Lois and Edgar. And besides, the squirrel was too bloody. It was a rush job. Gracie's work was meticulous. Careful. Thoughtful, somehow.

This feels more ominous.

It feels like a warning.

Gus fumes as she pictures Malachy snickering as he placed the dead squirrel by her door. A grotesque little message delivered on behalf of his boss, Wilfred Mutchmore, or perhaps his charming wife, Charlotte. She wouldn't put much past Mojo's grandmother. But what they don't realize is that dead shit just gets this girl going.

Sitting on her sofa across from her evidence wall, Gus clears her mind and travels across the wall, following lines and patterns, connecting dots. The bones found in the pond rocked Charlotte. And if Eva's diaries are to be believed, Poppy's mother did something terrible. Did she go to the bridge that October evening in Poppy's place? To send Leo away, or worse, to kill him? Do Wilfred and Charlotte know what she did?

Gus recalls the diary entry Eva made that night.

I watch the clock. It is almost time. It is the only way. I must do this for her.

If the Mutchmores know what happened that night, maybe that's why Charlotte called the bones an omen. But Poppy doesn't believe it's Leo, so the pieces don't really fit.

Unless Poppy's lying.

Gus is suddenly struck by a realization that should have come to her much sooner. *Damn avocado-brain.* There is someone who might know exactly what happened back in 1953. A potential eyewitness. And he lives in the Ambassador. The retired caretaker, Stanley Croft. Young Stanley delivered Leo's love notes to Poppy. He was their go-between. How had Gus not thought of this before? Stanley is her window into the past. A little rickety and time-worn, perhaps, but worth a look-see.

⌁

The next day is a warmish Friday. She spots a few crocuses peeking up through the snow at the park's edge. Coming back inside from their morning walk, Gus checks the listing on the lobby buzzer panel, confirming that the Croft siblings are in 107. She takes Levi upstairs, then heads back down the dim stairwell to the first floor. The past few weeks, Gus has felt a presence in the stairwell as if someone is lingering there, near the bottom. She hasn't seen anyone. More than once, on her way to do laundry, she's found the door propped by a brick. She's also seen signs of life. Wax drippings from a candle, crumbs, a discarded plastic water bottle, a stray mitten, an empty candy wrapper. Looks like a homeless person has taken refuge from the cold in the stairwell.

When she first saw the door propped, her mind had momentarily jumped to Tommy. Had he found her again? Was he lurking in the shadows? But just as quickly, she remembered that it couldn't be him. A few weeks earlier, she'd read a brief account in the local paper about the verdict in an appeal hearing for a man convicted of killing a Kemptville police officer. The judge reduced the sentence from murder to manslaughter. Gave him seven years less time served. The man's name was Tommy Oaks. She was relieved to know he was back in prison again.

It was a mistake to sleep with him, but she'd done that for herself. To soothe her own loneliness. She used him. And she got more than she bargained for.

But none of that matters now. She'll never see him again. He'll never know about the avocado. It isn't his. It's hers and hers alone.

Gus hadn't bothered telling Mr. Curry about her suspicion that someone might be sleeping in the stairwell. They were doing no harm, and she felt sad for whoever they were. She'd always had a soft spot for outsiders. Those living on the fringes of normal life, as if somehow they got left behind due to no fault of their own. Perhaps a wrong turn or a twist of fate led them astray.

Today, she leaves a box of Pop-Tarts at the bottom of the stairs, then heads to apartment 107 and knocks on the door.

The sound of her knocking splinters time. The fragments pierce her skin with painful memories. A child slams a bedroom door, angry with her mother. A policewoman knocks on her great-grandmother's door, bringing terrible news of a death. A heavy basement door closes, descending her into the blackness that is the present. A place in time that is so heavy it weighs on her chest. Crushing her. She can't breathe.

And then Gus does something she didn't think possible. She pushes the present away. Refusing to let it in.

And it goes. It leaves.

Despite the catastrophic pain surging through her body as

the baby contorts and battles for a way out, Gus finds herself able to reach out and open that impossible door that locked her in this prison. She pulls it open, and cloaked in the steely certainty of the past, in all that happened in the days leading to her confinement, she walks through that door and makes her way out of the subbasement and up to the first floor.

And now, right in front of her, is the door to Stanley and Alice's apartment.

It opens.

She is back where she belongs.

Feet firmly in the past.

And this time, she's staying there even if it kills her.

Fuck the present.

14

The Crofts

ALICE CROFT STANDS IN THE DOORWAY, SQUINTING. SHE'S NO more than five feet tall. Spandexed in neon green high-waisted leggings and a matching sleeveless tank top. Pink running shoes. Hands on hips. Skin dripping from under her biceps like webbed wings. She's tiny and trim. Looks to be in her eighties. They know each other from when the Crofts helped Gus clean Poppy's apartment after Gish's unpleasant demise. Gus has passed Alice in the lobby and seen her jogging in the park. Arms pumping, elbows high. A gangly bird. Emu-like. Alice sort of has an emu's face as well. Bulging eyes set far apart. Alice lifts the Coke-bottle lenses hanging from a chain around her neck and rests them on the bridge of her nose. She smiles as recognition dawns. Then she puts her hands in a prayer position and bows.

"Namaste," she coos.

Gus awkwardly returns the gesture.

"Namust—" Gus gives up. "Hi, it's Augusta from 305? Sorry to bother you, Miss Croft."

"No bother at all. I'm over the moon. Your timing couldn't

be better, don't you know? I just finished my morning sun salutations," says Alice, beaming.

Alice might not be a particularly handsome woman, but her airy nature is quite endearing. Gus smiles.

"Is Stanley home?" Gus asks.

Alice's smile quivers at the edges.

"He's still sleeping," she says, her bony shoulders slumping ever so slightly.

Alice was hoping the visitor had come to see her. Gus obliges.

"Actually, do you have time to chat, Miss Croft?" Gus asks.

Alice brightens and claps like a little girl invited to a birthday party. Gus figures why not. Alice might remember something from back then too. She would have been a young girl, maybe a preteen.

"Oh do call me Alice. Tea?" she offers, waving Gus inside.

Leaving the door open, she skips off into her apartment.

"It's oolong, don't you know?" she calls out.

Alice twitters about the kitchen with a sprightliness that belies her age. She's no doddering senior citizen. Gus takes a seat in the Crofts' sunny kitchen. A linoleum-topped table and two chairs are arranged under the window. The plastic cushions of the chairs are cracked. The table legs rusting. There's a medicinal smell in the air. Milk of magnesia. Gus's great-grandmother used to drink it daily, as she put it, *to keep things moving in the right direction*. On the table, a vase of synthetic daffodils is set between two souvenir place mats from Florida. Palm trees and bikini-clad girls sunning under beach umbrellas adorn the mats. On the fridge are flamingo-shaped magnets holding in place several faded family photos.

Alice downs a shaker cup of green liquid while she waits for the water in the kettle to boil. She sets out teacups and digestive cookies. Alice hasn't stopped talking since Gus sat down. It's as if she's been saving up, and now every thought in her head is tumbling out. She chirps on about the weather and the days getting longer and nights getting warmer. About her volunteer work with the Glebe Parks Committee. About the city's plan to install a pop-up bistro in the park this summer. About her fierce opposition to the plan. She pounds the table as she describes the idiocy of destroying a neighborhood park so that silly couples can drink wine and eat foie gras by the pond. Gus hasn't uttered a word in twenty minutes. She waits for an opening in which to steer the conversation toward the past.

The second Alice takes a sip of tea, Gus jumps in.

"So you've lived in the Ambassador Court your whole life?" Gus prompts.

It works.

Delight shines in her eyes as she tells Gus about growing up at the Ambassador. When she was little it was like living in a hotel. The building was so grand. She knew everyone who lived there, and everyone who came through, from the milkman to the postman. Her father, William Croft, was the caretaker for three decades. Her family had the keys to the kingdom, and she was the princess. She was allowed in places no one else was, like utility rooms and maintenance spaces, behind the scenes. She was even allowed on the rooftop, where her father built her a pigeon coop. She was allergic to dogs and cats, so he bought her the homing pigeons to care for. Her father was wonderful. He took her everywhere. Included her in everything. He taught her how to fix the boiler and change fuses and flush pipes, along with her brother.

Behind Alice, Gus notices some hooks hanging on the back of a cupboard door. On one hook, there's a large key ring holding multiple keys. On the others hang a pair of glasses and a man's watch. A small needlepoint artwork framed by a wooden hoop hangs above the hooks. The embroidery is adorned with pictures of tiny hammers and brooms and bears the words *Dearest Papa. The Caretaker of Our Hearts.* It's sweet and kind of weird. Like a little shrine to Alice's beloved father.

When Gus asks about her mother, Alice says she doesn't remember her. She died when Alice was two. But she does remember having a lovely childhood until her brother left for the military. She missed him so. She kept every one of his letters. A little over a year after Stanley left, Alice's father died from complications related to diabetes. Her saving grace was Stanley returning home to look after her and to take over his father's caretaking duties. Alice was thirteen. The siblings have shared the apartment since.

Alice takes a rare breath. Pauses and smiles, lost in some private thought. The quiet fills the space. Gus is about to ask Alice if she knew Leo when Alice launches back into her story.

"Stanley was always a good brother. He wrote me every week when he was away in the army. And when Daddy passed, he left it all to come back to take care of me. He loved me that much," she says. "I suppose he was meant to be a caretaker. He took care of everyone in the building. He always put the needs of others before his own, don't you know?"

As if on cue, Stanley appears in the kitchen doorway, yawning. He's wearing suede slippers and a velour robe over what looks like a long nightshirt. He looks like he stepped out of the pages of a Dickens novel. Alice leaps from her chair when she spots him. He and Alice are polar opposites. She's all bright and bubbling with energy whereas Stanley is pale and slow-moving.

"Well if it isn't the devil in blue suede slippers," she laughs, although there's a hint of disappointment in her eyes. She was enjoying Gus's undivided attention. Gus rises to greet Stanley, but Alice grips her arm and nods for her to stay seated.

"Give the old coot a sec," she says, rolling her eyes.

Gus stays put. Alice is the boss in this household.

"We've got company, dear," she says, loudly.

Stanley looks half-asleep and slightly bewildered as if he's shuffled into the wrong kitchen. His white hair is a bird's nest. His thin frame teeters as he tries to make sense of his surroundings. Alice pours him a glass of water, takes some pills from a prescription bottle, and hands them to him. He obediently puts the pills in his mouth and washes them down with water. With a great sigh, Stanley makes his way to the chair opposite Gus while Alice pops bread in the toaster.

"It's the girl from upstairs. August. She's come by for a visit," she shouts.

Gus smiles at Stanley. He nods as he settles his stiff bones into the chair.

"Augusta," Gus says, reaching for his hand. He weakly shakes hers.

"Augusta. Augusta, not August. I knew that," says Alice. "I've never been good with remembering names, don't you know? I have to say them over and over. Daddy used to tell me to say a person's name back to them and then I'd never forget, but I forget to do that and then I forget their name."

Gus doesn't acknowledge Alice's rant.

"Do you remember me, Mr. Croft? From Poppy's apartment?" says Gus, a little louder than she'd normally talk.

"You're the redhead," says Stanley.

"Stanley hasn't stopped going on about your hair since you helped us tidy up after that awful business with Poppy's kitty-cat," says Alice, busying herself buttering the popped toast.

Gus finds it amusing how Alice remembers the events. Gus helping them instead of the other way around. She's beginning to think Alice sees the world as it suits her. Which might not make her the most reliable narrator of decades-old events.

"How is Poppy?" asks Stanley. "I would visit, but I'm not the young man I used to be."

Alice slides a plate of buttered toast in front of Stanley, along with a knife and jar of jam.

"She's slowly getting better," says Gus.

"Quite the shocking experience," adds Alice.

She twists her face in mock horror.

"Oh I didn't mean to say that," she says, slapping her hand over her mouth.

"Her doctor thinks she'll be home soon," says Gus, ignoring Alice's attention seeking.

"That's good to hear," says Stanley.

Alice clatters about in the sink, washing her Magic Bullet. Stanley spreads jam slowly across his toast.

"I wanted to ask you," she says to Stanley, then remembers that Alice needs to be kept happy. "Actually, I wanted to ask both of you about Poppy's friend who disappeared back in 1953. I was hoping you might remember something from that night."

Alice darts to her brother's side and rests a hand on his shoulder.

"I understand you knew Leo." Gus looks at Stanley.

Stanley chews his toast, then swallows.

"I did" is all he says.

"Yes, Leo. He wasn't just Poppy's friend. We both knew him," she chimes in. "He used to help me feed the pigeons."

"On the night he disappeared, Poppy was waiting for a note from him. But she never got it," continues Gus, hoping to jog Stanley's memory. She glances at Alice, who shrugs.

"We wouldn't know anything about that," she says. "Back then, Poppy had her head in the clouds most of the time, so who's to know what was truth and what was a pretty girl's vanity run amok."

"How do you mean?" asks Gus.

"Well I'm not one to talk out of turn, but some girls just think all eyes are on them, don't you know?" she says, putting a hand on her hip and posing like she's at the end of a runway. "As if the rest of us were chopped liver. Oh it didn't bother me one lick. She lived in a fantasy world. She had romantic notions of being swept off her feet by some Prince Charming or some such nonsense. She thought every man was weak in the knees at the sight of her."

Gus doesn't quite know what to say. She could easily dismiss Alice's words as the jealousy of a young girl for her pretty teenaged neighbor, but Gus realizes that she's only heard this story from Poppy's perspective. Gus recalls how strong-minded Poppy can sometimes be and wonders if there's some truth to what Alice remembers and perhaps Poppy has convinced herself of some alternate reality.

"I mean, what is love really but two people, whoever they might be, knowing each other's insides, not fawning over their outsides," adds Alice with a slight air of superiority.

She crosses to the sink, grabs a dish towel, and begins to dry the Magic Bullet.

"Poppy didn't get the note," says Stanley softly, as if he knows it to be true.

Gus almost forgot Stanley was there, what with Alice's performance.

"So you remember that night," says Gus, turning her attention to the old man.

Even though Gus is well aware that Eva had that last note in her possession, Stanley might know how she got it.

"The milk door," says Stanley.

Alice turns to listen. She looks puzzled by the fact that he's got anything more to say.

"I used to put the notes inside their milk door. The milk doors were right outside the apartments in the wall. I'd wait until the milkman had come and gone, then I'd place it under the bottles. Poppy always fetched the milk for her mother," he says with unexpected clarity.

"But Eva found the note instead," says Gus.

Stanley looks at her, surprised that she knows that part of the story.

Alice twists the dish towel she's holding.

"She had come back from running errands and caught me hiding the note," he says, hesitating as if he's trying to recall that moment more clearly.

Gus flashes to an entry in Eva's diary.

After running into the Croft boy in the hall, I made minestrone soup seasoned with sleeping salts.

Alice flicks the dish towel, then lays it over the edge of the sink.

"Finish your toast, darling. You mustn't take your medicines on an empty stomach, don't you know?" she says loudly.

Stanley takes another bite.

"Did you tell Leo what happened?" Gus asks.

Stanley opens his mouth to speak, but Alice pipes up first.

"He went missing, so how could Stanley have told him about a silly note?" asks Alice.

Gus wishes Alice would fuck off.

"So Leo didn't know the note was intercepted?" Gus presses.

"He knew," says Stanley.

Alice takes away the remainder of her brother's toast and tosses the leftovers in the sink.

"You told him?" prompts Gus.

Alice flips a switch on the wall that triggers a horrible grinding noise. It takes a moment for Gus to realize she's turned on the garbage disposal. Gus stares at Alice. She smiles innocently, then nods as if she's just realized she's creating a racket. She turns off the disposal.

"I did. That was the last time we spoke. He should never have gone that night," says Stanley, eyes glistening.

Alice rushes over to her brother and clasps his shoulders.

"Oh, Stanley, sweetie," she coos.

"It was all my fault," he says.

The burden of that night clearly weighs heavily on him. Alice pats his shoulders.

"He blames himself for everything, this one does. He was just helping out a friend. He'd done all he could. He had his own obligations. Stanley left early the next morning, don't you know?" says Alice.

"Left?" asks Gus.

"Our Stanley was off to basic training in Borden, Ontario," she says.

The old man shrinks. Alice leans a bony hip against him.

"This one would give anyone the shirt off his back, wouldn't you, darling?" Alice says.

Gus wants to ask more about Poppy and Leo and the past, but she doesn't.

Stanley looks tired, and there's a finality to Alice's posture.

As Gus observes the siblings, side by side in their small apartment kitchen, Gus can sense the ease of their long companionship. They're like an old married couple or a well-worn pair of slippers. Comfortable and familiar. They've shared the same apartment for decades. They've fallen into routines of pills and tea and toast, and in Alice's case, sun salutations and jogging and community activism. And despite Alice's quirks

and somewhat controlling ways, Gus finds the siblings endearing. Alice is a lonely biddy with too much energy, and Stanley
is sweet and sad in his sagging nightshirt.

Later that afternoon, Gus is walking Levi through the park,
pondering her first official interview and sifting through what,
if anything, she's uncovered. Eva caught Stanley hiding the
note. That's how she came to have it. And Leo knew she'd
found it. What happened next is still a mystery, only it's starting
to sound like Eva and Leo both went to the park that night.

To the bridge then.

He should never have gone that night.

It's all my fault.

Lost in thought, Gus has made her way across the park
to the pond. Her feet have taken her there while her mind
wandered elsewhere. Now she's standing on the stone bridge.
From her apartment window, she's watched as the black pond
below has slowly expanded with the spring melt. Now only
fragile icy edges trim the water.

She looks down into the blackness and sees her reflection
from above. But it's her other face that looks back up at her.
That distant anguished face that is right now pressed, cheek
and jaw, against the cold stone floor of a locked basement
room.

She gasps and looks away.

She wills herself to keep walking. Gus steps carefully across
the bridge, heads away from the pond and the black water.
Gus and Levi hit the gravel path. She can hear the fine stones
crunching underfoot. Levi pulls on the leash, his nostrils flar-
ing in and out. He drops to one shoulder, letting his body fall
sideways. He wiggles on his back, eager to coat his fur with the
scent of decay emanating from the rotting leaves. Gus drags
the dog to his feet and pulls him toward the street. The leash
is tight around her fingers, cutting off the circulation. She

likes the feeling. It keeps her here. The smells, the feelings, the warmth of spring, the sound of the breeze.

She refuses to let go.

Gus grips the past and holds on tight.

The two of them climb the stone steps up to the sidewalk above the park.

Gus smiles.

She's in her happy place.

An old dog and the past at her side.

15

Ricker

GUS IS BRUSHING HER TEETH WHEN HER HAPPY PLACE DISsolves.

She hears a distant whimper.

Levi.

She drops her toothbrush and searches the apartment.

The bedroom. Living room. Kitchen.

Where is he?

"Levi," she shouts.

He whimpers again. The sound is coming from the hall outside her apartment. Her heart drops. She runs for the door. Did she leave him out there when they came back from their walk? She must have. He didn't bark or whine until now. He's been waiting patiently in the dim hallway, without food or water, for hours. Probably napping.

Gus flings open the door and is greeted by Levi's furry face. She kneels down and hugs his neck. He wags his tail and licks her cheek. She is overwhelmed with shame. She stares into his loving eyes. His forgiving, oblivious eyes. She's not ready to be a real mother.

Gus fills Levi's bowls with food and water. He laps up the water, clearly dehydrated. Then he eats, ravenous. She follows him to the bedroom and watches as he jumps on the bed, contentedly licking one paw then rubbing it against the sides of his floppy mouth. She sits on the bed and watches him until he falls asleep. Tears spill from her eyes for the first time in forever.

The floodgates open. Unlocked by out-of-control hormones. With her sense of purpose suddenly feeling paper thin, Gus is washed over by a deep loneliness that she hasn't felt since she was a child.

She cries for two weeks. Days blur past in a fog of wet tears. April rains join the pity party. She survives on frozen dinners and Honeycomb cereal until her gut rebels and she reluctantly adds carrots and apples and spinach salad to her diet, all of which are surprisingly palatable. Her body is telling her to take care of herself. She listens to it. Sometimes. Other times she downs cartons of milk and cans of cream soda then eventually combines the two into a frothy pink concoction. She lives in sweatpants, watches old movies, cries, stares out the window, cries, eats, cries. In the middle of her sob-fest, Gus tries to reach out to Poppy. A hospital administrator informs her that Poppy isn't taking phone calls and her visitors have been restricted to family members only. This doesn't help Gus's hormonal spiral. She misses Poppy.

But then one morning, the sun comes out, the tears wash through her, and a path is cleared. It's as if she's been rinsed by her own tears. Gus sees what she completely missed before. It was right there in front of her.

She knows what to do.

Step one, Gus takes a shower. The soap and water do wonders, washing away the rest of the weird weepy creature she'd become. Gus pairs a loose blouse with stretchy leggings and high black boots. The outfit is dressy enough for what she has planned. She looks at herself in the mirror. The person staring back is puffy-faced, but Gus recognizes her for the first time in days.

A few weeks back, when Mojo had been dragged off by her mother, the kid left behind her laptop and backpack. Mojo still hadn't come for them. Gus hadn't touched Alma. She'd left her alone to do her scanning.

Step two, Gus presses the space bar. Alma wakes up, but a password is needed to get inside. Gus had pretended not to be looking when Mojo had first logged on to her computer. She'd seen her type four letters but wasn't sure which ones. First she tries MOJO. Nope. Then ALMA. Yep. That was easy. The screen lights up. The little scanning wheel is still spinning. Gus clicks on it, but nothing appears. No results of the scan. It just keeps blinking at her. Then she does some harmless creeping. Clicking open desktop folders. One is full of random documents. Grade six homework. The other is a collection of family photos, meticulously labeled, likely research for Mojo's family tree project.

Among the photos is one of Mojo perched atop a pony. A wide HAPPY EIGHTH BIRTHDAY ribbon is draped across the pony's chest.

There's another of May and Ricker dancing at their lavish wedding.

One of Charlotte and Wilfred standing on either side of a baptismal font for May's christening. Charlotte looks about forty, Wilfred well into his fifties. Late to the parent game.

Another of Wilfred standing next to son-in-law Ricker, beneath the columned entryway of a red brick mansion embossed with the words FELIX MUTCHMORE FOUNDATION.

There is also the series of black-and-white photos taken from the family album.

One of Cora and Robert, dated 1921, standing with their

two children, Eva and Wilfred. The household help are lined up behind the family like deadpan marionettes in matching uniforms.

Another of young Robert, maybe twenty, wearing a chef's hat and holding a ladle. He looks to be standing at a makeshift soup kitchen in a large outdoor tent.

And there is the photo that Mojo had shown Gus before. The one of Cora with the Ladies' Benevolent Association posed in front of the orphanage they'd just opened. It is this photo's caption, specifically one of the names listed there, that clicks into a notch in Gus's brain. Waking it, just as she'd woken Alma from her black sleep.

Gus snaps photos using her phone of every image of the Mutchmore family. She needs documentation before heading out. Gus almost closes the laptop, but then remembers Mojo's warning.

You have to leave the laptop open or all the data will be lost.

Gus leaves the laptop exactly as Mojo had. Facing away from the sofa, angled at the wall. No sign that she touched it. Then she glances at her evidence wall, and that's when the second wheel clicks into place. She quickly cross-checks the photos on her phone.

Like a spindle in a combination lock, everything begins to line up and a theory takes shape.

Gus finds the address then sets out on foot toward Clemow Avenue with a theory firmly tucked in the back of her mind, ready to be tested.

As Gus makes her way down the busy sidewalk toward the headquarters of the Felix Mutchmore Foundation, an uneasiness curdles her stomach. And this time it's not the avocado.

It's the feeling she gets when she's about to stir up some shit. She likes the feeling.

Gus places a hand on the bump. It's larger, more solid than it was last week. She pulls out her phone and asks Siri how big it's supposed to be at twenty weeks. A small cantaloupe is the answer. It's hard to hide a cantaloupe under a thin raincoat. She notices the subtle change in the faces of strangers when they spot the bump. Shades of disapproval or surprise or empathy, as if they know what she's going through. But they don't. This is her fruit-littered path, not theirs. They live normal lives.

Gus has always felt more kinship with people on the fringes of normal. Outcasts like Gracie Halladay. Even Tommy was an outlier. A kid from a poor neighborhood made to do his brother's dirty work. He didn't get a shot at normal.

But despite never feeling like she fit in, lately Gus has been dogged by a strange and unfamiliar sensation. A new feeling. A feeling of connection to something. The glances from strangers passing by only deepen it. She feels oddly protective of the cantaloupe. She stares down the strangers, holding her head high. Most look away. She walks on, only now fully appreciating that she's not actually doing this alone. The two of them, mama and cantaloupe, are in this together. This knowing warms her breath and fuels her stride as she approaches the red brick mansion.

As she gets closer, Gus stops a moment to take it in. Above the massive front door is a gold sign engraved with a crest and the words FELIX MUTCHMORE FOUNDATION. The house is regal. Circa 1902, according to the date engraved in the stone frontage. A black limousine is parked off to the side of the curved lane. Malachy leans on the hood, reading a book. She was hoping not to run into him. He lifts his head. Spots her. His eyes are hidden by dark sunglasses, but his head tracks her as she steps onto the path leading to the house. He slowly places his book on the roof of the limo then moves in her direction, crossing the lawn and meeting her midway up the path.

He blocks the way.

"Ms. Monet," he says, as if he's been expecting her.

She tries to step past him, but he dodges and won't let her.

"You mind? I have an appointment," she says.

"I seriously doubt that, sweetheart," he answers, his Irish accent slithering across his tongue.

"What the fuck is wrong with you people?" she asks, this time trying to shoulder-check him out of her way.

He laughs as she rebounds off his hard torso.

Then he grips her arm. Hard.

"Let's take a little drive, shall we?" he says, pulling her across the grass toward the limo.

Gus scans the sidewalk. No witnesses. No one to help. Then she looks up at the mansion. She spots a blond woman on the second floor, squirting a spider plant that hangs in the window.

Gus loops her free arm under her belly, sticking it out so the bump protrudes. She contorts her face and stumbles to one knee, moaning.

Now it's Malachy who's looking up and down the street. He's thrown off by her sudden collapse. He tries to pull her to her feet. Gus squeezes her eyes shut, trying to make herself cry. All she can muster is some rapid panting like the kind she's seen pregnant women do in movies when they're going into labor. Malachy's red-faced. The woman in the window staring down at them looks horrified as she drops the spray bottle and disappears. Job done.

Moments later, Gus is inside the building, splayed out on a sofa in the lobby, drinking water from a paper cone. Turns out Blondie is the receptionist. She's hovering over Gus, asking if she needs an ambulance or wants her to call a friend.

Malachy lingers near the front door, hands in his pockets, not sure what to do. A door opens and footsteps echo down a hall. Someone's coming. Malachy stares at the floor as Ricker Stanfield and Wilfred Mutchmore enter the lobby. They stop dead in their tracks when they spot Gus.

"Ms. Billings?" says Ricker. Blondie nods toward Malachy as if that explains everything.

Wilfred stares at Gus.

"What in God's name is she doing here?" Wilfred says, turning purple.

Blondie looks like she's about to say something, but instead she abandons Gus and returns to her post behind a large mahogany counter. Malachy is a statue. Wilfred hobbles toward Gus, pointing a bony finger in her face. Gus tries to stand. The old man snatches the paper cone from her hand like she's a thief.

"How dare you come here. I'm sick of you poking your nose into my family's private affairs," he shouts. "Get the hell out before I call the police."

Wilfred spits on Gus as he talks. He looks like he might fall over. He's trembling.

Gus is stunned.

Ricker takes charge. He steers his father-in-law's shoulders away from Gus and eases the elder Mutchmore toward the exit, reassuring him the whole way that he'll handle it. Ricker hands Wilfred off to Malachy, who leads the old man outside. Blondie gives Ricker a weak smile. He ignores her, apologizes to Gus, and invites her to join him in his office if she's feeling up to it. He tells Blondie to bring in fresh coffee, then leads the way. Shaken but undeterred, Gus follows.

Ricker's elegant office smells of lemony polish and drips with brass and oak and leather-bound books. Glass cabinets display military medals and framed photographs of Ricker and Wilfred posing with important-looking people. There's a gigantic painting of Private Felix Mutchmore hanging over a stone fireplace. Vases of fresh lilies sit on the mantel, framing a gold clock that floats inside a crystal pedestal.

The Mutchmores have got money on top of their money.

The old-school stuffiness of the room seems more Grandpa Wilfred's style, but Ricker looks like he could make himself at home anywhere. He wears his expensive suit jacket open, one button on his shirt undone. No tie. Casual, cool, collected. He looks fifty-something. Kind of like a *GQ* model. Stylish haircut speckled with just the right amount of gray. Chiseled jawline dappled with carefully trimmed stubble. Gus can't help herself. She has a little crush.

She sits across from him sipping hot coffee while Ricker apologizes again for what he refers to as a *miscommunication*. Gus isn't sure what he really means. She's been threatened and yelled at and grabbed. The message seems pretty clear. Gus decides to let him make the first move. Ask her something. He settles into the leather chair behind his desk.

"Marjory tells us Poppy has you running errands for her," he says, playing with a letter opener on his desk.

Gus smiles, recognizing the dis. He brings to mind a snake, gently winding his way through the grass toward her. The hairs on her arms rise.

"I hope she's not overstepped," he adds.

"Actually, she hired me to investigate a disappearance," Gus answers flatly.

Ricker leans back in his chair. He smiles too.

"Ah, Leo. The jilted lover story. Yes, Poppy's been weaving that one for decades," he says casually.

"He didn't jilt her," Gus says, a little more aggressively than she meant.

"We were afraid this would happen," he says, almost to himself.

Gus narrows her eyes.

"I'm sorry you were drawn into Poppy's imaginings. She really can be quite engaging. Quite believable. Especially once she's found herself a new victim. No, victim's not the right word. You're no victim, I can see that. A confidante. Sadly, it's all a grand fabrication of a fragile mind, I'm afraid."

For a family who barely has anything to do with Poppy, they sure act like they know a lot about her. *Let's see how much they really know.*

"So it's all lies then? Leo and Poppy falling in love. Planning to elope. Eva discovering the truth. Hoping to stop it. And then, the night of October 31, 1953, Leo disappears and then years later a body turns up right where he was to meet Poppy. None of it happened?" she says, flinging words to see what sticks.

Ricker's calm expression remains unchanged, but she notices his pupils dilate. He licks his lower lip, then takes a deep breath.

"You are quite the detective," he says. "I underestimated you."

Gus knows she's not much of a detective. Knows she has a lot to learn about connecting dots. Knows that he's humoring her. But she also knows that a few of those dots that she's connected have brought her here. They've come together in a daisy chain of clues that link to Baby M.

Clue #1 was the caption at the bottom of the Ladies' Benevolent Association photograph, which named the man standing in the midst of the ladies as the architect of Children's Protestant Village. John Albert Ewart. Cross-checking the adoption records, Gus confirmed that Baby M was adopted by J. A. and E. W. Ewart. She'd barely noticed when Mojo was flitting from one document to another on her laptop, but the name had registered somewhere in the recesses of her brain and had popped up that morning like a beacon. She verified the name again on the forensics report identifying the bones as belonging to Leo Ewart.

Clue #2 was the date that leapt off the evidence wall. It was printed on the bottom of the photo booth images of a young Poppy and Leo. Taken on his birthday. August 2, 1953. He had just turned twenty-three, Poppy said. Cross-checking the birth certificate of Baby M, she couldn't believe she'd missed it. Baby M was born August 2, 1930. The day Leo Ewart was born.

Baby M is Leo.

Eva's son.

But Gus wants to be 100 percent certain.

She needs an inside source to confirm it, since Eva's name is nowhere on any of the documents. Gus was hoping Wilfred would be that source, since he was alive back then, but he wasn't exactly in a chatty mood, so Ricker will have to do. If Eva was indeed Leo's mother and she knew it, this explains her diary entries, her desire to see Poppy end her relationship with Leo, and quite possibly, her descent into madness. If Gus is right, Leo and Poppy were siblings.

She decides to lay her cards on the table.

"Poppy's mother, Eva, gave up a baby for adoption when she was young. I believe that baby was Leo. Leo Ewart," she says, not taking her eyes off Ricker.

He blinks, then rises and walks toward the mantel. He looks up at the painting of the foundation's namesake, then he turns to Gus. His expression is changed. Almost sad.

"Can I count on your discretion, Miss Monet?" he asks.

Gus nods.

"Yes. Leo was her bastard son," he says without emotion.

Gus shivers. She didn't expect a quick admission.

"When Eva was sixteen, she had an unfortunate dalliance with a young man who worked for her parents. As Wilfred explained it to me, in confidence, her mother, Cora, arranged a discreet adoption. Years later, as you discovered, fate intervened and brought Eva's daughter and son together. Eva found out and asked her brother for help. Wilfred opened his wallet. Leo was paid off and he moved on to greener pastures with a sizable wad of cash in his pocket," he says.

Gus is confused by this new information. It doesn't fit. They were in love. They planned to elope. Was Poppy wrong about Leo all along? Alice did say Poppy had her head in the clouds.

"You see, Miss Monet, Leo Ewart did not disappear. Every man has a price, and the Mutchmores ponied up. Sadly for Poppy, the price was highest. Her poor mother fell ill over the entire ordeal and Poppy was left all alone."

Gus feels sick. Could he be telling the truth? Has she been drawn in by an old woman's delusion? Will she eventually find out that Leo moved on, got married to someone else, and lived a life while Poppy wasted her own waiting for him?

Gus feels suddenly light-headed.

Ricker can see she's waning.

"Water?" he asks.

She shakes her head.

"I hope my father-in-law didn't cause you any distress," he says, glancing at her belly. "He values his family's privacy," he adds as he moves toward her, one hand outstretched as if he's ready to escort her out.

The meeting is over. Gus automatically rises, unable to think of anything more to say. Maybe he's not aware that U.M. was identified as Leo by the police. Maybe Ricker also knows it's not him because Leo was paid to go away decades ago.

There are too many dangling threads. Gus decides to pull at one of them.

"Your mother-in-law, Charlotte, called them an omen. The bones in the pond," she adds.

Ricker smiles as he leads her out of his office.

"My mother-in-law has premonitions every time she looks into the swirling foam of her morning latte," he says.

He walks Gus toward the lobby, down the wide hallway lined with portraits of prime ministers and royalty and governors general.

Blondie isn't at her desk, but a nameplate sitting on the counter says Beatrice Billings. The name rings a bell. Billings. That's the family biographer's last name. Braddish Billings. Boring Braddish from the gala. His wife, maybe. Seems the Mutchmore universe is tightly knit.

Ricker's shiny dress shoes click as they cross the lobby. Gus suddenly feels very small in the grand foyer. She looks up at the imposing family portrait that hangs above the sweeping staircase leading to the second floor. In the portrait are Robert and Cora Mutchmore with their three children, Felix, Eva, and Wilfred. Something about it strikes Gus as odd. Then she realizes what's off. In Mojo's speech about her family tree, she said Felix died in the war before Wilfred was born. And yet, there he is, added to the painting as if he were still alive when it was commissioned. A kind of weird photoshopped version of the family. Whole. Perfect.

Ricker follows her gaze. He hides a smirk. He thinks it's weird too.

"My wife's family can be a tad eccentric. They have an image they like to cultivate. It can be a bit much, I admit." He nods to the painting. "Despite being very much in the public eye, they prefer their personal lives be kept private. Perhaps they've overstated that desire in their dealings with you."

Gus appreciates the sort-of apology.

"I hope, for Poppy's sake, you'll be discreet when it comes to your findings and our conversation," he says. "The Mutchmores were wrong not to tell her all those years ago, but it would likely do her more harm than good now. But I'll leave that to your discretion."

They shake hands.

Gus knows he's right. Poppy can't know the truth about who Leo really was or that he might have left her for money. It would break her already damaged heart beyond repair.

"Is Poppy doing all right?" she asks, wishing she could see her, but almost glad she can't.

"My wife tells me she's receiving the very best care. Rest assured, Poppy will be back home soon and all this fuss will be behind us," he promises.

In that moment, she likes Ricker. His easy manner is comforting.

But as Gus walks back to the Ambassador, she begins to feel untethered from the truth.

The dots that seemed to connect now scatter. The daisy chain of clues now leads in some vague direction away from where she thought it was taking her.

Gus feels her investigation dissolving before it's really begun.

16

Mojo

WHEN SHE GETS HOME, GUS SLIPS HER HEAVY BODY AND MIND into a hot bubble bath. Ricker's words float to the surface. *I'll leave that to your discretion.* She doesn't want that burden. Poppy's family should be dealing with this. Not someone who's known her a few months. Levi rests his chin on the edge of the tub. Gus looks into his eyes.

"What do I tell Poppy?" she asks him.

Levi licks suds from her elbow.

"I could lie. Pretend I've hit a dead end. Say I'm not up to the job," she says.

But she was up to the task. She might have just found out what happened to Leo.

Gus sinks into the bubbles.

Eva's prominent family got rid of him. First giving him away when he was a child. And then paying him off when he fell for a sister he likely didn't even know he had. Scandal averted. Could it be that the Mutchmores have been motivated by a desire to protect Poppy as much as themselves? She had no future with Leo. And they lied to spare her.

Levi cocks one ear, then rises to his feet.

"What?" she says.

Levi sniffs the air.

Gus reaches for a towel and struggles to get out of the tub. Levi growls, then trots down the hall and into the living room, out of sight. Gus wraps herself in the towel.

"Levi," she calls out.

She hears a whimper. She waits. *Strange.*

"Dog," she calls louder.

Gus tiptoes down the hall, dripping. She rounds the corner and gasps, not expecting anyone to be there. Mojo is sitting on the floor, hugging Levi. The girl glances at Gus, tears streaming down her face, then she buries her nose in the dog's neck.

"I had nowhere else to go," she says, her words muffled.

A puddle forms around Gus's toes.

"Mummy was horrible. She slapped me right in the face, so I ran away," she gulps, pointing to a pink roller suitcase propped near the sofa.

Gus retreats to the bathroom to dry off. Mojo shouts from the living room.

"I knocked. Honest. The door was unlocked. Anyone could have come in, you know. That's not very safe if you ask me. Women who live alone always lock their doors."

Gus shakes water from her ears then throws on a robe. Clearly her pregnancy brain is overriding all else. Or at least muddling her thinking. Even the kid knows better than to leave your door unlocked.

Gus grabs each of them a cream soda and sits beside her on the sofa. Mojo rubs Levi's belly. He's lapping up the attention.

"Your parents will have the entire police force out looking for you," says Gus.

"Good," Mojo pouts.

"How did you get here?" Gus asks.

"Uber," says Mojo.

Gus stares at her.

"I set up a fake account with Mummy's credit card," she says. "It's not rocket surgery."

"You can't stay here," says Gus.

"I won't go back. I hate her. I hate both of them," she says, pulling Levi closer.

He snuggles against her.

"Don't you have a friend you could stay with? Or a relative? What about your grandma?" she presses.

Mojo's lip quivers.

"Levi's my friend, aren't you, boy?" she says to the dog, ignoring Gus. "Mummy doesn't like dogs. Or kids. She doesn't like anything. She told me she never wanted children. She really doesn't like you." This time she looks at Gus.

Now Gus understands why Mojo is here. To piss off Mummy dearest. Gus wonders how much the girl knows about the sordid branches of her family tree. She decides to find out.

"Did you know your family paid off Leo so he'd leave town?" Gus asks her.

Mojo stares at Gus.

"Poppy's Leo?" asks Mojo. "What? When?"

"You were right. Eva did give up a son. Baby M. He was a Mutchmore. But what I didn't know until today was that Baby M was Leo. Eva's son and Poppy's half-brother," Gus tells her.

Mojo's eyes bug out. She slaps her hand over her mouth.

"Poor Poppers. Does she know?" asks Mojo.

"No," says Gus. "And I don't think we should tell her."

"For sure it's her Leo?" she asks, not wanting to believe it.

Gus explains how the evidence first clicked into place.

And then how Mojo's father, Ricker, told her the truth today. Mojo goes quiet. She looks over at the evidence wall, then her eyes come to rest on her laptop sitting right where she left it. She flushes red.

"So that's it then. Case closed?" says Mojo loudly, pointing to the wall.

"None of it will bring Poppy any peace," Gus says, shaking her head. "When she comes home, I'll figure out what to tell her. Your dad's right. The truth will do her more harm than good."

"So it's over," says Mojo, again as if she's talking to someone down the hall. "That's good. I think you're right to give up."

Gus is confused as to why the girl's suddenly shouting her words. Is she hysterical?

Mojo is staring at Alma. The girl leans across the trunk and points to the laptop, which has been sitting there, open, ever since Mojo left it behind a few weeks ago. The girl looks at Gus then puts her finger to her lips. Her expression darkens. She rises and beckons Gus to follow her. Mojo leads her into the bedroom and closes the door. She turns to Gus.

"Daddy's lying," she whispers, looking around like someone can hear them.

Gus is confused. Before she can ask Mojo what she means, the kid spills her guts.

"And I've been lying too. I wasn't running a deep scan thingie like I said I was. It's a security app. Like a nanny-cam, and it's been watching you this whole time. They've been listening to you and they can see your evidence wall. They told me to point it that way. That's why I said not to touch it. They said you were taking advantage of Poppers and you were after her money and you were a scam artist. But I'm pretty sure they're lying. They don't care about her . . . or me," she says, tears pooling in her eyes.

Gus is dumbfounded and flustered and wants to crawl in a hole and hide.

"But if you were just here to spy on me, why were you helping me?" Gus stammers. "You found Baby M's records. You told me what your grandmother said about the bones."

"I wanted to help Poppy. I wanted to investigate. You're the first person who ever asked me to help on anything like that. And I'm good at it too. I thought I could help without them knowing," Mojo says.

"But why would you go ahead and set this thing up to watch me?" asks Gus, still not fully digesting the revelation.

"I had to set up the laptop just like they told me. I had to. They would know if I didn't and Mummy would have sent me away and I don't want to go live with our relatives in Maine even if they do live near the ocean," cries Mojo, tears spilling down her cheeks.

Gus can't move or think.

"They're scared of you," says Mojo.

Gus looks at her.

"And there's one thing on your wall that freaks them out the most," says Mojo, trying to redeem herself. "One question that Mummy and Daddy don't like. *Who are the babies?*"

A chill rattles Gus's spine and she pulls her robe close. She can't speak. Her mind churns with images of herself hormonally weeping for days while chisel-jawed Ricker looked on. She cringes thinking back to their meeting. Gus feels violated and pissed off in equal measure.

Gus sits on the bed, her knees weak.

"Tell me what he lied about," Gus asks, her throat dry.

"They didn't tell me that. Daddy was just telling Mummy how you came to his work and how he took care of it. He said you believed what he told you. I think he said something about loose ends."

They really do say anything in front of their kid.
What loose ends?

Her investigation. Her questions. Her relationship with Poppy. Are these the loose ends? The Mutchmores have been watching her, and clearly they want her to stop digging. But she's gravely underestimated them. They're willing to send their eleven-year-old daughter into enemy territory to set up a spy-cam. What kind of parents do that? What else are they capable of? Is it possible they tried to get rid of Poppy? Gus shudders at the thought.

"I found Malachy in Poppy's apartment. Do you think he was the one who tried to kill her?" Gus says, then instantly regrets it when she sees the look on Mojo's face.

Both hands fly up to cover her mouth. The girl can't speak. It's as if she's seeing her family for who they are and it frightens her. Gus suddenly feels deeply sorry for her. She's a kid. A pawn.

"Of, of course you don't know anything about that. And I could be wrong. I, I probably am," Gus stammers, trying to backtrack. "I'm being silly."

Then the girl stands up. She's remembered something.

"I know what they're about to do to Poppers," says Mojo, eyes glistening.

Gus's heart skips a beat.

"What?" Gus asks, not sure she wants to hear.

"They were fighting about it last night. They're gonna lock her up in a home for people who've lost their marbles. They're gonna sell her apartment and get rid of all her stuff. It's Grandpa Wilfred's idea, and Mummy's going along with it," she spits.

"That's horrible. They can't do that," says Gus, heart racing.

"Mummy said she got Poppers to sign some paper so they

could put her somewhere out of the way. Daddy said she was overreacting. And Mummy said they could lose everything. And then they yelled and said stuff that made no sense."

"What kind of paper?" asks Gus, trying to think it through.

"Mummy called it a power journey, something like that," she blubbers.

"Power of attorney," says Gus.

"That's bad, isn't it?" says Mojo, more tears streaming down her cheeks.

"When is this happening?" asks Gus.

"I don't know. I think they said next week," cries Mojo. "It's so not fair. Just 'cause you have the same DNA doesn't mean you should be allowed to lock someone up and throw away the key."

Mojo throws herself on the bedroom floor and thrashes about like she's having a fit. Levi pushes the door open and peeks into the bedroom. Too much drama for the old dog. He takes off.

After powering off the laptop, it takes Gus about an hour to calm the girl, get her tucked under a blanket on the sofa and asleep, thumb in her mouth. She looks so much younger than her eleven years.

Gus stays awake, pacing her living room into the wee hours. She reviews her notes, looks through the pages of Eva's diary, and flips through photos on her phone.

The Mutchmores are afraid. Gus and Poppy are the loose ends. They want Poppy out of the way and Gus off the case. But this doesn't scare Gus anymore. It only makes her more determined to forge ahead. She looks at her evidence wall.

What happened to Leo?

Whose bones were in the pond?

Who are the babies?

Gus aims to answer these lingering questions and not let anyone sidetrack her mission. These questions are her loose ends. And she won't stop until she finds out what's behind all the spying and lies and fear of losing everything. Gus makes a decision. She'll begin by pulling at the loose end that has the Mutchmores most freaked out.

Who are the babies?

An idea comes to her. It's triggered by something Mojo said earlier.

Just 'cause you have the same DNA doesn't mean you should be allowed to lock someone up and throw away the key.

A few weeks back in March, Gus had placed Poppy's locket in the picture frame box displaying the photo of her parents. She'd put it there for safekeeping, alongside her gun. The gun had since been hidden inside a bag of peas in the freezer. She'd moved it there when Mojo started coming around. Last thing she needed was for the kid to shoot herself in the foot. She'd also ordered some DNA kits, inspired by Mojo.

Now, Gus pulls the locket from the box and opens the tiny clasp. She examines the strands of Leo's hair. The instructions say there need to be roots if a hair sample is being sent in. It looks like there are roots on a couple of the strands but she's not sure. Gus places them in a container from one of the DNA kits. She fills out the forms and seals the kit in the pre-addressed envelope. It's worth a shot. Maybe Leo's DNA will shed some light on the truth and she won't have to rely on diaries, liars, and incomplete records.

Gus knows what her next move is, or rather who it is. Charlotte. She needs to talk to Mojo's grandmother. Alone. She's the Mutchmore who dangled those babies in the first place, and Gus wants to know why.

As the black sky outside her window edges toward daylight, it turns a milky and bleak gray. Mojo wakes and the two of them eat Honeycomb cereal and watch cartoons. Mojo picks up Gus's phone and asks for her passcode so she can add her number to Gus's contacts. Gus hesitates, then gives it to her. She can always change the passcode later. A sticky-eyed Levi makes an appearance from the bedroom. He stretches each limb, one by one, sending tiny tremors quivering through his spine. He yawns. Gus heads to the kitchen to feed him.

"What are we going to do about Poppers?" Mojo calls out.

"Ever heard of a double agent?" Gus says, peeking around the kitchen doorway.

The girl nods excitedly, chipmunk cheeks full of cereal.

They make a plan. Gus needs Mojo to spy on her parents. Tit for tat. She wants her to get intel on exactly when and where they're planning to shuttle Poppy off to. Mojo needs to be her eyes and ears like never before.

"And I need some alone time with your grandma. Any ideas?" Gus asks.

A loud knock at the front door interrupts their plotting. Mojo nearly chokes on her Honeycomb. Levi ambles to the door and barks. He never barks at the door. Something's up. Gus tiptoes close and peers through the peephole. Mojo follows her.

Shit.

It's a cop.

Mojo plasters herself against the wall of the hallway as Gus opens the door.

"Morning, ma'am. You Augusta Monet?" the man asks as Levi circles his legs.

"Yeah," she says, trying to sound casual. "What's up?"

"Is there a minor on the premises, first name Marjory, last name Mutchmore-Stanfield?" he asks, reading from an open notebook in his palm.

Gus's stomach clenches.

Levi licks the cop's shoes.

Mojo pops her head around the doorframe.

"That's me," says the eleven-year-old, smiling.

"Is there a problem, officer?" asks Gus.

He nudges the dog with his foot. Levi growls. He never growls. Gus grabs the dog by the collar and slides him into the apartment and down the hall. Levi stares at her like she's just swatted him. He lowers his chin to the floor and sulks.

The cop is talking to Mojo.

"Your parents reported you missing," he says.

Gus tries not to look like she's rushing back over.

"Sorry about that"—she nods toward the dog—"he loves people."

The cop's face is blank. Not a dog lover.

"Take a step back, ma'am," he says to Gus. She does.

Then he continues to address Mojo.

"Are you being held against your will by this woman?" he asks, moving his hand to rest casually on his gun belt.

Gus doesn't move a muscle.

What the fuck?

"Don't be a silly billy. She's my partner," says Mojo.

Gus cringes.

"Partner?" says the cop, eyebrows lifting.

"Yeah, we're partners in crime. Not that we do crimes. We solve them, together," explains Mojo.

Gus smiles through gritted teeth.

Please shut up. Mojo doesn't.

"We're detectives. See?" Mojo says, pointing to the evidence wall like that'll help.

Gus wishes she'd thought to assemble the evidence on her bedroom wall and not directly across from her front door for all to see. The cop looks at the wall. His expression is unusually vacuous, bordering on robotic. He's scary as fuck.

She needs to clarify things before this gets out of hand.

"It's a game we play, that's all. I'm her babysitter. I think there's been some misunderstanding. I'm a family friend. We met through a relative of hers who lives upstairs," she explains, trying to sound more grown-up than she feels.

"We did," Mojo adds.

"She showed up here late last night so I had to let her stay over," says Gus.

"I did," nods Mojo.

"We were just about to call her parents when you knocked," she says.

"We were," parrots Mojo.

"You didn't think to call them last night?" he asks.

"We didn't," says Mojo.

There's something off about the man. Levi sensed it. There's an emptiness in his eyes, like a part of him is hollowed out and could be filled up at any moment by something nasty.

Gus can't feel her toes. She's been fooled by a uniform before.

"Can I see your badge?" she asks, her voice scratchy.

He stares in a way that sets off more warning bells in her head. She should have kept her mouth shut. He moves his hand closer to his gun. It's a game. Then he shows her his badge and ID card. It looks real, but would she know? The name says Constable Taggart. He slowly puts it back into his pocket, then looks her in the eyes with that fucking blank face of his, saying nothing. She panics.

"I'm pregnant," Gus says, like the words are somehow a white flag.

"She is," adds Mojo automatically, pointing to Gus's belly. Then the kid looks up at Gus.

"You are?" she says, incredulous.

Gus doesn't take her gaze off Taggart. His eyes flit quickly to her belly then to Mojo.

"Get your things. You're coming with me, young lady," he says.

Mojo hops to it. She darts about the living room, gathering her things. She grabs her laptop and shoves it in the backpack she left at Gus's weeks ago.

"Where are you taking her?" demands Gus, suddenly afraid for the girl's safety.

"Down to the station for questioning," he says, deadpan.

Gus and Mojo freeze. Then Constable Taggart bursts out laughing.

It's more alarming than his stoneface.

"I'm taking her home," he says, clapping his hands together. "Chop, chop. Got more important things to do than chase after lost kids."

Gus doesn't know what to do so she just stands there watching as Mojo slings the backpack onto one shoulder and uprights her roller suitcase. The officer steps closer to Gus.

"Sleepovers with little girls, eh? Some folks might get the wrong idea about you. Some folks might think a person like that needs to be dealt with for good," he says softly in her ear.

Gus winces and moves away from him as Mojo heads out the door.

The Mutchmores aren't fucking around.

When the two of them are gone, Gus sits on the kitchen floor with her phone in her hand. Levi comes in and rests his chin on her leg. She calls the hospital. She needs to hear Poppy's voice, even if it's just to say hello. A woman picks up. An orderly or nurse. Poppy's sleeping. The voice is kind. She whispers as if she's standing next to Poppy. Tells Gus that she took her outside for a wheel around the grounds yesterday and her spirits were lifted by the fresh air. They hang up.

Some fresh air sounds good. Gus takes Levi for a long walk through the Glebe. It's warm out. First, she mails the DNA kit, then they head over the Lansdowne bridge and into Old Ottawa South. They walk down to Windsor Park on the Rideau River. Skirt the river's edge. Levi, nose to the ground, ambles happily along the putrid shoreline where wet, leafy debris has been unearthed with the snow's retreat. Green buds poke through soggy grass. Tulips and crocuses pop their heads up.

The seasons are shifting. Gus can feel it in the unstable gusts of warm wind. She can see it in the streaks of clouds that loop across the sky like superhighways. She's been here before. Crossing paths with people who seem willing to do anything to keep secrets buried. She's trespassed onto their land, opened their doors, and walked straight into the heart of what scares them most. And no matter who they send to whisper warnings in her ear, she's incapable of turning away once she's caught their scent. It's in her blood. Her mother was the same. There was no stopping her. A dog with a bone. She kept digging because she had to. Gus can feel that same pull.

She turns back, and as she does, she gets a cryptic text from Mojo.

Gus doesn't understand it.

Take an Uber. I put the app on your phone. You're welcome.

There's a file attached to the text. Gus opens it. It's an invitation to attend the Governor General's Investiture Ceremony for the Order of Military Merit and the Decorations for Bravery at Rideau Hall.

Garden party attire.

Admit one.

Ceremony at 4 P.M.

Saturday, April 17.

That's tomorrow.

Buffet dinner to follow.

RSVP.

Gus smiles. She's guessing Mojo's grandmother Charlotte will be in attendance.

Nice one, partner.

17

May

Playing with fire isn't as scary when you have an official invitation on your phone.

What's scary is not having a clue what garden party attire means.

Gus asks her best friend, Siri.

The answer? *Floral or pastel cocktail dress. Avoid animal prints.*

Gus's wardrobe is made up mostly of jeans, a few pairs of leggings, and a collection of tank tops, sweaters, and old T-shirts. Luckily most of her leggings are stretchy enough to still fit. Even if Gus knew where to buy a cocktail dress, she's not sure she could find one that would accommodate her growing midsection, so she decides to borrow one she saw in Poppy's closet. Gus heads upstairs Saturday morning and unlocks the door to Poppy's apartment. She hasn't been back since her encounter with the Irishman. The apartment smells different. It has that stale stillness of an uninhabited space, but there's now a faint smell of lavender clinging to the dusty air. Nothing looks out of place, but a few pieces of furniture look different. As if they've been moved then put back, only not exactly as they once were. She checks the bedrooms. Eva's is still locked. She chooses a loose-fitting pink floral dress from Poppy's room and borrows a string of pearls from her dresser and a tiny matching pearl-coated clutch. The dress is flowy. It hides the cantaloupe.

Gus locks the door of Poppy's apartment. She suddenly feels like she's being watched. Then she hears the faint groan of a floorboard. She looks down the windowless hall. It's darker than usual. A bulb must have burnt out. She can't make out the far end clearly.

Is someone there in the shadows?

"Hello?" she calls out.

Silence.

Gus takes a few steps backward, fumbles behind her for the stairwell door, then turns and runs. She takes the stairs two by two, and just as she's slipping into her apartment one floor below, she hears the whine of the stairwell door opening, one flight up.

Someone was there.

She waits behind her locked door, breathing heavily, staring through the peephole. No one comes out of the stairwell. She sighs. It was probably just the old building creaking with age.

An hour later, Gus is sitting in the back of an Uber heading down Colonel By Drive, then on to Sussex. They pass the National Gallery. A sculpture of a giant steel spider stands out front, hovering thirty feet above the sidewalk. The driver spots her glancing at it. He tells her the spider is called *Maman*. "It means 'mom' in French," he says.

It strikes Gus as odd that such an imposing and frightening figure could be a mother. She notices the spider is sheltering an egg sac. She thinks of her own mother, Shannon. How she could be both scary and warm. Protective and distant. Maybe the mama spider is a good omen, or at least she hopes so.

She needs some of her mother's steely resolve right about now. They continue along the Ottawa River, crossing the bridge into New Edinburgh, and finally pulling up to the front of the large stone and iron gates of Rideau Hall.

She jumps out. Two ceremonial guards in red uniforms with tall black fur hats stand guard out front. She feels like an impostor. A feeling she's getting used to. The guards look like they should be keeping watch outside Buckingham Palace, not the Governor General's residence in Canada. Gus can't help herself. She bows to one of them. Then she hurries awkwardly over to join a queue of guests waiting to check in with the official greeters just inside the gate. Not a Mutchmore in sight. A greeter glances at the invitation on her phone. He mumbles something about an RSVP, but before she can say anything, he waves her past.

Secret service types in dark suits hover on the fringes of the freshly cut lawns. They remind her of penguins, huddled together, heads bobbing, sizing up the arriving guests. She recognizes one of the penguins. It's Constable Taggart. Maybe they're all cops in plain clothes. Or maybe, like she thought, he's not really a cop. He hasn't seen her yet, and if he does it won't be pretty. She's now convinced more than ever that he's a Mutchmore lackey. Gus tries to blend in with the family ahead of her. But she still feels like a deer in an open clearing ready to be shot. She scans for cover.

Gus spots a group of reporters and camera guys off to one side under a white tent, angling for shots of the guests as they parade down the long driveway. The official residence is hidden by trees. It's some distance away, but if she sticks with the group, Taggart might not spot her. She heads toward the building, and despite the danger, Gus stops in her tracks when the residence comes into view. It's a gorgeous stone building with an enormous arching entryway. It's breathtaking. She suddenly becomes aware that she's lost her cover. The other guests have moved on. Cameras click.

"Hey, you!" someone calls out.

She's been caught. Gus picks up her pace. She starts to jog, trying to catch up to her surrogate family. Why are they walking so fast? And why is the Governor General's driveway so fucking long?

"Augusta?" shouts the voice again. It's coming from the white tent.

Someone knows her. She's going to be called out as a party crasher.

Gus glances over and spots a young man waving his arms like he's bringing in a jet. Why is he drawing attention to her? What does he want? She's too exposed out in the open. He steps from the shadow of the tent, and she recognizes him. It's the blogger she sat next to at the gala.

"It's me, Howard," he hollers.

Shut up, dude.

Gus has no choice but to make a beeline for Howard into the temporary refuge of the press tent. A secret service goon casually drifts in her direction, keeping a distant but watchful eye on the stray guest.

"Howard," Gus says, fake smiling and stepping under the shelter of the tent.

"Ms. Monet?" says Howard, with a little bow.

"Gimme one sec," he says to a photographer standing next to him. The guy shrugs and moves away.

"Are you covering the event for the *Mississippi Times*?" she asks, scanning the lawn for Taggart.

"*Kitchissippi Times*, you betcha. Society pages don't write themselves," he laughs, too loudly. Other reporters glance over. One nudges the photographer, who rolls his eyes.

"Outta your league, Baylis," one of them calls out. The others laugh.

Howard doesn't seem to notice. Or maybe it's that he doesn't care what they think.

She likes that about him.

"I knew you were special the moment I met you. You'd have to be to score an invite to this shindig," he smiles.

She notices his eyes flick down to her belly then quickly back up. Flowy dress isn't hiding the obvious.

"I'm nobody really," she shrugs.

"I don't think so," he says, a slight flush to his cheeks.

"Have the Mutchmores arrived yet?" she asks, trying to sound casual.

"You're with the guests of honor. Impressive. They're already inside sipping champers, no doubt," he says.

"Guests of honor?" she asks.

"The GG herself is presenting a Medal of Bravery to Felix Mutchmore. Posthumously. I hear little bro Wilfred is stepping up to accept."

That means Charlotte will definitely be here. Gus scans the arrival line of guests. She spots a distant cluster that she can insinuate herself into. She needs to kill time.

"Why decades after he died?" she asks.

"The family lobbied for years, ever since the hundredth anniversary of his death. Guess they finally got their way." Then he lowers his voice: "Between you and me, I think the timing's more than a little suspicious."

Howard looks around like he's got a scoop he doesn't want the other reporters to hear.

"Let's just say there's millions in land deals at stake. And the whole war hero story plays well with the city's deep-pocketed developers and zoning committee members."

Gus isn't sure what he's talking about.

Howard's eyes suddenly brighten.

"You think you could put in a good word for me with the Mutchmores? I'd kill for a one-on-one with the Ricker-meister," asks Howard, a bit too loudly.

Gus almost laughs at the notion that she would have pull with the Mutchmores.

"It's not really like that, Howard. We're not friends," she says.

The moment arrives for her to dive back into the guest line. She nods toward the line, indicating she's got to go.

"Smooth move, Howie," says the photographer.

Howard's face deflates and turns bright red.

"Oh I didn't mean you and I aren't friends," Gus stammers, seeing the look on Howard's face

"Look, forget I asked," he says quickly. "I'm sorry. I didn't mean to use you for your connections or anything. I'm not like that, really."

His fellow reporters seem amused at seeing Howard flustered.

"I should go." She motions toward the Hall.

He bows and waves her on her way with a grand sweeping gesture.

"I bid you adieu, fair lady," he says.

This sends a couple of the reporters into schoolyard fits of laughter. Silly as he is, Howard's quirky gallantry is sweet. She doesn't like that the other kids are mean to him. Gus starts to cross the lawn, then stops and doubles back. She walks right up to Howard and gives him a peck on the cheek.

"Nice to see you, Howard," she says, then runs off.

That shuts them up.

Gus joins the last of the guests for the final stretch of the long driveway. She passes under the archway and approaches the heavy wood-and-glass front doors that stand wide open.

A grand marble staircase flows from the large foyer. Beyond, she can see several guests taking their seats in a gold-curtained, chandeliered ballroom with baby blue walls. She spots Ricker in his seat. May is about to join him. Wilfred and Charlotte are standing near the front of the room. She steps across the marble threshold of Rideau Hall.

And that's when Augusta Monet and Wilfred Mutchmore lock eyes.

Then the shit hits the chandelier.

Wilfred staggers over to Ricker and May, scowling as he talks into Ricker's ear. May touches her father's shoulder. He flinches and pulls away from her hand. Ricker turns and nods to someone just inside the ballroom. Someone Gus can't see. Then she does. It's Malachy. The Irishman comes into view, exits the ballroom, and heads straight for Gus, his black eyes shining. She looks right then left. Spots her salvation. Gus dodges left before he can get to her and ducks into the ladies' room. Inside it's all satin stools and gilded mirrors and marble pillars. She locks herself in a stall and thankfully it's the kind with floor-to-ceiling walls and door. She's safe but trapped.

Someone enters. Heels click across the marble floor.

Gus looks for a window. No such luck. She contemplates staying in the stall until the ceremony is over and everyone's gone home. But that's not going to happen. Gus flushes the toilet under the pretense that she's not actually hiding. She opens the stall door, hoping some random guest has come in to freshen up. Nope.

May is standing facing the row of marble sinks with her back to Gus. Her purse sits on the counter. Gus can see her face in the mirror's reflection. Her expression is blank as she carefully removes her white gloves and slowly lays them across her purse, one on top of the other, as if arranging a display case in a fancy boutique.

Then suddenly and with surprising speed, May whirls around and lunges for Gus's throat, shoving her back against the marble pillar between the stalls. Gus's clutch goes flying from her hand. She feels the cantaloupe jump as if it was startled from a slumber. She opens her mouth for air but can't breathe. Tears fill her eyes. She claws at May's hands, but they only tighten around her neck, squeezing the pearl necklace into her windpipe. May's expression is oddly vacant. No fleck of empathy. Gus can smell May's lavender skin and minty breath as the lines around her mouth and eyes strain from the effort.

Gus has seen that kind of horrific resolve before.

On the face of a man in a video. A twisted, sadistic killer. Recorded when Gus was only eight. A video of her mother gasping for breath as she was strangled to death.

Gus feels herself losing consciousness. Her limbs feel anesthetized. A mind-numbing dread has her fast-beating heart fearing for her life, for the life of her unborn child.

Mama. Help me.

Then just as suddenly as she grabbed Gus's neck, May releases her grip. Poppy's necklace breaks apart and hangs loose. Some of the white pearls clatter to the floor like tiny applause. Gus sucks in great gulps of air and sinks to the floor in an awkward heap with her knees at odd angles.

May steps back and tilts her head like she's just hung a painting and is checking to see if it's straight. Her eyes are glassy.

Gus places one hand on her belly.

The two women's eyes meet in that moment and May sees the gesture for what it is. She gasps and blinks, as if she's snapped out of a trance. She looks around the marbled room like she can't quite process where she is. Then she stares down at her hands. They're trembling uncontrollably. She touches the blood on her wrists where Gus scratched her.

May turns away from Gus and approaches the mirror. She takes a deep breath, then she washes and dries her hands and wrists and puts on her white gloves. She opens her purse, pulls out a lipstick and retouches her lips, then gives herself a final once-over. May turns and spots something on the floor. She leans down and picks up the pearl clutch Gus had been carrying.

Gus can't stop panting like a half-drowned kitten. Can't shake off the shameful vulnerability of sitting helpless on the cold floor. She lets the tears come. A river runs down her cheeks and drips from her chin.

May speaks and Gus jumps.

"You're mistaken," May says, her voice thready.

Gus swallows, unable to make her mouth form words.

"You think you're someone special. But you're not," says May. "You're nothing."

Then May walks out of the ladies' room.

Gus lets out a small croaking sound. The rest of the pearls release from the strands of broken necklace hanging from her neck and roll across the cold marble. She can hear May's heels click, click, click across the foyer, echoing off the high ceilings and fading away as she returns to the grand hall where the Mutchmores are about to be honored.

All Gus can do is sit amongst the pearls.

18

Howard

MALACHY IS WAITING FOR HER WHEN SHE COMES OUT OF THE ladies' room. The ceremony is starting. The ballroom doors are closing. A voice reverberates from a loudspeaker. Gus wonders if it's the Governor General. She considers making a run for the ballroom, bursting through the doors and racing into the GG's arms. She could beg for asylum. Grab the mic. Tell them what May Mutchmore-Stanfield did to her. Create a scene in front of everyone gathered in that grand ballroom.

But she doesn't.

The GG has other things to worry about.

Like giving medals to brave soldiers.

Gus isn't brave. She doesn't make a break for it. Instead, she lets Malachy grab hold of her arm and escort her swiftly through the arched entryway. She feels powerless. And manhandled. Like she's being dragged through water, a fish flopping on the end of a hook. He steers her away from the driveway around the building toward a gate in the stone wall surrounding the property. Out of nowhere Taggart heads for them at a fast clip. When he reaches them, he hooks her other armpit.

The toes of her high heels skim the grass as she's lifted off her feet. She feels like a child who's been bad and is being hurried off to be punished. The other penguins smoke cigarettes and look away. None of their business.

Why is no one helping her?

Where are they taking her?

What are they going to do with her?

Her head is swimming with movie images of wood chippers and concrete hip waders and blood-soaked horse heads on white sheets.

What the fuck?

Linked together as if they're in a three-legged race, they squeeze through the narrow service gate that leads to a residential street, mansions on one side and the massive stone wall surrounding Rideau Hall on the other. Malachy's limo is parked in a long line of other waiting limos. Her captors scan for other drivers and pedestrians. Witnesses. The street is unmercifully deserted. No dog walkers or delivery men or members of the press or limo drivers.

Where the fuck is everyone?

A lone car heads in their direction at the far end of the street. Knowing they've only got seconds to get her out of sight, Malachy clicks the remote locks of his limo. He flings open the passenger-side back door and shoves her in as the car closes in. Gus tumbles to the floor of the limo, losing a shoe. Her knees burn on the carpet. Malachy slams the door behind her. She can hear muffled conversation, but she can't make out what they're saying.

Then the driver's-side back door opens. She's expecting Taggart or Malachy to jump in, but instead Howard's face appears. He holds out his hand. Gus grabs it and he pulls her from the limo. A sudden burst of adrenaline fuels her legs. She scrambles out the door and tumbles into Howard's waiting car.

She locks the passenger door. Sees Malachy and Taggart in the side view mirror racing around the limo toward her. Where's Howard? Then she hears a thud as Howard rolls awkwardly across the hood of his beat-up Honda Civic. He jumps in the driver's side as angry fists pound on her window and thump on the roof of the car. Howard peels away, his rear tires spitting stones into the faces of the assholes chasing after them.

Gus grips the seat with both hands, her heart racing. Driving with one hand on the wheel, Howard reaches across her and pulls her seatbelt over her body. He fastens it. His face is close to hers. His lips. His big brown eyes. His black hair brushes her cheek.

Gus stares at him, breathless.

"Who the fuck are those guys? I saw them drag you out the gate. I ran for my car and was going to follow you, but then they were just standing there so I thought, now or never." He shrugs.

Gus leans over and kisses him on the mouth.

The car momentarily bumps off the curb. They both jerk sideways.

Howard course corrects. His cheeks flush.

He grips the steering wheel, smiling ear to ear as they speed away.

Neither speaks for a few blocks. They watch the rearview mirrors. When they finally feel like no one is following them, Howard asks where she lives. Although Gus's breath and heart have begun to calm, she's still rattled. Her neck aches. She can't stop trembling. When she sees the Catherine Street exit that leads to Bank Street and the Glebe and the Ambassador, she asks Howard to skip the exit.

"Just keep driving," she says.

She needs to think.

Gus realizes that Malachy knows where she lives.

And there's somewhere else she needs to go right now. Howard stays on the Queensway. They reach the west end of the city as the afternoon sun blooms low in the April sky, full and orange. Gus spots the off-ramp leading south to the 416. She directs Howard to take the exit. A half hour from the Governor General's residence, they enter a gravel parking lot at a forested dog park called Bruce Pit. Gus asks Howard to park away from the other cars, near a steep incline that leads down to a lake below the parking lot.

They park and get out of the car. Then they sit together on the grassy hilltop. Gus tells Howard that this is where her mother died. Where she was murdered and then her car was rolled into the lake below with her body inside. Gus was in the back seat. She was eight. This place is where the worst thing that ever happened to her happened.

Howard listens. It feels good to talk about Shannon. Gus tells Howard all about her mother. How she bought her first house in Hintonburg when they moved to Ottawa. How Shannon liked to dance to music while she cooked and how her mother liked to sleep on the front porch on hot summer nights. And about her death.

Gus is surprised how easily she is able to share such intimate details about herself with a practical stranger, but it also feels right. Her mother's story needs to be known by more than just her.

She felt her mother's presence today in the ladies' room when May had her hands around her throat. Felt it more vividly than she has in years. There was a darkness in it that she'd never felt before, and Gus wanted to come out here to see if she could figure out why. But the place is empty. Her mother's not here.

"I'd like to go back to my apartment now," says Gus.

Her legs are stiff as she rises from the grass.

They've been sitting there for a couple of hours.

It's nearing sunset when they pull up to the Ambassador. Howard parks the Honda and insists on escorting Gus to her apartment. She's weak and pale and doesn't resist. He keeps glancing at the dark bruises on her throat and the red welts emerging on her upper arms. He guides her into the building. She's barefoot, having lost a shoe in the back of Malachy's limo. She carries the other in one hand as Howard leads her upstairs. So far so good. No sign of Malachy and Taggart lurking outside. No sign of anyone inside the dim hallways. She's glad of it because she's not sure she has any fight left in her. She's exhausted. Gus leans on Howard's arm as they approach her door. He takes her key and opens it for her and heads inside first.

The coast is clear, and from the way Levi wakes from his deep sleep, Gus can tell no one else has come in. Gus collapses into the sofa. Levi jumps up beside her and sniffs her swollen neck. She's shivering. Howard gets her a blanket. She can tell that he's trying not to look too closely at the evidence wall. For a guy who makes his living asking questions, Howard knows when not to. He tucks the blanket around her toes. He's kind of her hero right now.

"I'll make tea," he offers.

"Coffee?" she asks, nodding in the direction of the kitchen.

He gives her a thumbs-up and heads to the kitchen. Levi follows. She can hear Howard fumbling through cupboards for coffee and filters, cups, and spoons.

"How do you take it?" he calls out.

"Black," she says.

Then she hears him talking to Levi in a low voice, asking him if he's hungry and where his food's kept. She hears him try a few cupboards, then the fridge where she knows he'll find the Tupperware container labeled LEVI that contains the dog's rice and beef. Then she hears the dog eating loudly.

A few minutes later, Howard brings Gus a perfectly brewed cup of coffee. Now he's definitely her hero. He casually looks at the evidence wall again, then averts his eyes and looks out the window instead. Gus feels the familiar buzzy warmth of the caffeine seep into her bloodstream. It soothes her. Howard soothes her. She feels strangely at ease around him, even though she barely knows him.

"Guess you're wondering what's up with the wall?" she says, smiling.

He shrugs like he could take it or leave it.

"Well if you're not curious," she says, sipping her coffee.

"It's killing me. Spill," he says, sitting beside her.

"First, promise me you're not secretly working for the Mutchmores," she says, dead serious.

"I am not and have never been secretly in the employ of the Mutchmores," he says, hand to heart.

Gus laughs. Then she tells him everything. How she was hired by her neighbor to look into a decades-old disappearance when bones emerged from the pond outside the Ambassador. How Poppy assumed it was her long-lost love, Leo, but now she's convinced it isn't him.

Gus flings off the blanket, gets up off the sofa, and stands in front of the wall, pointing as she takes him through each piece of evidence.

Fast-forward several decades, and someone tries to kill Poppy. Her rich relatives, the Mutchmores, have been freaking out ever since. Gus shares how they've made threats, lied to her, spied on her, and attacked her. She thinks they even left a dead squirrel at her doorstep.

"What the—?" says Howard.

Gus shrugs.

"So back up. The bones aren't Leo?" he asks.

"The police think they are. He was wearing Leo's coat. Had his ID on him," she says.

Howard rises and comes over to examine the wall more closely.

"So you think it's the Mutchmores protecting their reputation, social standing, business interests? Everything?" he asks.

Fueled by coffee, they stand shoulder to shoulder staring at the wall.

"Yes, it's that, but there's so much more going on. A baby born out of wedlock decades ago hardly seems like the scandal that brings down an empire. For sure, the incest bit could tarnish the family crest, but Poppy's love affair ended before it even began. I can't see how any of this does irreparable damage to the almighty Mutchmore name," she says. "There's more going on here, Howard. I can feel it in my bones. I've only skimmed the surface and they know it."

"So you thought, why not poke the bear and show up at Rideau Hall as they're about to be anointed by the GG?" he asks, smiling.

"I was hoping to get Charlotte alone," she says. "It was worth a shot."

"I'm thinking maybe they've underestimated you, Ms. Monet?" he says, looking at the evidence wall.

Gus looks at Howard out of the corner of her eye. Something about his attentive expression, his openness to all possibilities, his warm, confident posture pulls at her heart. She's surprised by the feeling. She's attracted to Howard. Not her usual type. He's nerdy, yet doesn't carry himself like he is. He's not someone else's version of who he should be. He's his version. He's Howard. Gus hasn't met many people who seem so comfortable in their own skin. May and Ricker seem to have several versions of themselves, some they present at galas or in lemony-scented offices, others that come out in bathrooms when no one else is looking. Different masks for different occasions.

Howard is tracing one of the red lines on her wall with the tip of his finger. He's trying to feel his way through the evidence. Like she used to when she was looking for connections on her mother's evidence wall. The gesture makes her want to take his hand in hers. Instead, she sits back down on the sofa and sips her coffee.

"Who are the babies?" he says. "How does that fit with the rest?"

"Exactly, it doesn't. All the evidence connects to Leo and Poppy, except that as far as I can tell," says Gus. "That was something Charlotte said to me and I don't think it was a mistake. She said *stop asking about the babies*. Plural. She didn't mean the baby Eva gave up, she meant something else."

"That's why you went looking for her at Rideau Hall?" he adds.

"Yeah, only May and her grease monkeys got in the way," she says.

He turns to look at Gus, raising an eyebrow at the funny expression.

"I might know of another place you can run into Charlotte Mutchmore," he says.

Gus perks up.

"She's one of the Lucky Pennys," he says. "It's a book club run by a few society ladies. They meet at Zoe's Restaurant in the Château Laurier for high tea."

"How do you know this?" Gus asks.

"I did a writeup on the Pennys last year," he explains. "I get the real meaty assignments."

Gus grabs her notebook off the coffee table.

"Why Lucky Pennies?" she says, writing it down.

"That's Pennys with a *Y*," he says. "They're big Louise Penny fans. They've gone on all the tours. Three Pines Tour. Bury Your Dead Tour in Quebec City. They only read Canadian mysteries set in Canada. They're actually kind of militant about it."

"You're amazing," says Gus. "You know all kinds of things, Howard."

Howard smiles.

"I'll text you when they set a date for their next meetup if you like," he offers. "I'm still on their email list."

As Gus and Howard exchange numbers, she can't help yawning.

"And that's my cue. You need some rest," he says.

He's right. Gus can feel the heavy tug of sleep in her bones.

"I can stay," he offers. "On the sofa."

Gus shakes her head. She wants to be alone. She promises to lock the door. Levi will protect her. The dog lifts his head, one ear flipped on top of his head. He looks like he couldn't protect a flea. Howard ruffles the dog's furry head.

"You're sure you're okay?" he asks, glancing at her belly.

She reaches out and takes his hand in hers and squeezes it.

"Thanks, Howard, I'm good," she says, smiling.

Howard's ears turn red and roses bud on his cheeks.

"It's okay to ask," she says, resting her other hand on her belly.

"None of my business," he says, shaking his head.

It's the first time he's seemed uncomfortable.

"The father's out of the picture," she says. "He was a mistake."

Now she's blushing.

"As long as you two are okay," he says, nodding at her belly as he heads for the door.

Before leaving, Howard gives her one of his silly little bows. A few seconds after he shuts the door, there's a knock. A rhythmic door knock in five parts. She opens the door. It's Howard.

"You didn't lock it," he says.

She shuts the door and turns the deadbolt.

He knocks again. The same comical five-part knock.

Rat-tat-tatat-tat.

She knocks the response, smiling.

Tat-tat.

19

Ellie

GUS WAKES. SHE DOESN'T KNOW HOW LONG SHE'S BEEN ASLEEP, but she knows it hasn't been more than an hour. It's dark. A sliver of moonlight slants through her living room window, illuminating the photo booth images on her evidence wall. Illuminating Poppy. She's next to her boyfriend, Leo. She's eighteen. Smiling at a camera in a photo booth in 1953. The photo booth is long gone. Leo is long gone. And soon Poppy will be all but forgotten if the Mutchmores have their way.

Gus sits up. Her neck is tender and swollen. Her throat sore. She's still wearing the pink floral dress. She searches for her phone to book an Uber. Then it dawns on her. May has her phone. It was inside the pearl clutch May picked up and took from the ladies' room. Gus checks the time. It's only 9 P.M. Past visiting hours. The hospital will be quiet. Perfect. Gus changes out of the pink dress. She pulls on a pair of her stretchiest leggings and a turtleneck to hide the bruises. Levi stirs but doesn't wake. To be cautious, she takes the fire exit at the back of the building to avoid a possible stakeout at the front.

The evening is warm. Gus heads to the far end of the park and hops on a bus that's near empty. She's at the Civic Hospital in less than ten minutes. A couple of ambulances are parked near the emergency doors. An empty cop car sits next to them. A man dressed in scrubs leans against a wall, smoking. Gus enters the hospital, nods and smiles at a security guard who's more interested in his phone than her. She takes an elevator to the third floor, makes her way down the hallway, past an unattended nurse's station. So far so good. She gets to Poppy's room and is just about to enter when someone calls out from down the hall.

"Excuse me? Miss?"

Damn it. Gus stops and turns.

"Hi," she waves.

The young woman walks closer. She looks like a teenager. She's pushing a cart. She waves back.

"I don't think anyone's supposed to be up here?" she says, looking behind her.

"It's okay. I found the room. I've got it, thanks," says Gus with cheery finality as she pushes open the door to Poppy's room.

The room still looks occupied. Flowers sit on the windowsill, a few cards. There's a tray with a half-eaten meal sitting next to the bed. But the bed is empty and Poppy's purse is not on the side table.

Shit.

"The nurse has just gone downstairs for a quick sec," the girl says, her voice getting shrill.

She rolls her cart closer.

"Are you lost? This is the Geriatric Unit," she says.

"I'm pregnant," says Gus, tossing out her favorite go-to distraction.

"Maternity's on two," says the girl, glancing at Gus's belly.

"I was just looking in on a friend," says Gus.

"But it's way past visiting hours," says the girl, wide-eyed, like she's the one in trouble.

Gus sees that her cart is stacked with boxes of miniature chocolate bars, cans of pop, magazines, and newspapers. As the girl gets closer and passes under a light, Gus spots a name tag pinned to her chest that says Ellie.

"Ellie. That's pretty," Gus says.

The girl looks at her name tag, then smiles awkwardly.

"I'm Augusta," says Gus.

The girl's eyes soften and a lightbulb flickers inside them.

"You're Miss Honeywell's friend," says Ellie, like she's just aced a pop quiz.

"I am. You know Poppy," says Gus, pouncing on their common ground.

"Sure, she talked about you. She likes Coke Classic. She's sweet," says the girl.

"Do you know where she is?" Gus asks, her voice cracking.

"She's gone," Ellie says, "and Nurse Wootton is miffed."

Gus's heart sinks. She's too late. Blood rushes to her head and her vision dips in and out.

She grips the cart. The girl gasps.

"Did I say something wrong?" she says, looking more rattled than Gus. "Jujubes?" she offers, holding out a small package of candy.

Gus accepts. She rips open the bag, ravenous. She never did get that buffet dinner promised on the invitation.

"Thanks," she says, shoving the chewy candies in her mouth.

"They're my fav," the girl says.

Gus offers the package. The girl holds out her hand and Gus pours a bunch in her palm.

"Want a Sprite?" asks Ellie.

Gus shakes her head.

"Why was the nurse miffed?" Gus asks, nonchalantly.

"Nurse Wootton? They went to the cafeteria and after an hour when they didn't come back, she sent me to go look for them. Then she had to call the family. The girl just took off with Miss Honeywell," says Ellie. "It was a whole thing."

Mojo. She must have had the same idea as Gus. Get to Poppy before her parents do.

"When was this?" Gus asks.

"Like, a little over an hour ago. Nurse Wootton was called down to the chief of staff's office. I think she's in trouble," says Ellie, grimacing at the thought.

The elevator dings at the far end of the hallway. The two of them swivel their heads simultaneously in the direction of the opening doors. Four people step off the elevator. Despite the distance, Gus can tell right away who it is. May leads the way, followed closely by Ricker. They're still in their garden party attire. Bringing up the rear is Malachy and a woman in a nurse's uniform. Nurse Wootton, no doubt.

May stops in her tracks when she spots Gus. Ricker almost bumps into her. An eerie calm descends as if all the oxygen has been sucked from the hallway and everyone's suspended in zero gravity. May's hair bobs lightly on her shoulders. Ellie doesn't move. Nurse Wootton opens her mouth, but no sound comes out. Gus locks eyes with May.

Then Ellie lets out a nervous giggle and all hell breaks loose.

Malachy breaks into a sprint, dodging past May and Ricker. Gus pitches clumsily backward, spins around, and starts running for the far exit, her legs and arms pumping hard. She can hear the squeak, squeak, squeak of Malachy's shiny black shoes racing across the hospital floor. She reaches the exit door. The squeaking intensifies, gets louder, closer. She hip-checks the push bar, glancing back just in time to see Malachy become airborne, like a gymnast flying over a vault, only it's Ellie's cart that has somehow rolled into his path, prompting his aerial gymnastics.

Way to go, Ellie!

In the background, May and Ricker are gaping like a couple of wide-mouthed fish. Ellie's hands cover her face. The cart tips. Soda cans tumble and one bursts open. Malachy hits the floor spread eagle, chin bouncing off the hard floor, out cold as his body crashes into the wall. As the exit door shuts, Gus glimpses two of the Irishman's teeth bouncing across the linoleum in a shower of Coke Classic that sparkles in the fluorescent light.

Gus takes the stairs two by two. She bursts out of the ground-floor fire exit. She tries to orient herself quickly. She's on the wrong side of the building. The bus stop is on the far side. She spots a cab across a large public parking lot. She sprints into the lot. It's deserted except for an older couple struggling to use the pay machine. The moon is hidden behind clouds.

What are they doing out here in the dark?

The woman looks at Gus. Her eyes pleading. As if suddenly walking through water, Gus slows as a force greater than fear tugs at her heart. She feels sorry for the couple. Gus stops, turns back. Even though she knows it's not the time to be a Good Samaritan, she does it anyway.

To hell with the Mutchmores.

She helps the couple get their credit card into the machine properly and waits until their ticket prints. They thank her as she runs for the cab, but it's already pulling away from the curb. She tries to flag it, but it doesn't see her. Now her only option is to skirt the hospital and catch a bus, hoping the Mutchmores aren't on the hunt. Sirens yowl. The bus stop is up ahead. Not a bus in sight. She can't stand in the glass bus shelter. She'll be a sitting duck. It's too cold to hide out in someone's backyard until daylight. Panic rises in her throat and then a car pulls up right next to her. She nearly screams. It's the old couple from the parking lot. They offer her a ride home. She almost pulls the door off its hinges as she scrambles into their back seat. She sinks low. Tells them where she lives and away they go.

The farther they get from the Civic Hospital, the more Gus feels her heart rate slow and her mind unscramble. Mojo must have Poppy. She's probably taken her back to her apartment. She's safe. They can fix this. The Mutchmores can be stopped. She'll call the police. No. The press. Howard. A lawyer. Someone who can help Poppy. Surely there's a law against locking someone up against their will. Once the authorities see that Poppy is of sound mind, the Mutchmores won't have a leg to stand on. A psychiatrist, that's what she needs. No, a lawyer.

Her thoughts are jolted back to the car. It's going too fast. *Hold on.* They're on the Queensway. They're going the wrong way. For a split second, Gus thinks the couple are working for the Mutchmores and she's been totally duped, but then she realizes they're just lost. Turns out they thought the address she gave them was in Orleans, a suburb miles east of downtown. Gus patiently redirects them back toward the city. It takes the man half an hour to find an exit, turn around, and get back on track.

Gus feels like she's been chasing Poppy all night. It's even possible her friend was already safe at home when Gus set out for the hospital.

When the car finally pulls up to the Ambassador, it's been over an hour since they left the hospital. Gus is sick with worry, fearful the Mutchmores got here before her, but thrilled to finally be back. She thanks the couple for the lift and dashes to the front door.

Her mind races as she climbs the stairs to the top floor and makes her way to Poppy's apartment. Not bothering to knock, she pushes her key in the lock and tumbles inside.

"Poppy? Mojo? It's me," she calls out.

Her shrill voice echoes ahead of her as she runs down the hallway to the living room. Her words ricochet off the walls and bounce back at her, slapping her face with the cold hard truth. She stares at the empty living room.

Inconceivably, devastatingly empty.

She stumbles backward, teetering into the hall, bracing herself with one hand on the wall. Her fingers touch a fragment of paper held to the wall by a small lip of scotch tape. It's the torn corner from one of Poppy's lost pet signs. The rest have been ripped down. They're gone. Everything's gone. She stares at the tiny remnant of paper. A single faded word is visible on it.

Lost.

She gasps as the word stabs her in the heart.

20

Levi

WHEN? HOW?

Gus was in Poppy's apartment earlier that day to borrow a dress. It was brimming with furniture and carpets and lost pet signs and dishes and firewood and blankets and pillows and red velvet curtains. With all of Poppy's lovely belongings. In a matter of hours, it's all been removed. Taken. Disappeared.

As Gus locks the door to Poppy's apartment, she could almost laugh if she didn't feel like crying. She's been played. They held out a carrot. Lured her to the GG's garden party. Got her out of the Ambassador while they emptied Poppy's apartment. Was Mojo in on it? She sent Gus the invitation. And where is Poppy? What have they done with her?

Gus feels sick and confused. She heads down to her apartment and crawls into bed. Levi snuggles close. Gus doesn't think she'll be able to sleep, but it comes like a black wave that sweeps her away to the parking lot at Bruce Pit. She knows she's dreaming but she can't wake herself. She sees herself standing beside her mother's car. May comes up behind her and wraps a belt around her throat. She's lifted off her feet. Gus kicks, but she can't break free. Then May snaps her neck.

Gus wakes gasping for air. Levi is startled awake and barks in protest. She pets his head until he calms and rolls onto his back. It's dark outside her window. This night feels like it will never end. The bedroom is alive with dancing shadows that twist and float into shapes that look like faces, distorted and monstrous. Gus shuts her eyes tight. She lies awake the rest of the night, her mind going over the day's events, again and again, like a needle on a record, repeating and repeating.

Slowly, the morning light pushes the shadows to the corners and her monkey brain resets. She rises early and dresses. Levi won't get up, so she heads downstairs without him to do some digging. She finds Mr. Curry in the front lobby mopping the floors. Gus asks him if he knows anything. He does.

A moving company showed up yesterday afternoon with three trucks. He let them in. They emptied her place out in no time. He jokes that it was like a military operation. There must have been twenty guys. Packing, sealing boxes, handing them down the halls and stairwells like a chain gang. They used the back service lane and were gone in a few hours.

"Tell the old gal she'll be missed," he says.

Gus turns and finds Stanley and Alice right behind her. She's not sure how long they've been standing there.

"What's this now? Our Poppy has moved out?" says Alice, hands on hips.

Stanley looks dumbfounded.

"Not because she wanted to," says Gus, under her breath.

"Poor dear Poppy," coos Alice, grasping her brother's arm. "It's her health, isn't it?"

Gus doesn't feel like explaining but knows she should say something.

"Her family put her in a home," says Gus.

"This is what happens to old people, I'm afraid. Just the next to last stop on this journey we call life," says Alice, with all the wisdom of a greeting card.

Stanley looks dazed.

"Her family's doing what's best for her, I'm sure," pipes up Mr. Curry.

Gus glares at him. It's partly his fault. He let the movers in the building. He's an accomplice, for fuck's sake. And he thinks it's what's best for her. Being kidnapped and having all her possessions stolen. Gus has to stop herself from kicking Curry in the balls.

"And all her things?" asks Stanley out of the blue.

Alice rolls her eyes.

"Didn't you hear what Mr. Curry said? Movers took it all," she tells him loudly.

He ignores Alice and looks at Gus.

"Show me," he says.

"Not sure you should be going into her apartment without her there," says Curry.

Like he's one to talk. Gus ignores the super and leads the way.

"We're going to be late for church," whines Alice, but Stanley is uncharacteristically insistent. He follows Gus.

Stanley's life has largely been wrested from his hands. He probably just wants to steer his own ship this one time. Alice does everything for him. She gives him his pills, makes him his toast, takes him for walks. Poor old Stanley just wants to feel useful, like he was long ago as the building's caretaker. He wants to see with his own eyes instead of simply being told how things are. It takes a while for them to get up to the fourth floor. Stanley's creaky bones struggle against gravity as he climbs the flights of stairs. He's a lot like Levi.

They enter the apartment and are greeted by emptiness.

There are no curtains covering the windows. No carpets softening the harsh sunlight streaming across the bare floors. The trio wanders from room to room. Even the bedrooms have been stripped bare. Eva's, once a shrine to the past, is now a dead space where her pain and her dreams and her work once lived. Gus falters at the entrance to the empty kitchen. The floor is still blackened where Gish met her end. Cupboards stand open. The dumbwaiter sits empty. Drawers have been left crooked in their rails. Crumbs litter the countertop where the toaster once sat. Gus listens to the crackle and pop of the fridge, which is still plugged in. She opens it carefully, half expecting it to be rigged with a detonator to a bomb that blows her and Stanley and Alice to a million pieces that shower over Patterson Creek Park like confetti. There's no kaboom. Just a faint square stain where a milk carton once sat. She opens the freezer. It's empty. No frozen dinners.

Gus says her goodbyes to Stanley and Alice and goes down to her own apartment.

Opening the door, she stares at her evidence wall. It's been totally trashed. Everything's gone. All that remains are the red lines and questions written in red marker. The newspaper article, the forensics report, Leo's love notes, the photo booth images, and the pictures of Malachy and Gish are all gone. Gus can't believe her eyes. When did this happen? Was it like that when she woke up this morning? Or when she came in last night after finding Poppy's apartment empty? It could have been. She'd gone straight to bed, not even turning on the lights. She shivers at the thought of someone coming in while she was sleeping. But Levi would have barked. She looks around for the dog.

"Levi," she calls out.

She can't bear to look at the wall. It's happening again. The first evidence wall she created, her mother's evidence, was destroyed. And now this one has been wiped clean. History repeats until you finally hear what it's trying to tell you.

Back the fuck off.

Then Gus hears a ping. A text. Someone's in her apartment. It's coming from her kitchen. She inches toward the entrance and peeks into the room. There's no one there. But sitting on the counter next to her coffee cup is her phone. The one May took.

It's face down. It pings a second time.

Gus picks it up and slowly flips it over.

There's a text from an unknown number.

It's an address with an image below it.

Gus stares at the photo.

Her hand trembles so much she almost drops the phone.

In the photo a man is holding Levi by his collar.

The man is grinning.

Not a good grin.

A toothless, fat-lipped grin on a badly bruised face.

Malachy has her dog.

21

Netzke and Dewey

GUS GETS THE UBER DRIVER TO DROP HER A BLOCK FROM THE house. She watches the windows for an hour, hidden among the fronds of a willow on the far side of a small lake in a park. The house backs onto the lake. She can see people moving about inside, but no Levi. The address on Holmwood is in the exclusive southwest quadrant of the Glebe called Brown's Inlet, sandwiched between Queen Elizabeth Driveway, Lansdowne Park, and Fifth. It's a massive structure. A showy piece of modern architecture, all steel and glass, nothing like the stately brick and stone homes of the surrounding neighborhood. Its angular shape reminds Gus of a ship, its lines curving toward the water's edge. A series of tiered decks hang suspended above the inlet like giant concrete lily pads. It's the biggest house on the street. By design, no doubt.

Gus knows who lives there. May and Ricker.

She triple-checks that her gun is safely tucked in the interior pocket of her satchel. Then she takes a deep breath, skirts the park, and walks up the circular driveway to the front entrance. Before ringing the doorbell, she presses record on her phone's voice memo app. The door opens, and before she can say a word, Gus is beckoned inside by a butler. He was expecting her.

"They're waiting for you in the great room," he says.

He leads her across a foyer, through a library, and into a massive sunken living room that overlooks the inlet. Three large sofas and four armchairs are arranged around a massive brass-and-marble coffee table.

They are all there waiting. Except Mojo. It's grown-up time.

On one sofa, Wilfred, Charlotte, May, and Ricker have arranged themselves with the women seated and the men perched on the arms of the sofa. They look like they're posing for a family portrait. There are two men in suits Gus doesn't recognize. They're sitting across from the Mutchmores on a second sofa. One has a briefcase open beside him. A thick file folder sits on the coffee table in front of him. Taggart hovers in a corner. And there, nestled in one of the armchairs, is Poppy. Gus is speechless.

"Miss Monet has arrived," announces the butler, then he quickly leaves the room.

Gus feels her cheeks burning. She just wants her dog back. She wants to leave. She's not interested in some family meeting. She suddenly feels like that deer again. Caught in the sights of a rifle. All eyes are on her, except one person's. Poppy's blind eyes look vacant. She is gaunt and pale. She looks so much older than the last time Gus saw her. There's no sign she knows Gus is even there. She must have heard the butler say her name. But Poppy's chin doesn't lift in her direction. Indeed, Poppy barely moves. Gus wonders if she's been drugged.

Ricker gestures for Gus to take a seat on the empty sofa in the middle of the gathering. They've left that one empty for her and they've surrounded it on all sides.

She descends the steps into the great room but before she

can reach the bottom, Taggart moves in. He blocks her path. Then he pats her down. She doesn't resist. She's getting used to being manhandled. As he completes his search, she looks around for Malachy. No sign of him or Levi. Taggart takes her satchel without asking, pulls her phone from it, and stops the recording. He roots around inside, finds the keys to Poppy's apartment. He dangles them in the air so the two men in suits can see what he's found, then he pockets the keys and places her phone on the coffee table. No need confiscating it a second time, since they probably wiped the phone already. Taggart walks back to his corner with her satchel, the gun as yet undiscovered. She wonders if he feels the weight of it.

Gus sits. She wants to scream. Demand they turn over her dog. She doesn't.

The man with the briefcase takes charge. Introduces himself. But barely looks at her. He's the family lawyer. Miles Netzke. The guy next to him is his investigator. Pete Dewey. Everyone else has a role to play. Likely rehearsed before her arrival.

May plays the fretful, hand-wringing, soft-spoken heiress who is just looking out for her beloved family. Her performance is award-worthy because it's so far from who she really is. Her adoring husband, Ricker, plays the reassuring, supportive presence at her shoulder. Wilfred looks confused about his part in all this. He looks catatonic, like they've slipped him a few horse tranquilizers to make sure he doesn't go off script. His wife, Charlotte, fidgets with the silver bracelets encircling her thin wrists. With her husband relegated to a supporting role, she's left playing the matriarchal head of the family, clearly uncomfortable with whatever they have planned. Her hands vibrate, when she's not fidgeting. Gus is pretty sure she needs a drink, badly. Poppy is the heroine of the story. The tragic victim. Taggart's the muscle.

And, as it turns out, Gus is the villain.

Netzke is the one telling the story. He gets the ball rolling now that all the players have hit their marks. He opens the thick dossier in front of him. Says it's the final report of a private investigation undertaken by his firm on behalf of the Mutchmores. The report details the fraudulent behavior perpetrated by Augusta Monet to intentionally deceive Poppy Honeywell for personal and financial gain. He looks at Gus for the first time. Tells her the Mutchmores hope the matter can be dealt with in a discreet manner so as not to impact Miss Honeywell's already fragile health with the stress of a criminal trial.

Gus's mouth is dry. She's having trouble swallowing. She needs water. No one cares.

Netzke keeps going. He itemizes a list of stolen property and missing items that belong to Miss Honeywell. A dress, private documents, letters and photographs, and a rare and valuable pearl necklace and matching purse. Gus looks at May. She's stone-faced. Then there's the money. A suspicious transaction in the amount of one hundred thousand dollars was withdrawn from Miss Honeywell's account in the last twenty-four hours. Netzke has since discovered a deposit for that exact amount made to the account of Augusta Monet. He doesn't bother explaining how he got his hands on her bank records. May gasps on cue. The lawyer reassures her that the money has since been recovered.

Gus glances at her phone. She wishes Howard would call. He'd find this whole thing funny. But this is no laughing matter. Gus stays very still. She says nothing, hoping that in doing so, it'll be over quicker or she'll magically disappear.

Netzke pulls something from the dossier and slides it across the surface of the coffee table. It comes to rest in front of Gus. It's the Polaroid of Poppy's dead cat, Gish. He calls it evidence. Says it was found in Miss Monet's residence and points directly to her involvement in the electrocution of Poppy's cat and possible attempted murder of Miss Honeywell. This time Gus is the one to gasp.

May reaches over and touches Poppy's knee, bowing her head in dismay. Gus looks at Poppy. Her friend can't be buying this horseshit. A single tear escapes the corner of Poppy's eye. The old woman brushes it away and takes May's hand in hers. Poppy believes their lies. Her dear friend has turned against her. They're all against her.

Netzke pulls back on the murder accusation, saying that at the very least, he finds it strange that Miss Monet knew of the animal's demise and chose not to share this critical information with her friend. He goes on to say that the Mutchmores told her about her poor pet's fate. That they don't believe in hiding the truth from people they care about, even hard truths.

Up next, he produces the photo of Malachy standing outside the Mutchmores'. Further evidence that Gus has been surveilling the family for some time.

Seems they're using her own evidence wall to build a case against her.

Netzke asks Gus how long she'd been planning to insinuate herself into the Mutchmores' lives, into Poppy's life. It's not a question. Then he fills everyone in on what he believes her plan was. To gain Poppy's trust, to gain access to her residence when she wasn't there, to help herself to Poppy's valuables, all the while shamelessly impersonating a private investigator.

Netzke exchanges a look with Dewey. They've had a good chuckle over her efforts at amateur sleuthing. Gus speaks for the first time.

"Could I get some water?" she croaks.

Ricker snaps his fingers. Somewhere behind Gus water is poured into a glass that suddenly appears in front of her. The butler places the full water glass on a coaster, then noiselessly returns to his station. Gus swigs the entire glass, but nearly spits out the last gulp when Netzke slides his next piece of evidence in her direction.

It's a mug shot of Tommy Oaks.

Fuck me.

The lawyer rises slowly. This is his big moment. He's taller than he looked sitting down. He takes his time, pacing the room like he's about to make his final arguments in a court of law. Then he turns and jabs a finger in her direction.

"Yes, we know all about your convict lover. The father of your unborn child."

Gus would laugh if she didn't think she might throw up in the process. Ricker puts a comforting hand on May's shoulder. Charlotte grimaces and looks down at her lap. Poppy looks gray, defeated. Gus wants the fuckhead lawyer to stop talking. Not for her sake but for Poppy's. Her friend looks wrung out. Why are they making her endure this? She should be resting like Wilfred, who's fallen asleep on his perch.

But Netzke is just getting started.

"There's no point in denying any of this. Mr. Dewey, you spoke to Mr. Oaks, correct?"

Dewey nods. "I did indeed. He admitted to a secret rendezvous with Miss Monet last year when he was out of prison. Obviously you two did more than just meet." He looks at her belly. "He also informed me that Miss Monet was there when Constable Rory Rump was murdered."

"Did he now?" says Netzke with feigned surprise.

He pauses to make sure it's sinking in.

Gus picks up the empty water glass, drains it of the last drop, then places it back down, missing the coaster entirely. Her hand is shaking and the glass rattles against the coffee table like a mini drumroll. The cantaloupe shifts and Gus involuntarily puts her hand to her belly. Suddenly, Charlotte rises and leaves the room without a word. Ricker moves to stop her, but May takes his arm and forces him to stay put.

Netzke doesn't miss a beat. He won't let this minor defection throw him.

"We know Mr. Oaks is protecting you. We know you were his accomplice. If you weren't, why did you lie to Miss Honeywell about your pregnancy? Why tell her the baby's father is dead, if you had nothing to hide? Or was that all part of your scheme to take advantage of an old woman's kindness and vulnerability. To con her. Embezzle her of her fortune."

Gus's mouth hangs open. It's all lies. And Poppy's not rich. *Is she?*

Netzke knows what she's thinking.

"Oh don't look so surprised. We know you know about the inheritance. The one her mother refused so it was passed on to Poppy and held in trust until she turned thirty. You've known her bank account was well endowed from the very beginning. Indeed, it's obviously been the prize you've been eyeing this whole time," he says.

Something clicks and Gus realizes there could actually be some truth sprinkled amidst Netzke's lies. Poppy has managed to live in her apartment for decades without working. And the Mutchmores wouldn't have supported her for that long. They're not that generous. She's rich.

"We know you've found yourself a new boyfriend. Or should we say accomplice?" he adds.

Howard? Jesus Christ. Gus had been under the illusion that she's been investigating the Mutchmores, when this whole time they've been watching her every move.

"This is what you do, isn't it, Miss Monet? I mean, Oaks isn't the first criminal you've bedded?"

Gus can't feel her hands or feet or face. She knows who they're talking about.

They've dug up an arrest record from 2016 when she and her first boyfriend, Lars, got caught with unmarked cigarettes in the trunk of their car.

Gus isn't sure where they're going with all of this or what they're accusing her of.

But when he starts to talk about her mother, a police officer with a sordid past involving suspensions and kidnapping and demotions, that's when Netzke's inspired final act reaches its climax and begins to spiral out of control, becoming more dreamlike than real.

The Mutchmores' heads begin to grow. Their cheeks stretch and their foreheads bulge, then each of their balloon heads floats toward the loft ceiling, bobbing overhead like helium-filled party favors. Netzke and Dewey are suddenly prancing about the room, leaping from sofa to sofa, giggling as they trail pink and blue streamers behind them as if they're hosting some bizarre baby shower. The table is littered with presents, gift-wrapped with lost pet signs. The helium faces circle closer until she can't breathe.

Gus faints.

She wakes in the back seat of a limousine. It's moving fast. It's dark outside the windows of the vehicle, and she can't tell where they are. Through the cloudy glass divider between the front and back seats, she can see the blurry shape of the driver, but can't make out who it is. Taggart? Possibly Malachy? She leans her head back, closes her eyes, and lets whoever it is take her wherever he's taking her. Gus can't remember when she last ate but it doesn't really matter. He's probably going to kill her and bury her body in the woods.

The vehicle comes to a stop five minutes later. The driver doesn't get out, but the locks on the doors click open. She peers out the window.

They're in front of the Ambassador.

Gus spots her satchel next to her. She looks inside. Her phone is there. The gun is there too. Gus climbs out of the limo and it drives away.

She stands in the street, shivering. At first, she's unable to get her feet moving. Afraid what she might find in her apartment. But she has no choice. She unsticks herself and goes inside. Gus makes her way up the two flights of stairs, legs heavy and trembling.

She opens the door to her apartment.

It's dark.

She hears a noise in the bedroom.

A familiar padding of feet on the floor.

Then Levi appears, wagging his tail.

He heads for her outstretched arms.

She embraces him and he nuzzles her neck.

Her very happy, very lovely, old dog is alive and nothing else matters in that moment.

THIRD
TRIMESTER

22

Honey Locusts

TIME CREEPS ACROSS THE SKY UNSEEN. GUS KEEPS HER CUR-tains closed and installs a chain lock on the inside of her apartment door. She sleeps more than she's awake. She barely dreams, and when she does she's back in the Mutchmores' great room surrounded by giant balloon heads. Weeks wander by. Howard texts once in a while, and she texts back that she's not feeling well. She doesn't tell him what happened. No point. He can't do anything about it. It's over. She's slightly ashamed by the whole ordeal and more than a little shell-shocked. One morning she realizes she's missed her own birthday. It was May 2. It came and went, as did the rest of April and the entire month of May.

Out of nowhere it's June, and it's as if the days between her ordeal at the Mutchmores and now never happened. How is it that everything seems both at a standstill and racing forward all at the same time? Even the cantaloupe marches on—now a pineapple.

Gus also missed her last two monthly checkups with Doctor Chandra. Now the thought of being covered by a thin paper blanket in the cold, sterile exam room with her feet up in stirrups almost makes her cry.

Gus tries to ease her guilt about not taking better care of the pineapple by cleaning out her fridge, scrubbing it clean, then stocking it with bottles of green juice from Pure Kitchen. She chooses the ones labeled Nourish. The pineapple seems to like them even though they taste like grass.

As she suspected, the photos of her evidence wall were wiped from her phone by the Mutchmores' legal team. The documents they ripped down are likely tucked away in Netzke's dossier in some filing cabinet. What she most regrets losing are Poppy's precious love notes from Leo, and the photo booth images of the two young lovebirds. Gus hopes the Mutchmores kept them for her but doubts it. It breaks her heart to think that Poppy might have nothing tangible left of Leo. Then she remembers the locket. Gus digs it out of the picture box and places it around her neck for safekeeping. One day, she hopes she can give it back to Poppy.

What the Mutchmores don't know is that Gus has backup copies of all the photos from her phone. She uploaded them to the cloud a while back. Some lessons were learned from the past. The cloud seems like a faraway place for them to live. And that's where they might stay forever.

Another lesson she learned from the past is that people can put tracking software on phones. Lars once did it to keep tabs on her. She takes her phone to a local electronics repair shop and gets it cleaned. At least that's what the tech calls it when he finds the tracker and deactivates it.

Time is like Jell-O when you're terrified. Wobbly and dense. The days and hours lumber along almost unnoticed, only interrupted once when Howard sends her another text. This one is about the Lucky Pennys. Charlotte's book club is meeting in three days.

Sunday, June 13, at 3 p.m. at the Château Laurier tearoom.
She doesn't text him back.

She wants nothing to do with the Mutchmores ever again.

The evidence their lawyer presented, real or not, would be more than enough to get her into deep legal trouble. And if she's right, the Mutchmores know people. They have friends in high places. It would be her word against theirs, and they'd win. Siri has already told her that the punishment for embezzlement is a fine, prison time, or both. Gus can't risk going to jail. She could lose the pineapple. And Levi.

Backing off is the smart play. And she's pretty sure that's all the Mutchmores really want. That meeting had one purpose. To freak her the fuck out. That's why the lawyers and the frisking and the dognapping. It's why they sat her in the middle. Surrounded by the wolves. Intimidation 101.

Gus doesn't scare easily. Her usual MO is to get even more riled when provoked. But she's never had so much to lose before. Things are different now. She has someone she can't risk losing. Two someones—if you count Levi.

She tries to forget the ordeal with the Mutchmores, but her mind often wanders to her friend Poppy. She misses her. Wonders what they've done with her. The hurt look on Poppy's face was devastating. The idea that Poppy might think their friendship was fake pains her. Gus wanders up to Poppy's apartment late at night and listens at the door. The old building creaks and wind whistles and rattles windows, but no one lives there. There's a lockbox attached to the handle so real estate agents can show the place to prospective buyers. A sad reminder that someone new will move in one day. She sometimes sits outside Poppy's door and eats a frozen dinner. And in those moments when her loneliness feels like it might swallow her whole, Gus truly believes she may never see Poppy again.

It's the day after Howard's text, a warm Friday in June, when a glimmer of hope breaks through the darkness.

Gus gets a message.

A message in a bottle. Kind of.

She and Levi are nearing the end of their morning walk. Their last stop, as always, is to linger in the shady northwest corner of Patterson Creek Park near Lyon and Chamberlain. It's Levi's favorite spot, and he usually leads the way there. Gus lets him off leash so he's free to forage among the honey locusts. He likes to nibble the sticky, sweet flowers that have begun to bloom on the low-hanging branches. Even in winter when the trees were bare, he was drawn to this corner of the park. Something about the scratchy bark appealed to him, even before he knew the honey locusts had a sweet spring surprise in store. Poppy was the one who introduced them to the small thicket. A private spot most people didn't notice since the stone path in the park doesn't come this direction. Poppy and Leo used to meet amidst the seclusion of the honey locusts so her mother wouldn't see them.

This is where Gus finds the note wedged in the branches of one of the honey locusts. Levi doesn't see it. He's busy nibbling sweet buds. Gus spots it almost immediately. The bright pink color catches her eye. It's a can of cream soda. It's empty except for a note sticking out the top.

Dearest Augusta, I know they lied about you. I want you to find out why. Your friend, Poppy.

Gus stares at the note. She knows it's Poppy's handwriting. She once watched her feel her way across a sheet of paper with a ballpoint pen as she wrote out a short grocery list for Gus. At the time, Gus was amazed at her lovely penmanship. She wonders how long the note has been sitting in the tree. She's guessing Mojo was the one who put it there for Poppy. Surely

Poppy hadn't made her way to the park alone. Yes, it had to be Mojo.

Until this moment, Gus wasn't sure about Mojo's allegiances, but it looks like the kid might be on her side, and Poppy's. Maybe she did try to save Poppy from the hospital but got caught. Likely they've taken Mojo's phone away if that's the case.

Suddenly Gus feels a pain deep in her chest. But it's not the same dull ache she's felt for almost two months. It's the heart-wrenching joy of knowing that Poppy doesn't hate her. Gus examines the note, back and front. No details. No mention of where she is. No next steps or clues. Just a directive to do what she must. To figure it out. To risk everything.

I want you to find out why.

Likely the honey locusts are as close as Mojo could get to the Ambassador. The kid knew Gus and Levi came by here every day. She'd been here with them on their walks. She knew they'd see it eventually. The Mutchmores must be watching her. Gus smiles, picturing her little partner in crime sipping a cream soda as she walks across the park, then sidesteps casually into the trees for a moment to hide the can, reemerging before anyone knows what she's done.

Gus scans the park.

It's empty, and yet her heart is full to bursting.

23

Charlotte

Saturday, Gus texts Howard.

Can we meet?

He suggests they grab lunch at the Wild Oat on Bank since it's just a few blocks from where Gus lives. She knows the café but has never gone in. It's vegetarian and has a hippie vibe from the outside. Not her thing. But this isn't a date, so she agrees. This isn't about food. She needs Howard's help.

Gus gets there early. It's bustling. The place is rustic and warm like a log cabin. Paintings covering the walls. Local artists, according to the signs. There's a box of toys in one corner. Feels like the kind of place where people sit and talk instead of stare at their phones or laptops. She nabs a large triangular booth in the far corner where she can keep her back to the wall and one eye on the patrons, the other on the entrance and front windows.

Her paranoia is high, but so is her excitement.

As she sits waiting, Gus scans through the photos she downloaded back onto her phone from the cloud.

Howard bursts in and spots her. He waves with both

hands, a toothy grin spreading across his silly face. A line has formed at the order counter. Howard manages to catch everyone's attention with his showy entrance. His larger-than-life routine isn't exactly inconspicuous. She gives him a quick wave and he makes his way over, but not before chatting up the guy behind the counter, the chef prepping food in the open kitchen, and a couple of customers he knows in line.

"Ms. Augusta Monet," he says, bowing and knocking on the table in the same comical five-part knock he used on her door.

Rat-tat-tatat-tat.

She rolls her eyes and knocks the response on the table.

Tat-tat.

"Howard," she says, unable to stop smiling as he slides into the booth.

He comes all the way around the triangular bench so that he's seated right next to her.

"I highly recommend the Very Veggie Crepe with tahini," he says, pointing to the chalkboard menu above the open kitchen.

"Sounds yummy," she says, even though she's never tried tahini.

Howard slides in reverse out of the booth, jogs over to the chef, says something in her ear, then slides back in. Howard hasn't stopped buzzing since he arrived. She wonders how much coffee he's consumed today.

"You've been MIA," he says, wiping down the table with a wet wipe he's magically produced out of thin air.

"Sorry," she says.

"No more trouble with the M&Ms, I hope," he whispers, covering his mouth like a coach hiding his plays from the opposing team.

"M&Ms?" Gus asks as it dawns on her what he means.

"The Mutchmores," he says, looking around.

Howard eyes a bucket of knife-and-fork duos wrapped in paper napkins.

"We need utensils," he says, squirming out of the booth.

Gus grabs his arm and holds it. He stays put.

"Howard Baylis," she says firmly, like she's his mother. "I need you to sit still."

He stops squirming and sliding and talking and finally listens.

Gus tells him everything that's happened since she last saw him. About her late-night visit to the hospital after their escape from the GG's garden party. About Poppy's apartment being emptied. About Levi being taken and about her mock trial at Mutchmore manor. And finally, about finding the note in the locust tree and how she has to keep digging for Poppy's sake.

"Holy crow, I missed a lot," says Howard. "You got a plan?"

"Charlotte. She's not really one of them. She married into that family. I think she's the crack in their armor," she says, "but I can't be seen anywhere near her or they'll come after me for real."

Partway through her story, the chef quietly slipped the crepes and utensils onto the table. Howard was so caught up in her account, he barely noticed. But almost unconsciously, he cleaned his cutlery with wipes while she talked.

He's barely touched his lunch. Gus, on the other hand, has devoured hers while talking. Weirdly, she's starting to acquire a taste for vegetables, and this magical paste that is tahini is amazing. Or maybe it's just the pineapple who likes real food.

"You doing anything tomorrow, around three?" she asks.

"Let me guess. The Lucky Pennys?" he says.

She nods.

"I need your help, Howard," she says.

"I'm in," he answers without hesitating.

He takes a big bite of his crepe, tahini dripping down his chin.

"You don't even know what I'm asking you to do yet," she says.

"I'm in," he repeats.

Gus smiles.

They work out a plan. Howard will go in alone. He's the least likely of the two of them to be recognized by one of the Mutchmore thugs. If Charlotte is in the company of Malachy or Taggart, he'll lie low until he can get her alone. Hopefully, he can casually bump into her in the hotel lobby before she goes into Zoe's. He'll remind her of the article he wrote about the Pennys then slip her his card. All very innocent. Only there'll be a note on the back of the card that hopefully only Charlotte reads.

Can we talk? By the hotel pool. 5 tonight.—Augusta

∽✺∾

Charlotte walks through the revolving doors with Malachy shadowing her. Howard is hiding behind a bust of Sir Wilfrid Laurier. Charlotte's eye is drawn to the sculpture, and she immediately spots Howard peering out from behind it. Recognition flits across her face. Then Howard sees her slip the paperback in her hand inside her coat pocket. She turns to Malachy, showing him her empty hands. Howard can hear her echoing voice telling him to go back to the car to get the book she forgot. When Malachy heads outside to retrieve it, Howard crosses the marble floor and approaches Charlotte. He's about to launch into his planned speech when she cuts him off.

"You're her friend," she says. "You were with her at the gala. I believe you were trying to distract me so the two of them could get away from me."

Apparently, Charlotte wasn't as drunk as she looked.
Howard nods apologetically.

"I was being quite the bitch," she adds dryly.

Howard smiles awkwardly.

"Is your friend well? Is the baby all right?" she asks, shame wilting her voice.

Howard nods again, then tries to get back on script. He hands her his card. She flips it over and reads the note, then looks up at him for a moment as if pondering her options.

"I do love to swim," she says, almost to herself, "and when you're lucky enough to be a Mutchmore, you can have an entire pool closed for your pleasure if you so choose."

She turns as if to leave, then has another thought that she tosses in Howard's direction.

"Our hired man isn't one for water sports. He'll be waiting in the car."

Charlotte walks over to the front desk, speaks to the concierge. Malachy returns empty-handed. Howard ducks behind Sir Wil. Charlotte glares at Malachy like he's a complete incompetent, then strides across the lobby and into Zoe's to meet the Lucky Pennys, pulling the book from her pocket as she enters the tearoom. Malachy shifts uncomfortably then decides to wait outside instead of following her.

Howard walks over to the concierge.

"Hey there, I'm a guest at the hotel. Can you remind me what the pool hours are?" he asks. The uniformed man checks his wristwatch and smiles.

"Ah, I'm afraid the pool is closing early today, sir. At five P.M. For maintenance." He adds, "You might have time for a quick dip."

Howard's impressed. Considering this regal old hotel has catered to the likes of Lady Diana and the Rolling Stones, Howard is surprised Charlotte Mutchmore has enough clout to shift its operations. Then he laughs to himself, remembering that the Mutchmores own the joint.

Howard thanks the man and heads for the Sussex Street side exit to avoid Malachy. He's not sure if the chauffeur got a good look at him when he rescued Gus outside the GG's residence, but better safe than sorry. Howard texts Gus as he walks away from the hotel.

You're on.

❧

The pool at the Château Laurier was built in 1930. It hasn't changed much in nine decades. Same art deco design with big globe lamps hanging from the tall ceilings, an ornate fountain at one end, and decorative balconies overlooking the sixty-foot saltwater pool. Gus stands in the shadows on one of the balconies. She watches as the staff clear the pool of guests, hose down the deck, then lock the doors as they leave. At 5 P.M., Charlotte emerges from the women's changeroom wearing the white linen dress and high heels she wore to tea. Her coat draped over one arm. Gus presses record on her phone's voice memo app and steps out from the shadows to the railing, hiding the phone from view. Charlotte spots her, then casts her gaze down to the pool's shimmering surface.

"I used to bring May here Saturday mornings when she was a little girl," she says, her voice reverberating off the high ceilings. It sounds like Charlotte is right next to Gus instead of thirty feet away. Perfect for her recording.

"Thanks for meeting me," says Gus.

"She loved the water. A fish. I couldn't get her to come out," says Charlotte, softly to herself. "May was sweet once. But her heart has hardened so much that I can't talk to her anymore."

Gus is hoping Charlotte didn't agree to meet so she could

take a trip down memory lane. She has so many questions. She starts with the most obvious.

"Is Poppy okay?" she asks.

"Okay?" Charlotte says as if the word is beneath her. "As *okay* as any of the Mutchmore women could be, I suppose."

Not helpful.

"Has your husband locked her away yet? That's what he's planning, isn't he?"

"Hah, you are a dramatic little thing. Seems you already know the answer to your question," she says.

"Where is she?" says Gus, a little more aggressively than she meant.

"Not to worry. She has a lovely new home. Dearest Poppy is safe and sound," she says.

"I'd like to see for myself," says Gus.

"That's not happening," answers Charlotte.

Gus is getting nowhere. She changes tack.

"And the babies?" Gus asks. "Why did you tell me to stop asking about them?"

Charlotte looks up at Gus.

"I'd like to be clear about something, young lady. I am not here to help you. I am here for my granddaughter," she says. "I want you to help her."

"Mojo?" Gus asks.

"Marjory?" says Charlotte, then she looks away again.

The weight of her coat seems too much for her thin arm. She takes a deep breath and walks over to a row of reclining chairs near the pool's edge. Her heels clack on the hard deck. She sits down and places her coat beside her.

"We tried for years to have a child. Wilfred so wanted a son to carry on his legacy. Fertility treatments finally brought us our miracle baby. Alas, May wasn't a boy. The curse, you see. Then last year, May's cervical cancer left her barren. No sons for her either. That was her entire worth. The only value she had to her father. May had the makings of a formidable businesswoman. Smart as a whip. Ambitious and educated. All of her talents squandered. She's been relegated to ladies' luncheons and managing the household staff. Ricker runs the foundation, but he's not blood. Wilfred has always had a blind spot when it comes to the fairer sex. And most tragically, he never really saw his daughter for who she was or could have become. May tried, but she could never catch her father's eye long enough. Now, she's lost to him, to me, to herself. That sweetness she had as a little girl has all but disappeared, twisting into something dark and angry. I fear the same fate lies ahead for my granddaughter. The burden falls to her, you see. Marjory is her grandfather's last hope to carry on the Mutchmore bloodline," she says, her voice flagging. "Like it needs carrying on."

"And the babies?" Gus tries again.

"The babies are the rot in the family tree. The poison," she says.

"Were they Eva's babies? Did she have twins?" Gus asks.

Charlotte laughs then goes quiet.

"No" is all she says with a sigh.

Charlotte slips off her shoes, rises, and walks over to the pool. She sits at the edge, dipping one hand in the water as if to gauge the temperature. Gus watches her. Charlotte's tiring, so Gus doesn't push. She's come for a reason and Gus decides to let her find her way toward it.

"We have all become like one who is unclean, and all our righteous deeds are like a polluted garment," she says, moving her fingertips through the water.

Gus is pretty sure Charlotte just quoted the Bible. She's beginning to think the woman's sanity is slipping. Then Charlotte looks up at Gus, clear-eyed.

"I want you to bring down the Mutchmores," she says. "I want the whole damn thing to crumble to dust."

Here it comes.

"I cannot stand idly by and watch as my granddaughter becomes the next to pay for her great-grandfather's sins," Charlotte says. "I was always made to believe that Eva was the bad seed, but I was wrong. I only learned the truth very recently. She sacrificed so much. She had no choice but to do something horrific. Something no mother should have to do, and in the end, it drove her completely mad. She confessed her sins to Wilfred and he turned his back on her. And now he's unburdened himself and told me what she did. I know now that Eva and Poppy and May have paid a terrible price for being women in that wretched family. I paid it too. I will not see Marjory led to the slaughter."

The old woman lifts herself up off the pool deck. She stands on shaky legs. She looks spent. Whatever she's got on the Mutchmores spells their doom. It's the reason they were so freaked out by Gus's investigation. But it's clear that Charlotte is struggling to reveal all. Gus tries to help her out.

"She killed Leo," says Gus.

"There are worse things than murder," says Charlotte.

Gus waits for her to say more, but she doesn't. Charlotte is a Mutchmore by marriage only, but betraying family isn't a straight road. Now that she's embarked upon it, she appears to be riddled with guilt and near exhaustion. Gus keeps her mouth shut and her recording going. Slowly Charlotte finds a way around her reluctance and into a story.

"There was a great fire back in 1900 in these parts. It was spring. The fire started in a chimney in a house in Hull. It spread to more than half that city's dwellings. Then the wind sent burning embers across the river into Ottawa, where it flattened a quarter of that city. Most of the devastation was along the swath of small wood houses crowding LeBreton Flats, all the way to Dow's Lake. Miraculously, the fire only took seven souls. But the final toll of this tragedy was yet to be felt. You see, the homeless numbered fifteen thousand. The already impoverished families were forced to spend that winter in tent cities on the high, exposed land of the Flats. Disease took hundreds more.

"That fire is where it began. I don't know exactly what happened. That's for you to find out. I know my husband's parents, Robert and Cora Mutchmore, owned that land on LeBreton Flats. Wilfred said that before his mother died, she confessed a great sin to him. A sin forged in the fire of 1900. Wilfred never shared her secret with me. But just last year, he said something upon waking from a nightmare. He said his father made a deal with the devil in the ashes of that fire. He said the babies were the currency. When I heard you talking to Poppy about a baby, I thought you might be treading where you shouldn't. I was foolishly trying to protect my family. But since hearing the truth about Eva, about how Wilfred abandoned her when she needed him most, I'm done with that now. You find out the terms of that deal, and I believe the very whisper of it will burn the Mutchmores to the ground."

Charlotte puts on her shoes, picks up her coat, and heads for the women's changeroom. Gus expects her to turn or stop or say something else, but she doesn't.

"Whose babies are they?" hollers Gus.

Charlotte leaves the pool without another word.

Gus's mind is reeling. Her thoughts tumble back to another fire. The Elgin fire, which scorched the heart of a small town, turning it into an uninhabitable ghost town. Gus feels the past licking at her heels. Looping over and over upon itself. Retelling the same stories and sending her the same warnings, in the hope that she gets the message or learns the lesson this time. Another devastating fire. Another pile of ashes in which the truth lies buried.

Alone in the cavernous room, Gus stops the recording on her phone.

She turns to leave but hears a changeroom door open. Gus steps into the shadows of the balcony just as Malachy comes out of the men's changeroom. She stands still as a statue. The sight of him sends spiders crawling down her spine. He steps onto the pool deck. Scans the room. Looks up at the balcony. She stops breathing. He stares into the shadows for an eternity. She's positive he can't see her if she doesn't move. She tries to stop her body from shaking. He scans the far balcony then retreats into the changeroom.

As the door closes behind him, her cell phone chimes. A text.

Gus doesn't wait to see if Malachy heard it. She runs to the end of the balcony, pushes open the glass doors, and races down the mezzanine to the far exit. She doesn't stop running until she's outside the building, around the corner, and down in the parking garage. She spots Howard. He's waiting beside his Honda. They jump in the car.

"You got my text?" he asks.

"That was you?" she says, out of breath.

She looks at the phone.

Found limo. No sign of Malachy. Watch out.

Had the Irishman overheard Charlotte and Gus? They can't be sure.

Howard drives up the long ramp leading to the street, passing a row of town cars and limos parked in reserved spots alongside the Château. As they reach the top, they pass Malachy and Charlotte. He's holding the door of the limo open as she climbs in. Gus slumps low in her seat. Malachy closes the door behind Charlotte, walks to the driver's side of the limo, and glances at the passing Honda. Howard checks his rearview mirror.

Malachy looks in their direction as the Honda merges into traffic on Wellington.

Howard loses sight of the chauffeur and focuses on the road ahead.

❧

Later that evening, Howard and Gus take a long walk with Levi. They make their way over the Flora Footbridge, along Colonel By Drive, crossing back on the Corktown Footbridge. They come full circle back to the Glebe, talking the whole way. Gus plays Howard the recording of Charlotte. The curse, the poison, Eva, the fire, and Charlotte's desire to chop down the family tree. All of it Howard finds bizarre and unexpected and fascinating.

As they walk side by side, Gus realizes she doesn't want to do this alone. She can't anymore. And even though her head tells her to tread carefully, she knows she needs Howard's help to bring down the Mutchmores. He's a journalist. He knows how to track down leads and interview sources, and when the time comes, he can make sure the story gets out there. Her head is in a tug-of-war with her heart and gut. Both are telling her he's a good guy.

She stops walking. Howard looks at her. Levi looks at her. Then she decides to go for it. Gus shares everything she's thinking and feeling about the Mutchmores, and about Howard.

Howard listens until she's done. Then without hesitating, he tells her he's all in. He always is. And true to form, the kid inside him is bubbling over with silly energy, while the weird old man inside him is minding his manners. Reassuring Gus that he has no evil ulterior motive, unless winning the Pulitzer qualifies. She laughs. Gus watches as Howard babbles away, far too loudly, his gangly frame bouncing along the path. She admires how light he is. How he seems to fit in the world even though he's an odd duck. Howard is who he says he is. She likes that most about him. No bullshit. No mask. She trusts him. This sudden realization floods her with unfamiliar warmth. As they approach the edge of the park near the Ambassador, she knows this is a rare feeling for her. To trust in someone. To let go.

It's just gone 8 P.M. The sun is low and orange. It's mid-June and the days are long. Levi gets sidetracked by a broken branch. He lies down with it. He wants to have a chew and he won't budge. Gus suggests they sit a moment on a bench by the pond. She's tired. The pineapple is prodding her ribs. Demanding her attention, her body, her resources, her focus. As thirty weeks become forty, she's going to need Howard's brain power. She looks at Howard playing tug-of-war with Levi. In that moment, she can imagine something more. The shape of it dances in the glow of the golden hour, vague and slightly magical.

She closes her eyes and red shadows meander across her eyelids.

Her mother's hand lightly caresses her hair.

Honey Pie, Shannon whispers softly in Gus's ear.

24

Dr. Braddish Billings

THE FOLLOWING DAY, GUS AND HOWARD GET TO WORK. THEY meet for lunch at one of the cool restaurants on Howard's *best of* list. He seems to have found a favorite place to eat in every neighborhood. This one is Lexington Smokehouse in Westboro. It's well away from the Glebe and hopefully the Mutchmores. It has tall booths for maximum privacy, and they serve the best barbecue jackfruit in the city, according to Howard. Gus has never heard of jackfruit. As Howard wipes off his cutlery, he tells her that Buddhist monks used to dye their robes with the orange-reddish extract from jackfruit wood chips. She rolls her eyes at Howard's encyclopedic brain.

She wonders to herself if a jackfruit is as big as a pineapple.

Over lunch, they review the photos on her phone, listen to the recording of Charlotte again, and then they brainstorm next steps. Gus pulls out her notebook.

"Okay, we know there was a fire in 1900. We know Robert Mutchmore made a deal with the devil around that time. Babies were the currency. We also know his son Felix was born that year. The one who died in the war in 1916. We also know years later his daughter, Eva, had a baby boy she gave up for adoption," says Gus.

"But how does the deal with the devil connect to Robert's children, Felix, Eva, and Wilfred? Or does it?" says Howard.

"Exactly. We think Eva's baby is Leo. And that's why she sabotaged Poppy's elopement and got rid of Leo. But we still don't know what happened that night by the pond, where Leo is, or who's in the pond—or for that matter, where they've put Poppy," says Gus.

"Or why Charlotte called the bones an omen," says Howard.

"Or if bones have anything to do with the fire," she adds, tossing her pen. "We know fuck all, Howard."

"That much we do know," he laughs.

They both bite into their sandwiches. Turns out jackfruit tastes a lot like pulled pork when it's smothered in barbecue sauce.

"You know who doesn't know fuck all?" he says, cheeks full of food.

Gus shrugs and chews.

"That historian guy. The one who was sitting at our table at the gala. I've seen him around. He's at all the Mutchmore shindigs. If anyone knows about that family it's—"

Gus cuts him off.

"Boring Braddish!" she exclaims, spitting jackfruit. "Why didn't I think of that?"

And from there, inside the privacy of their booth, a plan comes together. They order dessert as they fine-tune the way forward. Gus gets the chocolate peanut butter cheesecake. Howard gets the vegan version made with cashew butter.

And of course, Howard knows all about the cheesecakes. Just like the forget-me-nots and the Lucky Pennys and the jackfruit. Howard knows that the young woman serving them is named Susie and that the cheesecakes are made special order by her aunt Noreen, who started out baking them for family, but as word spread about her sweet creations, a homegrown business was born. Now Aunt Noreen supplies restaurants all across the city, still baking them from scratch in her home kitchen.

Gus realizes that what fascinates Howard are not things, but people and the stories they hold. She can relate. It's why she's drawn to the past. That's where the stories of people she once knew still live. For Howard those stories seem to ground him in the real world. Connect him to whatever he's doing or eating or seeing. For Gus, they do the opposite. They take her away.

They finish their cheesecakes and their plan.

Divide and conquer.

Gus is going to track down Braddish Billings to follow up on Charlotte's lead. See what he knows about the family's connection to the historic fire. Meanwhile, Howard's assignment is to find out what the Mutchmores have done with Poppy. Howard knows a guy in the records room at the Royal Ottawa Mental Health Centre. Even if they got power of attorney, the Mutchmores would still have to submit a psych evaluation, real or doctored, to have Poppy committed. All such records from across the region land in the Royal Ottawa database, no matter where the patient ends up. And the guy owes Howard a favor.

Howard drives Gus back to the Glebe. They park in front of the Ambassador and agree to get together first thing the next morning to report what they've learned. It feels like the most natural thing in the world to lean over and kiss Howard. She lingers, her lips on his. He returns her kiss. She squeezes his hand, then gets out of the Honda and waves as he pulls away from the curb.

Maybe if they hadn't kissed, she would have noticed the

limo parked across the street. Maybe if Howard hadn't been distracted by her unexpected show of affection, he would have heard the engine turn over or caught sight of the limo pulling into traffic a few cars behind him. But when a feeling is beginning to grow between two people, it can quicken the pulse and tingle the skin and block the senses. She didn't see and he didn't hear.

Gus goes up to her apartment. She gets the scoop from Siri. Braddish is a history professor at Carleton University. She browses the course calendar and discovers that he's teaching a first-year history course in Southam Hall from 1 to 4 P.M. today. Gus catches a bus to the campus, buys the book she needs at the university bookstore, then waits for the students to file out of the lecture hall at 4. She enters the large hall. It's a theater space. He's alone on a stage at the bottom of a series of tiered rows of fixed chairs, each attached to its own folding tray. He's standing behind a large table, gathering his laptop and papers. She's done her homework and has her prop in hand.

"Excuse me. Are you Braddish Billings?" she calls out, descending the lecture hall steps.

"Doctor," he says, without looking up.

"Wow, this is such a thrill. Could you autograph my book, Dr. Billings?" she says, holding up a copy of his book, *The Life and Legacy of Robert Mutchmore*.

Braddish looks up, but not at her. His eyes are on his book. He refuses her pen. He has a better one.

"Name?" he asks, pressing the pen to the title page.

"Shannon," she says. It's the first name that comes to her.

She tells him she's a freshman. A history major. She drops a couple of his colleagues' names and mentions some courses she's taking. Blah, blah, bullshit from course descriptions on the university's website. She tells him she can't wait to take his course in third year. He's practically famous and such an expert on Canadian history. Especially as it relates to the founding families of the nation's capital, like the Mutchmores. She tells him she's doing a paper on the great Ottawa fire of 1900, and she thought maybe she could pick his brain.

As icing on the cake, she adds, "It would be an honor if you could share your insights."

His ego sufficiently fluffed, Braddish sits on the edge of his lecture table and launches into a lengthy yawn-fest about his connection to the Mutchmores and how he came to be their official biographer. She finally gets him to focus on the fire. He looks anywhere but at her. As if he can't be bothered connecting with a lowly first-year student. As if she's not important enough to have her presence fully acknowledged.

He tells her about the fire. It happened on April 26, 1900. Gus takes notes, only interrupting to ask a question or two when he strays too far from the Mutchmores, which isn't often. He seems obsessed with the family, dropping hints along the way that he's more than a historian to them. He's a trusted friend.

Braddish's story is less about homes and lives ruined and more about the financial cost to some of Ottawa's wealthiest business owners. Apparently, his view of history is seen through a highbrow lens. Lumber magnate J. R. Booth was hardest hit, losing over a million dollars in lumber piles and stables. No mention of the people who died. The Mutchmores fared better, he tells her. They were well insured and quickly began designing new plans for an improved housing development on the LeBreton site. Plans that were eventually abandoned as city planners and land developers squabbled for years over zoning bylaws. He muses that much of that land remains undeveloped to this day.

He defends Robert Mutchmore due to his considerable

youth. Robert was newly married, had only recently inherited his father's holdings. He did his best. And over time, he became a leader and a role model in the community. It's not as though the Mutchmores abandoned their tenants, Braddish tells her. In fact, they rolled up their sleeves. The couple founded a relief committee and volunteered their time in the encampments, helping the sick, dishing out food to thousands left homeless. They weren't afraid to get their hands dirty.

Gus wonders if Braddish equates poverty with dirt.

The couple also donated large sums of money to the poor. The local newspaper published a list of every single donor to the relief efforts, from twenty-five cents to ten thousand dollars. Robert and Cora Mutchmore topped the list, having donated more than even the local banks and government. Their efforts saw millions of dollars raised in that first year alone. Businesses, churches, courthouses, a post office, banks, hotels, mills were all rebuilt with that money.

"This was the most significant time period in young Robert's life, a time when the seed of benevolence was planted in his heart. The tragedies he witnessed in 1900 led him to his true purpose. To serve. His eldest son was born the year of that fire, and I believe that also shaped the man he was to become. When Felix died in the war, Robert's altruistic path was carried forth when he created a foundation in his son's name. And, as they say, the rest is history. The Mutchmore family legacy was forged in that fire," he says.

Gus is struck by these words. The very words Charlotte used. Only in her story it was sin that was forged in the great fire. Perhaps sin is the legacy.

Gus wonders if Braddish knows more than he's saying. He has spent his career studying this family. Talking to them, writing about them, watching them. Establishing himself as the preeminent Mutchmore biographer. He must know some of their secrets. But as he goes on, painting an almost superhuman portrait of his hero, Robert, Gus realizes that Braddish is so invested in the Mutchmore myth, even if he knew their darkest secrets, divulging them would only bring his life's work into question. His opus cannot risk being tarnished. It's all he has. The fact that Braddish has bothered to spend a half hour talking to some student tells her as much.

It's possible he knows nothing. That he's in the dark as much as she is. They've used him to tell the story they want out there. A carefully curated tale of heroism and altruism. It's probably earned them a whack of goodwill, and cash, and influence, and a Medal of Bravery.

Gus tries a different approach. She starts with a little prod.

"What can you tell me about his daughter, Eva? I heard she gave up a baby for adoption, right? A son? When she was just a teenager? Must have been quite the scandal"—she looks down at her notes as if it's written there—"for the foundation and all."

Braddish seems to have momentarily lost his ability to speak, incredibly. Gus looks up. He's looking at her, as if seeing her for the first time. His eyes flit to her pregnant belly. A tiny glimmer of recognition ignites his dark pupils.

"Have we met?" he asks.

Gus shrugs, wondering if he remembers her from the gala.

He lets it go, regains his composure, and pivots to indignation.

"Downstairs gossip, nothing more," he huffs. "When you reach the heights of the Mutchmores, you inevitably have a few rats in the kitchen, spreading filth. But I assure you there was no scandal," he says, as if she's just spit in his face.

Clearly, Gus has struck a nerve. Before she can get a word out, he continues his rant.

"The Mutchmores raised their children to be upstanding

citizens with a proper sense of right and wrong. They had private tutors, a nanny, the best schooling. There were no unwanted babies. Ridiculous. I'll have you know, the Mutchmores were beyond charitable. They even took on their nanny's son as a houseboy, showing their children that everyone deserves a fair shake. Generous to a fault. Cora always gave full credit for their refined manners to the children's nanny, Mrs. Trichborne."

Gus makes a note. That name rings a loud bell, but she's got to stay tuned in to the task at hand while Braddish is still talking to her. She'll figure the name out later.

Time to up the voltage.

"So Robert and his wife liked to help people. Did that include helping people get babies?" she asks, hoping this not-so-subtle jolt lights him up.

It works.

"I don't know what you're implying, young lady. Are you talking about Cora's involvement with the Benevolent Association's orphanage?" he asks.

"I heard the Mutchmores were selling babies or something," she says.

Braddish stares at her. He's lost for words, and from the look on his face, it's clear he knows nothing.

His left eye twitches with recognition.

"We have met," he says, his tone icy.

"Oh I'd remember if we had," she says, forcing a smile.

Just then, the door at the top of the lecture hall moans on its hinges. Someone has come in. Gus looks up. Despite the distance separating them, Gus recognizes the woman standing at the top of the theater.

Shit.

It's Blondie. Beatrice Billings. Ricker's receptionist. When she'd noticed her nameplate at the foundation, Gus had assumed they were related, but this confirms it.

Gus turns to face Braddish, her back to Beatrice. Gus can't let her see her face.

"I'll be right with you, Bea," he calls.

"I've made you late. I'll go," Gus says, hurriedly shaking his hand as she scans for alternate exits.

She spots one in the wings of the stage.

She can hear the woman's footfalls descending the steps.

"I've been waiting for thirty minutes outside, brother," Beatrice snaps.

Gus heads for the exit, in the opposite direction of Beatrice.

"Yes, yes, don't fuss. I've been counseling a rather ill-informed student," he says.

Then Braddish calls out to Gus, "Miss? Oh miss? You forgot your book."

Gus pauses. She turns to see Braddish holding out the signed biography of Robert Mutchmore. Beatrice is next to him, looking at her.

Double shit.

Gus spins on her heel and walks out the exit door.

25

Rabbit

BACK AT THE AMBASSADOR, GUS GRABS HER MAIL ON THE way in. She wolfs down a frozen dinner of beef Stroganoff, then downs the bottle of green juice she bought on her way home. While leafing through junk mail and overdue bills, one piece catches her eye. It's the results from the DNA testing company where she sent Leo's hair. She'd completely forgotten about it. Gus rips open the envelope.

The truth is starting to show itself.

Or has it already been on display and she just didn't see it?

She tucks the DNA results away. For now, she'll keep them to herself. She needs to know the whole story before revealing what she's learned.

Gus examines the images on her phone as she follows a train of thought. She flips through the ones of the Mutchmore family album. There's a particular photo that interests her most. She finds it. It's a photo of Robert and Cora Mutchmore. She zooms in. It's dated 1921. The couple is standing with their two children, Eva and Wilfred. The help are lined up behind the family.

For the first time, she looks closely at the staff. She hadn't really taken them in before. She'd been so focused on the Mutchmores. There are ten staff. Four men, six women. One of the men has a familiar face. He's about twenty. She flips through her other photos and spots the same face. It appears in the 1953 newspaper story about The Trichborne Group. In the article, he's older, but it's Teddy Trichborne. Same thin frame. Unmistakable dark eyebrows, long nose, and square jaw. The man standing behind the Mutchmores is a younger Teddy. There he is, one of their staff. And then thirty-some years later, he's standing in front of his own staff, now the head of a company. Light-years from where he began.

That's why the Trichborne name sounded familiar when Braddish mentioned the nanny. Poppy had said the name once too, and it was right there on the caption of the newspaper article from 1953. No wonder it rang a bell. Braddish said the nanny had a son who the Mutchmores took on as a houseboy. Teddy's that son. Gus examines the faces of the female staff members. It's hard to tell which one is Teddy's mother. She's guessing it's the one standing closest to the children. Right behind little Eva and Wilfred. That's where they'd place the nanny.

Poppy said Teddy was a family friend of her mother's. He was the one who introduced Leo and Poppy. This must be how Eva and Teddy first became friends. When Teddy worked for Eva's parents, the Mutchmores. Then years later, Teddy had a business of his own and hired Leo.

A theory based on bits and pieces begins to take shape in Gus's brain. It's murky, so she lets it ruminate. She's eager to go over everything with Howard. Bounce her theory off him to see if it sticks. But she decides against calling or texting him tonight. They just saw each other earlier at lunch and what with the kiss and all, she doesn't want him to get the wrong idea. That kiss probably threw him. She'll see him first thing tomorrow as planned.

But all evening her mind stays with Howard. With their kiss. Seems it threw her too. She replays the moment. Her hand touching his. The warmth of his breath. The whole thing was unexpected, just like Howard. He's not her type at all. And yet, there's something about him that tugs at her heart. He's sweet and has impeccable manners. And he's a good kisser. Lost in thought, Gus's body warms as she imagines what it would be like to do more than just kiss Howard.

A hot flash suddenly coats her in sweat. Her Howard fantasy dissolves as her hormones take control. Her skin hot, her mind restless, her belly feeling larger than it did just moments earlier, Gus decides to take Levi outside for a pee before bed, mostly so she can cool down.

Gus pulls on her running shoes and a jean jacket. Levi instantly perks up as she grabs his leash. Then a noise stops them both. The floor in the hall groans as if someone is standing just outside the door. Levi sniffs the threshold. Gus leans close and looks through the peephole. A shadow moves across the far wall. Gus gasps and jumps back. She wasn't really expecting anyone to be out there.

Fuck this.

She grabs the gun from her satchel and heads for the door. She releases the chain, turns the lock, and opens the door, gun raised. Levi and Gus both peer down the hall, one way then the other. The stairwell door moves slightly. Levi bolts for the door. Gus races after him. They burst into the stairwell. She hears something below, leaps down the steps two by two, but when she reaches the bottom, the dark stairwell is empty. Except for one thing. There's a small bundle of cloth on the bottom step. She picks it up and unrolls it. Inside she finds a couple of large sewing needles, some rough twine, a knife, a roll of gauze, and some cotton balls. A makeshift first-aid kit. She rolls it back up and leaves it in the corner behind the stairs, realizing it probably belongs to the homeless person who hangs out there. Maybe that's who was lingering in the halls, meaning no harm.

Levi catches up, making it to the bottom, panting, tail wagging. She picks up his leash, tucks the gun in the pocket of her jean jacket, and the two of them head outside. They're at the back of the building next to the park entrance. A streetlight sends a beam across the dumpsters. She looks toward the park. A figure limps across the bridge, momentarily passing through the light of a lamp, then disappearing into darkness.

Gus and Levi enter the park. They cross over the bridge. There's no one around. They loop the park, pass a couple out for a night run, but no one else.

No Malachy. No Taggart. No Mutchmore.

Her hormones are playing tricks on her.

Gus looks up at the silhouette of the Ambassador looming in the clear night sky. A half moon hovers over its shoulder. Maybe it was a ghost. The ghost that haunted Eva. The building's definitely creepy. It's a hundred years old, so of course its lights flicker and its old bones groan from time to time. Gus now wonders if she even saw a shadow. She can't believe she's out chasing ghosts. Clearly, she needs sleep. They head back to the apartment once Levi's done his business.

Upon their return, they find a gruesome gift sitting outside their door. Brown with a white tail. A dead rabbit that someone's tried to clean up and stitch back to normal. As normal as Frankensteinian roadkill can be. This time she manages to keep Levi away from the carcass. She chucks it down the garbage chute and quickly goes inside, locking her door. If this is another dispatch from the Mutchmores, then they must already know she's back on the scent. Maybe Charlotte confessed to their secret meeting. Maybe Malachy did hear them talking at the pool. Maybe Beatrice called Ricker the second she saw Gus.

Or maybe this is something else, from someone else.

Gus barely sleeps, one ear listening for intruders, one eye on the alert for ghosts.

Morning brings with it bright sunshine and an ominous, uneasy feeling. Even Levi seems restless. He sniffs near the door where the scent of dead rabbit lingers. Gus showers, brews coffee, feeds the dog, then pours herself a bowl of Honeycomb. She pours a second bowl and heads down to the bottom of the stairwell, where she leaves it next to the first-aid kit she found last night.

By eleven, Howard hasn't shown.

He's not answering her texts.

Gus tries not to worry. Maybe his car broke down or he got sidetracked at work.

She putters, changes the sheets on her bed, does the dishes, makes a grocery list, stares out the window, and checks to see if her phone's volume is on for the fifth time.

Nothing can stop the sense of foreboding that she woke with from festering into full-blown panic.

Something has happened to Howard.

She waits until noon. Morning ticks over and he's a no-show. She hasn't known Howard long, but she does know this is not like him. He's too polite. He'd never blow her off or forget their plans. Then Gus realizes how little she really knows about him.

She has no idea where Howard lives.

She looks up the contact info for the offices of the *Kitchissippi Times*. Calls and asks for Howard. A woman tells her he's not in. Gus asks for his home address. The woman says they don't give out that kind of information. Gus hangs up.

She writes down the paper's address. The offices are in City Centre, an industrial retail space and office tower at the edge of Hintonburg. Gus knows it well. She lived just a few blocks away with her mother years ago.

Back then, City Centre was a rundown row of warehouse bays, half of them abandoned. But as she walks toward the tower, past the curved warehouse, she marvels at the place. It's transformed. There's a hipster café in one of the bays with a big patio out front, a microbrewery in another, a dance studio, an art gallery, paid parking. Like the surrounding neighborhood, it's been dusted off, repaved, and reimagined for some cool, young crowd who likes oat milk lattes and avocado toast and truffle oil on their pizza.

Gus doesn't get it. But then, she's not cool. Never has been.

She has a sudden longing for the City Centre of her childhood. The concrete eyesore where half the bays were either empty or occupied by strange businesses with no signs on their doors other than KEEP OUT or PRIVATE or NO TRESPASSING. People came and went, sometimes pulling suitcases on wheels, or they hung around outside smoking. There was a mystery and a danger to the place back then. Her mom told her not to play around there, but she'd ride her bike through the concrete underpass leading from the bike path into the belly of City Centre. The underpass smelled of urine and oil. People sometimes slept there under tarp tents or inside cardboard boxes the size of fridges. She'd collect discarded bottles behind the warehouse, returning them for pocket change to the 7-Eleven. She'd buy jawbreakers or sponge toffee that she'd hide in her room, since her mother said they'd rot her teeth.

Gus enters the office tower and takes the elevator to the fifth floor. Up to the suite shared by several local papers. The door's propped open. There's no reception. Just a bunch of desks and a few people hunched over computer keyboards. A woman is wiping off a whiteboard in the far corner. Gus is wearing the tight leggings and T-shirt she purposely chose for maximum impact. Her belly is impossible to miss, but no one seems to notice her walk in. She recognizes a guy sitting nearby. He's the photographer from the GG's garden party. She approaches him. He looks up, glancing at her belly. His face brightens as if he recognizes her.

"I'm looking for Howard Baylis," she says.

He sits back in his chair.

"You and me both," he says. "We've got an assignment and he's not answering his cell."

"I need his home address," she says, not interested in small talk.

"I'm afraid I can't—" he starts, but she cuts him off.

"I need to talk to him. It's important," she says, making a show of touching her belly.

The photographer's mouth drops open. He seems momentarily lost for words.

"Oh," he says.

"It's personal," she adds.

He looks around.

"I'm sorry. It's policy. Can't have nutjobs coming after . . . I mean people. I didn't mean you were a nutjob," he stammers.

Gus decides the only thing to do is cry. Turns out to be quite easy these days.

He flushes red and holds out a box of tissues.

Gus takes one and wipes her tears, then blows her nose, loudly. Other people in the office are now looking over at them and muttering. The photographer wants her gone.

"I guess I could make an exception," he says, grabbing a green Post-it.

Gus has discovered that most people have visceral reactions to a pregnant belly. Curiosity, sympathy, discomfort, envy—

there's always a strong reaction. And that reaction usually throws them off balance just enough to get the results she wants.

The photographer hands her the Post-it note with Howard's address.

"Tell him Andy says he should charge his frickin' cell phone," the photographer says.

Gus can't make out what's being said, but as the elevator doors close she can hear the murmur of gossip coming from the fifth-floor suite, likely Andy telling anyone within earshot about Howard and his baby mama. She'll have to apologize to Howard when she finds him.

If she finds him.

A lump forms in her throat as she sits in the back seat of an Uber on her way to the Ossington address in Old Ottawa South. She texts him again. Nothing. She asks the driver to wait out front. It's a huge three-story brick house with a two-level wood veranda attached to the front. Gus wonders if Howard is staying with a relative. An aunt or uncle. He once told her his parents owned a winery in Prince Edward County near Picton, so this can't be their house. There's no Honda in the driveway. She knocks on the front door. Then rings the bell. She can hear its chimes ringing inside.

Is this Howard's house?

No one answers. She signals to the Uber driver, asking him to wait, then she goes around back. There's a flower garden along the back fence, a garage and tool shed, a hammock on a stand, a tidy back patio, a series of recycling and garbage bins arranged neatly alongside the house, but no sign of Howard. Gus peeks into the small window of the garage. No car in there either. She tries to control her rising panic.

"You won't find anyone home," someone calls out. Gus jumps. She turns and spots the neighbor out sweeping her back porch.

"He's gone to see his folks, I expect," says the woman, mid-seventies, round face, smiling eyes.

Gus nods to the woman.

"Why do you say that? Did Howard say something to you?" she asks, hopeful this is true and Andy's right. Howard simply forgot to charge his phone.

"No. But he didn't come home last night. And I know he doesn't have a girl. Howard always brings in my bins after the garbage collectors have come, but they were still out there, so I had to bring them in myself. He hadn't even put his own out. I expect he's gone down to visit his Mum and Dad," she says. "He's a good lad. But he should've let me know just the same."

"Thank you," says Gus, trying to stop tears from bursting from her eyes.

"Shall I tell him who came by?" she asks, obviously curious.

"No thanks," says Gus, rushing off.

"It's no trouble," the woman calls out, a little too eagerly.

As the Uber driver takes her back across town, everything blurs past in a kaleidoscope of flashing lights and teeming sidewalks. She can see her own face in the reflections of store windows. She feels sick and wants to stop the car, but suddenly they're back at the Ambassador.

Gus is desperate to be alone, but even more desperate not to be. As she climbs the stairwell to the third floor, she feels like she might throw up. She should have told his coworkers he was missing. She'll call the police. And tell them what? A man she barely knows didn't show up for a meeting and isn't answering his phone?

Where are you, Howard?

Gus enters the hallway leading to her apartment and there he is.

Crumpled in a heap against her door.

"Howard!" she screams, her heart leaping to her throat.

Howard looks up. Through one eye. The other is swollen shut. His face is mincemeat. He's been beaten black-and-blue. Gus falls to her knees in front of him and gently cups his battered face in her hands.

"Oh, Howard," she cries.

"Sorry I'm late," he says through split lips.

He smiles weakly.

It's not until Gus has cleaned and dressed his wounds, tucked him into her bed, and brought him a handful of Tylenol and a bag of ice wrapped in a dish towel for his eye that he tells her what happened.

Last night he went to the Royal Ottawa. He'd just seen his buddy in records and was heading back to his car in the underground parking garage when he was jumped from behind. He fell to the concrete. It was dark, so he didn't see their faces, but there were two of them. They laid into him with boots until he blacked out. One of them spoke with an Irish accent so he's pretty sure he knows who it was.

Malachy and Taggart.

Howard came to hours later, not sure what day it was or where he was. They'd put him in the trunk of his Honda with his smashed phone. He kicked his way through the back seats since his old car didn't have a release lever inside the trunk. He saw that he was still parked in the underground garage, so he drove himself right to her place, knowing she'd be worried. He'd buzzed her apartment but when she didn't answer, he'd gone around back and snuck in the fire exit, which he'd found propped open by a brick.

Howard admits the chauffeur got a good look at his license plate as they left the Château the other day. He didn't want to worry her. He figures they were tailing him. Gus recalls their kiss outside the Ambassador. Were they watching

then? Is that when they followed Howard? Is this her fault?
She should have been more careful.

Levi comes into the bedroom. Ever since they staggered
into the apartment, the dog's kept his distance, as if he's not
sure what's happened to Howard or doesn't recognize his distorted face. Levi ambles into the room but doesn't jump up on
the bed. His nostrils are doing overtime. Sniffing the mix of
blood and antiseptic in the air. He rests his chin on the duvet
and stares at Howard.

"It's Howard, you old fool," she says to Levi.

Levi bats his eyes but doesn't move any closer.

Gus sits on the bed and tells Howard about her meeting
with Braddish.

"Sounds like the Mutchmores haven't exactly handed him
the keys to the family's secrets," says Howard, then coughs
and holds his ribs.

"You sure you don't need a doctor?" she asks.

"You can't put a cast on broken ribs," he says, wheezing
slightly. "I'll be fine."

"I'm so sorry," she says.

"Don't be. I should've had my head up," he tells her. "I
was distracted by what I'd found out."

"Did you find out where they've taken Poppy?"

"Nope. They must have done it on the hush-hush. Zero
paper trail. My guy in records couldn't even find a physician's
report or a psych eval. Not even a Certificate of Involuntary
Admission, which they have to file with the Consent and Capacity Board to have her committed. She's not in the system."
He adds, "They're good."

"But what does all that mean?" she asks.

"It means the Mutchmores found a private facility willing
to bend the rules," he says.

"So we're back to square one," sighs Gus, her heart sinking.

"Not exactly," he smiles, pausing like he's waiting for a drumroll.

Gus raises an eyebrow.

"We did find something really interesting. We came across some archived records dating back a few decades, and guess whose name was all over them?" he says with a lopsided grin.

Gus can't help but smile back. He looks ridiculous.

"Eva Honeywell," he beams, proud of his big reveal.

"Poppy's mother, Eva?" asks Gus, wide-eyed.

"Yup. There's a record of her being committed in December 1953. She was being treated by this Doctor Brine dude in Brockville. His notes are all there. He goes into how she was super agitated and delusional when she first arrived. She said she was seeing ghosts. Specifically, the ghost of her dead son. She's described as barely functioning. Totally psychotic. Brine put her on meds, and the delusions got even more elaborate. Then Eva started to say that her son's death was the fault of one person. A guy she called Pug. At one point, she confessed to murdering Pug as revenge for what he'd done to her son. She said no one would ever find the body because she'd hidden it in Australia, and all the secrets were hidden along with him. Brine had even looked into it and found out that Eva had never left the country. She never even had a passport. He concluded that her delusions were likely incurable, and Pug was an imaginary villain she'd invented to help her cope with whatever plagued her. He recommended she remain in their care for the rest of her life."

Gus stares at Howard.

He's breathless from going over his findings. Gus tells him about the DNA results that arrived in the mail.

"So it all lines up. And if the son wasn't a delusion, maybe the rest of it's true, and that's the big secret the Mutchmores want buried. Eva killed someone."

"Teddy Trichborne," says Gus.

"Who?" he asks.

"Pug. That was Eva's nickname for her friend Teddy Trichborne. He worked for the Mutchmores when Eva was young. Years later, he introduced Leo and Poppy. I think you're right, Howard. She was telling the truth. Eva killed Teddy Trichborne," Gus says, then she remembers something. "She said as much."

Gus reaches under the mattress and pulls out Eva's diary. She flips to the final entry.

"The dark hood knows what I have done. Who I discarded, who I deceived, who I killed." She looks up.

"Pug," says Howard.

"We're on to something, Howard," she says, taking his hand in hers.

"Where are the records? Did you make copies?" she asks.

He looks at her and she knows. The copies were taken by Malachy and Taggart, and likely they've already got their hands on the originals.

Gus remembers something Charlotte said.

There are worse things than murder.

They sit quietly together awhile. They mull the evidence. Ponder next steps. Both knowing they can't stop now.

Levi whines and circles the bed. He nudges Gus with his warm nose.

"I should take him for a walk while it's still light out," she says.

"I'll come with." He tries to get up, but his sore ribs force him to stay put.

"I've got my pepper spray," she says, when what she really means is she's got her gun.

"Keep your head up," he says.

She nods.

"Give you a chance to get some rest. Plus it's been a couple of days since I checked the honey locusts," she says.

"Is that code for something?" he asks.

Gus smiles.

"Trees in the park where I found a note once. I check them every so often, just in case."

∞

The next day, Gus gets a terse call from Doctor Chandra's receptionist. She wants to know if Gus is coming to her appointment today. If not, they're going to remove her from their patient list to make room for someone who actually shows up. Gus doesn't like the idea of being removed. Set adrift to do this pregnancy thing on her own. Howard assures her he'll be fine alone, so she decides to go.

The waiting room at the small Glebe health clinic on Third Avenue is packed with pregnant women of all shapes and sizes. Some bellies hang low, others high and wide. Gus feels like she doesn't belong in their glowing midst. She's the only mother-to-be who is not wearing official maternity wear. The only one in black. The others are all in bright yellows or pinks or florals with kangaroo pouches in their slacks that lovingly hug their unborn babies. Gus wears skin-tight leggings with the waistband tucked uncomfortably under her belly and a tight T-shirt, the largest one she owns.

Doctor Chandra is surprised to see Gus. It's been four months since she last saw her, and Gus is due in just over two. At least the doctor remembers her.

"Better late term than never," says Chandra with a shrug.

The doctor gets down to business. She feels Gus's belly and confirms that the baby is in the right position. When Gus looks at her blankly, she says, *Head down.* The doctor checks her feet for swelling, asks how she's been feeling, and listens to the baby's heartbeat. It's strong. She lets Gus listen too. The rapid chugging reminds her of a tiny locomotive engine.

"It won't be long now before you two meet," smiles Chandra as she types a few notes on her laptop.

The reality of the doctor's words hits Gus hard. She's become so used to having the pineapple along for the ride, she almost forgot it is going to be an actual baby one day.

They won't always be one.

Of course they won't.

They will be two.

Gus barely hears the rest of Doctor Chandra's advice about what to expect when she goes into labor and how to reach her. Only fragments of her words penetrate Gus's faraway mind.

All she can think about is the little train heading toward its destination at rapid speed.

26

Belleville

THROUGH THE SCORCHING HEAT OF JULY AND INTO AUGUST, Gus and Howard continue their investigation, carefully and quietly digging. Howard begins to heal, gets a new phone, takes a leave of absence from work. The pineapple becomes a watermelon.

And then one day, unexpectedly, after two months of checking the honey locusts on her daily walks with Levi, Gus finds another pink can perched in the branches.

The note inside is short and to the point.

> *They've locked her up and I know how to get her out.*
> *Hampshire Care Home in Belleville.*
> *Meet us across the street in Corby Park.*
> *2 pm, August 15.*
> *Bring a getaway car.*
>
>   *—Mojo*

They leave for Belleville early Sunday morning. August 15. The drive is a little over two and a half hours from

Ottawa. It's good to be on the road again. Out of the city. The summer breeze is thick with sweet milkweed. Driving south on the 416, Levi has his nose out the back window. Gus is reminded of the road trips she and the dog took three years earlier, tracking the scent of another cold case. Back then it was just the two of them driving along the highway as strobes of sunlight bounced off the windshield of her great-grandmother's Buick. Past the groves of white spruce that slowly gave way to a patchwork of rolling cornfields.

Today, they're in Howard's Honda. The Buick took its last gasp a year ago, and she sold it for scrap. They're passing those same green stalks topped with golden tassels. But the view feels different. More expansive. Sort of like her belly. Everything looks sharper and brighter. She can almost see the corn growing. Maybe it's because Howard is with them. Maybe it's because he's driving, and this time Gus can look around or at least look more closely at what she missed before, when her mind was full of thoughts of her mother's death. Today, her mind is also full, but it's lighter. The heaviness of that dark August is slowly lifting with time.

Before hitting the highway, they stopped for gas. Gus went into the gas station convenience store for a quick bathroom break and to stock up on snacks while Howard filled the tank. It gave her a chance to make sure the gun was easily accessible inside her satchel. She wasn't going anywhere without it these days.

She bought water, two bags of chips, a six-pack of chocolate bars, and string cheese.

The watermelon was always hungry these days.

She also bought a map of Eastern Ontario. They both have mapping apps on their phones, but she's always been more comfortable with the real thing. Howard goes with it.

Gus folds the map open to their route and now it rests on

top of the watermelon. She runs her finger over it when they pass an exit to a town, when they cross the Rideau River and when they merge onto the 401. The map grounds her. Almost as if her finger is guiding them safely toward their destination.

All they have are a day, time, and place written on a cryptic note. They assume they'll be meeting Mojo and Poppy. Corby Park at 2 P.M. They looked it up. It's a public rose garden in the old east village section of Belleville across from the home. Gus isn't surprised the M&Ms have shipped Poppy off to another city. And Howard was right, Hampshire Care Home is private. According to their website, it's an exclusive facility catering to a select group of discerning seniors who need complex care. *Whatever the fuck that means.* The website goes on and on about their secure, fully escorted, upscale services. Translation: you need money to get in, but you can't get out.

"Sounds like the Hotel California," says Gus.

Howard laughs. It's good to see him laugh without it hurting. His ribs are on the mend, his bruises have shifted from purple to yellow, and his left eye has resurfaced as the swelling retreated and the broken flesh healed.

The last two months, they've gotten closer. She'd been surprised by how she'd felt when she thought something horrible had happened to him. As the grip on her heart eased, as Howard got stronger and healthier, she realized her feelings for him were deepening with each passing day.

They arrive early to scout the park from the car, circling it twice. It runs the length of a city block, boxed in by heritage homes to the north and south, and open at two ends, east and west. There's a rose-shaped fountain in the center of the park, framed by benches and lampposts. Rose beds are spread in assorted shapes across the lawns. A wrought-iron fence surrounds the park, and pathways weave toward gates that lead out to two streets. On the east side is Ann Street, where Hampshire Care Home sits across the road. On the west side is William Street, where nineteenth-century homes sit along a residential avenue lined with maples and oaks. They park on William in the shade of a large oak with a view across the rose garden toward the home. They roll the windows down and munch on chips and wait.

Levi wakes. Gus puts on his leash and lets him out for a pee on the grassy median by the sidewalk. He wants to bolt through the open gate of the garden, but she holds him tight. He pees, jumps back in, and rests his chin between their seats. She doesn't bother to remove the leash. Gus gives him a chip. She pours water into her palm, lets him lap it up, then the old dog rolls onto his back and closes his eyes. Howard leans over the seat and rubs his belly until he falls asleep.

Their plan is thin at best. Howard will keep watch and be on the ready with the car running. Gus will grab Poppy and Mojo as soon as they show. The rest is a crapshoot. May and Ricker might be close. Mojo might not be able to get Poppy to the park. Poppy might be too sick to manage a quick getaway. The whole thing might be a wild goose chase or a trap. The possibilities bounce around her brain. Gus stares out the window, biting her fingernails. Howard gently touches her hand. She jumps, then realizes her finger is bleeding. She's chewed away the skin around her thumb. He hands her a wet wipe from his endless stash.

"Do you feel it?" he says.

"The feeling that we're being set up?" she asks.

"No, the roses. They have powerful energy fields, you know," he says.

Gus smiles, knowing he's about to launch into one of his Howardisms to distract her.

"Tell me," she says.

"See, roses vibrate at this electrical frequency that's higher than any other flower. In fact, the essential oil of a rose vibrates at a rate three times higher than the human brain."

"Is that why they say 'Wake up and smell the roses'?" she asks.

Howard doesn't laugh. He's staring across the garden.

Gus turns to look at what's got his eyes transfixed. It's Mojo. She's crossing the road in front of the care home, heading toward the garden. Beside her, Poppy is being pushed in a wheelchair by a very tall, thin nurse in a light-blue uniform. A nurse who looks like she could leap tall buildings in a single bound if she had to. Super Nurse. Shadowing this trio are two men wearing matching beige short-sleeved coveralls. Even from a hundred yards away, their biceps and necks look gargantuan. They're oddly similar. Like twins. Twin bouncers moonlighting as orderlies.

Gus looks at Howard, then back toward the group as they come through the gate. Mojo skips ahead, scanning the park. She spots Gus. With her back to the entourage, she waves Gus off. It's a frantic wave that says, *Abort. Abort.* Gus shakes her head. *No.*

The bouncers hang back. They lean on the fence, light cigarettes, and wait by the gate. Mojo goes back to the nurse and says something. The nurse nods and hands the wheelchair off to Mojo, who begins pushing Poppy toward the fountain. The nurse follows for a few paces, then decides to take a seat on a bench and lets the pair walk ahead.

It's now or never. Gus grabs her satchel and goes for it. She climbs out of the Honda, leaves the door open, and enters the west gate. She acts casual like she's just come to smell the roses. Doesn't look at Poppy and Mojo. She wanders toward the beds near the fountain, taking it slow. Gus wonders how long it will take them to get Poppy into the front seat.

She looks back at Howard. They'll have to ditch the wheel-chair. She nods. He nods back.

But then out of nowhere, Mojo is screaming and running full speed, pushing the wheelchair. Poppy is hanging on for dear life.

"Cover me," Mojo hollers as she steers toward the car.

Gus is stunned. Frozen. Then she clues in to what Mojo means. She needs Gus to buy them time. Super Nurse looks up, confused. She doesn't don a cape and leap into action like Gus thought she would. Instead she motions to the twins. They drop their smokes and haul ass across the park. They can really move for musclemen. And they're crossing the park too fast. Gus looks back at the car. Mojo is clearing the gate. Howard is out of the car, dashing around to the passenger side, ready to load Poppy inside.

"Levi," yells Gus.

Levi scrambles over the seat and out the passenger door, trailing his leash behind him. He runs to her, as fast as his old legs will go. She grabs his leash, releases the extension button, and starts racing across the lawn, heading straight into the path of the twins who are making a beeline for the Honda. Levi bounds along, trying to keep up, energized by this unexpected playtime.

Super Nurse stands and spots them. Too late to realize Gus is not some random flower-sniffer. The nurse is helpless to stop what's about to happen.

Gus narrowly misses crashing into the twins, who don't see her approach their flank. When they do, it's too late. She crosses in front of them, and the leash extending behind Gus catches the twins at their shins, sending them both hurtling into a bed of pink roses. Levi tumbles onto the grass as the leash is yanked tight. Gus lets go so he doesn't get dragged or hurt. The dog clambers to his feet, shakes himself off, and spots the fountain. He loves water. Before she can catch hold of him, Levi dodges out of reach and races for the fountain. The dog can smell water a mile away. He barrels toward the nurse who's now standing in front of the fountain. As the twins try to disentangle themselves from the thorny bushes, a look of terror flashes across the nurse's face as the dog charges her. She loses her footing and tumbles backward into the fountain, her long legs sticking out like a toppled ostrich. Levi happily jumps into the water with her. She wails like a drowning kitten.

Gus looks in the direction of the car. The wheelchair is tipped over. Left empty on the sidewalk. The Honda is gone. She can't believe her eyes, but the twins have freed themselves from the rose bushes, and there's no time to think. She's got seconds. Gus shakes off the shock of being abandoned and springs into action. She races for Levi. He's standing in the fountain, shaking his entire body, sending a spray of water into the nurse's face. Her eyes are shut and her arms are flailing about. Gus reaches the fountain, grabs the leash, and together Levi and Gus run for the east gate. The twins give chase. She takes the center path. The most direct route out of the park. But the twins are faster than a fully pregnant woman and an old dog. The twins split up, each taking one of the curving paths on either side of her. They get to the gate first, blocking the way out.

Levi and Gus stop in their tracks.

One twin closes the iron gate and the other moves in, fists clenched, tiny thorns protruding from his forehead. He aims to take her down with force, and it doesn't look like the watermelon is going to stop him. Gus looks quickly behind her. A soaking wet, very angry Super Nurse is blocking any possible retreat. They're surrounded. Levi whimpers.

Gus reaches inside her satchel and grabs the gun. The

gun she hasn't told Howard about. She points the barrel at
the twin closing in on her and he stops in his tracks. His
Adam's apple quivers. She gestures for the twins to join the
nurse. They do, moving like molasses away from the gate.
Her hands are shaking as she slowly turns, keeping the gun
aimed in their direction. Now with her back to Ann Street
and the Hampshire Care Home, she inches toward the gate.
Behind the threesome, the rose garden looks breathtaking, as
if all the blooms have opened in one beautiful yawn to the
sun. Gus suddenly feels the world shift under her feet.

What the fuck am I doing?

She's pointing a gun at a bunch of health care workers.
She's kidnapping an old woman, or at the very least, she's
orchestrating a prison break. Has she lost her mind? Behind
her, there's probably an army of orderlies advancing at this
very moment. The Mutchmores likely leading the charge.
She has nowhere to go and no one to back her up.

Then, she hears the beeps.

Beep-beep-be-beep-beep.

It's Howard.

Tires squeal behind her as a vehicle comes to a rapid stop.
Gun still trained on the Hampshire trio, Gus lets go of the
leash, and with her free hand she opens the gate. Levi bolts
for the car and she follows, walking backward. She feels behind her for the passenger door. It bumps her leg, already
open for her. Levi jumps in first. He scrambles into the back
with Poppy and Mojo. Then Gus eases herself into the passenger seat, finally lowering the gun and slamming the door.

"Hit it," she says to Howard.

He guns it down Ann Street, sending gravel airborne in
their wake.

She watches in the side view mirror as the twins and Super Nurse race across the road to the Hampshire Care Home to report the escape of Poppy Honeywell and crew.

Howard doesn't say anything as she tucks the gun back inside her satchel. He focuses on the road ahead and getting out of town. Gus reaches over the seat and squeezes Poppy's hand. The old woman smiles and squeezes her hand back.

A very soggy Levi snuggles between Poppy and Mojo.

It's not until they're back on the 401 and are heading toward Ottawa that anyone speaks.

"That was so awesome," says Mojo.

27

Teddy

IN THE WEEKS BEFORE THEY RESCUED POPPY, GUS AND HOW-ard had been working in the shadows to unearth the history of Teddy Trichborne. Howard's beating had probably been enough to satisfy the Mutchmores for the moment, but the pair weren't taking any chances. They were being extra careful. If they were being watched, Gus and Howard were hopeful that nothing they'd done since her visit to Braddish had sent up any more red flags. They watched their backs. They never took the same route twice. Gus kept up with her daily routines of dog walks and outings to get groceries, and she even kept up with her monthly doctor appointments. They always worked separately in different records offices or libraries or archives across the city. They stayed apart most of the time, but kept in almost constant touch, texting multiple times a day and using code words, just in case.

Jackfruit meant they should meet at the Lexington. *Leprechaun* meant Malachy had been spotted. *Mama Bear* was May and *Papa Bear* was Ricker. Charlotte was *Lucky Penny*. And *wet wipes* was their code name for danger. An SOS of sorts.

They even set up their phones so they could track each other's locations.

Gus was happy. She couldn't help it. She was worried for Poppy, but she knew their efforts were inching them toward a truth that would help her friend. Even if parts of that truth might be hard to swallow, she knew Poppy wanted it all to come out, and that gave Gus a sense of purpose and direction she hadn't felt since her investigation began. Code words, research, digging into the past. It all felt so natural. Like this was what she was meant to be doing. Gus felt like she was growing up a little more each day. Like her cells were reorganizing themselves so she could take on something bigger than herself.

Howard and Gus began to piece together a life by wading through a thick and winding trail of birth records and school records, newspaper articles, corporate documents, zoning applications, bidding and tender lists, and customs manifests.

The life of Teddy Trichborne.

He was born in 1900. His father, Calvin Trichborne, was listed among the casualties who died after the great fire. Cause of death: dysentery. The Trichbornes were among the poor who lived in the tent city that sprung up from the destruction. Teddy was registered at Bank Street School in 1906. And there was a record of him attending high school at Ottawa Collegiate Institute on Lisgar in 1914. His mother was Annie Trichborne. Her records of employment list her as being a nanny from 1916 to 1923, when her job description changed to housemaid until her death in 1929. Teddy's employment records listed his job as houseboy from 1916 to 1929. Both were employed in the Mutchmore household. Teddy worked there well into his late twenties, leaving soon after his mother's death.

It seemed 1930 was a turning point for young Teddy. Maybe losing his mother inspired him to do more with his life. Or maybe staying at the household where she worked was too painful. The documents didn't reveal reasons or motivations, just the facts. In 1930 his employment with the Mutchmores ended.

His name resurfaced in corporate documents filed five years later, when Trichborne Enterprises was born. Six years later, the business became The Trichborne Group, as his staff and holdings grew. Through the forties Teddy made a name for himself, sitting on boards of trade, business associations, and chambers of commerce, often alongside Robert Mutchmore and, following Robert's death, his son Wilfred, who took over his father's company in the late forties. Newspaper articles from the day hinted at a friendly competitiveness between the two entrepreneurs, Teddy and Wilfred. Although one *Maclean's* article about the next generation of wealthy Canadian philanthropists featured Wilfred Mutchmore at the top of their list. The profile on the do-gooder entrepreneur didn't pull any punches in describing his bitter rivalry with Teddy. The two had a history of getting into nasty bidding wars over lucrative land development projects, often going head-to-head when acquiring talent, property, or businesses. Despite ongoing feuds, both men's fortunes seemed on the rise. From all accounts, they sounded unstoppable.

Until November 1953 when The Trichborne Group board of directors unceremoniously fired CEO Teddy Trichborne at their board meeting. The vote was unanimous. He retained his minority interest in the company but would no longer be involved in day-to-day operations, said the annual report to shareholders. No specific reason was given. It appeared as though Teddy left or was tossed from his own company. Again, the facts didn't tell the whole story, but it looked like things were unraveling for Teddy.

That's when Teddy's trail went cold. Gus found a passenger list for a ship called the *Empress of Canada* that left the port of Montreal bound for Liverpool, England, in November 1953. Teddy Trichborne was listed as a first-class passenger on the ship's manifest. Yet customs records in the UK didn't mention anyone by the name of Teddy Trichborne among the passengers who disembarked the ship a week later. Handwritten records being what they were, it was unclear if he ever boarded the ship in the first place, if he just didn't make it across the ocean, or if his arrival was simply missed.

Nothing in their archival research connected Eva and Teddy in the years after he left the Mutchmore household. All they had was Eva's mention of a meeting with Pug in her diary. What Gus and Howard found most intriguing was that a houseboy went on to build a company successful enough to compete with his former employers.

They both knew there was more to the story. Gus also had a feeling about the M&Ms. They didn't strike her as the sort of people who encouraged or appreciated healthy competition. They wouldn't have mentored young Teddy. They would have looked down on him no matter what he'd accomplished, because he came from nothing.

But if Teddy was murdered, were the Mutchmores in the thick of it? Everything Howard and Gus had managed to dig up only skimmed the surface. Corporate records were pokerfaced. They let you know who did what, but they didn't reveal why. The whys were locked away in the hearts of those long dead.

But not everyone was dead.

And now that they had rescued Poppy, the time had come to tell her everything.

28

Australia

ON THE DRIVE BACK TO OTTAWA, THE HIGH FROM THEIR AD-venture in Belleville slowly got sucked from the car like air from a balloon. They realized that Gus had been seen. Mojo was deep in it. They knew all eyes would be on the Ambassador and on Howard's house. The police would probably be looking for them and for the car. They had to get out of sight and fast. Lie low somewhere until things cooled off.

Howard had an idea.

He had an apartment he'd bought a while back and now rented on Airbnb. A loft, actually. If they could get there unseen, it was the perfect place for them to hunker down safely. No one was booked right now, so it was empty. Gus stared at him. This was the first she'd heard of any loft. Howard was uncharacteristically uncomfortable, almost embarrassed. He explained. When he was in college, his parents won the provincial lottery. A pretty big windfall. They'd always dreamed of running their own winery, and now they could. When they left town, they gave him the family home and a sizable chunk of cash, which he invested in the loft. His ears flushed red.

"It's okay, Howard. Being rich isn't a crime," Gus said, reassuring him she didn't see him any differently.

Mojo leaned over the seat between them and chimed in with "I'm rich too," then she went back to petting Levi.

Later that evening, they parked the Honda in the underground lot and took the elevator to the penthouse level, which was only accessible with Howard's private keycard. They entered the modern open-concept loft with floor-to-ceiling windows and a huge sectional sofa in the center of the living area with views of the Gatineau Hills. The place was chic and beautifully decorated. That's when Gus realized there was so much more to learn about Howard, and she had no doubt he had even more surprises up his sleeve.

&

That was a week ago.

The four desperados have been holed up in Howard's three-bedroom loft in the Byward Market ever since. They haven't left. They've had all their meals delivered, bought extra clothing online, and have only stepped outside into the interior courtyard to take Levi for short walks. The building is a fortress, with security systems that include fingerprint access, delivery drop-off stalls, and cameras everywhere.

It's been exactly seven days since Gus pulled a gun on the staff of the Hampshire Care Home. Seven days since Mojo boarded a VIA Rail train to Belleville without telling anyone and made a surprise visit to see Poppy, then begged the duty nurse to let her take Poppy across the street to the rose garden. Seven days and no mention in the news. Not a blip on any of the police scanners that Howard monitors. No amber alerts or silver alerts, no bulletins or social media posts. Nothing on any of the news feeds that Howard follows.

Zip.

The silence is almost more chilling than if they knew the cops were involved. It means the Mutchmores have locked it down and they're on the hunt. Likely using back channels and PIs and their own goons, Malachy and Taggart, to smoke them out of hiding. No doubt they've already ransacked Gus's place, questioned Mojo's schoolmates, leaned on Howard's colleagues and neighbors, and put surveillance on both the Ambassador and his house on Ossington. But Howard is confident they won't find the loft. He doesn't like his money to be a thing, so his colleagues don't even know about it. He goes online and changes his Airbnb listing so his real name isn't listed as the host.

Mojo seems okay. A lot calmer than she was back in March. Maybe in the five months since, she's grown up a little. Maybe she's had to. The girl plays fetch with Levi down the hallway of the loft, cuddles with Poppy on the sofa, and watches reruns of *Gilmore Girls* on the big-screen TV, describing everything that's happening so Poppy gets the full picture. There's no going back for the eleven-year-old. Or is she twelve now? Gus has no idea. She knows what the girl did must weigh heavily on her tiny frame. She betrayed her parents. Ran away. Conspired with the enemy. Got Poppy out of the home where they'd put her. They must be furious with her. Gus never got the warm and fuzzies from either of Mojo's parents, but she also knows most kids will forgive their folks anything. But Mojo hasn't asked to go home, hasn't even wanted to reach out. Maybe she's too scared to. Gus is glad Mojo has Poppy. She's her family now. Only once does the girl mention missing her Gramma Char-Char.

On the seventh day of their self-imposed hideout, Gus finally works up the courage to have her heart-to-heart with Poppy. Her old friend's eyes have brightened. She's rested now. Her cheeks are rosy once again. She looks well. Their talk goes better than expected. It feels like old times. Their conversation picks up with the easy rhythm of those evenings when Gus used to climb the stairs to Poppy's apartment and they'd share dinner by the fireside. Those winter nights seem so long ago, and yet it's been less than a year.

Gus holds Poppy's hand in hers and tells her what she knows and what she suspects. She tells her everything about Gish and Leo and Eva and the babies. She tells her what May did to her in the GG's fancy ladies' room and how Charlotte came clean by the pool. She tells her all about their investigation into Teddy, including the part about Eva's delusional confession to her doctor that she killed him.

Poppy listens quietly, occasionally asking questions, but mostly she sits quite still, one finely wrinkled hand gently stroking Levi's furry brow. The dog is stretched out on the sofa next to her, his head in her lap. When Gus finishes her story, Poppy turns to her and reaches a hand up to touch Gus's cheek as if she wants to feel the expression on her face. Gus flushes at the intimacy of her touch. The motherly feel of it pulls at her heart.

"You've done a good job, love," she says.

Gus smiles as Poppy lowers her hand.

"And you're sure about Leo?" Poppy asks. "That he was my half-brother?"

Gus hands Poppy the locket she's been keeping for her.

"I'm sure. I had his hair tested. It's a sibling match to your DNA," she says.

Poppy looks momentarily confused, then she remembers.

"Ah yes, Mojo's school project," says Poppy.

"She collected your entire family's DNA," adds Gus.

"I'm so sorry, my dear child," Poppy says.

"You have nothing to be sorry about. I'm sorry," Gus says.

"No. I should never have gotten you into this dang mess," she says.

"I wanted to do it," says Gus.

"And I should never have let them treat you the way they did, with those horrid lawyers," Poppy says, her voice cracking. "I was so drugged all I could do was sit there."

"It's okay; in the end they didn't hurt me or Levi. And Howard's all right now. What they did to you is a million times worse. They took everything from you," says Gus. "All of your beautiful things."

A single tear appears at the corner of Poppy's left eye, then rolls down her cheek, leaving a shiny trail across her time-swept skin.

"We're going to get it all back, I swear to you, Poppy," says Gus.

"You've got pluck, Augusta Monet," says Poppy, smiling.

Mojo has crept up behind the sofa. She pops her head between them and they nearly jump out of their skin, including Levi.

"Okay, now it's your turn, Poppers. You have to tell her everything," the girl chirps, one hand lightly pinching Poppy's shoulder.

Poppy pats Mojo's hand.

"You mean about Pug," the old woman says.

"Yeppers," sings Mojo as she tips over the sofa and wedges herself between them.

Levi gets pushed off the sofa as they spread out. He huffs and ambles off to sun by the window.

"What about Pug?" asks Gus, ears perked.

Sitting on a stool at the kitchen island, Howard, who's been doing some research on his laptop, swivels to face them.

"Anyone want popcorn?" he calls from across the room, oblivious to the precipice they have just reached.

"Me, me," shouts Mojo, jutting one arm in the air.

"Marjory. Why don't you give Hughes a hand," says Poppy.

Poppy has taken to calling him Hughes ever since their escapade in Belleville and the revelation that he has money. She also finds the nickname fitting, since Howard tends to be a bit hyper-focused on germs, and so was Howard Hughes. Poppy enjoys teasing him. Mojo does too.

"Howard Hughes likes to snooze," Mojo sings as she skips across to the kitchen.

And then, with the snap and crackle of popping corn in the background, Poppy tells Gus about her very worst fear. That her mother, Eva, was indeed a murderer. She never wanted to believe it. But now it looks like it could be true, from everything Gus has told her.

In November, after Leo's disappearance, Teddy Trichborne came to the Ambassador. He was looking for Eva. He didn't look well at all. Gray and sick. Eva wasn't home. Poppy's field of vision was narrowing fast, but she could still see enough to know he was upset. He asked her to come with him to the rooftop of the Ambassador. Something about the pigeons and a message he wanted to send, he said. But once up there, he became erratic and hostile, as if whatever ailed him was fueling a rage deep in his soul. He told Poppy that she was the message. She would have to pay for what her mother had done. It was the only way that Eva would feel the pain that he felt.

He said that the rest of the Mutchmores would be next. He had some dirt on them that he should have given to the press years ago, but he foolishly thought things would turn out differently. Now he was going to bring them all down with what he knew. And Poppy would be the first to pay for their sins.

She was terrified. He kept moving closer, backing her toward the roof's edge. Then he lunged at her, grabbing her shoulders. She heard a strange clack, like wood snapping in a fire. He let go, fell to his knees, then crumpled forward in a heap. Her mother was behind him, a bloody brick in her raised hand. Eva told Poppy to go back to their apartment. To stay there. Poppy did.

Her mother came home hours later. Eva never spoke of Teddy again and never told Poppy what happened that night, but she wasn't the same after that day.

"For a long time, I believed my mother had just knocked him unconscious and he'd gone away once he came to. I should have told you about it, but I honestly didn't think it had anything to do with Leo," says Poppy.

"She wrote in her diary about killing someone," says Gus, gently. "And when Howard saw the hospital records where she confessed to her doctor that she'd killed Pug, we thought it might be true, but we still weren't sure. Her own doctor didn't believe it. He thought Eva conjured up ghosts, and when she told him she'd hidden Pug's body in Australia, they thought it was all pure fantasy."

Poppy jumps a little as if something sharp has pricked her skin.

"Oh dang it," says Poppy.

Levi lifts his head.

"What is it?" asks Gus.

Suddenly, Mojo is back. She squeezes between them, a bowl of popcorn on her lap.

"Get your hot popcorn!" she shouts, shoving a handful in her mouth.

Gus glares. The girl looks from Gus to Poppy.

"What?" says Mojo.

"She said Australia?" asks Poppy, looking disoriented.

"No, I said popcorn," says Mojo, interrupting again.

Gus puts her hand over Mojo's mouth.

"What about Australia?" says Gus.

Howard walks over, listening. Levi approaches and sits at Mojo's feet. He can smell the popcorn or maybe he senses that something's up.

"That's what we used to call the storage locker in the subbasement. One time, my mother said she was going down under to get something from our locker. I asked if she was going to Australia. She laughed and from then on we called the locker Australia. I did love making her laugh," says Poppy, her eyes glistening.

Gus removes her hand from Mojo's mouth.

"So Pug's been in the basement this whole time?" Mojo blurts out, bits of popcorn flying from her mouth.

Levi skillfully snaps a kernel from the air.

"It would have been cleaned out years ago," says Gus.

"Should have been. It was left up to the residents to empty their lockers. We were given notices and all, but we never bothered. And then they closed off the subbasement and anything left behind was sealed up for good," says Poppy.

"And the elevator? Did it go all the way down to the subbasement?" ponders Howard.

"It did at that time," says Poppy.

"That's how she got him down there," says Gus, following Howard's train of thought.

Howard and Gus lock eyes.

They're both thinking the same thing.

Time to take a trip down under.

BIRTH

29

Mr. Curry

THEY KNOW IT'S RISKY GOING BACK TO THE AMBASSADOR. And Poppy isn't sure she wants them to go, but part of her needs to know what her mother did, one way or another. Gus understands that push and pull of wanting to know, yet fearing what you'll find out. More than that, Poppy wants to know why Teddy tried to push her off the roof. Perhaps they'll find nothing. Perhaps there's no Pug and no secrets and it really was all a delusion. In the end, they agree it's worth a shot. The lead is too big to ignore. But they have to do this right.

Gus and Howard take their time formulating a plan. The Mutchmores are likely waiting for them to come out of hiding. Watching and waiting. If they're going back to the Ambassador, they can't be seen or caught. They decide to go in the middle of the night, under cover of darkness, and find a way in the back of the building. Plan B is to go in the front. But that's a last resort. They organize supplies and a van rental. Everything is arranged online and delivered to the loft. The whole operation takes a few days to come together. Even the van is dropped off. It's agreed, after a whole lot of whining from Mojo, that only Gus and Howard will make the trip. And it's also agreed, after a whole lot of whining from Gus, that they'll leave her gun behind. Howard insists that they'll be in far worse trouble if they have to use it. He'd rather run than shoot. Gus relents.

Poppy fills them in on a few logistics. They would need a master key to get into the subbasement storage room and into the locker itself. Her keys are long gone. There are no windows down there, but they might be able to break in if they have the right tools. Poppy describes the rough location of the storage room as she remembers it. They'll be looking for locker 14. Then Gus remembers seeing keys hanging on a hook in Alice and Stanley's kitchen. Keys that belonged to her caretaker father. Master keys. Gus will deal with that part.

Next, they'll have to find a way into the subbasement, which was closed off years ago. The elevator doesn't go down there anymore. Back then, its mechanics were altered so it wouldn't. The stairwells are barricaded down to that level too. Once they do get down there, they'll find the locker, see what's what, gather evidence if there is any, and get out as fast as they can, the same way they came in.

If they get separated, their plan is to meet at the west entrance of Patterson Creek Park. If Howard can get to the van, he'll pull up to the park's entrance on Lyon Street. If he can't, they'll meet on foot and figure it out from there. Hopefully, it won't come to that.

It's been more than a week since the Poppy-napping. The M&Ms may have given up on finding Gus and Poppy. But they won't stop looking for their daughter. They've likely got someone watching the front door of the Ambassador. But maybe not the back. If they're careful, Howard and Gus can get in and out before anyone knows they've been there.

But even the best-laid plans can't foresee tits on a bull.

It's 3 A.M. when they pull into an empty parking lot off Rosebery. The lot is behind a commercial building next to the Ambassador Court. It butts up against the service lane behind the apartment building, where two large dumpsters sit next to the service doors and fire exit. They park in the shadows, then squeeze through a gap in the fence separating the lot and lane. They have Gus's keys and some disguises if there's no other choice but to use the front entrance. Howard carries a backpack of supplies. Luckily, they find the fire exit propped open a crack. A brick wedged in the door. The homeless person must be back. They're in.

Howard waits in the stairwell while Gus goes to the first-floor apartment of Alice and Stanley Croft. She knocks. At first lightly. When no one comes to the door, she hammers a little harder. The sound feels like a booming echo that reverberates through the entire building.

Finally, Alice answers, blurry-eyed and wearing a nightgown and matching floral nightcap. She doesn't look her usual vibrant self. Smaller and faded. Older than her eighty-some years, yet also looking like a little girl blinking at the hall light.

"Augusta Monet?" she says, squinting.

"I'm so sorry to wake you at this crazy hour, Alice, but I really, really need your help. It's my pregnant brain. I was out for a walk, and I've locked myself out of my apartment and Mr. Curry isn't answering his door. I feel so silly. I was wondering if you might have a key?" she begs.

Alice looks baffled.

"Like one of your father's old keys? A master key from way back?" hints Gus.

Gus puts on her most desperate face and shuffles from foot to foot like she's got to pee.

"You took a walk in the middle of the night?" asks Alice. "Without your dog?"

"I'm up all hours these days. You know," she says, pointing to her belly.

Alice blinks several times.

"No, I don't," says Alice.

Gus gives Alice a feeble smile.

"I really have to pee," says Gus.

Alice waves Gus inside. She offers her the use of their bathroom. Gus pretends to use it then finds Alice in the kitchen. The woman doesn't seem in a hurry to give Gus the keys hanging behind her. She insists Gus sit for a minute at the table. With a sinking feeling, Gus realizes that Alice wants the company now that she's up. Gus keeps her cool as Alice offers to make tea.

"I really just want to go to bed," she says, attempting a yawn.

Just hand over the fucking keys.

Alice doesn't. Instead she leans against the counter like she's settling in for a chat. "A man was looking for you. A police officer. He said he needed to reach you urgently. Did he find you?"

Taggart.

"Nice fellow. He wasn't too busy for a cup of tea," Alice adds, a pout to her lower lip.

"He did find me, and it turned out to be nothing in the end," says Gus.

Alice doesn't seem convinced. "I haven't seen you around lately. Have you been away?" Alice asks.

What's with the third degree?

Gus's cheeks flush. She has to restrain herself from pushing past Alice, grabbing the keys, and bolting. Instead she rises and smiles politely.

"I went home to see my parents for a couple of days," Gus lies.

"Oh that's right, the police officer said he knew your mother. He said she was worried about you," Alice adds.

Gus swallows hard.

"Is she excited to be a grandmother?" she asks.

A little corner of Gus's heart breaks.

"She is," Gus says.

"And that boy I've seen you with. I assume he's the father?" Alice asks.

Jesus Christ, enough.

"Howard?" Gus immediately regrets saying his name out loud. "He's just a friend."

And he's not a boy.

"Howard. The officer asked about a Howard, and he sounded a lot like that boy, don't you know," says Alice with a gossipy lilt to her voice.

"He did? What did he say?" she asks, keeping her tone super carefree.

"He described him. Tall, dark hair, dark skin. He said he was a person of interest, whatever that means. He wasn't at liberty to say. That's why your mother was worried and why he was looking for you," Alice says, becoming more awake and excited with every word.

"Yes, I know. It was all a big misunderstanding. I squared it away with my mum."

"Are you sure you're all right, dear? You're not in trouble, are you?" Alice persists.

"No, not at all. Don't you worry. I just locked myself out"—she nods to the keys behind Alice—"but I do need some rest."

Give me the motherfucking keys.

Alice reaches behind her and unhooks the key ring. Before she can remove one of the keys, Gus takes the entire ring from her hand.

"Oh," says Alice.

"I'm not feeling so well," Gus says, brushing past Alice. "Thank you so much. And I'm sorry to have bothered you at this hour."

Alice follows her to the door.

"I'm happy I could help. That Mr. Curry is as useless as tits on a bull," she laughs.

Alice's odd insult would turn out to be an apt description. Gus heads into the hallway.

"I'll bring these back later," Gus says, walking away.

"You know you can always knock on my door, day or night. And don't let some silly boy ruin your life. Not ever," she calls out.

Gus wishes Alice would lower her voice. She'll wake the neighbors. One of them being Mr. Curry. That's the last thing she needs. Gus heads into the stairwell. Alice is watching with expectant eyes, like a child waiting to be picked for a team.

Gus gives her a little wave, then slams the door.

Howard is leaning against the stairwell wall.

"How'd it go?" he asks.

Gus holds out the key ring.

They head down to the basement level. They already know the stairwell leading to the subbasement is barricaded with old furniture and wood planks. There's too much debris in the way to get through safely. They'll find another way. They enter the basement and make their way through the narrow halls. Past the storage rooms built to replace the old ones when the subbasement was permanently boarded up. Past the laundry room where the fluorescent light flickers on. They both jump but then realize it's just the motion sensor. They reach a door marked UTILITY ROOM. Worth a look. Gus finds the key that fits the lock and they step inside. They search the room. They find a stockpile of cleaning equipment, cans of paint, and old garbage bins. There are sewer and water lines running up one wall and electrical panels with breakers on another. Then Howard finds something hidden behind the large boiler.

It's a trapdoor.

This could be it.

Without a word, they spring into action.

Gus pulls on the handle. It won't budge.

Howard searches around for a tool.

He finds a crowbar.

Gus holds the backpack of supplies.

Howard pries open the hatch and swings the trapdoor to one side.

They both lean in, gazing into the dark hole beneath.

They can make out the top of a narrow and steep staircase leading down some long-forgotten maintenance shaft.

Jackpot. They've found a way into the subbasement.

Howard shines his phone's flashlight down the shaft. The metal staircase looks prehistoric. The shaft is laced with dense cobwebs. Crumbled pieces of brick litter the floor below. They decide Howard will go first to test the staircase. He straps on the backpack. Gus will follow if it's sound. He doesn't tell her to stay put while he goes ahead to find the locker. In fact, Howard never questions whether or not Gus can do something. Never makes her feel like the watermelon is a reason for her to be sidelined. This is her investigation. He's along for the ride, and he's not about to stop her from missing out on any of it.

She loves that about him.

And even though she can no longer see her feet and she

has to pee every hour, she also feels healthier and more alive than she has in a long time. A lot of this has to do with Howard. He never calls attention to it, but she knows he's been taking care of her ever since they arrived at the loft. He does it with subtle gestures. He fills up her water glass whenever it's empty. He puts vitamin D, calcium, and iron pills in a tiny dish next to her morning coffee. Vitamins he ordered online. He sneaks salad onto her dinner plate. And he insists she sleep in the king bed with all the pillows she needs. Meanwhile he's on the living room sofa. Mojo in one room, Poppy in another. He doesn't make a thing of taking care of her. He just does it. No hidden motive. No pressure. No expectations.

Howard makes it to the bottom of the staircase. No steps crumble. No alarms sound.

"Catch," she says, tossing down the keys so her hands are free.

Just as she's about to place one foot on the first step, Gus hears someone coming.

A voice calls out.

"Hello? Who's in there?"

Damn it.

It's Mr. Curry. He's outside in the hall. The utility door is open a crack. He's seen it.

Gus looks at Howard. He nods. She closes the hatch.

When Mr. Curry enters the utility room, Gus has her back to him. She's standing in front of the electrical panel, one hand resting on a breaker. He's surprised to find her down there in the middle of the night but seems to buy her story. She lost power in her apartment, tried him first, then found the utility room unlocked, so she thought she'd try fixing it herself. And she just did. The breaker to her apartment has been flipped and everything's fine now. She points at the panel as evidence.

Mr. Curry tells her he heard voices upstairs and thought

he'd have a look around. He seems less concerned about her messing around in the utility room than he is about her overdue rent. She still hasn't paid for August. It's already the twenty-fifth. Curry thinks the middle of the night is a perfect time to get into it. He tells her he'll be forced to evict her if she doesn't pay up soon. As they head out of the utility room, Gus tries to distract him so he forgets to lock it.

"Do you think the wiring's faulty or something?" she asks.

"You trying to get out of paying your rent?" he asks.

"No, I was just wondering why it happened," she says.

"You plugged in too many things. Bloody young people and their devices," he mumbles.

Then he turns his back on her and fiddles with his giant ring of keys. It feels like it's taking him forever. Gus almost walks away but doesn't. She's worried Howard might open the hatch and make a noise. Finally Curry finds the right key, but he's having a hard time actually locking the door. Alice was right. He is as useless as tits on a bull. Gus wants to scream and push him aside and use Alice's keys, but then she remembers dropping them down to Howard. His struggle ends as the lock clicks.

Curry escorts her from the basement. He spots the brick in the fire exit and kicks it out, closing the door and ranting about filthy vagrants. He watches her as she pretends to make her way up to her third-floor apartment. Finally he heads through the door back to his apartment on the first floor.

Gus is halfway up the stairwell. She's tempted to check in on her apartment. See what damage the M&Ms have done. But then she remembers that her apartment keys are tucked in Howard's backpack. *He's got all the fucking keys.* Without a way back into the locked utility room, Gus sees only two options. Try to squeeze through the debris blocking the stairwell or wait by the utility door and hope Howard comes looking for her. She opts for the latter since she's not exactly sized for squeezing through small spaces.

As Gus retraces her steps back down, someone enters the stairwell below. Gus flattens against the wall. She hears footsteps coming up the stairs. *Is it Curry again?* She ducks onto the second-floor landing, eases the door closed behind her, then races to the opposite stairwell. She makes it through the door before whoever it is reaches the second floor. Gus bounds down the stairs, heart racing. *Who the fuck is creeping around the building at 4 A.M.?* Gus enters the basement, reorients herself, finds the passage that leads to the west side of the building, turns the corner, and heads for the utility room. She knocks.

"Howard, it's me," she scream-whispers.

She hears the basement door open around the corner, footsteps approaching. The lock clicks on the door of the utility room. It opens and she squeezes inside.

"Someone's coming," she whispers.

Howard closes the door and turns the lock. They stay quiet. Standing very still. Gus is breathing heavily. Their faces are close. Howard slips his hand in hers. Gus looks up at Howard. Their lips are almost touching as the footsteps near the door, pause, then move on, fading into the distance.

They're both through the hatch and down the metal staircase in minutes. They follow Poppy's directions along a narrow passageway toward the old storage room. It's clear no one has come down here in years. Spiders and rodents have taken up residence. Left alone, they've made the subbasement their home. Vines hanging from light fixtures that no longer work loop across the ceiling like decorative garlands. Mossy fungus forms soft carpets that squish underfoot, spewing out the pungent smell of decay and rat droppings. The subbasement is a windowless cavern, the only light coming from the flashlights on their phones. The place feels otherworldly. A soundproofed, sunless planet with not a blip of service reaching their phones.

The storage room door isn't locked. Why would it be? They find locker 14. It is locked. Gus tries a few keys before finding the right one. She turns the lock. Dust and shards of rotten wood fall away from the frame as she opens the door.

The locker is pitch-black.

Gus swings the beam of her flashlight toward the locker's interior.

They both peer inside.

30

Pug

AT FIRST, IT LOOKS EXACTLY LIKE A STORAGE LOCKER THAT was abandoned decades ago should look. There's a few moldy cardboard boxes folded in a stack. There's a child's bicycle, a collection of empty picture frames, a pair of rusty ice skates, and a rolled-up carpet. Everything is colorless because it's covered in a thick cloak of gray dust. She shines the light in the corners. There's nothing else in there.

Then Howard nods toward the carpet. Gus tips her head in agreement.

They position their phones against the opposite wall, the flashlights aimed at the locker. Gus pockets the keys. Howard sets down the backpack and pulls out two sets of latex gloves from a side pocket. He hands one set to Gus. Gloves on, sleeves rolled up, they look like a couple of doctors ready for surgery. Howard steps inside the locker and grabs the far end of the carpet. He coughs from the dust. Gus grabs the end closest to the door. Together they carefully lift the carpet out of the locker. They place it on the floor. It stinks of decay.

Howard gently pushes the side of the carpet. As it rolls open the moldy inner layers partially disintegrate to dust.

Pug is inside. At least they figure it's him. Who else would be down under?

Only Pug isn't Pug anymore. He's just a collection of bones wearing tattered bits of Teddy's clothes.

They both stare at the skeleton cradled in the remnants of the carpet.

Even though Gus knew they were looking for Teddy Trichborne's remains, she could also picture him walking up the gangplank of a ship about to cross the Atlantic in 1953. Both fates seemed entirely possible until this very moment. Howard checks Teddy's coat pockets. Also not really a coat anymore. Just bits of fabric in the shape of a coat. Amongst the dusty threads he finds a leather wallet. Teddy Trichborne's ID is inside along with a first-class ticket for the *Empress of Canada*.

Gus suddenly feels sorry for him. Sad that he ended up in the bowels of an old apartment building wrapped in a carpet instead of standing on a ship's deck with the salty air in his nostrils and the sun on his face. Howard tries to move one of Teddy's arms, but it breaks free from the rest of him. He gently places it back where it belongs.

"We should probably not touch him," she tells Howard.

"Right. It's a crime scene," he agrees.

"DNA and all," she adds.

Gus has a theory she's been mulling over since they dug into Teddy's history. The fact that he worked at the Mutch-mores' when Eva got pregnant as a teenager might make Teddy the father. Maybe that's why he took Leo under his wing. Because he knew Leo was his son. But if that's true, why introduce Leo to Poppy, knowing they were half siblings? Maybe he didn't think they would fall in love. Or maybe in some twisted way, he hoped they would. That part she's not sure about, but DNA might verify some of the story.

"So, an anonymous call to the police?" she suggests.

"Sounds about right," he answers.

They both look at each other in the dim light.

"Or we could take him with us," says Gus, testing the waters.

"It's a really old crime scene," says Howard.

"It's not like anyone is looking for him," adds Gus.

They stare at Teddy's bones.

"So Pug comes with us, then?" says Gus, making sure they're on the same page.

"Sounds about right," says Howard.

They do their best to disassemble Teddy. Howard manages to fit all the bones into the backpack, except the skull. Gus carries that in one of the plastic grocery bags they brought along in case they needed to carry a bunch of evidence inconspicuously. They gather their supplies and head back the way they came. At the utility room door, they listen for signs of life. Nothing. The coast seems to be clear now. They slowly head down the hallway, through the basement, and up the stairs to the fire exit. When they open the door, the sky is brighter than they expected. The operation took longer than planned because of Alice and Curry. Sunrise is edging close. Gus scans the service lane. Almost as if she planned it, Alice jogs through the gate leading from Patterson Creek Park. She's wearing one of her neon spandex outfits and running shoes. She stops short when she spots Gus at the door.

"Oh! Oh! Hold the door," she shouts, running over.

Damn it, Alice.

"Keep going," Gus says to Howard. He slips past her and crosses the lane, moving fast and not looking back. He's through the fence and heading for the van before Alice can get a good look at him. Gus realizes she forgot to hand him Teddy's skull in the plastic bag.

"Oh my goodness, you saved my life. I was going to have to go all the way around to the front, and I'm plumb tuckered out," says Alice, panting.

"Look at you out before the crack of dawn," smiles Gus, stepping outside and holding the door wide for Alice.

"Who was that?" asks Alice, watching the van pull out of the parking lot.

"Who, him? A repair man from Hydro Ottawa. I had an electrical issue. It's all fixed now. I was just seeing him out," says Gus.

"Good, let's get inside. There's a chill that's quite refreshing when you're moving but not so much when you're standing about, don't you know," says Alice as she enters the building.

Gus wants to leave, but she feels stuck, so she goes back inside. Alice trots ahead, yammering away.

"I love running this time of day. I have the park all to myself. No bloody dogs nipping at my heels," chirps Alice. "Oh, I don't mean your lovely Levi. Where is that dog anyway? Haven't seen him in a dog's age." She giggles. "Ha, see what I did there?"

Gus changes the subject as they climb the stairs together.

"I'm glad we've run into each other. I can give you your keys back now," she says, reaching in the pocket of her jean jacket and handing Alice the key ring.

Alice stares at the dirty latex gloves that are still on Gus's hands and the plastic bag she's holding. The one containing Teddy's skull. Gus stares at them too.

"I was at the grocery store. Germs," she says. Then she continues up the stairs past Alice.

"You've had quite the busy morning. Already out for a

walk, done repairs, and groceries," says Alice. "I didn't think grocery stores were open this early."

"Lucky for me they are. I had a craving. Watermelon," says Gus, holding up the bag.

Alice tilts her head like she's trying to figure Gus out. Then she appears to give up.

"Namaste," Alice says with a little bow.

"Namaste," says Gus, returning the gesture.

Alice heads through the door to the first floor.

Gus goes up one flight, then decides to wait on the landing a few minutes so she can be sure Alice has gone inside her apartment. She'd better text Howard to let him know she'll meet him in a few minutes across the park like they planned. She pats her pockets. Can't find her phone. Then she remembers where she left it. Right now her phone's flashlight is shining on locker 14. She hadn't even noticed it as they left the storage room. She was too distracted by the mission and the bones and the skull she was carrying.

But Gus also knows they didn't bother locking the utility room behind them, so she could easily go back and get it. It'll only take a few minutes now that she knows the way. She can grab her phone and be across the park before the sun fully rises.

It did seem important enough to go back for at the time.

Her phone, this palm-size device that carries her photos, that speaks to her in a humorless voice, that acts like a clock and a stopwatch and a compass and a flashlight. This device that she'd become quite attached to. It really did seem worth rescuing. Worth going into that subbasement alone to find.

But it wasn't.

Gus does find her phone exactly where she left it. It's leaning against the brick wall across from locker 14. She finds something else as well. Caught in the beam of light, she spots an object they hadn't noticed in their hurry to get out of the subbasement. Lying in the dusty bits of carpet that they left spread across the storage room floor is a small cloth bag. At the time, it must have looked like a fragment from Teddy's clothing that fell from his bones or a remnant of the carpet. But as she picks it up and examines it more closely, Gus sees that it's not a random bit of fabric. It's heavier. It's a small pouch tied with ribbon. Her flashlight beam is fading, so she pockets the newfound object and heads for the staircase. Halfway down the first hallway, she falters.

Has she gone the wrong way? Did she get turned around?

Then Gus hears a noise. A rat? A footstep? Is someone else down here? Gus feels her heart skip a beat. She holds her breath. She turns off her flashlight. She keeps moving forward, her hand tracing the wall like a blind woman. She tries to pick up her pace, but stumbles on a loose brick. She turns the flashlight back on and spots a doorway up ahead. Has she found her way back? It looks like it, but then everything looks the same. She steps through the door hoping it leads to the room with the metal staircase. It doesn't. It's a dead end.

She turns and stumbles, teetering into the brick wall. Smacking her head hard. Momentarily dazed, she looks up just as the door to the room slams shut and a lock clicks. Dread circles her like a hideous black monster dancing in the dark, mocking her stupidity. She is trapped. Shivers rack her body. The monster howls—or is it her own screaming that rings in her ears and rips her throat raw?

Gus knew this moment would come.

She tried to build a world made entirely of the past. Methodically retracing every movement and word and thought, every walk in the park, every meal at one of Howard's favorite restaurants, every piece of evidence they dug up, every moment they shared, but the monster was always going to find its way in. Find a crack in her mind. The past is too fragile to hold close for so long. And the past only leads in one direction. To the present. The walls were always going to crumble. The cracks were always going to give way. The past was always going to catch up to the present. And the monster was always going to walk in and brush its cold, stony-hearted cheek against hers.

Gus is back in her subbasement prison.

Back right where she started.

Only now she knows how she got here.

She has nowhere left to go but straight into the pain.

31

Hughes

WHAT SHE DOESN'T KNOW IS THAT IN THAT VERY MOMENT Howard is looking for her.

When Gus got held up by Alice, he drove the van straight to Lyon Street and waited at the edge of Patterson Creek Park. When she didn't show at the rendezvous point after a half hour, he tried to keep his cool. He sent texts. Nothing. He tried tracking her phone, but the app just kept saying her location wasn't available. He did the only thing he could. He stuck to the plan and waited. The last thing he saw was her holding the door for Alice. Maybe she got sidetracked by the woman. She'd be along any minute.

An hour comes and goes. The August sun slips above the horizon. 6:15 A.M.

As he watches the park, a man plays fetch with his dog. A woman and child cycle down a path. Ducks mingle at the pond's edge. It's Wednesday. The world is waking up. It's getting light, and they've now lost the cover of darkness.

Where is she?

He shouldn't have gone ahead.

He shouldn't have left her.

Howard waits another forty-five minutes. He calls the loft to see if they've heard anything from Gus. Mojo answers. They haven't heard a peep. Mojo has a million questions. She wants to know what they found in Australia, what's taking so long, and where's Gus. Then Poppy comes on the line. She's livid.

"Don't you come back here without our girl, Hughes," she says, then hangs up.

Howard feels like a scolded child. He suddenly sees the futility of having stuck to the plan, and feels incredibly stupid for having waited so long despite the voice screaming in his head for him to do something. Anything. Now he might be too late. He's sweating buckets.

It's 7 A.M., and the sun is even higher and hotter. Howard cranks the air-conditioning and drives back to the parking lot off Rosebery. There's no sign of Gus behind the Ambassador. The brick that was propping the exit door has been tossed near the dumpster. He can't get in that way. Then he remembers something. Howard searches the backpack and finds Gus's apartment keys. He can get inside.

But the only way in is through the front door.

Plan B.

Howard jumps out of the van. He sticks the decal they ordered online to the side door. M&M Pest Control. Then he gets into the back of the van, puts on one of the disguises they got on eBay, and climbs into the driver's seat. Anger and fear battle for control of his brain and body. His hands shake. He's terror stricken that he's wasted precious time. Maybe Gus was grabbed an hour ago by Malachy or Taggart or both. Maybe they caught her in the park when she was trying to get to him. It's all his fault.

Howard pushes the waves of panic into the pit of his stomach, grips the steering wheel, and channels his anger. He focuses on finding Gus. He drives around the block and pulls up in front of the Ambassador. He spots a black SUV parked down the street. Tinted windows.

It's now or never.

He leaves the van running and hops out of the air-conditioning. Howard is hit by a wall of thick humidity. It doesn't help that he's wearing disposable hooded coveralls, safety goggles, a respirator mask, and rubber gloves. He's also got a four-gallon tank strapped to his back and a sprayer wand in his hand. They didn't fully think through this whole pest control getup. Howard heads for the front entrance of the Ambassador. He strides toward the door like he knows exactly where he's going. Confidence. That's all it takes to sell a disguise.

But confidence and humidity don't go together. The mask fogs up and he can't see. He can't get the key in the front door. A sudden surge of claustrophobia makes Howard panic. He turns and looks at the SUV. Big mistake. He quickly looks away, but he hears the engine turn over. The bloody keys aren't working. Howard hears tires squeal.

Shit.

They're coming for him. He abandons his futile attempt to get into the building and stumbles for the side door of the van. He flails for the handle and manages to open the door as the SUV speeds toward him. It lurches right up to the nose of the van, screeching to a halt.

With nowhere to run, Howard rips off his goggles and mask and rushes toward the SUV and its occupants as they jump out on either side. Two men. He doesn't recognize either. They both wear wrinkled shirts. One has coffee stains down the front of his. He's damn sure they're not tourists looking for directions. Howard unleashes a spray of pink paint from the wand. The Pepto-Bismol-colored deluge covers both men. The wide spray also coats the front windshield, hood, and roof of the SUV. Howard's glad he picked the high-voltage wand with the six-foot spray capacity. It does a fuck of a job. The pink rain buys him enough time to yank the tank off his back, toss it in the van, jump in the front seat, and slam the vehicle into reverse. He guns it backward down the street. He checks the driver's-side mirror. A city bus is heading straight for him. Howard cranks the wheel. The van donuts, narrowly missing the bus. Howard shifts into drive and heads south on Bank. In his rearview mirror he can see the two pink men standing in the middle of the street, stunned and dripping.

Howard was hoping it was Malachy or Taggart in the SUV and not a couple of hired PIs. That means goons number one and two are still out there somewhere. Howard takes Bank all the way to Fifth then circles back to Lyon. He parks, changes out of the coveralls, pulls the decal off the van. They'll be looking for the van. The pink PIs have probably called it in. He leaves the keys in the driver's side wheel well and a note face down on the dash for Gus, then he enters the park on foot. Even if no one's got their hands on Gus yet, backup is definitely on the way now that Howard's made a splash.

But he can't abandon Gus if she's still inside the Ambassador. He needs to find another way in. Maybe he can break in through one of the lower floor apartment windows that face the park. But as Howard approaches the Ambassador, he's caught off guard. The park is busier than expected. The lower windows are too visible. Someone might notice a guy climbing through a window. Then he spots a police officer coming down the stairs leading into the park. Howard ducks into the bushes near the gate by the Ambassador. He immediately regrets not walking through the gate. Now he's trapped. He pushes himself deeper into the bushes so no one can see him. Another police officer arrives from another direction with a dog. Then another. Howard is certain they're about to search the park with their sniffer dogs when the cops start doing training drills with the dogs. This goes on for what feels like hours. Up and down the common. Back and forth, drill after drill. The group even stops to eat sandwiches one of them brought in a cooler.

What the fuck?

Howard's losing his mind. He's been up all night. He's stuck in the bushes. He's overheating. Getting delirious. His legs are cramping.

After way too much chitchat, the police and their dogs finally disband just after 2 P.M.

Howard emerges from the bushes, stiff and furious. A young woman in a ragged ski vest, hoodie, and grubby jeans passes him. She's overdressed for the heat. She must be homeless and has to wear all her possessions. She goes through the gate that leads to the alley behind the Ambassador. He watches as she approaches the fire exit. She pulls something from her pocket. Howard follows. He moves low and fast, as if he's dodging snipers on the rooftop. She has a screwdriver in her hand and she's wedging it into the frame of the door. The door pops open and she goes inside. Howard bolts for the door, but it shuts behind her. He knocks lightly. The door opens a crack. The woman has her hood pulled over her head. She reminds him of a sulky teenager, face downturned. Hidden. She lets him inside. The two of them stand there. Her head bowed. Neither sure what to do next. Then she offers him a piece of licorice. Her fingernails are filthy.

"I'm good. You keep it," he says, trying to get past her.

She blocks his way and holds out the licorice.

He stares at it. He can almost see the bacteria crawling all over it.

She taps him in the chest with the red stick of candy.

Instinctively, Howard swats her hand away.

She jolts, and he glimpses her face as her hood shifts back. Her hollow, frightened eyes look on the verge of tears. Howard feels badly. He takes the licorice and tries to smile.

Her face brightens and she nods for him to try it.

He takes a small bite from the tip of the licorice and chews. "Yum," he says.

She laughs and dangles another piece in his face.

He's done wasting time.

"I'm good with just the one piece, thanks. I'll see you around," he says.

Howard slides past her and climbs the stairs two at a time. As soon as he's up one flight he tosses the licorice and spits out the piece in his mouth. He reaches the third floor and cracks the stairwell door to check the hall. It's empty. He scoots to Gus's door, uses her key to unlock it, and slips inside, closing the door behind him. Then he breathes.

He's expecting the place to be trashed, but the apartment looks the same as the last time he was there. Only not. The sofa cushions have been lifted and not put back properly. The stuff on top of the trunk Gus uses as a coffee table is gathered in the center instead of spread out. Someone's searched the place and tried to make it look like they didn't. But he can tell that was days ago. The air doesn't smell or feel like it's been disturbed in some time. Before he even calls out her name, he knows she's not there.

"Gus? It's Howard," he tries anyway.

He checks the bedroom. The closets. The bathroom.

Someone's definitely been snooping around.

Howard checks the kitchen. That's when his stomach lurches. At first he thinks the homeless woman has poisoned him, then he remembers he hasn't eaten in hours. He checks the cupboards. All he can find is a box of strawberry Pop-Tarts. Against his better judgment, he eats a couple. He opens the fridge and downs a cream soda, making a mental note to himself to buy Gus a book on basic nutrition. Now that he's jacked up on sugar, Howard's next step is to find Alice. Maybe Gus is with her for some reason. If not, Alice might know where Gus was headed.

On his way out of the kitchen, Howard trips on a cupboard door propped against the wall. It's sitting on the floor. Ripped off its hinges, by the looks of it. Howard looks up at the cupboard that's missing the door, but it's not a cupboard at all. It's a compartment inside a shaft. From the roof of the small compartment, a strand of red hair dangles from a piece of cloth. Howard freezes. He knows that red hair. He leans closer. The words *wet wipes* are scratched into the floor of the compartment. An SOS.

There's a pulley. It's a dumbwaiter.

Howard grabs the pulley and hauls the dumbwaiter upward so that it's out of the way. He grabs his phone, turns on the flashlight, and sticks his head and one arm into the shaft. He shines the beam down the shaft. It's deep. Very deep. It goes all the way down.

Holy shit.

Howard knows where she is.

"Gus," he hollers down the shaft.

Nothing. And there's no time to waste.

First, he tries the utility room in the basement level. It's locked. His only other option is the stairwell. He'll have to clear a path and squeeze through. He props the fire exit wide open with a few bricks. Then he starts with the larger pieces of furniture. He uses a wood plank to lever a sofa out of the way, then he tosses the smaller items out into the lane. The young woman hovers on the stairs, watching. He's making progress along one wall of the stairwell, but he doesn't realize the crazy racket he's making. The fog of adrenaline has made him deaf to the noise and numb to the scrapes and cuts from random nails and sharp edges. His shirt is torn and his hands are bleeding, but he's unable to stop. He needs to get to Gus. It's not long before Mr. Curry comes racing into the stairwell, mop in hand. He starts hollering.

"You no-good vagrants. What have you done? Get the fuck out," he says, swatting the woman like she's a rat.

Howard snaps out of it. He looks down at his bloody, filthy hands and realizes how bad this looks. Curry comes at him.

"You don't understand. I have to get down there. Someone's down there," he says.

Curry clocks Howard across the head with the mop.

"Fuck off," says Curry.

Howard is dazed. The woman takes his arm and pulls him outside. She drags him behind the dumpsters.

"I'm calling the bloody police," shouts Mr. Curry as he slams the exit door.

Howard runs for the door and bangs on it.

"Fuck, fuck, fuck," says Howard.

The young woman tugs on his sleeve.

"I have to get back in there," he says, pulling away from her.

She motions for him to follow her as she walks away.

He doesn't.

Instead, Howard leans against the door, trying to catch his breath. Blood drips from his temple. He dabs at it with one grubby hand. Checks his pockets and finds a small baggie of wet wipes. He pulls one out and dabs his head as he watches the woman disappear down a narrow alley next to the service lane. He sighs and follows.

Howard turns the corner into the alley and she's standing

there, pointing at a large wood box. He walks over. She pulls a pair of tweezers from her pocket, picks the padlock on the box, yanks off the lock, and flips the box open. She points inside. Howard looks into the box. But it's not a box at all. It's a metal chute leading down into the building. He's not sure what it is. Then a little historical nugget comes dancing into his sore head. Some of the city's original nineteenth-century buildings used to store wood for the residents for their fireplaces. This is an old wood chute. They don't use them anymore. It looks deep. It looks like it goes all the way to the subbasement. It's a way in. Howard looks at the woman. Her dark eyes look directly into his. She tips her head to one side, encouraging him to get in.

Howard pulls his phone from his pocket.

"Can you speak?" he asks her.

She nods.

"English?" he presses.

"Yes," she says in a small voice.

He dials 911 and hands the woman his phone. He tells her to say they need an ambulance.

"Tell them a pregnant woman's in trouble."

Then he sits on the edge and swings his legs over the box.

Here goes nothing.

Howard lets go and launches himself off the edge. He rockets down the chute and lands in a pile of rotten wood. It's like landing on a soggy mattress. Howard rolls off the pile and brushes himself off. He checks his limbs for injuries. Except for a few more scratches, he's unscathed.

In the pitch black, he searches the subbasement, feeling his way with his hands. It feels like a maze. His eyes slowly adjust. After a while, he can make out shapes and shadows. Something runs across his foot and he stifles a scream. At one point he passes a door that he's positive he passed five min-

utes earlier. He's going in circles. Then he hears a very faint
sound. He moves toward it. It grows louder as he gets closer.
It's the sound of someone knocking.

A five-part knock.

Rat-tat-tatat-tat.

It's her. It's Gus.

He finds another door by following the sound. The tapping
is coming from inside. He tries the handle. It's locked. Howard
backs up, then pushes off the wall and slams his shoulder into
the door. It holds, but something splinters. He tries again. This
time he kicks. The door gives slightly, but still holds. He kicks
again. And again. On the fourth kick, the door busts from
one of its rusty hinges and hangs sideways from the splintered
frame. He steps over the door and into the dark room. He
finds Gus on the floor. She's lying on her side, one arm outstretched. In her hand is a brick that she's tapping over and
over against a rusty pipe.

Rat-tat-tatat-tat.

Rat-tat-tatat-tat.

She doesn't appear to have heard him kick the door down
or to see him kneeling next to her. She just keeps tapping.
He gently takes the brick from her hand and taps the reply.

Tat-tat.

This seems to bring her around. She looks up at him for
the first time.

Howard bursts into tears.

"There you are," he sobs.

Gus doesn't remember how they got out of the subbasement. She doesn't remember the firemen or the paramedics.
She remembers the feeling of being rocked as people lifted
her. She remembers Howard talking to her as they rode in the
ambulance. He was telling her all about the five-part knock.

How it was from a song written in 1899 by Charles Hale. A call-and-response couplet, he said. Howard even sang her the lyrics.

Shave and a haircut, two bits.

After that everything went quiet.

Her eyelids got heavy.

Howard's voice faded.

And Gus had only one thought before she drifted off.

Why wasn't the baby crying?

32

Pearly Everlasting

WHEN SHE WAKES, GUS DOESN'T OPEN HER EYES. SHE LIES very still. She's not sure she wants to wake up. To know. She wiggles her fingers. Then her toes. Then slowly opens her eyes, fluttering the lids. Gradually her pupils adjust to the soft light from the lamp next to her. A curtain runs along one side of the bed. A tube leads from a plastic bag of clear liquid hanging from a stand then disappears under a piece of tape on the back of her hand. A machine beeps. A voice echoes over a distant intercom. She's in a hospital.

Gus turns her head to take in the rest of the room. Howard is sitting in a plastic armchair by a window. He's absorbed in reading something. He looks terrible. A purple bruise spiders out from a square dressing stuck to his temple with surgical tape. He's got bandages wrapped around several fingers. She doesn't let him know she's awake. She watches him.

A butterfly flutters just outside the window behind him. It's a monarch. Orange wings webbed with black and trimmed by white dots. It lands on the sill and delicately hovers there, moving its wings in a slow rhythm just over his shoulder.

Then the monarch flies away, taking Gus along with it.

She is eight. Walking in a meadow with her mother. They know the place well. They come to the wildlife garden next to Dominion Arboretum every Sunday to walk and explore. In the summer they hike the road that loops the tree-lined avenues, then enter the forest path and make their way to the butterfly meadow. It's a grassy field hidden in the forest, sheltered from the wind by surrounding trees but open to the sun. It's light and airy. Perfect for butterflies. Shannon counts how many different butterflies she can spot, and Gus hunts for names. She finds them printed on tags dotted across the field. The tags sit on top of tall sticks. Placed there by members of the Ottawa Field-Naturalists' Club, who tend the garden and plant the wildflowers. Gus loves the names of the flowers. She calls them out to her mother, each one more magical than the last.

Oxeye daisies. Queen Anne's lace. Joe Pye weed. Black-eyed Susans.

Each a newfound friend.

She looks over at her mother just as a monarch alights on Shannon's hand. Her mother stands perfectly still, watching the creature with a look in her eyes that Gus has never seen before, as if she's seeing into the future. Her mother seems a million miles away in that moment. Gus wants to run across the field and join them. The monarch and her mother. But she knows if she does she'll ruin it. Her mother is so still. So unreachable. Gus can't bear it. Can't bear the distance between them. She calls out another name, very loudly.

Pearly everlasting.

Her mother jumps, and the butterfly startles and flies away.

Gus is startled too. Back to her hospital bed, but her mother's face lingers. She aches for her. Like she does whenever Shannon comes unexpectedly close. Then she suddenly aches for someone else. Gus touches her belly. The watermelon's gone.

"You're back," says Howard, rushing to her side.

"Where is she?" Gus says.

Howard hesitates just long enough to send a painful shockwave through her heart.

"Is she dead?" she says, gripping his forearm.

"I don't know," he says.

Gus's anguish turns to confusion.

"I"—he shakes his head—"I don't know."

"What do you know, Howard?" she demands, sitting up in bed.

Howard tells her everything that happened since they got separated.

How he finally found her six hours ago. He tells her about the towels and the blood that were in the room with her. How he searched the room and found nothing but her phone. There was no baby. The fire department knocked down the barricade to the subbasement. The homeless woman told them where they were. At the hospital, the emergency room doctor told the cops Gus had given birth a few hours earlier. They had already searched her apartment and were coming back this morning to question her. Howard had kept his mouth shut. Played dumb. He didn't know how to explain what they'd been doing in the subbasement.

"She's alive," says Gus, knowing it to be true.

Howard takes her hand.

"Someone helped deliver the baby," Howard says.

"And that's who has her," she says, willing it to be so.

Her mind is racing. Who knew she was in the subbasement? Whoever locked her down there has her baby. She tries to remember, but she can't.

"Do you think the Mutchmores could have taken her, or Malachy?" she asks.

"I don't know," says Howard.

"Damn it," she huffs.

Gus pulls the tube from her arm.

"We have to do something. We have to find her," she says.

He doesn't try to stop her as she gets out of the bed. There's no point.

Gus feels surprisingly strong despite all she's been through.

"Where are my clothes?" she asks.

"I don't think you want to wear those," he says, visibly slumping.

Howard points to a plastic bag below the windowsill.

Gus steadies herself, walks to the bag, sifts through the bloody clothes. Pulls out her jean jacket. It's the only thing not bloodstained. As she pulls it over her hospital gown, she notices the papers that Howard was reading when she woke. They're scattered on the sill. It looks like a stack of old letters.

"What are these?" she asks.

"Letters. They were in your jacket pocket," he says.

Gus spots the faded ribbon and cloth bag next to the letters. She recognizes them. She found them lying in the storage room on Eva's carpet.

Howard walks over to her. He stares at his feet.

"What's wrong?" she asks.

"I should have gone looking for the baby. I fucked up. But I couldn't leave you. I had to know you were okay. I didn't want you to wake up alone and not know what was going on. I fucking fucked up," he says, eyes glistening.

"Howard, you didn't fuck up." She pulls him close. "You found me."

Gus kisses him. He tastes like coffee. The kiss calms her.

Steadies her heart. As Gus hugs Howard tight, there's the sound of a ping. It's her phone. A text. They both look at the phone sitting on the table next to the bed.

Last night when he was feeling incredibly useless, Howard had wandered down to the hospital concourse and bought a charger. He'd powered her phone for her while she slept. It was the least he could do.

Gus lunges for the phone and stares at the screen.

There's one incoming message. No words. Just a photo.

"It's from you," she says to Howard.

He never did get his phone back from the homeless woman. She was AWOL when they were brought out of the building by the firemen.

Howard moves closer to Gus. They both stare at the image. It's a photo, taken from a distance, of a woman leaving a Giant Tiger department store. She's carrying a plastic bag. A teddy bear and a white packet stick out the top of the bag. Gus zooms in on the words printed on the packet.

Huggies for Newborns.

Diapers.

Gus and Howard look at each other.

They know who has her baby.

They're out of the hospital and in the back seat of an Uber before anyone knows they're gone. The driver doesn't bat an eye at Gus's paper gown.

"Flat or bubbles?" is all he asks.

Gus downs three bottles of fancy water on the drive over. She has a moment of déjà vu. The same feeling she had when she was riding in the back seat of the old couple's car after running away from the Mutchmores at the hospital. She can't remember how long ago that was. Weeks, months. Time has a way of folding in on itself when the world starts spinning too fast.

Howard keeps asking Gus if she's okay. She tells him that whatever the hospital pumped into her veins is working. She tries texting Howard's phone, but gets nothing back. She tries tracking the phone, but its location is unknown. It must be turned off or out of juice.

As they approach the apartment building, Howard says they need a game plan. What with the chaos of yesterday, the odds are good that the Ambassador is being watched. As the Uber pulls up to the building, Howard tells him to go around back. Gus says no. The front entrance is good. Gus tells Howard to follow her lead, and she's suddenly out of the vehicle. Howard has no choice but to jump out too. Gus is pushing her key in the front door when someone lays on a car horn. Howard turns to see Malachy dodging the honking car as he races across the street straight at them. Gus gets the door open. They squeeze inside and pull it shut just as Malachy reaches for the handle. The Irishman pulls but it's locked. Malachy slams his fist against the glass. Howard gives the Irishman a one-fingered salute.

Gus and Howard run down the first-floor hall and bang on the apartment door.

After several loud bangs, Stanley opens the door.

"Where's Alice?" says Gus, trying to see over Stanley's shoulder.

Stanley looks confused. Like he's been woken from a nap. Gus is vibrating.

"We need to talk to your sister. It's urgent," Gus barks.

Howard gently holds Gus's hand so she doesn't knock the old man down.

"She's not home," Stanley says. "Is everything all right?"

"No, everything's not all right," says Gus, becoming more shrill.

Stanley sways a little and rubs his eyes.

Howard puts his arm around Gus, trying to steady her.

"When did you last see her, Mr. Croft?" asks Howard quietly, playing the good cop.

"We didn't have toast this morning," offers Stanley.

"So you haven't seen her today?" says Howard.

Gus feels like the world is moving in slow motion.

"I think last night. Maybe. Yes," Stanley says, deliberately finding his words.

His brain seems to be rummaging for scraps.

Gus is ready to scream. *How can Howard be so calm?*

"So last night you saw her, then?" Howard prompts.

Gus bites her lip.

"Not last night," says Stanley.

Howard squeezes Gus's arm. He's waiting for Stanley to remember something.

"Alice was busy with her project, I suppose," he mumbles.

What fucking project?

Gus can't seem to get her mouth to form words any longer.

"Stanley!" Howard barks, startling the old man.

That's more like it.

"Tell us about this project?" says Howard, now the bad cop.

Stanley's eyes focus. Then he points up.

"Alice has been repairing her old coops so she can raise pigeons again," he says.

Gus shudders as his words bring memories rushing toward her.

Alice talking about her father building her a pigeon coop when she was a child.

Poppy telling her that Teddy lured her to the rooftop to see the pigeons.

Alice is on the roof.

33

Alice

ALICE HAS HER BACK TO THEM WHEN THEY OPEN THE DOOR. She's not in her usual neon workout gear. She's wearing a thin cotton dress. Yellow with white polka dots. She doesn't turn around despite the loud slam of the door as it closes behind Gus and Howard. She only flinches. She's standing next to the broken remnants of what must have been the old pigeon coops. She's holding something in her arms.

Gus wants to run over but Howard stops her. He nods toward the roof's edge.

Alice is too close.

"I bet you didn't know that pigeons mate for life," Alice says in a soft voice.

Howard motions to Gus that he's going to circle the coop and come up beside Alice.

Gus slowly walks toward her.

"I just want my baby back," says Gus. "It can be our secret. It's just you and me up here. No one else has to know."

"They always come back home, don't you know. But you

have to train them when they're young, or they fly away forever," muses Alice, as she gently sways then turns to face her.

Gus's heart sinks. It's not a baby that Alice has cradled in her arms. It's a teddy bear.

Alice takes in Gus's strange outfit.

"What have you done with her, Alice?" Gus pleads.

Alice looks ghostly white.

"Doesn't everyone deserve a mate? And a baby," says Alice, her voice squeaking.

"I understand. You just wanted a baby of your own," says Gus softly.

Alice smirks.

"You're a liar. You don't understand. You tricked me to get my keys. And I saw you with that boy. You pretended he was some repairman. You don't deserve her. I do. I brought her into the world. But that awful street woman took her from me. And now I have no one," she says.

"What woman?" demands Gus.

Alice catches sight of Howard through the coop.

"Him." Alice points. "More lies. Why does everyone have to lie?"

She stumbles and teeters backward, arms flailing. The teddy bear falls from her arms and disappears over the roof's edge. Howard freezes. Alice falls onto her backside, landing on the lip of the roof. Gus isn't sure what to do. She looks into the compartments of the coop. There's an empty basket, a baby bottle, and the open packet of diapers. No baby. She meets Howard's eyes and shakes her head. He stays put.

"Please," begs Gus, not daring to move any closer to Alice.

Alice's shoulders slump and tears roll down her cheeks. She doesn't bother brushing them away. She lets her gaze drift.

"He said he loved me. But he was pretending. It was always Poppy he loved. He was going to run away with her and leave me. I went to stop him. I didn't mean to hit him so hard. I didn't know. I only saw his face as he fell into the water," she says.

Alice looks like she's slowly shrinking.

"You killed Leo? You were just a child," says Gus.

Alice's eyes dart toward Gus.

"I was nearly thirteen," she snaps. "And no one would have ever, ever, ever found out if it weren't for Poppy. And you. I heard everything her mother said to him before she walked away. That Leo was Poppy's brother. It was disgusting. Poppy always thought she was so special. But he was destined to be with me, not her. And then you came along and everything started to change. I saw how happy he was when she started coming out of her apartment. When she went to that party. It was only a matter of time. I couldn't let her take him from me again. Then you two went out for a walk, and that was my chance. She got what she deserved."

Gus is trying to make sense of what Alice is telling her.

Then an image pops into Gus's head. She's in Alice and Stanley's kitchen. There are family photos on the fridge behind Alice. Under magnets. Polaroids. The picture of Gish dead on Poppy's kitchen floor was taken with a Polaroid. Alice had master keys. She could get into Poppy's apartment any time she wanted.

"Why would you want to hurt Poppy?" Gus asks.

"Because he loved her more than me," she says. "I could see it in his eyes."

"Whose eyes?" Gus asks.

"Leo's," she says.

Howard and Gus exchange a look. Both are dumbfounded.

"Leo's alive," says Gus, more to Howard than Alice.

"Stanley," says Howard as it comes to them simultaneously.

"But you said you saw him fall into the pond." Gus turns to Alice.

"He was wearing Leo's coat. He had his back to me. I thought it was Leo. He was holding Leo's suitcase. It was all there in the note. I peeked at the note before Stanley put it in the milk door. They were going to elope. I knew where they were meeting. But Stanley didn't tell me that everything had changed. That he and Leo had a plan. I saw his face when he fell. It was my brother. I killed my own brother," she says, her voice trailing to a whisper.

Howard stays put and Gus moves closer to Alice.

"It's okay, Alice," says Gus. "Let's go find the baby. It's not too late. You can make this right."

"I tried to make it right. I didn't mean to lock you down there. I was following you and it just happened. All your lies. I just wanted you to stop. Stop helping Poppy. Stop lying. But I knew I'd been bad. You were with child. So I went back. I had no idea the baby was already coming. I was the one who helped you. I helped the baby. I made it right," she says, looking up at the sky.

"You did," says Gus, stepping closer.

Alice looks at Gus then glances past her with a look of surprise.

Alice rises to her feet. Gus doesn't dare move.

"I thought you loved me," Alice whispers, still looking past Gus.

A strangely contented expression settles across the old woman's face.

"I'm sorry," says Alice, then she steps backward, off the edge of the roof.

"No!" Gus yells as she reaches for Alice's arm, but she's too late. She misses.

Gus almost goes over herself. There's a sickening thud from below. Alice is gone. Howard grabs hold of Gus and pulls her away from the edge. Gus doubles over, trying to catch her breath, her heart throbbing in her chest.

"We have to move," Howard says, looking around.

They hear a scream from the street below. A car skidding and another person shouting.

"Gus," insists Howard.

She rights herself and they turn for the door. Stanley is there, in his housecoat and slippers. He heard everything.

"Do you know where the baby is?" Howard asks.

The old man shakes his head. Tears in his eyes. He doesn't know.

"Go," he says softly.

In that moment, Gus sees a flash of Leo. The young man in the photo booth images.

They leave him there and enter the stairwell, but they can already hear footsteps coming up from below.

"Someone call 911," a voice yells.

They can't be seen.

"My apartment. We can hide there," she says between heavy breaths.

Sirens are already wailing in the distance. They duck onto the third-floor landing and into her apartment. It no longer has that stale scent of an unoccupied space. The police have been there. Or maybe someone else. Howard is on high alert. He quickly checks the bedroom and bathroom while Gus sits on the sofa to catch her breath. Howard comes back into the living room. They stare at each other a moment, then Gus rises and rushes over to hug Howard. She buries her face in his chest.

And that's when they hear it. A small sound coming from the kitchen.

A tiny cooing sound.

Gus lifts her head. They both rush to the kitchen.

And there, swaddled in a blanket and tucked neatly inside the dumbwaiter compartment, is a one-day-old baby. Gus's baby. The child is reaching one tiny hand toward the strand of red hair dangling above her. Howard's cell phone lies next to her.

The baby's green eyes blink as she looks at Gus.

Her hair is golden with a hint of auburn.

She's absolutely, stunningly, perfectly beautiful.

34

Little One

LEVI HAD WHINNIED AND WIGGLED HIS BODY WITH DELIGHT at the sight of Gus coming back to him after being gone nearly two days. With gentle curiosity, he had sniffed the bundle in her arms and hadn't left their side since.

Gus and Howard weren't sure how it happened, but it looked like the homeless woman had been following Alice and somehow got the baby away from her. The woman had Howard's phone—later they found a picture on the phone of the baby in the dumbwaiter. It was in another text to Gus that never got sent. Her way of telling them where the baby was, only the phone appeared to have died before it went through. They'd been lucky to find the baby. Lucky they'd been forced to hide out in Gus's apartment. Even luckier still to have slipped out of the Ambassador unseen.

With paramedics and police and a crowd of bystanders and neighbors surrounding the Ambassador, out front and in the service alley, they'd made their way down to the first floor and slipped into the Crofts' unlocked apartment. They were banking on the fact that when Stanley followed them up to

the roof, he hadn't bothered locking his door. They were right.
They found the apartment empty. More than likely he was
outside talking to the police. They climbed out a bedroom
window facing the park then skirted the tree line and made
their way to the west end, where the van still sat waiting. The
park was mercifully quiet. Just a solo dog walker who barely
glanced at them. Gus had changed out of her paper gown
back at her apartment, and the baby was tucked inside her jean
jacket. They looked like a couple out for a hurried walk.

The keys were still in the wheel well. A parking ticket
was jammed under the windshield wiper. A backpack of
bones was still sitting in the cargo space and Howard's note
was still on the dash.

Don't wait for me. Go back to the loft. I love you.—Howard

Howard hadn't wanted her to go looking for him if she'd
made it back to the van before him. They didn't talk about
the other words on the note. There was no time.

And it was only when they were crossing Bank Street and
were able to look toward the Ambassador that they saw Poppy
and Mojo. They had both completely forgotten to call them.
Poppy must have insisted that she and Mojo head down to the
Ambassador when an entire day and night had gone by since
Howard's last call. The two must have seen all the commotion
and rushed into the fray to make sure Gus and Howard were
okay.

And that's when they were caught.

From three blocks away, Gus could see them being led
across the street by Malachy and Taggart. Mojo was squirming.
Beyond them was a crowd of onlookers and flashing lights and
police tape and pink paint splattered on the road. That was the
last time they saw them.

Before heading back to Howard's loft, Gus asked him to
make a stop.

The mothers-to-be in the waiting room craned their necks to get a glimpse of the bundle in Gus's arms. Despite the ordeal of the past few hours, she felt her own motherly glow now outmatched most of theirs by a mile. The receptionist glared at her, not sure why Gus was standing in front of her without an appointment. But when Doctor Chandra emerged from her exam room, she let out a high-pitched squeal that made the receptionist jump out of her skin. Chandra was overjoyed to see Gus and her newborn, and more than a little surprised.

"I knew you were a one-woman show," she giggled, ushering them into the exam room.

Chandra gave the baby and Gus thorough examinations before declaring them both fit as fiddles. Apparently, the baby had been well taken care of in her first hours. Washed and fed by a woman with so much love to give that it consumed her. Gus offered vague answers to the doctor's questions, telling her the baby had come so fast she had no choice but to deliver it at home, with her boyfriend's help. Chandra tells her to be sure to register the baby's birth. She gives her the paperwork she'll need to do it, then the bubbly doctor sends the two of them on their way.

❧

That was a week ago.

Safe at the loft, the present has never been more vibrant and lovely and real. Gus stares at the new life sleeping peacefully in her arms. Warmth envelops her. She feels like a storm has raged through her body, leaving her forever changed in its wake. Her heart has been set adrift, outside her body, yet she's happy and her heart is too. It now belongs entirely to someone else.

Howard doesn't hover. He cooks and walks Levi. He does

some digging into a new lead but keeps what he finds to himself for now. He also tries to keep an eye on how much trouble they might be in. He checks out the Ottawa Police website. Finds the *Persons to Identify* page, where a blurry picture of him and Gus is featured. They're outside the Civic Hospital, caught on some surveillance camera. The image is captioned *assistance with an investigation*. Howard scans a few of the other *persons* pictured on the page. Their captions seem far worse and more specific. *Assault. Theft. Witnesses to murder. Fraud. Shooting. Robbery.* At least their caption doesn't include words like *death* or *child endangerment* or *kidnapping* or *firearms offense* or *break and enter* or *disturbing the scene of a crime* or *interfering with human remains*, all of which they've been involved with in one way or another in the past few weeks. No doubt the police have been to his house, and maybe his workplace, since he gave the officers his real name at the hospital. But so far no one seems to know about the loft, so they can breathe easy for the moment.

Howard finds a small article in a local paper about the suicide of eighty-year-old Alice Croft. Her brother is quoted as saying she hadn't been herself lately. He would know. There's no mention in the article that two people came looking for her just before she fell from the roof or that he witnessed her confess to killing her own brother before she fell. Stanley left out those parts. He's been hiding the truth for decades. He's good at lying. Or rather, Leo is good at it.

Howard looks into Stanley Croft. He finds his military records. He joined up in 1953. He did his basic training at Camp Borden in Ontario but returned home a year later when his father died. Howard finds a picture of the young soldier posing with fellow cadets. He compares it to the photo booth images of Leo and Poppy on Gus's phone. Looks like the same guy.

One day out of nowhere, Gus asks Howard a question.

"Tell me what you found out about Stanley?" she says, sitting next to him on the sofa.

Howard smiles. She's been watching him and knows he's been up to something. Still, he's a little caught off guard by her interest. Lately, she's been so laser-focused on one person. Her wide-eyed wonder at the tiny being she created hasn't faded, but her fear of breaking her or not feeding her enough or leaving her alone in the fancy crib Howard ordered online—those worries have softened. Gus hasn't named the baby yet. She simply calls her Little One. She's learned how to support the baby's neck when she holds her, how to breastfeed and burp and change her and rock her to sleep. Gus is slowly figuring out how to be a mother. Or at least, she's found a steady rhythm that works for the two of them.

Levi believes himself the protector of this new, odd-smelling creature. He sleeps under the baby's crib. He brings over her stuffed toys when he finds one of hers mixed with his on the floor, and he paces when Gus bathes her in the large kitchen sink. And right now, he's nestled as close as he can get to where the baby has fallen asleep on Howard's shoulder.

"He definitely joined the Canadian Forces in fifty-three like they said he did," he answers.

Gus looks through the photo evidence and the military records. His first physical performance test and exam is among them. It makes no mention of a missing toe. How did he get away with that?

Gus recalls why Poppy believed so strongly that the body in the pond couldn't be her Leo.

Leo was missing a toe on his left foot. I'm betting a toe can't magically rematerialize.

She examines the photos. It's him. It's Leo.

"So Leo took Stanley's place in the military," says Gus, the wheels turning. "Maybe when Stanley and Leo swapped coats that night, their IDs were in their coats. And maybe the swap was only meant to be temporary, and things went wrong, as we know."

Gus flashes to what Alice said on the roof.

Stanley didn't tell me that everything had changed. That he and Leo had a new plan.

"Why didn't he just run away with Poppy instead of joining the army?" asks Howard.

"We'll have to ask him," says Gus.

Her mind flutters to Poppy. All their efforts to contact Mojo and Poppy have failed this past week. And Gus has been so caught up in baby care that she's forgotten that her friend doesn't even know Leo is alive. She'll be so happy. But then, maybe not. Howard verbalizes what she's thinking.

"Leo has been lying to Poppy for decades. He's lived in the same building, pretending to be someone else. I know she's blind, but how did she not know his voice?"

Gus has a fleeting recollection of something Poppy once said about Leo.

He loved to make her laugh by doing impersonations of their favorite screen actors.

"She heard Stanley's voice. Leo was a good mimic. He and Stanley must have looked enough alike that no one questioned it when he came back a year later," says Gus.

"I guess people believe something when there's no reason not to," adds Howard.

"And Alice went along with it, so who was going to question it?" asks Gus.

"Leo started selling the lie the moment he joined the army and wrote letters back home to Stanley's father and Alice," says Howard.

Gus likes feeling her mind come alive with the familiar

flutter of excitement as a mystery from long ago begins to come out into the light.

"Speaking of letters," she says, "at the hospital, you were reading some letters."

Howard raises an eyebrow. "You don't miss a thing, do you?"

Not wanting to disturb the baby on his shoulder or Levi snoring next to him, he tells Gus to get the protein powder from the cupboard.

"You need a shake right now?" she asks.

"Trust me," he says, smiling.

She opens the cupboard and grabs the large tub of powder. It feels light. She sits next to him and opens it. No powder. Just a cloth bag tied with faded ribbon. Gus gives Howard a look. She's impressed.

"We don't want those getting into the wrong hands," he says.

"Why not?" she asks as she pulls the ribbon and dumps the letters from the bag onto the sofa between them.

"I've been waiting for the right time to show you these," he says.

"What are they?" she asks.

"Secret letters between two mothers," he tells her.

She looks at the worn edges of the folded letters.

"These letters are the answer we've been looking for," he says.

"To what?" she asks.

"To the Mutchmores' deepest, darkest secret," he says.

"*Who are the babies?*" they both say at the same time.

Gus gets shivers. She sifts through the pile, skimming the words on the pages. There are more than a dozen letters from Cora Mutchmore to Annie Trichborne. Howard tells her they span sixteen years, from late 1901 to 1916. The letters are written on cream-colored stationery with an elegant water-mark of purple lilies trailing down one side of the notepaper. It's lovely stationery, fitting the wife of a wealthy industrialist.

Gus reads every word of every letter, faded but legible. And like she is with most artifacts of the past, Gus is charmed by the swirling ink of the fountain pen on the old-fashioned paper. By the intimate smudges and the fragile creases where Cora carefully folded the letters.

The letters are mundane for the most part. Mother-to-mother, yearly updates about ordinary life at the Mutchmore household, mostly musings about a child growing up and becoming a strong, young lad. A son. Felix. But the first few letters are anything but ordinary.

When Gus is done reading, she looks up at Howard.

"This is the poison," she says, nodding to the letters.

"Yup. The sins of the great-grandfather," says Howard.

"The curse Charlotte was talking about. This is what she meant. This is what brings them down," Gus says, her excitement building.

"Yup," says Howard, lightly patting the baby's back.

"And you're going to be the one to do it, Howard," she says, her eyes full of fire.

35

Poison Lilies

HINTS HAD BEEN DANGLING IN FRONT OF HER ALL ALONG. SHE knew their birthdates. They were born the same year. The year of the great fire. Both were boys. Their mothers knew each other. One became the other's nanny. And then there was that family photo in which the help were lined up behind the Mutchmores, nothing more than wallpaper.

In many ways, that photo said it all.

It was hard to tell which of the women standing in the back row next to Teddy was his mother. But he did bear a resemblance to someone else in the photo. Someone in the foreground. Cora Mutchmore. Similar long, aristocratic nose and dark hair.

But it was the DNA results that sealed the deal.

Teddy's bones proved rich genetic material. Howard had ordered a kit from Easy23DNA.com when they'd first returned to the loft. The company was one of the few offering to test bone fragments from cremated remains. They sent a small piece of Teddy in an envelope for testing. If you paid more, you could get results in three days. Howard paid more.

Seventy-two hours later, the results arrived by courier. Howard had been sitting on the results for a few days, and the
letters, waiting for Gus to be ready.

Gus is ready.

Thanks to Mojo's family tree project, the Mutchmore
database was fertile ground. They got several hits. Teddy was
definitely related to Poppy, May, and Mojo. One of the best
matches was to Wilfred's DNA, confirming that they were
brothers from the same parents. But the closest match revealed
the truly dark depths of the Mutchmore family secrets. The
devastating truth of who Leo's father was.

Now that they're both up to speed, Gus and Howard set
a final plan in motion.

Howard begins writing his blog post. He's going to include scans of the DNA results and of the beautiful, lily-
patterned correspondences from Cora. It all proves that what
he's written is true. The lab results are the science that backs
it up, and the letters tell the story of the babies. The rot in
the family tree. The poison. Howard even gives the letters a
nickname. He calls them the *Poison Lilies*. It's fitting. They
are equal parts toxic and tender.

The story begins in 1900. It was the days following
the great fire that flattened much of LeBreton Flats. Robert Mutchmore was handing out meals at a makeshift soup
kitchen when he had a chance encounter with one of his
tenants who'd lost everything in the fire. Calvin Trichborne.
Calvin happened to be carrying his one-month-old son,
Teddy, that day. Robert remarked that his own son was about
the same age. Only Teddy Trichborne was a robust, rosy-
cheeked boy. Robert's son, Felix, was not. He was small and
sickly. A weakling, Robert called him.

Cora's first letter to Annie recounts this meeting along
with her husband's growing obsession with Teddy. Her letters

come across as if she's trying to justify what her husband did next. She writes that he always blamed himself for his son's poor health. Her child suffered side effects of syphilis passed through the womb because of Robert's indiscretions. Robert couldn't stand weakness. He could barely look at his own child. Cora believed her husband's scorn would have scarred the child for life. She says the boy is much better off being raised by someone else. Perhaps Cora wrote the letters to ease her guilt over giving up her firstborn son, but whatever her reasons, she was doing it in secret. Cora warns Annie that no one can ever know of their correspondences, especially their husbands. They agree to stay in touch. It appears the two kept up an exchange of letters for years.

Cora reflects upon what happened that spring of 1900 in one particularly painful letter. The two fathers came to an arrangement. Calvin was paid a large sum of money. Enough to buy a small home for his family. In return, he would exchange his healthy son for a weak one. The babies were swapped. The mothers were not told until it was done. Teddy Trichborne became Felix, and Felix Mutchmore was now Teddy. Cora was powerless, as was Annie.

The robust baby grew into a strong, healthy young man. He was Robert's pride and joy. At sixteen, Felix lied about his age, joined the war effort, and was killed in action. The Mutchmores were devastated.

The boy who became Teddy had a difficult start in life. His father died a year later amid the filth and disease of the tent city. Dysentery. By then he'd gambled away all of the money his benefactor had given him. Annie raised Teddy as best she could. She made sure he went to school when he wasn't sick. His health wavered from one illness to another. He was often bullied for being small and feeble. She tried to protect him, but she worked three jobs and was rarely home.

Cora never offered Annie money or assistance, until the death of her precious son, Felix. In one of her last letters, Cora begs Annie to come work as her daughter's nanny. She insists that Annie can live in the servants' quarters with her son. It's clear Cora is distressed by Felix's death and wants to be close to her birth son, Teddy. She'd lost the son she raised, but her real son was still alive. Annie must have finally agreed, because Cora laid out the terms of their new arrangement in a final letter written in 1916.

Howard writes a damning finale to his blog post. He exposes the fact that the Felix Mutchmore Foundation is built upon a lie. A secret baby swap. A business transaction in which firstborn sons were used as currency. The Mutchmores have banked on their dead son's legacy and name for generations. Holding him up as a war hero. Garnering donations, securing funding, winning contracts, making lucrative land deals—all based on a falsehood.

Howard also finds a number of discrepancies in the city's public records relating to housing developments financed by the Felix Mutchmore Foundation. Millions in private and public monies were raised by the foundation for veterans' housing and a veterans' hospice that, it appears, were never built. He even tracks down ribbon-cutting ceremony images of Wilfred and Ricker standing on heaps of dirt that remain just that to this day. Howard ends with the kicker: the letters were found buried with a body. A body left in a basement for decades. The body of their forsaken son, Teddy.

Did the Mutchmores murder Teddy Trichborne to hide the truth?

A cliffhanger.

Howard doesn't offer up evidence pointing to Eva as the one who killed Teddy. There's no point. Eva's long gone, and it would only hurt Poppy.

Howard's post goes live on Thursday, September 9, at 9 A.M. By 3 P.M., it's been viewed a total of six times.

Howard's blog doesn't exactly have a huge following, but he was expecting a bang not a whimper. One loyal reader leaves a comment.

When did you start writing fiction, Howard? I love how you use real names and historic facts to add local color. Nice touch creating mock-ups of documents.

There were three likes, but no shares.

Howard is deflated.

But then he has an idea. He cites Braddish Billings as a source and tags him. That does it. Braddish is incensed. He posts an angry response in the comments. Then he shares his rabid denial across all his social media feeds. He's got a lot of followers, and a lot of them are his students. They like to share. Braddish also links to the offending article just so that everyone is clear about where his outrage is directed. Gus and Howard doubt he realizes what he's just done to the Mutchmores. The post goes viral.

By week's end, Howard's post has been shared hundreds of thousands of times. It's been syndicated by Post Media across their national digital network, then it gets picked up by the *Washington Post* and goes international. Gus and Howard are interviewed by a reporter from the *New York Times* researching an article about profit-making schemes among nonprofits.

Some influential donors to the Felix Mutchmore Foundation are less than thrilled at being associated with the growing scandal. In early October, the foundation offices are raided by the RCMP. It's on the evening news. Boxes of documents, including financial records, and computers are confiscated. In the days that follow, rumors swirl in the media of a larger investigation unfolding. One involving mismanagement of charitable funds, inappropriate spending, missing donations, and political interference in land deals and development bids that go back decades. Mama Bear and Papa Bear are detained as they try to board an international flight to the Caymans. Their lawyers claim they were going on vacation. Their passports are confiscated, and they're placed under house arrest until a court date is set. Charges are pending.

The Mutchmores are done.

36

Stanley

WHEN GUS'S EVIDENCE WALL WAS RIPPED DOWN BY MALachy, he delivered the documents to the Mutchmores. In secret, Charlotte had hidden away the love notes belonging to Poppy. She'd since returned them to their rightful owner.

The Poison Lilies, on the other hand, belonged to no one.

Gus imagines that if those letters were strung together on a wall, they would read like one long correspondence reaching across generations and decades, connecting that original sin made by two fathers to the tragic fates that befell their sons and daughters. A few words written on paper was all it took to fell the family tree.

Poppy's apartment has been reassembled, almost exactly as it once was. Charlotte took care of that too. She made sure the family didn't sell the apartment or any of Poppy's possessions. And Poppy was beyond grateful. She didn't want the place changed or updated. She wanted her old curtains hung and her favorite carpets laid. She wanted her sofa positioned by the fireplace exactly where it was and her mother's room restored and locked. Mojo, who was now living with her grandmother, had come over to help Poppy get things just right.

The past may have revealed itself, but Poppy seems to have no desire to live without its familiar patterns and shapes. It's all she's ever known and it's all she needs. She is settled.

Save for one thing.

Leo.

She hasn't seen him since she found out that Stanley is actually Leo. She's carefully avoided contact. But now that she's ready, Poppy has asked Gus to be there for the reunion. The old woman is not bitter or sad or angry. She's more nervous and curious. Gus is as well. They both want to hear his side of the story. Poppy knows what Gus has told her, but she wants to hear it from the source. She needs to know why. The eighteen-year-old inside her needs to know.

Gus invites Howard to come too. He's as much a part of this as she is, now. But he insists on watching the baby for her so she can go alone. It started with her and Poppy, and it should end with them. Howard's sweet selflessness tugs at her heart.

Poppy and Leo pick a date.

October 31.

Sixty-eight years to the day from when they were to elope.

It's a cold October evening. Gus arrives early so she and Poppy can ready themselves. She brings Levi along. The dog has been loving their familiar visits up to Poppy's apartment since they returned to the Ambassador. When Poppy paid her everything she owed her and more, Gus was able to cover her overdue rent and move back into her apartment with the baby. Howard did hint that they could both come live with him in his house on Ossington, but Gus wanted to be close to Poppy for the moment, in case she needed her. In his usual considerate way, Howard helped out, setting up the crib in a corner of Gus's bedroom without a hint of being hurt by her choice. Howard rented out the loft and moved back to his house. The loft had been a lovely oasis in the sky for a while. And a good hideout. But it was always meant to be temporary. Life had to get back to normal at some point.

Gus sits next to Poppy on the sofa, and Levi settles into his spot by the fireplace. The windows have frosted over. The fire casts a warm glow in the heart of the dark room. It's almost as if nothing has changed, and yet everything has. Sparks dance in Poppy's eyes. Her new kitten stares at Levi from its perch on the mantel. The cat's still not sure about him. She's keeping her distance for now. She growls softly. Levi could care less. He's in his happy place.

"Dang it, Mary Pickford. You be nice to our Levi," says Poppy.

Poppy is wearing a pink cashmere sweater and gray slacks. Her long hair hangs loose on her shoulders. She's also wearing the locket Leo gave her. She looks beautiful, and quite well, considering all she's been through. The two distract themselves by discussing possible names for the baby. Poppy suggests Bette or Greta or Marlene. She clearly has a thing for old Hollywood movie stars. They share the news of the day. Gus tells Poppy about Howard's new job writing for the *Globe and Mail*. Poppy tells Gus that Mojo has decided she wants to become a private detective when she grows up. Just like Gus.

When they run out of things to say, they let the quiet envelop them like they used to. Levi's snoring fills the comfortable silence with its rhythmic song. Soft breaths in and out. The past joins in. It reverberates around them. But it's no longer a sad song that fills this room. Perhaps when the movers put everything back in place, and inadvertently removed layers of dust, they also brushed off the longing and loss that once coated Poppy's belongings.

The room feels a little lighter every time Gus visits. And so does Poppy.

There's a knock at the door.

Poppy bristles ever so slightly but doesn't move to get the door. Gus touches her arm lightly and rises to greet the visitor.

Gus lets him in. Stanley is still Stanley in Gus's eyes. A ninety-one-year-old man with a shuffling step and a wandering mind. But as he sits in the armchair across from Poppy and sinks deeply into the cushions, she sees someone else behind those sagging eyelids. A young man.

When Gus first met Stanley, she thought him a bit lost. She assumed it was simply the ravages of time. An old man nearing the end of his life, losing his faculties. But now she sees that Leo has also endured a lifetime separated from his true love. He might have only lived four floors away from her, but it must have felt like a chasmic gap. One he could not bridge. His heart must have broken every time he saw her.

"You look very well, Poppy," he says softly.

"Tell me about that night, Stanley," she says.

There will be no small talk, and she's not using his real name. Gus takes a seat next to Poppy. She's suddenly worried that her friend hasn't fully grasped the truth of who he is.

The old man's eyes water and he appears to stop breathing. He turns an odd shade of purple. He looks ashamed and slightly stunned. Gus shifts and clears her throat, wishing she could disappear. The intimacy of the moment is unbearable.

"I'm sorry," he says finally.

He's breathing, thank Christ.

"Please tell me," Poppy insists.

He sinks lower into the armchair and then, casting his eyes upward, he drops into the past. Gus can almost see the years dancing before his pupils. It's probably just the firelight, but in that moment, he becomes Leo. Words flow from his lips like they never did from Stanley's.

"I wrote you a note telling you when and where to meet me. I gave you the signal from the park. The red cap at noon. Later that day, Stan came looking for me. He was upset. He told me your mother had found the note and he was certain she was going to the park that night. I knew she was only going to try to put an end to our relationship, so Stan and I came up with a plan. He was scheduled to leave in the morning on a bus for basic training. It was perfect. He would be long gone before anyone would know of his part in our plan. By then, we would have eloped and it would be too late to stop us."

Gus flashes to Alice's words.

But Stanley didn't tell me that everything had changed. That he and Leo had a plan.

"Our plan was to switch coats, and he would go in my place to the park, to keep Eva there long enough for me to get you out of the apartment. People always said Stan and I looked alike. He was taller but we had similar builds, same hair color, so we thought we could pull it off. Stan made sure the side door was left open so I could sneak in and collect you before Eva came back. We planned to meet up later—switch coats and travel bags and go our separate ways.

"But you didn't answer the door to your apartment. I knocked and knocked. I thought you'd found the note that Eva intercepted, and you'd gone to the park. I ran there as fast as I could. But you weren't there. Your mother was. She was talking to Stan. He stood on the bridge, holding my suitcase, wearing my coat, his back to her. Eva thought it was me. We'd broken the lamp over the bridge, so it was dark. He kept his back to her, buying us time. But then I heard her say something that drew me closer. She was talking about the orphanage where I was sent as a baby. My ears perked up when I heard the name. Then she told him that she was my mother and that she'd given me up for adoption. She couldn't have known the name of the orphanage unless she was my mother. I knew then that I was your brother.

"I was devastated. I stumbled off into the park, dazed. I didn't know what to do or where you were. I was truly lost. Then I heard footsteps behind me. I turned. Eva was coming in my direction. I hid in the bushes. She passed by me. She was crying. That's when I heard the splash. We both heard it. She raced back to the bridge. I followed her at a distance. Stan was in the water, floating, sinking. He was under in seconds. She ran toward the bridge, then she stopped in her tracks, turned, and ran off," he says.

Gus now sees why Eva thought her son was dead. She truly believed that the man on the bridge was Leo. She watched his body disappear into the pond. Maybe she thought he took his own life at hearing the news, and she blamed herself. She also didn't try to save him.

"I didn't know what had happened or why Stan had gone into the water, but I had to get him out. He was my friend. I jumped in but I couldn't find him. The pond was bottomless. It was as if it had swallowed him whole. I dove and dove, nearly drowning myself, but he was gone. I finally dragged myself from the pond. Before leaving town, I did leave you a note. I had to. So you'd move on. There was no going back. All I could do was . . ."

Gus remembers that last note written on blue paper.

I'm sorry. Please forget about me. —Leo

Poppy's hand rests on her heart as if she's trying to hold it inside her chest.

"You took his place," she says.

"I had Stan's rucksack and bus ticket. I was wearing his coat. I even had his ID. I owed him my life. I took his seat on that bus and I took his place in the army. It was the least I could do. Stan and I looked enough alike that no one questioned it. No one knew him at basic training. I did come back once on a weekend pass. It was late December. Just before Christmas. I wanted to know that you were okay. I hung around the park, hoping to catch a glimpse of you, but Eva spotted me, so I was forced to leave without seeing you," he says.

Gus feels for Eva. She saw Leo and believed he was a ghost because she was certain she'd watched him drown two months earlier.

"I wrote to Stanley's family from basic training so his father and sister wouldn't wonder about him. Alice didn't know the letters were from me, at least I didn't think she did at the time. We corresponded. I felt like I had everyone fooled. There was even this one compassionate army doctor who agreed not to report the fact that I was missing a toe. I told him it happened when I was a kid, and it didn't affect my physical abilities. He fudged the paperwork and made it so I wouldn't be discharged or put on a desk. I hoped one day to get posted overseas and never come back, but then Mr. Croft died, and everything changed.

"I owed it to Stan to take care of his little sister, and I owed it to his father for the son he'd lost because of me. At that point, I was used to pretending to be Stan. Alice said she didn't care. She helped everyone believe I was who I said I was.

"I was *changed a little by my time away*, was what she told them if they raised an eyebrow. I even convinced you. I had to. Your heart needed to move on, to forget you ever knew me," he says.

Poppy lowers her hand from her heart. It's the first time she's moved in forever. Mary Pickford jumps into her lap and rubs her furry head under Poppy's chin.

"I came back for Alice, but I stayed for you," he says to Poppy.

Gus doesn't say a word. She looks from Poppy to Leo.

Then Poppy looks up and smiles.

"It's been a long time, Leo," she says.

37

Bly

GUS KNOWS THE PAST ISN'T DONE WITH HER.

She knows this partly because of something Howard tells her about the homeless woman. How she offered him licorice. That was Gracie Halladay's favorite. Gus found packages of licorice in the attic room in that big house outside Elgin, Ontario, where the strange young woman was living for several years. It's probably just a coincidence. That and the dead animals left at her door. Just a pattern repeating. The past does that. It revisits. Like a déjà vu. Whoever she was, Gus owes her for rescuing her and her baby. She sometimes checks the stairwell, but there's been no sign of the woman. It's as if she were a ghost who stopped by for a time, looked out for her, and now she's moved on.

They hand over all of their evidence to the RCMP task force investigating the Mutchmores, including the letters and Teddy's bones. His skull is still missing. Lost somewhere in the depths of the Ambassador subbasement, likely tucked in a dark corner never to be found again. Gus and Howard both give witness statements to the task force. They're also questioned by the Ottawa police about their part in disturbing evidence at a crime scene and about the unusual circumstances surrounding her child's birth. In the end, they're cleared of any wrongdoing and the birth is officially registered at city hall.

Some two months after she was born, Gus's daughter has a name.

NAME: Bly Shannon Monet

MOTHER: Augusta Maggie Monet

FATHER: Tommy Oaks

Gus names her daughter after one of her heroes, Nellie Bly. The name suits little Bly. She is curious and strong-willed like her namesake. She's forever touching or reaching or gazing with wide eyes at the world around her. She has a strong will and an even stronger grip.

The name also means "gentle" and "happy." She is that.

Gus doesn't hesitate putting Tommy's name on the birth certificate. She won't hide the truth from Bly. Ever. Her daughter will know where she comes from and who her father is. DNA cannot be denied. Cora and Robert tried that, and look where it got them. The son they rejected, who spent his life trying to prove to them he was worthy of the Mutchmore name, was the one who helped destroy that name in the end. And yet, it is that same DNA that now bonds Poppy and Leo as siblings.

The two of them have become inseparable. They see each other every day for walks in the park; in the afternoons, Leo reads the newspaper to Poppy; and on Sundays, they do the *New York Times* crossword puzzle. They've found their way past what tore them apart and discovered a new way to love each other. As friends and companions. And amazingly, Poppy's sight has begun to return. She laughs about it. Says that being electrocuted somehow rewired her optic nerves.

Gus thinks otherwise.

She believes love has healed Poppy's eyes.

Bly is living proof that love is an inexplicably powerful force. The strength of it catches Gus off guard each time Bly crinkles her nose when Levi licks her face or smiles as she notices the sunlight dancing on the ceiling. Gus wonders if DNA is a two-way street. If it can be passed from the baby to the mother as well. A tiny chain of molecules that Bly wrapped around Gus's heart before she left the womb. She wonders if her mother felt this same tug. Perhaps it's what inspired Cora to write to Annie about her son. She was pulled by a force beyond her control.

Another force pulls at Gus. Another kind of love. Poppy no longer needs her close by. It's time for her to let herself be pulled in a new direction.

❧

They meet in the arboretum on a warm autumn Sunday. Howard pushes the stroller. Bly is cooing and pointing at a pair of mallards flying overhead. Howard tells the baby that the ducks will be heading south any day now. She spits up. He wipes her chin with a wet wipe he just happens to have in his pocket. Gus and Howard continue to walk side by side down the gravel road, past the tall pines that curve toward Dow's Lake. A golden carpet of needles covers the road. Levi ambles ahead, nosing the fallen leaves, tail swishing. He circles a small tree set apart from the pines. Its leaves have turned a golden apricot color.

"It's a katsura tree," says Howard. "Sometimes called a caramel tree."

Gus catches the tree's sweet scent. It smells like cotton candy. She crouches, gathers a handful of the buttery leaves, and brings them to her nose. She smiles.

"They're native to Japan," Howard says.

Gus brings the handful of leaves over to Bly and puts them to her nose. The baby takes one and tries to eat it. Gus pulls it gently from her mouth.

She turns to Howard. He is watching them. She knows that look. And even though her father died before she was born, Gus can picture him looking at her and her mother in that very same way.

The past in all its forms runs through her veins. It is alive. She has longed for it, and she has tried to escape it. She has been driven to dig into it until her fingers bleed and her body aches. It has haunted her and toyed with her and stalked her.

But in this moment, she sees it in a new light.

The past is not somewhere else. It is right here.

No, the past is not done with her, and it never will be.

It is all around her. It lives in the smell of a caramel tree, in the pink flush of her baby's chubby cheeks, in the gray whiskers above Levi's old eyes, and in the face of the lovely man standing next to her. It is everywhere.

Gus takes Howard's hand in hers.

She is home.

Acknowledgments

POISON LILIES IS A STORY ABOUT FAMILY—THOSE WE'RE BORN into and those we create along the way. When my world got very small, like everyone's did for a while, it was made entirely big enough and full enough and safe enough by my wonderful family—my husband, my mother, my daughter and her lovely fella, my sister and hers, my brother and his, Vivi and Grace, Jamie and Sarah, Sue and Lori, Jen and Mike, and their people. These relatives and friends grounded me as I worried and wondered and walked, then began to write again.

Gus and Levi have become part of that family, as have the many talented, kind, and wise folks who continue to support me as I make my way. I couldn't do this without my amazing agent, David Halpern. He's simply the best. I also want to thank his team, in particular Janet Oshiro, for always cheering me on.

I am grateful for the terrific group at HarperCollins who've shared this journey with me from the beginning. My editor, Sarah Stein, is considerate, enthusiastic, responsive, and open to all my ideas. She's been a dream to work with. I feel lucky to even say I have a team backing me up at Harper, but I do! Thank you to Lisa Erickson, Kristin Cipolla, Hayley Salmon, Alicia Tan, Alice Tibbetts, Lauren Morocco, Mike Mason, and all the amazing copyeditors, proofreaders, designers, and marketing folks—everyone who works so carefully and passionately to bring my novels into the world.

I'd like to thank Stephen Parolini (aka the Novel Doctor) for his sage advice on the early manuscript, as well as my fearless first readers—Alex and Jamie—whose excitement, love, and brilliant insights fueled and enriched those early drafts.

Thank you to all the wonderful booksellers and champions who gave my debut novel, *Dark August*, such tremendous support. A big shout-out goes to Bridget at Books on Beechwood in Ottawa; Alison from Beggars Banquet Books in Gananoque; Bethany Beach Books in Delaware; Sweet Reads; Leo from Zen Habits; Tammy from Rowdy Kittens; Capital Crime Writers; Ottawa International Writers Festival; Blomkvist Wannabes from Words Worth Books in Waterloo; Autumn and Miranda from Topeka and Shawnee County Public Library in Kansas; Vicki and Laura Lee from Rideau Lakes Public Library in Elgin, Ontario; Sara at A Mighty Blaze; Canadian Book Enablers; the amazing Hannah and Hank of First Chapter Fun; Mary from *Ottawa at Home* magazine; the "Halldon Place" Book Club; as well as podcasters Hank from *Author Stories*, Laura of *What to Read Next*, and Courtney and Bailey of *Soul and Wit*. All of you helped launch my first book in a time of virtual meetups and online book clubs. In doing so, you helped my novel travel the world when I couldn't.

A final thank-you goes out to those very special readers who took the time to send me personal notes and letters expressing your love for all things Gus and Levi. Your words touched my heart and each of you connected me to a world beyond my writing—a world of readers and book lovers. A family of another kind. I thank you for that.

About the Author

KATIE TALLO GREW UP IN OTTAWA, ONTARIO. AFTER STUDY-
ing film and English at Carleton University and television
broadcasting at Algonquin College, she was invited to attend
the prestigious Women in the Director's Chair in Banff. For
almost three decades, Katie has had an award-winning career as a screenwriter and director of short films, documen-
taries, feature films, and television series. In 2013, she won
the Mslexia Novel Competition in the United Kingdom for
unpublished fiction. Katie made her debut with the international bestselling novel *Dark August*. She continues to work
in video production while also writing novels. Katie has a
daughter and lives with her husband in the Wellington West
neighborhood of Ottawa, Ontario.

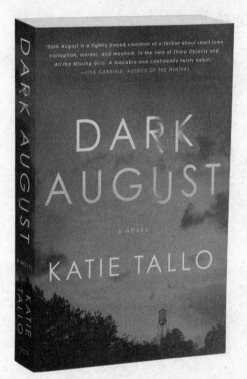